Murder in the Weird . . .

I flipped open the folder without speaking. Nothing like autopsy photos to start the day.

Murdock leaned back in his chair. "Victim's been ID'd as a street worker named Gamelyn Danaan Sidhe. Only been around a couple of months. One arrest for hustling. So what are you thinking?"

"Nothing," I said.

"Come on, Connor," he said, stretching his arms behind his head. "I'm not asking you for a name. What's this starting to shape into? If it were your basic murdering psycho, I'd say we have a disassociative personality acting out anger against victims who represent some kind of past psychological trauma."

I couldn't resist smirking. "And what makes you think you're wrong?"

He laughed. "I'm not saying I am. But given his choice of fairy prostitutes, his use of wards, and the ritualized placement of the stone, I'd say there's a layer to him that you might enlighten me on."

unshapely things

mark del franco

WITHDRAWN

ACE BOOKS, NEW YORK

THE BERKLEY PUBLISHING GROUP
Published by the Penguin Group
Penguin Group (USA) Inc.
375 Hudson Street, New York, New York 10014, USA
Penguin Group (Canada), 90 Eglinton Avenue East, Suite 700, Toronto, Ontario M4P 2Y3, Canada
(a division of Pearson Penguin Canada Inc.)
Penguin Books Ltd., 80 Strand, London WC2R 0RL, England
Penguin Group Ireland, 25 St. Stephen's Green, Dublin 2, Ireland (a division of Penguin Books Ltd.)
Penguin Group (Australia), 250 Camberwell Road, Camberwell, Victoria 3124, Australia
(a division of Pearson Australia Group Pty. Ltd.)
Penguin Books India Pvt. Ltd., 11 Community Centre, Panchsheel Park, New Delhi—110 017, India
Penguin Group (NZ), Cnr. Airborne and Rosedale Roads, Albany, Auckland 1310, New Zealand
(a division of Pearson New Zealand Ltd.)
Penguin Books (South Africa) (Pty.) Ltd., 24 Sturdee Avenue, Rosebank, Johannesburg 2196,
South Africa

Penguin Books Ltd., Registered Offices: 80 Strand, London WC2R 0RL, England

This is a work of fiction. Names, characters, places, and incidents either are the product of the author's imagination or are used fictitiously, and any resemblance to actual persons, living or dead, business establishments, events, or locales is entirely coincidental. The publisher does not have any control over and does not assume any responsibility for author or third-party websites or their content.

UNSHAPELY THINGS

An Ace Book / published by arrangement with the author

PRINTING HISTORY
Ace mass-market edition / February 2007

Copyright © 2007 by Mark Del Franco.
Cover art by Jaime DeJesus.
Interior text design by Tiffany Estreicher.

ISBN: 978-0-441-01477-4

ACE
Ace Books are published by The Berkley Publishing Group,
a division of Penguin Group (USA) Inc.,
375 Hudson Street, New York, New York 10014.
ACE and the "A" design are trademarks belonging to Penguin Group (USA) Inc.

PRINTED IN THE UNITED STATES OF AMERICA

10 9 8 7 6 5 4 3

*To Mom and Dad, who have waited.
And to my partner, Jack Custy, who never
expected to live with fairies and elves and the
occasional vampire, yet does so willingly.*

acknowledgments

I may have written this novel, but others made it a book. Many thanks to my agent, Andrew Zack; my editor, Anne Sowards; and my copyeditor, Sara Schwager. Officer Carol Ann Liguori of the NYPD provided great information regarding police procedures. They have made this a better book with their input and advice.

I am lucky to have a supportive crowd of friends and family. Thanks to: Paul Carroll, John Liguori, Andrew Schieffelin, Marianne Cutler, Sandy Bardsley, and Caedwyn (who is so cute); Becky Hemperly, Susan Altman, Kristin Lofblad, Rich Paradis, Robyn Renahan, Susan Hileman, and George Carner; Bess Hochstein and Kipp Lynch; Grace Polivka, who was That Teacher; my fabulous sisters Jody, Teresa, and Michele, who make me laugh and always share secrets; my grandmother Josephine Amore Del Franco, who would have loved this, except for the swearing; and to Jezebel, who sat faithfully beside me through the entire creation, and who is sorely missed.

A special thanks to Francine Woodbury, who Knows Stuff, always has beer and coffee, and has an uncanny knack for reminding me of things I forgot and telling me things I never knew, but needed.

The wrong of unshapely things
is a wrong too great to be told

—W. B. Yeats

1

The alley was slick with rain and a rainbow-hued slop I didn't want to think about. As I ducked under the yellow crime scene tape, something brown oozed away from my feet, and I almost tripped trying to avoid slipping on it. Flashing lights illuminated the dark end of the alley where an ambulance van and a couple of police cars waited. About forty people milled around, a good three-quarters of whom probably had no other reason to be there than to check out the latest victim.

As I came around the nearest car, Detective Lieutenant Leo Murdock of the Boston P.D. waved me over. "Hey, Connor, it's another fairy," he said.

Fairy. Not that there was anything wrong with that, I thought sardonically. Not down by the docks of the Weird, where a dead fairy in the middle of the night was becoming all too common. He didn't have to tell me anyway. I had smelled the blood back when I turned the corner from the main street.

"Same MO?" I asked. We walked over to where the medical examiner crouched, doing nothing to the body.

Murdock shrugged. "You tell me."

The naked body lay on its back staring up at the empty night sky. He was a pale-skinned male, not particularly well-endowed, but you can never really tell when someone's dead and leaking blood all over the place. Blood still dripped from the edges of his split-open torso, the lights glittering on the pool it formed around his waist. A shock of long white-blond hair fanned out around his head, little bits of organ tissue flecking it. At the center of the wound in his chest, a gaping hole showed the mangled evidence of a missing heart. His wings lay flat against the ground, a ward stone resting on each of them.

I nudged the medical examiner out of the way and crouched. The rank smell of alcohol wafted up from the body. Damn fairies never learned. They so much as look at a bottle, and they're drunk, but they still keep drinking the stuff. Putting on a latex glove, I eased a couple of exposed arteries aside and found the small stone I expected. I felt an odd null zone to my left and glanced up at Murdock. His holstered gun hovered over my head.

"Back off, buddy," I said. "Your gun's screwing me up."

Murdock put on an embarrassed face as he stepped off a ways. He never remembered about cold iron, and I never remembered to remind him, so I guess we both were to blame. As soon as he was a few feet away, the essences started to assert themselves. Nothing unusual, just the dead guy, maybe another fairy with him earlier in the evening, maybe an elf or two. His crotch reeked of human. He must have had a busy night—usually humans barely register.

Other than the heart, nothing else seemed to be missing. A slash across his right palm looked like a defense wound. It wasn't too deep and glanced off to the side. Probably too drunk to put up much of a fight. A couple of rings on each finger and most of the toes. The killer hadn't been interested in money.

I glanced around. The alley was a classic dead end, all the doors and lower windows boarded up tight. As I started to get up, I caught sight of something red shoved between a dumpster and a box. It looked too clean to have been there very long. I stepped carefully around the body and leaned in. It was some kind of fabric with residue of the same essence as the dead guy. "Bag this and check the dumpster," I said to no one in particular.

As I started to turn away, I paused, sensing something. The dumpster sat against a blank brick wall. I climbed up on it and inhaled. Bingo. A flit. Flit essence fades fast, so it couldn't have been there very long. I mentally kicked myself as I jumped down on the pavement. I hadn't thought to check very high up at the other crime scenes.

"Any flits around when your guys showed up?" I asked Murdock.

He shook his head. "Body was found by someone who called 911. People were everywhere when we got here."

I just nodded. Didn't mean anything in particular. If a flit was here when the cops arrived, people would have remembered it. Flits made it their business not to be seen too often. They were pretty good at it, camouflaging their scent, too, unless they had no reason to. Like if they didn't think anyone would look for them fifteen feet above a rank-smelling dumpster. It was a small lead, no pun intended, and I knew just who to go to ask about it. I decided not to tell Murdock. It was bad enough that he didn't understand why I couldn't just wave a magic wand to solve these things. No use having him terrorize the flit population if it was just a coincidence.

"It's the same MO," I said. I snapped off the latex glove.

Murdock nodded and frowned. A lot of people think Murdock's dismissive. I knew him well enough to know that he cared about the freaks in the Weird. He'd been on the detail too long not to be able to transfer out anytime he wanted. But he didn't. Just another thing I admired about him.

We walked back to his car. "You want to wait for a lift?" he asked.

"Nah, even I'm not that lazy. It's just a couple of blocks."

He turned back to the crowd at the barricades. "Suit yourself. I'll send you the file."

"Thanks," I said.

At the end of the alley, I pushed my way through the motley crew of gawkers that were held back by a police barricade. A huge woman, easily seven feet, towered over everyone, her hair flowing up even higher, tight green spandex straining against an enormous bust. I shook my head. Someone once said when it comes to murder, there's always a woman. I didn't think so in this case, though. Besides, in the Weird, half the time you didn't know if the woman in front of you was the real thing or even what species she was.

As I made my way through the maze of streets, I couldn't help but think what a waste it all was. Every time the papers said things were getting better, I knew it was a lie. As long as there were desperate people, there would be the Weird. And as long as the Weird existed, I had a reason to get up in the morning. So maybe it wasn't such a bad thing, at least for me. I never fooled myself into thinking I did more than gnaw around the edges. Even before my accident, I only kept the flashpoints from turning into conflagrations like everybody else did. I may not work in the big power leagues anymore, but I still pull my weight even if now I'm poor Connor Grey, crippled druid. At least I didn't have to deal with the politics of the Ward Guild anymore. And they do send disability checks.

My career at the Guild had been moving pretty fine. The Ward Guild monitors the fey—the druids and fairies, and the elves and dwarves—and acts as a policing agency as well as a diplomatic corp. Every city with a major concentration of fey has a Guildhouse that serves as headquarters for the locals. Ultimately, all the Guildhouses report to the top in Ireland. Good old Maeve, High Queen Mucky-Muck at Tara.

I miss some of it though. The money. The big apartment. A date any night of the week if I wanted. My picture in the paper. In my time, I got to handle most of the high-profile crime investigations. But that's over. All gone now. Washed away the moment I met up with an environmentalist elf at the nuclear reactor. Asshole had a power ring he didn't know how to use. He lost control, and some kind of feedback loop with the reactor happened. The next thing I know I'm waking up in the intensive care unit at Avalon Memorial with a migraine and most of my abilities gone. I could have cared less that the entire Northeast power grid went down. Nobody died. Not even the stupid elf.

The doctors are baffled. They know the problem is a dark smudgy mass in the middle of my brain, but they can't figure out if it's organic or not. No diagnostic, technological or otherwise, has been able to penetrate it. They offered to go in physically and look, but no one knows enough about the interface between living tissue and ability for me to trust them. They can use someone else to experiment on and get back to me. Having the power ring would go a long way toward helping figure it out, but it disappeared with the elf. I'd wish the jerk were dead if I didn't hope to find him someday. I just hope Murdock isn't around when I do. He'd just go all ethical on me and stop me from killing the guy. But then, he's just as upset about the whole situation as I am. Or at least thinks he is.

Murdock's a good guy. Sometimes too good for his own good. He knows I won't take charity, but that doesn't stop him from dangling interesting cases in front of me. The system was set up for the Guild to handle any crimes involving the fey—meaning anyone with the ability to manipulate essence—while the municipal police retained their usual jurisdiction over everyday humans. The way everything plays out, though, is that the Guild wants only fey-on-fey cases. The glory cases. Petty crimes, whether they involve fey or not, get punted to the local P.D. Whenever the Guild considers a crime a human matter, and most times it does, Murdock's unit picks up the slack. Human police have to take care of the Weird because the Guild doesn't much care about the fey here, unless someone important gets caught doing something. Between the disability and the occasional check Murdock squeaks out of his consultant account, I can pay the rent.

I hit the front door of my building just as dawn started creeping up. Home is an old mill warehouse in the twilight zone at the edge of the Weird, barely describable as converted. The elevator up to the fifth floor is slower than walking, but I usually don't bother with the stairs. It's cheap and it's quiet and the neighbors are not prone to scrying in the middle of the night, which wakes me up. Most of the other tenants are retirees and art students, and I think we still have dwarves in the basement, though I haven't seen them in a while. My apartment's on the top floor corner. I used to have a cool retro sanctum sanctorum, but now I make do with a one bedroom overlooking a rotting pier. The view of the harbor beyond that is nice, though.

I do my living in the main room, the larger one, and my working in the smaller one, which sits at the corner of the building. That way I can work without the sun coming up in my eyes in the morning and have a view of the Boston skyline and the airport from my desk. They make ample diversion anytime, day or night.

I slipped into the squeaky chair in front of my computer and booted up. Opening the case notes, I gave the new victim his own database file, made notes on the scene and the body, and plotted the crime scene location in the map file. Murdock would send me more particulars as soon as he had them. Tonight's victim was number three in a weekly cycle, so Avalon Memorial had agreed to give any new cases top priority. Big of them.

The latest victim could have been either of the first two. Male fairy, prostitute by trade, found in a remote alley with his heart missing. A stone was placed in the chest cavity and ward stones set on his wings. The ward stones I could figure. Even a drunk fairy could manage some kind of flight, so the perpetrator needed the wards to nullify the wings. The stones were obviously some kind of talismanic replacement but not part of any ritual I ever knew. They weren't charged with anything, either, except normal body essence. If any real power were involved, the residue would have lasted a lot longer than the time I took to get to the scene.

I leaned back in the chair and skimmed the bookshelf that ran around the room along the top of the wall. Ancient leather spines fought for space with cheap trade paperbacks in a profusion of incantation primers, spellcaster workbooks, grimoires, rune dictionaries, pronunciation guides for fourteen languages—three of them technically dead and one that never was—and a complete set of first edition Lloyd Alexander. The ritual I needed to know very likely lay buried somewhere in the pages. As I contemplated an old Celtic handbook of spells perched close to the edge, I decided three hours' sleep was way too few for ogham reading—or anything else.

I got up and went into the kitchen galley off the living room. The fridge bulb made it abundantly clear I needed to get some groceries. I pulled out a thimble-size bottle with a little yellow point of light in it. "Glow bees" most people called them, the poor man's sending. Humans with fey friends used them mostly, though they didn't work for everyone. Even when they did, the average human had to hold them for a couple of hours to get a decent charge on them. Email was quicker. I have to use them now. Most of my sendings go astray these days.

I slipped it in my pocket to warm it up. By the time I got the futon open, my pants were humming. As I took the bottle back out, the little light danced up and down inside, emitting its characteristic faint buzz. Carefully, I took off the lid and cupped the ball of light in my hands. I brought my hands to my lips and said, "Stinkwort. The Waybread. Noon." Opening my hands, the glow bee shot up and hovered a moment, then popped through the window.

I crashed on the futon and was asleep before the morning news began. Four hours later, I was seated in The Waybread, eating lunch for breakfast. A Chinese couple had opened the place a few years back, hoping to tap into the elf market. They didn't know honeycomb pie from scallion pancakes, but the burgers were pretty decent. It catered mostly to teenage tourists on a day jaunt to the bad-ass part of town. I liked it because I wasn't likely to run into anyone I know. Most of the friends I had left had better taste.

Noon came and went. I sat twiddling a coffee straw and watching the completely human crowd. Every time the door opened, their heads would bob up only to return to their plates without a wing or pointy ear sighting. No one bothered me. Druids aren't obviously different. We look human but have more sensory abilities and, of course, can tap into essence. After another twenty minutes, my bladder would no longer stand being ignored. I went to the restroom.

I was just about to take care of business when a voice over my head observed, "At least you're not sitting down."

Above me twelve inches of loincloth-clad flit hovered, tawny-colored arms crossed, face pinched, wings spread in dark pink anger. "Stinkwort, what the hell took you so long?" I asked.

He moved down in front of my face. "Me? It's about time you came in here. What the hell were you thinking sitting out there with all those people? How long do you think it would have been before that bunch started with the cameras? You think I have nothing better to do than pose for some human?"

"Sorry. I was hungry." I looked down, then back up. "Um, can you give me a sec?"

Stinkwort glanced down and flipped his shaggy blond head with scorn. "Fine. I'll be in the alley." He winked out. He winked back in. "And stop calling me Stinkwort." He winked out again.

True to his word, I found him sitting on a crate in the narrow passage behind The Waybread. He hovered up as I came out the back door so that we were able to face each other. He was still pretty angry. "So what do you need, oh great and powerless one?"

I frowned. "That's pretty low even for you, Stinky."

"Call me Joe," he said. "If you can't keep that straight, I'm out of here."

Nothing amuses me more than an angry flit. They try so hard to be menacing, an oxymoron when it involves wings that are blue or yellow or, in Stinkwort's case, pink. Especially pink. He had a point though. Stinkwort is an awful name. Whatever his mother was thinking when she gave it to him, she's keeping it to herself.

"Okay, Joe. I'm sorry. About the restaurant. About your name. About what I just paid for lunch. Can we call it a truce?"

He stared at me a moment, long, bushy eyebrows hanging over glittering eyes. Then he did the smile, the one that keeps on going from ear to ear. "What can I do for you, Connor?"

"I need some help on these fairy murders." Joe blanched, hovering back in fear. "Wait!" I said. "Don't bug out on me!" Flits can be so, well, flitty.

He paused, looking at me suspiciously. "What can I do about it?"

"A flit was at the last murder, maybe the others," I said, before he changed his mind. "Have you heard anything?"

He kept looking at me, a sour expression on his face. "That's all anyone's talking about."

"But have you heard anyone say they were there?"

He shook his head. "No one would say so if they were. If the murderer can kill one of the Dananns . . ." He left the rest unsaid, surprisingly. Most of the fairy folk think their own special people are the best of all possible fairy, all the others a sad imitation to be tolerated and pitied. Flits, especially, can be sensitive about their place in the universe. For Joe to come close to admitting that killing a Danaan fairy is harder than killing a flit showed how shaken up he was.

"I know a flit was at the most recent one," I said again. "I don't know if it was with the victim or the murderer, but it's the only lead I've had."

"No flit would stand by for murder," he said. He scowled again. "Did you say 'it'?"

"Okay, given," I said. "But I don't know if *he* or *she* knows the murderer and stumbled upon him in the act this time, or if it was a friend of the victim."

Joe considered for a moment, tapping his chin. "Everyone's upset. People are talking of hiding 'til it's over." He pursed his lips then. "You said 'it' again."

I smiled my best you're-the-best-Joe smile. "But you know people, right? People who would know of an upset flit?"

"I just said everyone's upset. What are you, deaf now, too?"

"Well, maybe someone who's upset in a different way. Like maybe someone who saw something. Look, if it's out of your league, Joe, I'll understand. I can try and find someone else."

He did this funny little annoyed dance. "I didn't say I couldn't find out."

I beamed at him. "That's great, Joe. If you hear anything that might help, let me know."

He studied me for a moment, eyeing me up and down. "So, how are you feeling?"

I shrugged. I knew what he was asking. "The same. No change."

He nodded absently, trying not to show too much concern. Joe was at the hospital when I woke up from the accident. He peered up the alley as though something very interesting were happening in the next trash heap. I didn't see anything, but flits look at the world differently. "I haven't seen you around. I was wondering what you were up to," he said.

"Sulking," I said with a smirk. I was pretty sure he was lying. For all I knew, Joe could have been ten feet behind me for weeks, and I wouldn't have known. He never stays away for long. Actually, I should say he never hides from me very long. I realized years ago that he watched me a lot. He's pretty good at staying out of sight, but every once in a while he makes an oblique reference to something in my life that I didn't think he'd been present for. His clan was from the west end of Devon in the old country—old, as in most of them were originally from Faerie—and those folks tended to attach themselves to families. I've known him since I was a kid, and I know he knew my parents before that. Besides, his favorite cookies always disappear out of my apartment, and I rarely eat them.

Joe huffed a little. "You should go dancing," he said. He winked. "I could set you up with a date."

I did laugh then. It was an old joke between us. The last time I let Joe fix me up was high school. I spent two hours with a troll who talked all the way through *Star Wars*. "I'll work that department on my own, thanks."

He kept glancing up the alley and getting twitchy. Too exposed probably. "Well, look, I gotta go. If a flit is involved, I'll find it."

"Thanks, Joe. Um, did you say 'it'?"

He barked at me like a dog and winked out. People who don't have much exposure to flits think it's some incredibly marvelous interaction. They're just people though. A little eccentric, maybe, but still just people who happen to wink in and out of sight. And they're harder to reach than someone without call waiting. If they don't want to talk, they don't, and they're not just a little bit paranoid. But then, if I were less than a foot tall, I'd be careful where I went, too.

I strolled up the alley to Old Northern Avenue, the main drag of the neighborhood. Most people called it the Avenue, but if you lived in the Weird, you earned the right to facetiously call it "Oh No" in casual conversation because that's what the uninitiated often say when they get in over their heads down here. Thirty or so years ago if someone said an entire residential neighborhood of sorts would be thriving on the waterfront in this part of town, you would have said they were crazy. An odd mishmash of warehouses and parking lots had turned into loft apartments and new, albeit sometimes indecipherable, businesses. Most of the property is owned by dwarf syndicates who thought they'd make a killing if the state built a new tunnel ac-3cess to the airport on the other side of the harbor. But, as usual, the syndicates got a little too greedy and started renting out space to the fey folk to increase their profits in the meantime. Before they knew it, tenant unions cropped up and killed the tunnel plans. Now the dwarves are stuck with the property. Eviction isn't much of an option for them since many of their tenants have a penchant for turning them into stone when negotiations get nasty. It's illegal, of course, but the city doesn't have the money or the ability to trace every spell cast in a rental dispute. So the dwarves content themselves with raising rents whenever they can. They pretty much have a stranglehold on the construction business in the area, though, so I guess it eventually balances out for them.

Banners in red and yellow and orange fluttered from wires hung across the Avenue as far as I could see. Even the streetlights had giant sun-shaped pinwheels spinning on top of them. Midsummer's Day was just a couple of weeks away. Fey folk and wannabes and hangers-on would descend on the Weird like a druid fog and dance and drink until beer came out their noses or they were arrested, whichever came first. Absolute madness would take possession of the entire neighborhood for twenty-four hours. It's a week of Mardi Gras insanity crammed into a day.

The Avenue was fairly empty. Since morning is not the favorite time of day in this part of town, business picks up around early afternoon. I opened a newspaper box on the corner and grabbed a copy of *Weird Times*, the local rag. TUESDAY KILLER STRIKES AGAIN the headline screamed. I stifled a groan. It didn't take Sherlock Holmes to notice the timing of the murders, but I hated when the press gave criminals catchy monikers. For the rest of the case, I wouldn't be able to not think of this psycho as the Tuesday Killer. I scanned the article and was relieved to see that not all the evidence had gotten out yet. Everyone knew the victims were fairies and the hearts were missing. Given the weekly time frame that was developing, even a novice could tell some kind of ritual was being played out. The reporter speculated about a couple of theories, all of which I had thought of after the second murder and discarded five minutes later. No mention was made of the stones. They were the one thing Murdock and I had managed to keep quiet, and so far it seemed to be working.

The day after a crime is one of the best times to hit up sources for dirt before they calm down and realize they can barter their information for higher prices later. Given the lives the victims led, it was still too early to find their associates. Murdock wouldn't have a file on the latest victim for me yet, and I prefer to do book research at night. That left running things down the old-fashioned way.

I crossed the Avenue and cut down a small side street. Calvin Place is just a little connector street between two main drags. In better days, it had no better days. Time was marked by small service establishments that went in and out of business with the change of year. Near the middle of the north side sat one shop that had remained in place for decades with a single owner. Its wooden facade had turned ashen from lack of paint and the large plate-glass windows were so soot-stained you couldn't see inside. The sign that ran the length of the building had been installed sometime in the 1950s and hadn't been updated since: BELGOR'S NOTIONS, POTIONS, AND THEURGIC DEVICES. Half the letters were missing and a newer metal sign had been nailed just under it: CHECKS CASHED. As I opened the door, a little bell fixed to the inside rang mournfully.

At first glance, dust seemed to be the major item for sale. The space was crammed with wooden bookcases rising twelve feet high, leaning toward each other in the dim ochre light as though browsing each other's wares. Yellowed boxes with faded names, blue glass jars with odd shapes, old hardcover books with no titles, and innumerable rocks, crystals, and baubles filled the shelves in no discernible order, most everything covered with the detritus of time. Here and there the subtle hint of something True lingered in the air, or something that was powerful at one time, but now just a faded shell of its former glory. As I moved along to the back, the unmistakable odor of unwashed elf hit me like a fist in the face. It's a lot like burnt cinnamon and not remotely pleasurable.

In front of the back wall stood a counter cluttered with piles of newspaper, receipts, and street flyers leaning against an old manual cash register. A coffee mug filled with warped wooden sticks had a label that said "Yew Wands, 10 cents," and, from the looks of them, that's all they were worth. The back wall was lined with videocassettes for rental, most of them low-rent skin flicks, and rolls of lottery tickets. I picked up and examined a small jar of newt eyes in vinegar that was half-hidden under a carton of cigarettes.

The curtain in the corner parted, and the amazing immensity of Belgor shifted his way ponderously into the room. No one lived in the Weird for any length of time without knowing, or knowing of, Belgor. He primarily dealt with the lower rungs of the neighborhood, which is to say considerably downmarket, operating a small numbers operation and occasionally fencing stolen goods. He kept himself lowkey, just low enough to avoid any particular attention by the Ward Guild but not enough to avoid the occasional surprise visit from the Boston P.D. No one ever found anything though. I had enough on him to make his life miserable if I wanted, but as long as he feeds me decent information when I need it, I let him slide. It annoys the hell out of Murdock that I won't help put him away, but you make your compromises where you do. I try to mollify them both by coming in alone in the middle of the afternoon so Murdock doesn't have to know where I've gotten my stuff, and Belgor doesn't have to be embarrassed by my presence in front of his latenight customers.

The obese elf rested his thick hands on the counter and his fleshy, sallow face split with a patented cold smile. He had the long, pointy ears that come with extreme old age in elves and didn't bother to pluck the bristly hairs that grew out the ends. Not surprising from someone who was hygienically challenged. "Good evening, Mr. Grey. What can I do for you?"

"It's the middle of the day, Belgor. You should wash your windows more than once a decade."

I pulled a ward stone out of my pocket and placed it on the counter. It was dead, just a short obelisk about three inches high, poorly finished in black and gray stone with just enough iron in it to make it useful for minor work. It was one of the ones found with the second victim, no different from the others that had been left behind. "Do you happen to know where this might have been purchased?" I asked.

Belgor pumped his lips at the sight of the rock, not deigning to touch it. "You know as well as I do, Mr. Grey, that this is standard off-the-shelf inferior merchandise. It could have been purchased anywhere between here and Southie. Most of my customers would not have the energy to overcome the flaws in it."

He had a point. Cheap ward stones were counterproductive. It took more energy to make them work properly than a finely tuned stone. If the killer were moving through a crowd with a good charged ward, someone would be bound to notice. A poor stone, crudely charged, would slip by most people until it was needed—say, on a drunk fairy. Someone with a fair amount of ability would be able to pull it off subtly.

"Yeah, I guess you're right," I said.

"Terrible about these murders. Have you any leads?"

I like the way he just drops that he knows I'm working. Doesn't take Belgor long to hear much of anything. "I'm following a couple of things."

He pretended to pick dust off the counter. "I could be in a position to make a nice commission on the sale of some high-quality chargeable selenite. Selenite has a long and odd history of usage. An odd gentleman came to visit me several months ago inquiring if I had such a thing." He chuckled and waved his hands about. "If only my humble shop could be so stocked," he said with practiced modesty.

I did my best not to look too eager. Unless the Guild, which had agreed to do a scan on the heart stones, had let the information leak out, only Murdock knew that the stones were selenite.

"How long ago was this?"

"About six months. I remember it was before Yule." He pursed his lips. "He was about your height, and young. But at my age, everyone seems young." Belgor tapped his nose. "My senses are not what they used to be. His essence was very odd. I thought he was an elf by first glance, but his ears were misshapen."

"Misshapen?"

He wiggled his own pointed appendages. "Like yours."

"Call me if he shows up again. I'll see if I can help. I'll stop by again."

He bowed his head. "I shall look forward to it," he said, looking anything but.

"Have a good night," I said sarcastically. Outside on the sidewalk, I forced myself to sneeze to clear my nose of body odor. Belgor did very little for my growing animosity toward elves who do stupid things. I didn't think he knew more than he said. He's a shrewd operator. Wouldn't have lasted as long as he has if he weren't. He wouldn't be so stupid as to hint he knew about the stones if he knew the murderer. I could have pressed him on it, but now that I had confirmed his guess about the stones, he would keep his eyes open.

2

A pounding on the door woke me at the crack of noon. I sat up in bed, rubbing my fist into my eye and wondering what had died in my mouth to make it taste the way it did. The knocking started up again, and I put on a robe and opened the door. Murdock sauntered in like a cop.

"Do you know what time it is?" I asked. I hate waking up. I opened the refrigerator. Seltzer water, condiments, and glow bees. I had to go shopping. Every night the last thing I do is set up the coffeemaker to save a minute and a half. I hit the ON button. Murdock knows the routine. He didn't say a word while I disappeared into the bathroom. The only thing that kills that morning shag rug feeling from a six-pack of Guinness is an extra dose of Crest, and the only thing that kills the Crest is black coffee. I didn't come out until I knew it was ready. Murdock was in the study flipping through an herb dictionary. I slipped on a pair of jeans and yesterday's T-shirt and joined him. The squeak of my computer chair sliced through my head.

I took a gulp of hot coffee, met Murdock's eyes, and smiled thinly.

He smiled, shaking his head. "How can you sleep half the day away?"

"Same way most people sleep the night away," I said. I hardly came from a line of farmers and never saw much value in dawn except as a sign that maybe I had stayed up late again. Murdock had probably been up too many hours already for me to think about.

He tossed a folder on the desk next to me, the edge of some paper and a compact disc sliding out. "This week's victim. We're still waiting for serology, but it will probably confirm alcohol and trace user drugs like the others. I took the liberty of putting the photos on disc for you."

I flipped open the folder without speaking. Nothing like autopsy photos to start the day. Murdock leaned back in his chair, looking as fresh in his white shirt, classic red tie, and barely creased tan gabardine pants as if he had just dressed. "Victim's been ID'd as a street worker named Gamelyn Danann Sidhe. Only been around a couple of months. One arrest for hustling."

Gamelyn's face stared out from a head shot with that disconcerting glassy stare of the dead, narrow fine features, hair so pale that his eyebrows barely showed. He looked young for a Danann, a hundred or younger, probably a runaway, or one of those fools who think humans are a fascination to experience.

"So what are you thinking?" he asked.

It wasn't a general question. Murdock's own admitted fascination with fey folk drew him to the Weird and kept him there. The more you got to know, the more there was to know. Years ago, when I thought of such things, human curiosity annoyed me no end. I used to think being a druid was no different than anything else. Just a different set of skills. Not every druid excelled at his craft, just like not every human or fairy or elf. But that was before I lost most of my ability, before I learned what it was like not to be able to do things. Before I understood that only if you could make a spell work could you bring true intuition to understanding how someone else's spell worked. Now I only have the intuition and limited ability. I have to confess to a certain amount of anger about it. But at least I had that. Humans had neither, no matter how many books they studied. It's a mystery to them in the truest sense, in the ancient theological sense. And like all mysteries, they hold out hope that the answers are easy if you know the secret. So Murdock, with all the sincerity in the world, asks me every time what do I, who has been granted access to the mysteries by dint of birth, know.

"Nothing," I said.

"Come on, Connor," he said, stretching his arms behind his head. "I'm not asking you for a name. What's this starting to shape into? If it were your basic psycho, I'd say we have a disassociative personality acting out anger against victims who represent some kind of psychological trauma from the murderer's past. The trauma most likely occurred at a young age. The act of the murder is his way of taking control. Even without the evidence of aggressive removal of the hearts, he's likely to be male. Given all the victims are male prostitutes who service male customers, I'd consider that the killer was likely molested by a male, possibly a relative."

I couldn't resist smirking. "And what makes you think you're wrong?"

He laughed. "I'm not saying I am. But given his choice of fairy prostitutes, his use of wards, and the ritualized placement of the stone, I'd say there's a layer to him that you might enlighten me on." It was his turn to smirk and mine to laugh.

"All right, fine," I said. "Given that the wards have to be charged, it's not likely he's human. He might have bought a charged ward, but there's no room for error if the fairy is strong enough to resist. He might get lucky once, but three times leads me to think some kind of enchantment is used even before the alley is reached. So that leads me to believe the killer is fey. I've already told you that I sensed human, elf, and fairy essence on the victims, which narrows the possibilities to elf or fairy. It's clearly a performed ritual, one I've never heard of. Most rituals are very proscribed. The methodical enactment of the murders supports that. The heart is considered the power center, so power is either being gained or taken away. Blood rites, particularly involving people, are very old, and were supplanted by symbolism long ago, much as Christians use wine for blood. If it is a real ritual, the killer would either have to be very old or have access to old knowledge."

Murdock cocked his head to one side and squinted at me. "What do you mean 'if ' it's a real ritual?"

I smiled back at him. "He may have no other motive other than a disassociative personality taking control from the perpetrator of his childhood trauma. Other than the wards, I haven't sensed any expenditure of power that a ritual might entail. Just because he's fey doesn't mean the ritual does anything. It could just mean he has his own ritual for killing fairies."

Murdock blew air through his lips. "Great."

"And . . . he just might be finished," I said. "It's an outside chance. There've been three murders. Even if the ritual's not real, the killer could still be operating within fey parameters. Three is a very powerful number. The first token stone was dark, almost black, the second, gray, and the last white. A nice balance. He might be done."

Murdock scratched his head, then smoothed his hair again. "Is this your way of saying that magic isn't always magic?"

I sipped my coffee. "No. Just that there are no magic answers. And stop calling it magic. It's manipulated essence. That's all."

He stood up. "So we work it like a regular case, solve it with forensics and witnesses and evidence."

I couldn't resist. "On the other hand, the ritual could be real. If I find the ritual, we find the motive, and if we find the motive, we might have the killer."

Murdock shook his head, laughing. "I don't know if you're trying to drive me crazy or just get more consulting fees."

I poked my cheek out with my tongue. "Both have their appeal."

He jerked his head at the door. "Let's go. We have to meet someone."

I rummaged on the floor for a pair of socks. I hadn't even taken a shower, so I wasn't going to worry about dirty socks. I threw on a baseball cap, grabbed a long leather jacket, and we left the building. I slid into the passenger seat of Murdocks's car right on a poorly disguised romance novel. We all have our embarrassing secrets. For all his immaculateness, Murdock's car was a pigsty. Newspaper, take-out bags, and napkins mounted in the well on the passenger side to the point that the mats underneath were actually clean because they rarely had feet on them. Club invitations and gum wrappers littered the dashboard. It was why he couldn't keep a partner for more than a few months at a time. I think he does it on purpose.

"So, where am I going?" I asked.

"Talk to a couple of guys," he said, snaking the car in and out of the dumpsters behind my building to avoid the one-way street in front. "Street kids. The photos of the barricades show them at the first and third scenes."

He leaned across, opened the glove compartment, and handed me two photos. Two heads were circled in each, one a tall blond boy wearing a green tunic and a bow and quiver, the other shoulder height to the first and wearing some kind of dress and a black wig tied with a red sash. The blond looked familiar, but if Murdock hadn't told me they were both male, I'd never have guessed. At least not from the photos.

"Do you know them?" I asked.

"A little. They're runaways, been living the life to get by. No trouble as far as I know," he said. He made the turn onto Pittsburgh and cut into the next alley. He pulled up behind one of a series of boarded-up buildings. We got out of the car. Murdock scanned up and down the alley as he slipped on his sports coat. "Maybe they haven't been caught yet," he said.

He walked up to a door covered with several pine planks and pulled. It popped open easily on its hinges, boards and all. Murdock gave me a crooked smile and walked into the darkened hallway.

I stood behind him, apprehension creeping up my back. I never carried a gun, even when I was in the Guild. Didn't need one then. Even with extra senses and body-warding abilities, though, you can't stop that adrenaline rush that comes from stepping into blind situations. A faint prickling sensation ran over my face as I called up a weak body shield. At one time, the shield was amazingly tough. It wasn't much now, mostly my head and just patches on the chest and arms, and it would never stop a bullet. If someone threw something at me, like a fist or a brick, the force of the blow would be slightly blunted. It worked more for comfort than usefulness these days.

Sunlight penetrated just past the threshold, showing a debris-strewn hallway trailing off into black. The odor of mildew hung in the air. A door slammed not far off and a blazing high-voltage light snapped on in our faces. Instinctively, I dove for the floor.

Murdock looked down at me and burst out laughing. "What the hell are you doing?" he said.

"Who is it?" a voice demanded.

Murdock turned away from me and held his hand up to protect his eyes. "Turn off the damned light, Robin!" The light went out to be replaced by a dimmer bare bulb in the ceiling. Murdock shook his head.

I stood up, brushing dirt off my coat. "You could have warned me," I said.

He just kept chuckling as he led the way down the hall to a door at the end. When we reached it, it opened slightly, then all the way. A tall thin boy clothed in jeans and a white T-shirt faced us, long, blond hair framing a strikingly hand-some face. His eyes were wary as he backed away, and we stepped into the room. Another boy stood in the corner, his face incredibly feminine, with just the hint of applied color on his eyes. He wore a long shift in light blue with a match-ing piece of fabric tied around his dark hair. Most of the room was taken up by two narrow beds, the walls decorated with old posters, hanging fabric, and some standard house-hold good luck charms. The far wall was partially covered by a thick maroon velvet curtain, behind which neatly arranged clothes could be seen on shelves and hooks.

Murdock lifted his chin at the blond. "This is Robin, and that's Shay," he said. I just nodded as Murdock sat down in the only chair. He leaned back and smiled at the kid in the corner. "How's it going, Shay? Still doing the Snow White gig?"

Shay crossed his arms and frowned. "No. The damned dwarves quit. They said their cut wasn't enough." He rolled his eyes. "Like standing around watching takes effort."

Murdock shrugged. "Too bad. I heard you were making quite a name for yourself."

Shay draped himself on the nearest bed. "Who is this, Detective Murdock?"

"A friend. You can call him Connor."

Robin arched an eyebrow, a small cocky smile twitch-ing at one corner of his mouth. I was tempted to slap him. "*The* Connor, as in Connor Grey? I thought no one ever met you."

"Consider yourself met," I said. I stared right back at him, but he held my gaze. I was impressed.

Shay walked toward me with an exaggerated languidness.

"I've seen your picture in the paper. You're much more handsome in person. I don't usually go for tall, dark-haired types, but you have very pretty eyes. Aqua."

"They're just blue, thanks," I said. The kid was a hoot.

He smiled and strolled back to the other side of the room. "You were at the murder," he said. Robin shot him an annoyed look.

"So were you," said Murdock.

Robin moved closer to Shay's bed. "A lot of people were there," he said.

"Yeah, but a lot of people were not at two murder scenes," Murdock said. The two of them looked studiously at their hands. "You want to explain that?" Murdock prompted.

Shay busied his hands with the chenille on the bedspread.

"You know they happened right near here. We were on our way home," said Robin. He nervously ran his fingers through those long blond strands. His expression stayed suspicious though.

"Bad luck," Shay whispered. He darted his eyes at me, then away to examine a poster on the wall, an old Deco print of a ship coming into port. Stylish optimism. " 'Turning and turning in the widening gyre.' Isn't that the way of it?" he murmured.

My heart caught a moment. I couldn't help it. Something about the kid, his pretty little woman face on a man's little body and the sadness in his voice. I didn't think it was an act. For a moment, I heard what must have driven him here and maybe what kept him here.

Murdock leaned forward. "Do you want to tell me something, Shay?" he asked softly. I could tell Murdock had felt it, too. Is that what kept him in the Weird?

Shay just stared at us solemnly. He reached up and removed his head scarf, shaking out long, brown hair. "It's the way Robin said. We were on our way home." Robin seemed to relax a little. "The first time," Shay continued.

"Shay! No!" Robin said, spinning away from us.

Shay tapped his arm. "It's all right." Robin reached out and held his hand. Shay fixed us with a defiant eye. "We were looking for Gamelyn the second time."

"You knew him?" Murdock asked.

Shay nodded. "I met him at the Flitterbug. He was sweet. Too sweet for that place. And drunk, like they all are when they first come here. A man kept buying him drinks. He made me nervous. I tried to talk Gamelyn into going home, but he said he was fine. They left together. I started to follow, but Robin came back, and we talked for a bit. Then I got nervous again, and we went looking for Gamelyn. We were about to give up when I thought I saw Gamelyn's friend go down an alley."

"What friend?" Murdock asked.

"A flit. She usually came around to talk to Gamelyn."

"Was the murderer still there?"

Shay shook his head, and his voice went soft. "When we got to the alley we . . . we found him and called the police. They'd only been gone about twenty minutes, but I guess that was all the time he needed."

"Could you identify him?"

Shay considered for a moment. "Probably. The Flitterbug is kind of dark. Not everyone goes someplace else, if you know what I mean. He looked old. Mean. I think he was fey."

"What kind of fey?"

"I don't know," he said. "One of the fairies or maybe a druid. He made my skin crawl. I never felt like that around the fey before. I didn't like him. And his voice. His voice sounded like someone took a saw to a violin. I would remember that voice."

"Tell me about the flit," I said.

Shay shrugged again. "I don't know her name if that's what you mean. She seemed shy. She only talked to Gamelyn. Half the time, I didn't even know she was around. She liked to curl up on his shoulder under his hair. She was tiny, maybe four or five inches tall."

"What color were her wings?"

"A pale yellow. That's why I didn't always notice her. Gamelyn had such lovely blond hair, like morning sunlight," said Shay.

"And you have no idea where she's from?"

Shay shook his head. "No. Like I said, she only spoke to Gamelyn."

Murdock cleared his throat. "Where were you, Robin?"

The kid became very still as he glared at us. "I was busy," he said. I didn't need to ask, and Murdock let it drop.

Murdock stood up. "I'll need you to come down to the station. I want you to work with a police artist."

Robin turned away. "Shay's lying. He didn't see anything. He's just looking for attention."

Shay rose from the bed and came around to the other side. He took Robin's hand and tugged it. "It's okay, Robin. Detective Murdock won't let anything happen to me. We'll do this favor for him. And for Gamelyn." He threw Murdock a flirty little look. "We may need his help someday."

I could see just the hint of a smile playing on Murdock's lips. He was too indulgent sometimes. Shay did have a certain amount of charm though. We walked back to the alley while Robin and Shay locked their door. On the floor in the corner, Shay placed a small protection ward that looked like some of Belgor's merchandise. I didn't have the heart to tell them it was only decorative.

I stood aside as they got in the car. Murdock leaned across the seat to look at me through the passenger window. "You coming?"

"No. I'll catch up with you later."

He straightened up in the seat and started the car. I stared down the alley after he drove off. Even in the stark light of day, the buildings could not muster more color than brick, and gray, and faded yellow. Rain-soaked paper and rotting leaves lined the gutters where the occasional weed fought to take root. Under a crisp blue June sky, it was just a melancholy, depressing place. But when day turned to night, melancholy turned to menace. Shadows lengthened and the gray deepened, hiding danger and calling fear. And two young men called it home.

I shivered, whether from my thoughts or the light breeze wasn't clear.

As I made my way up to the Avenue, a group of teenage boys came swaggering up the sidewalk, dressed in baggy jeans and red T-shirts. They didn't speak to each other, more interested in looking menacing as they scanned the street. They didn't part around me, but made a point of jostling me as they passed. Their essences were human, one of the xenophobic gangs that liked to show the human presence on the Avenue. They had their own colorful names, but most people just called them the xenos. I suppressed my annoyance because I wasn't in the mood to provoke them. Their organizing principles centered on conspiracy theories about secret fey alliances controlling the government. They were prejudiced thugs who preyed on the drunk and the drugged. They made damn sure they didn't try anything with any fey who had real power.

I hit the groceria on the corner of my street and picked up some nice sodium-rich deli meats, bread, some sundries, and a bag of Oreos in case Joe stopped in.

Back in my loft, I poured myself a cup of stale coffee and sat at the computer staring out the window. I didn't really believe the Tuesday Killer was finished. Murdock was right. The killer was trying to accomplish something even if he had a disassociated personality. Anyone who carved a heart out of a body had to be damned disassociated. Whatever it was, someone, somewhere was bound to know about it.

I pulled down a concordance of ancient druidic ceremonial writings. It was a nice little reference but only partially helpful. The druids themselves rarely wrote anything down, and most of the existing material was secondhand. Of that, even less was available to the general public. I counted myself lucky to have my own copies of high holiday ceremonies as well as the divination series put out by Modern Library back in the sixties before the Ward Guild shut them down. Most everything else I knew came from the classical oral training I had learned in camp. And that was stuff I kept meaning to put on the computer. The only heart removal references were the usual anecdotal junk that no one's ever proved, and even that didn't include the rituals themselves. I tossed the book aside.

Even if the ceremony were druidic, I kept coming back to who could know such a thing. Modern druids considered the old sacrifice stories a lie to discredit them, so they would hardly be candidates for passing down the information. A controversy flared up a few years back when it was discovered that an orthodox sect in northern Maine occasionally chewed raw meat for divination. The Ward Guild even investigated, but no evidence of anything illegal turned up. If anyone did know an ancient blood ritual, it would be them. But only a few were left, pretty ancient themselves, and not likely to be hitting on prostitutes without raising an eyebrow, even in the Weird. I didn't relish driving up to the Canadian border to find out.

I stretched back in the chair. The Guild had an excellent database. Even though I was no longer on staff, I could get in. Practically everyone in the place builds a back door into the computer systems on the remote chance they'll get the old access denied. Sure, they made a monthly security sweep, but if you had enough computer knowledge and enough ability to ward against detection, they weren't likely to find you. I had both at one time. My wards were still in place, at least the last time I checked.

I glanced at the computer. It was coming on two o'clock. After lunch, people kicked back and played a bit, a little solitaire, a little esoteric research, maybe a cyber quickie.

I could hide in the crowd of odd file requests for at least an hour before everyone got back to real work. On the other hand, if I just punched in for blood rites, I might get a security flag. With people on duty during the day, I might be picked up faster. As I debated risking access and possible detection, a more obvious approach occurred to me, and I picked up the phone.

"I've been expecting your call for days, darling," Briallen said when she answered.

I smiled into the receiver. "You could have called, you know," I said.

She laughed, her rich, throaty voice giving me the thrill it always did, especially if I were the one to make her laugh. Briallen verch Gwyll ab Gwyll was bawdy but nice, strong but sensitive, dynamic yet subtle, and one of the most powerful beings I have ever met. A pretty damn good cook on top of it, though I always make certain to ask before I sample from her stove. She's one of those people you're proud to know and flattered that they give you the time of day.

"I know I could have called, but at my age one likes to have her abilities confirmed. You haven't been by in ages."

"I've been, um, busy," I said, chagrined.

"You've been brooding again," she said. It was a statement of fact.

"Yeah, well . . ." My voice trailed off.

"Life's an ass, sweetie, you just have to bite it."

"I know, I know," I said, laughing. "I need a favor."

"You're working on the murders," she said. Again, just a statement. Between the people Briallen knows and the things she just knew, little escaped her. I filled her in on what I had so far, everything. If I couldn't take Briallen into my confidence, there was no one in the world I could.

"Danann hearts," she murmured. "I have a couple of thoughts, but I will only open those dusty old books on one condition: You must come for dinner."

"I owe you more than that," I said.

"Only if you bore me, darling, and you haven't yet. Call me in a day or so." She disconnected abruptly like she always did. I sat smiling at the phone for a moment. Briallen was many things: druidess, teacher, researcher, and, most importantly, friend. She was the other person at the hospital when I woke up. She also had one of the best private libraries on this side of the Atlantic.

I called up my database files and ran down the patterns. All three murders were localized off the Avenue. Ragnell Danann Sidhe, the first victim, was found in an alley two blocks away from where Pach Danann Sidhe, the second victim, was discovered. The latest victim, Gamelyn, had landed one block over. On the one hand, it was not surprising. Most illegal activity in the Weird happened in the alleys. On the other hand, I couldn't discount the possibility that something other than prostitution was a connection. A fey committing the murders might very well live in the area.

Stillings and Pittsburgh Streets connected the Avenue to Congress Street, forming an elongated rectangle. Most nights, cars circled the block with people jumping in and out like an endless merry-go-round. Ragnell worked the street, notably Stillings near Congress, but Pach worked out of a dive called the Flitterbug on the Avenue. After the conversation with Shay and Robin, I added Gamelyn's connection to the bar. Murdock had been running down the victims' associates. So far no one remembered anything unusual the night of the murders. Tuesdays tended to be quiet. Not many customers, not many witnesses.

Nothing unique was coming up on the clothing found at the scene. So many hairs and fibers were showing up, the Boston P.D. was still cataloging the tunic Ragnell wore on the night of his death. The forensics lab was not exactly rushing, and a little race resentment slowed the process. Very few fey folk were on the force, and the human contingent tended to want to focus on human problems. More politics at play.

Pach was covered with makeup and lotion smears from trying to hide bruises, obviously too poor to afford even a modest glamour stone. If he had not met his death at the hands of a murderer, he would have found it at the end of a needle soon.

And now Gamelyn, a young Danann, recently arrived from parts unknown. It was too soon to have much of anything on him except he was in good health when he died. And drunk.

Annoyed, I snapped off the computer. Staring at their gutted torsos made my own chest hurt. I prowled the apartment, trying to figure the twists that lead people down the paths they take. How does anyone end up a dead whore? What loss starts the slide? Physical looks? Love? Money? Power?

I pulled off my clothes and jumped in the shower, blasting myself with hot water. The heat penetrating under my skin felt cruelly satisfying. I wanted to burn away the frustration. I turned up the water temperature to match the heat of the anger spreading over me. I could not comprehend the stupidity that drives the fey. All the power they could ever want, and they wallowed in the muck of the Weird. I've heard the reasons, if they can be called that, the mere dalliance that most of them consider the depravity they cause and find. The inconsequentiality of sex in races that rarely gave birth. The resilience of bodies that lived for centuries. I'd heard all that and more. But it all rings hollow when toted up against the waste and pain and death.

As I stood naked, my skin nearly blistering, I knew I did not want to miss a minute accorded me. Not when I had no idea if I had anything stretching beyond an average human life span. Sometimes I imagined I could feel the thing in my head, like a cancer perhaps, dividing and replicating over and over, pushing every last ounce of ability out of my body. I'd barely lived forty years, nearly a childhood for my race, but I still wanted more, while fools risk their lives for the novelty of a high or a bed.

I gave myself a blast of cold water and shouted at the shock of it. The towel felt deliciously rough against my skin as I dried off. As I wrapped myself in a robe, I realized that pummeling my body with extreme temperatures was no different than the way others punished their bodies to soothe their inner emotions. It was all a matter of degree and rationality. I was just trying to feel alive. Just like them. I hated moments when I recognized my own kinship with the people who frustrated me. They only reminded me of why I loved the Weird. I made some fresh coffee and turned the computer back on.

3

While my ancestors had the luxury of tramping through forests and waging war to keep in shape, I had to resort to the tedium of bench-pressing three times a week. Jim's Gym was a nice little hole-in-the-wall just over the Congress Street bridge from the Weird. I liked it because I generally didn't know anyone there, it smelled like a gym, and it didn't have a juice bar. The clientele tended to be eclectic, from financiers to truck drivers, and mostly human. The common denominator was a good solid workout ethic with no prima donnas. The only mirrors at Jim's are in the locker room.

I had started working out to restore muscle tone after my hospital stay. I kept to myself, using the small weights I could manage then. It is amazing how weak lying in bed can make you. That was how I met Murdock. We'd exchanged the usual nonconversational gym etiquette before, the nods hello and shaking of heads when someone emitted gratuitous grunting. A year or so ago, in one of those fits of overreaching conceit I'm prone to way too often, I used too much weight and found myself pinned to the weight bench. In a further bit of pride, I didn't call out for help but lay there hoping I would get enough energy back to heave the bar off my chest without tipping the weights in a clatter to the floor.

Murdock's upside-down face appeared above me with just the flicker of the smirk I've since come to know too well. "Need help?"

"Yeah," I gasped, and a partnership was born. We started working out together after that, him giving me workout tips and me telling him about the fey folk. Things just progressed from there.

Friday afternoon was one of our usual workout times. I was getting off the treadmill when Murdock walked in, late as usual. He was dressed in his standard gear, regulation white T-shirt and nylon running pants. Even wearing clothes designed to sweat in, he looked freshly ironed.

We got down to it. Our routine ran smoothly, long practiced, with little conversation. Once we started working together on cases, work talk at the gym became taboo. I liked being able to get my aggressions out, not continue them. On the other hand, Murdock felt no need for such separations. He's got to be the most balanced human I've ever met. Either that, or I haven't figured out what's wrong with him yet.

Once we had showered and changed, Murdock suggested we go for an early dinner. It was unusually warm when we stepped out of the gym, so we decided to walk to the North End for Italian. The late rush-hour traffic zipped through the heart of the financial district. Some of the British fairies and German elves discovered a knack for the stock market in the early eighties and sparked a downtown renaissance of sorts. While many of the fey folk frowned upon the newfound fascination with wealth, few humans complained about the new businesses and the taxes they generated. Besides, the old parking garage in the middle of

Post Office Square was now buried under a nice fairy garden and that was definitely an improvement.

We found a small restaurant off the tourist route with comfortable booths and middle-aged waitresses. Murdock liked to carbo-load after a good workout. While we were waiting for our orders, he slid an envelope over to me. Opening it, I found a police artist sketch.

"Shay's sketch?" I asked. Murdock nodded. The sketch showed a bald man, dark eyes slightly tilted, almost Asian, and a straight nose, both attributes I would have expected of several of the elven races. But his ears were smooth, not pointed, and he had full lips, which could be just about any race but elven. As usual with these sketches, the face had a crudeness about. If you squinted the right way, it would look like anyone from your next-door neighbor to the emperor of Japan.

"Not very helpful," Murdock said, as the waitress served our orders.

I dug into my pasta. "I don't know. It pretty much eliminates elves, dwarves, and trolls. And flits, of course. How old does Shay think he is?"

"If he were human, he thinks about fifty," Murdock said.

I frowned. "Fifty? For one of the fey folk to look like a human fifty, he'd have to be pretty old. Most of that generation tend to stay in Ireland or Britain. They don't like the US."

Murdock shrugged. "That fits. You said the ritual was probably old."

"When I said that, I was talking a couple of thousand years, Murdock. Fey folk that old are few and far between."

"But this eliminates elves, right? We know it's a fairy now."

It was my turn to shrug. "Like I said before, it's not likely he's human, but that doesn't mean he's not. I'm comfortable assuming he's a fairy for now, though. Keeping the stone tokens under wraps seems to be working," I said.

Murdock's lips compressed into a thin line, and he distractedly rubbed the edge of the table. "I have some bad news about the stones. We sent them to the Guild for examination. They were receipted into inventory and when I called to follow up, they said they couldn't find them. They're missing."

I looked at my watch. It was coming up on eight-thirty. No way I could get any staff on the phone this late on a Friday. "Dammit, Murdock, why didn't you tell me earlier? I could have called before everyone went home."

Murdock was silent as the waitress dropped off the check. "I was just calling to confirm they got the new one. Connor, you know how it is. They haven't told us a thing about the other stones. I don't think they even looked at them yet. I didn't tell you earlier because you'd just get pissed off, and you're annoying to work out with when I bring up work."

I leaned back in my seat and rubbed my hands over my face. He was right, of course. The Guild spends its time on its own priorities first. Fairies in the Weird were on the lowest rung as far they were concerned, and prostitutes somewhere even lower. Maeve was none too pleased at the turn of events that dumped the fey in the modern world. As High Queen of the Seelie Court that rules over all fairies, she had sent out an edict long ago that people who venture outside of sanctioned territory were on their own. Part of the reason the rulers of the fey set up the Ward Guild was to handle the really egregious situations, but the Guild decided what those were. They gave token support to the local police on crimes they did not directly handle, just like the local police gave token support to fairy crimes they were stuck with. The end result is a lot of unresolved petty crime and, yes, dead fey folk some people think got what they deserved. That meant people, both human and fey, caught in the middle of official jurisdiction fights had to rely on whomever they could for justice. Murdock and I were on our own more often than we liked.

"The good news is that three dead bodies seem to have gotten the mayor's attention. He's about to authorize a task force," he said.

I smiled slyly. "Do I hear the sound of the Murdock brothers riding to the rescue?" Murdock comes from a big police family. Between friends and family, Sunday dinner at his father's house looks like roll call.

"Maybe," he said. "It's my case, but I don't see staff coming my way. Mostly, it'll be more uniforms on the street. He's more worried about tourist dollars and anti-fey protesters than the murders. The festival's right around the corner."

I nodded. Midsummer was two weeks away. What had its ancient roots in celebratory dancing had mutated into one long, wild party. Practically every religion ever had some kind of holiday associated with it, and every year the party got bigger. The Weird, as the local neighborhood with the highest concentration of pagans, became a nexus for the gatherings. It was a nightmare for residents, but it also brought huge amounts of money into the local economy. At least it wasn't England. No one in their right mind goes near Stonehenge for Midsummer. Some drugged-up fools always decide it's time to resurrect human sacrifices, and they're not picky about the virgin thing. It had become the longest day of the year in more ways than one.

"I don't want to think about Midsummer. I'm more interested in next Tuesday," I said.

We walked out into the evening twilight. Sunset had brought with it an early chill. Murdock stepped with his cop swagger, eyes instinctively scanning the sidewalk as though every passerby had some secret motive. We reached the Old Northern Avenue bridge and paused halfway, leaning in among the industrial girders to look at the water. Early-evening foot traffic passed behind us with little idea that we were probably the only ones in the city trying to figure out who had killed three people less than a mile away.

Across the channel, you could see the corner of my loft near the edge of what is still called Fan Pier. Around the turn of the century the pier, which was really filled-in harbor, was a railroad storage facility and switching station that from a height looked like a giant handheld fan. Hence the name. As the years went by, the rail yard shrank, and shacks and warehouses went up. It made the kind of picturesque jumble of shoreline that urban renewers just love to raze for luxury housing.

"What about a connection to the festival?" Murdock asked.

I gazed down at the rich gray water. Little bits of foam and debris spun slowly beneath our feet. "I don't see a connection yet. The Forest King is obvious. He dies on the summer solstice, completing the cycle of birth and death. But that's one person killed and pretty much a voluntary community event."

"Maybe just one person is doing the killing and the rest are keeping quiet about it," he suggested.

"Maybe. But I think we would hear about it. Of the sacrifice rituals I know, it doesn't make sense to go after fairies. Faith and belief by the sacrifice is just as important as the slayer's. I'm missing something. I just haven't figured out what."

"Want to hear what Shay thinks?" Murdock asked.

I rolled my eyes. "Sure, why not."

"Elves. He thinks it's connected to the old fairy/elf feud because if there were bad blood among the fairies, he would have heard about it." I cocked a doubtful eyebrow at him. Murdock just shrugged and smiled. "I wouldn't underestimate him, Connor. He may be young, but he's lasted a lot longer than a lot of kids his age."

Whenever something bad happened to elves or fairies, someone always brought up the tension between the two races. When the fey began to appear around 1900, fairies and elves were at war but reached a truce of sorts when they found themselves here instead of in what everyone calls Faerie. "Convergence" is the accepted term for the merging of the two worlds, and arguments still rage over whose world is the real one. The fact remains that the fey definitely came from someplace else, a place where time ran differently, and they had not faded into myth and legend. Whichever, in both places, elves and fairies didn't like each other very much. In fact, the two sides were currently meeting in Ireland for a Fey Summit to try to iron out their continuing differences.

"So, what's Shay's story?"

"Shay's of legal age, but he's a runaway, if you ask me. No boy that looks like a woman could have had it easy growing up," said Murdock.

Mildly surprised, I glanced over at him. "Murdock, I would have thought by now you would be over the gender thing."

"I didn't say *I'd* hassle him, Connor. I grew up here. I'm just stating a fact. Believe it or not, there are some places in this country where the fey don't live. You forget that not everyone is comfortable with fey folk, never mind the whole pansexual stuff."

He was right. Being fey and growing up in one of the highest concentrations of fey folk in the US, it's easy to forget the hinterlands are out there. Though the fey more often fall into opposite sex relationships, they're fairly indifferent to biology. Briallen tells me it has to do with low fertility and long lives. Promiscuity is hardly frowned upon when it often is the only way to propagate the species. Since the likelihood of producing children is so low, sex becomes more about the relationship and less about procreation. Extremely long lives leave plenty of time to breed if someone wants to try. No one would have thought anything strange about Shay in the schools I went to.

Murdock pushed away from the bridge railing, and we resumed walking. "He was born in Boston, but there's no other info before last year. He's either got a sealed juvie record somewhere, or he was clean. He's gonna get snagged on a soliciting rap eventually. It's just a matter of time."

"And Robin?"

Once over the bridge, we were officially back in the Weird. We crossed over Sleeper Street, which I lived on the end of, and walked slowly along the sidewalks of the Avenue, passing the packed parking lot of the Barking Crab, a seafood restaurant that had been around so long it was an institution. No one went there for the ambience except in a kitschy kind of way, but the food was incredible. If you lived nearby, you left it to the tourists and suburbanites on the weekends. We kept going up the street to where the local shops and bars began.

"Robin's story is a little different," Murdock said. "He's got a short soliciting rap sheet. No drugs as far as I can tell. Been on the losing end of a fight now and then. If you ask me, he provokes at least half the trouble he gets in. He's at that bulletproof age and has a nasty disposition to go with it."

"Yeah, I noticed," I said sarcastically.

"What else do we have to go on?" Murdock asked.

I hesitated before answering. Before I went to bed the night before, I had sent Joe a glow bee with the flit information from Shay, but hadn't heard back from him. I still hadn't told Murdock about the flit I sensed at the murder scene. Tossing it around in my head, I decided to come clean.

He frowned and shook his head. "That's cold, Connor. I never hold back on you."

"I wasn't really holding back, Murdock. I wasn't sure it was relevant and didn't want to sidetrack you."

He stopped to examine a window display of parade masks for the festival. Ogre, troll, wolf, and snake masks faced off against fairy, elf, and forest animals. Most of them were covered with glitter or feathers for that extra festive touch. "I could have given you names of flits that hang with the hookers."

That startled me. "You can track flits? They're pretty secretive."

Murdock walked away. "Newsflash, Connor: They hang with people who aren't," he said over his shoulder. His voice had the low, flat quality it gets when he's angry.

"I'm sorry, Murdock. I made a bad call. It won't happen again."

He stopped and stared at me a moment. I could tell he was trying to decide how angry to be. He settled for annoyed. "You have to remember you're not the Guild hotshot anymore, Connor. I'm not saying that to make you feel bad. I'm saying it because I don't want to find out this has all been passing time until you get your ability back. Partners have to trust each other. You can have all the glory you want, but not at my expense."

"That's a little thick over a minor slip-up, don't you think?"

He shrugged. "Minor turns into major eventually. I don't want that to happen."

"Okay. I won't do that again."

He nodded firmly. "Good. You know how I feel about loyalty." Murdock glanced at his watch and began walking again. He had checked his watch several times since we left the restaurant.

"Are you meeting someone?" I asked. We joined the early-evening crowd making its way into the neighborhood. At this point in the evening, they were people catching a show down at the old theater and some middle-aged folks who get a thrill at being near the edge. They'd all be gone by ten o'clock. That's when the people who really owned the place took over.

Murdock looked around without meeting my gaze. "It's just a drink."

"Anyone I know?"

"No, she's nice," he said.

"Very funny," I said. "Where are you meeting?"

"The Ro'Ro'." The Rose Rose was what someone's Irish mother would call a nice place just off the Avenue on B Street. It had warm wooden booths around a main seating area that was filled with little tables cozy for four. Behind a beveled-glass partition was a long mahogany bar for more serious drinking. It was well lit, not too smoky, and had great entertainment, from bands to a cappella singers. It's what the Weird could be if someone cared more about it.

"Oh, so it's serious," I teased.

"It's just a drink. She's there with some friends," he said.

We reached the intersection of Pittsburgh Street and stopped. Murdock was obviously not inviting me along. We hadn't quite gotten to the point in our friendship where we partied together. Admittedly, I had never asked Murdock to join me for a night on the town. The only places I went served beer, shots, and fistfights, not the kind of situation a detective likes to find himself in without police backup. I wasn't exactly looking for potential relationships at this point of my life either. I knew Murdock well enough to know he could be respecting the fact that I might be uncomfortable in a date atmosphere since I hadn't seen anyone in a while, or he could be tacitly making the point that I didn't invite him so he wasn't inviting me. Probably both. He was rather efficient. He was also nice enough not to tell me to buzz off. We stood awkwardly on the corner as though waiting for something to happen.

"Well, I guess I'll catch up with you later," I finally said.

"Call me if you think of anything. Have a good night." And he was off into the crosswalk.

I made my way back up the Avenue until I came to the

mask store. Murdock wasn't too far off when he brought up the Guild. It was a cutthroat environment. High levels of ability tended to come with high-maintenance personalities that did not necessarily enjoy working together. Competition for recognition and promotion was fierce. You played your cards close to the vest and only tipped the hand on a need-to-know basis. The payoff is money, stardom, and power. The risk is simply failure at all three. You could fall a lot faster and further than you could rise. I had been damned good at it.

If the truth be known, I had been gunning for the top. The Top. Guildmaster of Boston. Throughout the last century, most of the Guildmasters have been fairies, reflecting the fact that the Seelie Court paid the bills. No elf had ever run the place and probably never would. For all the talk of truce, the old animosity between elves and fairy remained strong. A handful of druids and druidesses had had short tenures. Enough to make me think I could do it.

But then, as they say, tragedy struck. My security clearance was revoked before I even left the hospital. The Guild has strict rules that allow only those with high-level ability to have high-level access. A year later I lost my Beacon Hill condo, but most of my so-called friends stopped calling long before then. The only people that stood by me were Stinkwort, Briallen, my family, and some casual acquaintances from outside the Guild.

The more I thought about it, the more I realized what Murdock said was true. I wasn't used to working with somebody, never mind as the junior partner. I might have more knowledge about fey folk, but he brought sanctioned authority to the table. Without him, I was just a loose cannon neither the Guild nor the Boston P.D. wanted. And without either of them, I was just a washed-up druid with no prospects.

Turning away from the store, I could see the Flitterbug on the opposite side of the street. Above its dark red metal door hung a dim sign with three sets of wings that flickered more from dying neon than artistic effect. Most people walked right past it, on their way to more brightly lit bars of marginally higher repute. I crossed the street against traffic to a hail of car horns.

As I pulled on the door, I sensed a warding, vague and subtle, that was quickly washed away by the essences that escaped from within. Many fey places used them, mostly as protection charms, to keep away bad influences. Of course, bad influence is a matter of perspective. They could be keyed to just about anything, from police badges to specific people, depending on need and ability of the warder. For the Flitterbug, I sensed it was more likely the boys in blue.

A sense of staleness overwhelmed my senses as I stepped inside, and the door closed behind me. Stale beer. Stale smoke. Stale sweat. Residual essences of all manner of people lingered in the air. The entire room ran about fifty feet back. The place was dark, halogen lights purposefully providing little illumination beyond their fixed spots, and red and blue lasers crisscrossed the ceiling. A sound system played house music very loudly to an empty dance floor right near the front. A row of cramped cocktail tables fit along one wall, which consisted of one long banquette of indeterminate color. The opposite wall was taken up by the bar itself.

It was early yet, just a couple of elves at a table talking. The Flitterbug was one of those places that saw most of its action when the majority of the population was home sleeping.

I went to the bar, where a dwarf stood wiping down the pitted wooden surface. He was about three and half feet tall and wore Levi's with an old black T-shirt. His gnarled features had a sooty cast, as though he had just toiled up out of a coal mine without washing. Some kind of gel plastered dark hair to his head, the side part razor-sharp in the dim light.

"I'll have a Guinness," I said. His eyes flickered up at me a moment, then he walked down the elevated planking behind the bar to the taps. He returned with the smallest beer I'd seen in a long time. He went back to his wiping.

"You work here this week?" I asked.

He shrugged. "Yeah."

I pulled the police sketch out and slid it near him. "Recognize him?"

He looked over my shoulder to check out the elves. "You didn't pay for your beer," he said without pausing his fruitless cleaning. I placed a ten on the bar next to the sketch. The bill disappeared into his pocket in one smooth motion. "He looks like every other old geezer that hobbles in here."

"He has an odd voice. Maybe kind of screechy or raspy?" I said.

The dwarf shrugged again. "I need more than that." I placed another ten on the bar. "Yeah, I think I remember someone like that."

"Remember which day?"

He finally gave up with the rag and gave me a long, considered look. A sly smile came over his face. "You act like Guild, but you don't look it. I'm thinking you want me to say 'Tuesday.' How about another beer, friend?"

I hadn't touched the first. I didn't think I would, which is saying something considering some of the places I've passed the evening. I put another ten down. Murdock was going to kill me when I turned in the expense report. The bill disappeared. "He was in here last Tuesday. I saw him talking to a street kid named Shay, then the dopey kid that got killed."

"Shay? Guy that looks like a girl?" I said.

The bartender nodded. "And a little bitch, too. Some friends of mine worked with him for a while, but he was holding out on them."

I pursed my lips in thought a moment. "Ever seen them together before?"

He shrugged and began wiping down the bar again. "Naw. Just that night. Seen the guy before though. He was in here a lot last fall. Always sat in the corner. Didn't drink. Just looked. Then he disappeared. We get all kinds in here, but he just felt creepy. I may not be in your league, but I can sense a fairy from a druid from a toad. I don't know what the hell this guy was, but he wasn't normal."

"Thanks," I said. Without another word, he went to the far end of the bar and continued wiping.

I was intrigued that Shay hadn't mentioned he had talked with the presumed suspect. I wondered whether he had something to hide and, if he did, why he would come forward with information that might reveal it. Murdock had cautioned me not to underestimate him. When he said that, he had meant it as a compliment to the kid. Now I didn't think he'd be so sure that was a good thing.

Back on the sidewalk, I hunched my shoulders against the spring chill. It had reached the point in the evening when the neighborhood paused, taking a deep breath as the yuppie crowd left for safer entertainment, while the people who truly called the place home crawled out into the night. As I moved along the street, the faces that passed were a little more grim or desperate or secretive. The voices of groups seemed louder, as though the sound of laughter itself could ward off danger. Traffic slowed as cars cruised for a quick connection for drugs or a warm body.

As if on cue, a shout went up across the street. People hustled themselves away from a boarded-up storefront like rats abandoning ship. I could see a small cluster of men, boys actually, arms flailing about in a classic brawl. I was halfway across the street before I remembered things like this were no longer my first line of business. Plus I was alone.

One of the boys became airborne and landed on a parked

car. I heard a string of curses in German, and the object of their pounding came into view. A dwarf swung his fists like anvils, and another two guys went flying. The remaining hoods circled around him just out of reach. Xenos out for a little bashing. Seeing it was four on one, I decided, outnumbered or not, I had to dive in. Just as I stepped up on the curb, my ride to the rescue was cut short. Three more dwarves came running toward the scene, shouting for all they were worth. The remaining gang members rethought their stupidity and ran off.

"I could've handled them," the dwarf said to his new-found comrades.

"Yeah, well, you shouldn't've had to," said one of them. They walked away grumbling.

Back in my apartment, I dropped onto the futon and watched TV until I could almost recite the news myself. Seelie Court and the Teutonic Consortium were in their final round of talks at the Fey Summit in Ireland. Several key issues remained to be resolved, notably the autonomy of elfin and dwarvish colonies in eastern Germany and the structure of a proposed Fey Court having authority over both parties. The Celtic and Teutonic fey had been fighting forever, it seemed. Territorial wars that began centuries ago had mutated into ideological political differences. The Convergence at the turn of the last century complicated the issues significantly, with the Teutonic Consortium demanding more funds allocated to research affecting a return to Faerie and the Seelie Court pressuring the Consortium to confront the issues of living in this new reality. The only issue on which both parties agreed was that neither could pursue their primary agendas without the other. The Fey Summit was only the most recent attempt to avoid all-out war.

A small reference to the murders came in the context of the mayor's decision to put a greater police presence on the streets. But even then, the murders were mentioned almost as an aside, the report instead focusing on traffic control during the festival. If the killer was looking for notoriety, he picked the wrong victims. I finally just turned the set off and went to bed for a restless sleep, disturbed by dreams bordering on nightmares.

4

First thing Saturday, I took a run along the waterfront. Between the gym and the running, I'd gotten myself in the best physical shape I'd ever been in. I took a complicated path along crumbling sea walls, wooden planks thrown across gaps between piers, cracked-pavement parking lots, and rusting rail tracks. The area's history can be read in the remnants of old buildings and twisted alleys marking the neighborhood's evolution from a fishing ground to a working port to a train yard to a warehouse district to, finally, the Weird.

The neighborhood's current residents left their imprint everywhere. Spirit jars crowded along building gutters; random graffiti resolved itself into ogham if you knew how to read it; boards and stones inscribed with old runes lay obscured by weeds; and spent candle stubs littered the docks like confetti. Sometimes the various charms, tokens, and wards gave off such a resonance that I could feel a static discharge lifting the hairs on my arms and legs.

It was one of those early-June mornings that tease you

with the promise of summer, the sunlight warm on your face, the sky a rich blue. The wind off the harbor usually knocks the temperature down to a steady chill, but that day it barely registered. My route took me down into South Boston, which those raised there proudly called Southie. It's an old Irish neighborhood, born of the famine in the old country that brought a deluge of immigrants. No surprise the fey folk gravitated to Boston after them. I ran past men washing their cars and kids playing in the streets while middle-aged women chatted in front of the grocery store. All the things that transpire in a nice neighborhood in a perfect world.

I hit the end of the causeway boulevard out to Fort Independence. The old Revolutionary War fortification sits at the end of a spit with a strategic view of the city. Proper residents call it Castle Island, in deference to the fact that it was once actually an island before all the landfill projects connected it to the rest of the neighborhood. To the uninitiated, the old fort looks like a castle, with its granite sides and five batteries. On summer weekends after Memorial Day, costumed tour guides provide a little local color about the interior portions. Gauging the crowd trooping out for the views, I decided to skip the fort and loop back through Southie to my apartment.

I slid into my chair before the computer. During my run, I had considered whether I might be approaching the ritual aspect of the murder from the wrong direction. The correct solution to a problem is often the simplest one: If a ritual popped up in a murder scene, then there had to be a tidy proscribed ritual written down somewhere to explain it. A fine premise, provided, of course, you had a way of researching every conceivable ritual. That was where the trail became a bramble. Everything is simply not written down.

But a ritual is merely a means to an end. With the right amount of ability, the correct elements at hand, and the will to use them both, any number of people can perform the same ritual, but for very different ends. I had gotten so focused on the "how" of the Tuesday Killer, I had lost track of the "why."

After my accident, I threw myself into figuring out what was wrong with me. Like everyone who has ever had a serious physical ailment, I started reading and researching until I was more of an expert than the experts. And I came to the same conclusion they had: diagnosis unknown. The biggest problem was that I had a physical ailment that wasn't particularly physical. The darkness in my mind had no mass, no real physical manifestation other than an unexplainable blackness that showed up in every conceivable diagnostic available. Whatever it was, it short-circuited my attempts to activate my abilities on any appreciable level. If I pushed it, my mind felt like it was shattering into shards of glass. Push it far enough, and I blacked out. That fact led me to the assumption that the mass was some kind of energy intimately linked to the essence of being fey.

One shelf of my study was crammed with books dedicated solely to the question of essence. In every age people have examined the issue of what made the fey fey. That interest had accelerated in the last century as more and more humans had the opportunity to join the investigation. At the risk of sounding elitist, the modern druids tended to have some of the best philosophical writings on the subject. We have a long history of researching the world around us.

I pulled down a slim volume called *The Essence of Essence*. Briallen had given it to me long ago because it was a particular favorite of hers. The unknown author, who I suspected was actually Briallen, took a spiritual approach, heavy on the connectivity of all things. The crux of the discussion poses that everything, organic and inorganic, has an intangible form of energy we have come to call essence, from the most powerful fairy queen to the lowliest pebble. Inorganic matter tends to hold essence uniformly throughout.

What prompted me to open the book, though, was its claim that living beings, by virtue of their organic nature, have their essence centered in one place. The heart.

Because of the nature of the murders, I had speculated to Murdock that the ritual might involve the giving or taking of power. Most fey know intuitively that the heart holds the essence of their being. The mind might activate our abilities, but the power is drawn from one of the most protected organs in the body. We can feel it whenever we cast the yew rod, breathe over a scrying pool, or summon a friend.

But I had sensed no ritual residue at either the second or third murder scenes. Murdock hadn't called me in until the second murder, but given how things had been playing out, I doubted there was anything at the first scene I would have picked up. The key, as far as I was concerned, was that the hearts were taken. On the basest level, serial killers like to keep souvenirs of their deeds. It gives them a sense of accomplishment and power. Factor in the essence issue and the fact that the removed hearts would retain their power for quite a while, and Power in a more real sense came into play.

My chair protested with a loud squeal as I sat bolt upright. There was no residual ritual magic at the scenes. Maybe the killings weren't the ritual. I had been sitting around trying to understand the reason why the garden was weeded when the herbs were in the pot. The murders could have merely been a means of acquiring hearts for something else. I spun my chair back to the books lining the far wall, ready to dive into researching this new line of thought, when I heard the very loud sound of someone clearing his throat in the next room. As I jumped up, my body warding came up so suddenly the back of my head screamed in protest. I stepped into the living room.

Stinkwort sat on the edge of the kitchen counter with a half-eaten Oreo in his hand. "Got any milk?" he asked around a mouthful of cookie.

Anger and relief swept over me as I murmured the short

incantation that dissipated the body ward. It was one of a very few spells I could still work. "Can't you knock?" I said.

He took another bite. "I suppose if I used doors, I would," he said. While he had no problem going in my cabinets, Joe hated touching the refrigerator, claiming something about the cold felt unnatural. It was just a bunch of bull as far as I was concerned. He just likes it when I serve him things. I poured him some milk in a shot glass.

"Make that two glasses," he said.

I crossed my arms and looked down at him munching away. "Why?"

Joe stopped and looked around puzzled. He put the remains of his cookie down, stood up, and began walking along the counter, peering among the canisters. He stopped on the side of the coffeemaker and said something too softly for me to hear. He reached his hand out. "No, really, it's okay," he said.

A bright yellow wing moved into view. A small face darted out, then back.

"Come, there's milk," Joe said in Cornish.

A small flit stepped out. She had bright yellow wings, larger in proportion to her body than Joe's were to his, but she had only a little over half his height. Very pale blond hair hung smoothly down to her waist, almost obscuring her light green tunic. Her skin was so white, it seemed translucent. She regarded me gravely with large green eyes but didn't move any farther.

"This is Tansy," Stinkwort said.

At the sound of her name, she glanced at Joe. Spreading her hands out from her waist with the palms forward, she bowed toward me, and said, "*De da.*"

"*De da,* Tansy," I said, returning the formal bow when Joe introduced me.

Joe looked up at me. "She doesn't speak English very well."

I smiled reassuringly at her. "She's a wee thing, isn't she? Are you sure she's the right one?"

Joe rolled his eyes in annoyance. "I have spent the last quarter day listening to her ramble about the merits of spring grass. Trust me, I wouldn't have bothered if she weren't the right one."

"*Pan wreugh why debry?*" she said in a thick rustic accent.

"Cookies and milk," Joe said, snapping his fingers at me.

I pinched my lips and smiled at him at the same time as I poured another shot glass. I pulled the open package of cookies out of the cabinet and put them on the counter. Tansy immediately took one and began eating as she stared around the apartment.

I watched her trail to the coffeemaker, sniff it, and wrinkle her nose. "I can barely understand her. What's her clan affiliation?"

Joe shrugged and shook his head in unconcealed disdain. "Her clan name has something to do with wattle and daub, which fits because she's as thick as mud."

I couldn't help chuckling. While Stinkwort would never concede a pecking order among the fairy races, he had no problem using one in his own species. Flits are pretty tight-lipped about their social structures, but I had long ago surmised that Stinkwort came from an important family. Not royalty—I'm sure he would have let me know that—but important in some way.

"Can she understand me?"

Lifting his head from the shot glass, Joe gulped, a little drop of milk suspended from his nose. "She's trying to learn English. If you have a few decades, I'm sure you will be able to communicate quite effectively."

"Are you here to help or just eat?" I said.

Joe threw his hands in the air. "You said find her. You said nothing about liking her."

"Okay, fine. Ask her if she knew Gamelyn Danann

Sidhe." At the mention of the third victim's name, Tansy straightened up and looked at me.

"I think she understood that one," said Joe dryly.

"Ask her if she was with him last Tuesday," I said.

"*A wrussta gweles Gamelyn war Tuesday?*" Joe said.

Tansy stared intently at her hand, counting on her fingers. After a long pause, she nodded vigorously. "*Me a wrug gweles.*"

"Did she see the man Gamelyn left with?" I asked.

"*A wrussta gweles an den gans Gamelyn?*" asked Joe.

"*Me a wrug gweles,*" she said again.

"What did he look like?"

She paused after listening to Joe, screwing her face up in thought. "*Bras ha ska ew den,*" she said, then in halting English, "He . . . sick me . . . yes? . . . *ef a wrug ow claf vy.*"

"She says he was a big man that made her sick," Joe said.

"Was he fey?"

"*Ska,*" Tansy spat.

Joe fluttered off the counter in surprise, then settled back down. "She says he was just wrong," said Joe.

"Wrong? How?"

For a few moments, they argued, Joe seeming to insist on something and Tansy repeating herself. She began to flailing her arms and shouting in angry frustration. "*Ska! Ska na ew an den. Ska ew an pysky! Ska ew an aelf! Ska! Me na wra gothvos!*"

Joe and I backed away from her. Her rapid-fire speech was indecipherable to me. Joe shook his head in confusion. "She says he was wrong like a fey, not human, I think. She's an idiot, Connor. All she keeps saying is that he's bad."

"Did she see him kill Gamelyn?"

Tansy covered her face when Joe asked her. She began to cry as she spoke, her words garbled by sobs. Joe leaned in to listen, straining to make out what she was saying. "She says Gamelyn asked her to wait for him outside the bar, but she followed him anyway. When she found them in the alley, Gamelyn was on the ground and the man had a knife. He saw her and sent her away."

It took me a moment for that to sink in. "Sent her away? You mean he spelled her away?" I said. Joe nodded. "Well, that definitely rules out human." I went into my study and retrieved Shay's artist sketch from the folder. Coming back to the kitchen, I held it up for Tansy. "Is this the man?"

She hissed at the paper and backed away, muttering and waving her hands. Joe's eyes went wide. "Stop! Stop!" he yelled at her. The sketch burst into flames in my hands. I dropped it and stamped out the fire on the floor. When I looked up they were both gone. Joe came back almost instantly.

"She's upset," he said. He took another cookie.

I fell into a chair in the living room and stared at the ceiling. "I guess we know Shay's sketch is accurate."

"Either that or she's afraid of paper," Joe said.

I didn't rise to his bait. "Would you be able to find her again?"

Joe dropped his jaw. "Whatever for? She's got a head like a bubble."

"She's a witness, Joe. She might be a better witness than Shay." I told him what the bartender had said about him.

Joe shrugged. "So—he didn't lie. He just didn't tell you everything. That's a crime?"

"No," I conceded. "But it undermines his credibility. He's already got one strike against him as a prostitute."

"Oh, I see. Mud brain will be much better in a court. It's no wonder the fey find this country so amusing."

I closed my eyes and rubbed them. "I am not about to debate the American judicial system with you, Joe. If Murdock needs her, can you find her again?"

"Sure. I found her when I didn't know her, didn't I? She won't be hard to keep track of."

I looked at him in thought for a moment. "You don't

happen to know how someone might use a fairy heart for its essence, do you?"

He looked down at the floor, idly swinging his feet. If there's one thing flits like less than being around people larger than they are, it's talking about dead fey. As near immortals, it's not a subject they find captivating. "There is no honor in such a thing, Connor. No fey would do it, not even the sad brothers of Unseelie would break such a rule. Destroying someone in the nobility of battle is just. Enslaving their spirit is outside the turning of the Wheel. It would destroy everything."

A light shiver ran across my skin. Joe was rarely so serious. "Are you saying it can be done?" I asked quietly.

He hovered up from the counter. "No. The world is still here, isn't it? I have to go." He vanished. A moment later, he popped back in again. "By the way, you need more cookies." And then he was gone.

I cleaned up the white flaky residue from the fire and wandered back into the study, perusing the bookshelves. Most of the titles on essence were philosophical discussions or medical theories. The books on rituals were on process. I could not recall a single book on using someone else's essence. Employing the essence of animals, stones, or plants abounded in rituals, were even the point of rituals in general. In all my years of training, I had never come across any discussion of using fey in rituals. Even the old druid sacrifice stories always talked about human children, usually males, as the sacrifice. But the essences of children were weak, and in humans almost negligible.

I felt a thrill of excitement. Druidic lore had always been an oral tradition dependent on teaching and self-discovery. You moved up in rank only when you were judged ready or had enough intuitive knowledge to discover the next level of mystery on your own. It was a way of managing powerful knowledge so that it could only be used with the wisdom of experience. If everything were simply written down, the temptation to run before you could walk would be enormous. The silence over fey sacrifices had to be secret knowledge, never to be spoken to the unready or written down for the unwary.

Which meant I had no easy way to learn the reasons for the silence. Such knowledge was passed on in a chain of trust, from teacher to student. It wasn't likely that I could walk up to someone and ask. My old mentors were gone, journeying in their own paths. I could track them down, but that would take time I didn't have. I had to see if I could convince Briallen to tell me.

I turned toward the living room a moment before I heard the knock on my door. Anxiety clenched my chest, like it did whenever something unexpected happened. I had made a lot of enemies when I worked for the Guild, people who would have been only too happy to find me in my current more vulnerable condition. The Guild had given me some wards to guard the house, mostly warning beacons. The ones around the windows made them less susceptible to breakage or long-range casting. I had felt none of them go off. And nobody had rung the building buzzer downstairs.

I moved quietly into the living room, listening. The only sound was the distant drone of a plane taking off from the airport. The knock came again, no different than the first time, no more urgent. Maybe it was a neighbor. "Who is it?" I finally said.

"Keeva," came the muffled reply.

Chagrined, I shook my head and opened the door. Keeva macNeve lounged against the opposite wall, the barest hint of a smile on her face. The wards hadn't gone off because she had set them up for me before I moved in. The lock on the building front door certainly wouldn't have deterred her.

Keeva was tall for a fairy woman, almost my height, with lush red hair that cascaded over her shoulders. A touch of haughtiness kept her finely drawn features from being truly beautiful; her green eyes were a bit too cool, her dark lips a bit too thin. We had had a modest flirtation when we first met, nothing serious. But then we got to know each other better, or that is to say, I got to know her better, and the attraction dimmed. She was smart enough to detect the change and didn't pursue. When I'm being kind, I describe her as carnivorous. I take no responsibility for what I might say if she comes up in conversation when I'm drunk.

"Well, hello," I said, managing a smile.

She pushed away from the wall, letting her own smile go a little wider. Not much. We stood looking at each other. "Hello. Aren't you going to ask me in?"

I stepped back and gestured into the room. She walked by me in a faint cloud of honeysuckle, a glamour hiding her wings. Most fairies wear glamours in public—usually they don't like the attention their wings tend to attract otherwise. The form-fitting black jumpsuit she wore seemed genuine though. If I looked closely, I could see a slight shimmer on the back obscuring where her wings began. She walked to the window and stared out for a moment before turning to face me.

"Honestly, Connor, it can't be so bad that you have to live here, can it?"

"Oh, so this is a social call?" I said, smiling to take the sting out of it.

She chuckled, inspecting the armchair briefly before sitting. "How are you? Any change?" Her voice had a neutral tone that conveyed neither sympathy nor indifference.

I didn't want to be rude and stand at the door, so I sat in the chair facing her. "None. So, what brings you to the other side of the channel, Keeva? It's not like you to just stop by."

"Believe it or not, I was actually in the neighborhood. I have some friends coming in for Midsummer, and they want to see the Weird. I thought it'd be fun to have dinner down here, so I'm trying a couple of restaurants out. Any recommendations?"

I couldn't help hesitating. Keeva macNeve just having lunch in the Weird is like the Queen of England nipping into the pub for a pint. "The Barking Crab's always good and safe. It gets a nice mix," I said. I didn't need to mention that every city guide recommended the place. The last thing I wanted was Keeva's cronies invading my favorite dinner haunts.

She nodded absently, obviously not caring. "You haven't been by the Guildhouse lately. I thought you might like an update. Bergen Vize was spotted in Bavaria a number of times a month ago. There has been an increase in eco-terrorist activity around the Black Forest."

I cocked my head to the side. Of all people, Keeva mac-Neve had taken on the investigation into my accident. I still hadn't been able to find out if she was assigned to it or requested it. Vize was the jerk with the ring that screwed up my head. Every couple of months, I checked in with Keeva, and it was usually the same useless information with only the location changed. Sometimes he was in London, sometimes Germany. In the States, he seemed to favor California and the Southwest. He was never in New England. I decided to play my part in the charade. "Has anyone gotten close to him?"

Keeva shook her head, of course. "We're trying, Connor. You know he's tough."

I nodded. "So you're still working for macDuin?"

A brief flush of rose colored her cheeks, a physical reaction she either didn't know she had or couldn't control. Lorcan macDuin was head of the Community Liaison Office, the Guild department that monitored local crime. When we were partners, Keeva and I shared a mutual frustration with his poor management skills. Ultimately, it was macDuin who decided whether the Guild would get involved in a fey incident.

During World War II, the elves of Germany actively supported the Nazis, hoping that an Axis victory would help them re-create their Faerie kingdoms in the Convergent world. Lorcan, like many fairies who wanted to go back to Faerie, had been a sympathizer, which made him an outsider in the upper echelons at the Guild. Not something that was openly discussed in the more recent times of political rapprochement between the races. He knew what people thought, though, so he tended to overcompensate with a little more zeal than called for. Keeva chafed under him, knowing full well he couldn't advance her career because of his own circumstances.

She shifted in her chair, crossing her legs. "Yes. Mac-Duin is macDuin. You know how it is."

I nodded. People were hesitant to criticize their superiors openly if they thought it could get back to them. The worst relationship could often be the stepping-stone to something better. "So what are you working on?" I asked again.

She shrugged. "Besides Vize, nothing interesting. I have a missing person right now that I'm hoping to wrap up."

"Anything I can help you with?"

She smiled charitably. "I'm handling it, Connor."

She stood up and wandered about the room, touching a book here, adjusting a picture frame there. She paused by the kitchen counter. Fairies do not have the ability to sense essence very effectively, but with Joe and Tansy so recently there, Keeva probably felt something. She turned back to me, brushing her hands together. "You should clean up these crumbs."

She made her way back to the windows. She glanced at something to her left so that I could see her in profile. She really would be something without that bitter tinge to her mouth. "What about you? I heard you were working on this serial murder thing. What's the status?"

I hesitated, realizing this was why Keeva had just happened to drop in. She confirmed my suspicion when she didn't acknowledge the lengthening silence. "We have a small lead, a possible eyewitness."

She dropped herself back in the armchair. "I read that in the reports."

That surprised me. "Is the Guild investigating?" I asked.

She ran her fingers idly through those long red tresses. "No, it's just the standard review to keep macDuin apprised. Your name caught my eye, of course, so I read the file. What's not in the report?"

I smiled at her, and she smiled back. "What if I told you it might be a fey-on-fey situation?"

She arched an eyebrow. "Might or is?"

"I'm still leaning toward 'might.' The human witness said the guy felt funny, like something was wrong with him."

"That's it? A human prostitute thinks he can sense essence, and you're thinking it's fey?

I shrugged. "Another witness may have placed him in a local bar. A fey witness."

"Working for one of the meat joints, no doubt," she said.

I clenched my teeth at the barely concealed scorn in her voice. It was a ploy of Keeva's I had fallen for a few times earlier in our acquaintance. She would express skepticism in my theories in an effort to demoralize me. I would reveal everything I knew to prove myself, which played right into her hands. She was not above making someone feel like an idiot while she co-opted an investigation. I wasn't about to tell her about Tansy.

"The fey may not be the best witness, but it's all we have right now. Why the interest?"

She shrugged. "Professional curiosity. And personal. You're wasted down here, Connor. All you have to do is ask, and I can get you a position in research."

I pretended to consider it, again. From all directions, the idea was foul. I'd be working for people I used to supervise and working on cases I was assigned instead of those I requested. If I had taken some half-ass support position, I would never have gotten any respect even if my abilities came back. I'd be considered tainted goods, which people probably thought anyway. And I certainly didn't want to be beholden to Keeva macNeve. It was bad enough competing with her. I didn't want to do her paperwork.

"No, thanks," I said. "I'd prefer to see how things work out first."

She stood up and spread her hands. "Okay. You can't say I didn't offer. I should be going. If there's anything I can help you with, let me know."

I walked her the few steps to the door. "I will. If this does turn out to be fey-on-fey, you'll be the first to know."

She smiled smugly. "Yes, I will be. It'll probably end up my case."

We chuckled in feigned companionship. She patted me on the shoulder and sauntered away. I coldly watched her back until she turned down the stairs.

It occurred to me that with her connections, Keeva might have known one of the victim's families. Naming fairies Danann Sidhe bordered on calling them Smith. Sidhe, obviously, was a race affiliation and Danann indicated the clan. Occasionally, someone connected to the royal line would call themselves Aes Sidhe to distinguish themselves from the commoners. More often, though, they used family names. I knew Keeva's full name, for instance, was Caoimhe ap Laoire mac Niamh Aes Sidhe; she had anglicized the spelling for ease and went by her grandfather's name for prestige. Niamh was very well connected in the old country, something Keeva had no problem mentioning.

I closed the door and went in to my computer. Opening the database, I quickly scrolled through the victim profiles. The dead faces of Pach, Ragnell, and Gamelyn stared out at me. I wondered what about them could have possibly interested the Guild in general and Keeva in particular. Their appeal to the killer fell into neat categories of appearance, profession, gender, and race. I glanced through their bios, but the information was slight. Pach and Ragnell had been in town long enough to get arrested, but not Gamelyn. I realized that two pieces of information about all of them were missing: where exactly they were from in Ireland and who were their next of kin.

The odds of all three victims having a high profile connection seemed slim, and someone knowing that even more so. I leaned back in the chair. If all the victims were royalty, the Guild would have stepped in long ago if only to protect the family's privacy. On the other hand, the Guild taking an interest in prostitutes would draw attention immediately. I chuckled to myself. What a lovely irony if the Guild were trapped between its own arrogance and indifference. And after all my snide remarks about the Guild not wanting to get involved in the case, the irony of my suspicions about their interest was not lost on me.

Fairies fallen on hard times tended not to broadcast their family names. Blood honor and all that. If a royal link hadn't turned up in the previous arrest records, it probably wasn't going to. Except for Gamelyn. He hadn't been arrested. And Keeva didn't decide to show up until after he died. Maybe he was a one-shot, another high roller slumming at the wrong time and place. I'd have to get Murdock to look into it.

While I waited for fresh coffee to brew, I munched on the one cookie Joe had been nice enough to leave. The revulsion on Tansy's face at the sight of the artist's sketch popped into my mind. Even the lowliest flit liked a little adventure, but she had gotten more than she bargained for. I could still smell the odor of burnt paper. As I poured my coffee, I wondered why Tansy kept calling the killer "*ska*." My Cornish was sketchy at best, but I had to have at least as good a vocabulary as a peasant flit. I knew the general word for bad was "*drog*." I didn't know *ska* at all and hadn't thought to ask Joe before he left.

As I mentally arranged the rest of my day, I decided it

was time to check in with Briallen and see if she could fit some of these pieces together. I could take the opportunity to ask her about fey essence in ritual, too. That thought drove me back into the study for more reading. If I was going to ask her for training help, the last thing I wanted was for her to catch me not knowing enough.

5

Sunday mornings are for coffee, the newspaper, and, apparently, waiting on the corner of Newbury and Dartmouth for half-a-damned-hour because Murdock was late. Some people know who's calling when their phone rings at midnight. I know it's Murdock when my phone rings at seven o'clock on Sunday morning. He knows he's the only person I won't kill for doing it because I'd have his father and brothers after me, not to mention the entire Boston P.D.

Even on a warm morning, Newbury Street was quiet. The exclusive boutiques didn't open until ten o'clock or so. The couture fashion parade would start around noon, the cool and the neo-hip strutting their disposable-income purchases while jabbering into the latest in cell phone technology. Most of the people walking about were Back Bay residents retrieving their *Boston Sunday Globe*s and cups of ready-made coffee. They wouldn't be caught dead here in their designer sweat suits in a few hours.

Across the way from me stood the old Prince School. It had gone derelict when the area population started focusing more on having BMWs than having kids and had been a favorite haunt for squatters until a developer decided to turn it into condominiums. Before the owners understood with whom they were dealing, the entire basement had been leased by fey folk, who dubbed it The Artifactory. It's said that the vendors inside provide almost everything fey legally available and, if you had the right connections, a few things that weren't. Human kids liked to hang out watching all manner of folk enter and leave, but they rarely bothered anyone. You only need an itching rash once to convince you staring is rude.

Murdock appeared from around the corner, strolling nonchalantly like he was on time. He gave me a pleasant smile. "Sorry I'm late. Mass went long."

Murdock at Catholic mass, the earliest one on Sunday. Not something I could easily visualize, but also not something he gave me reason to criticize. The Roman Catholic Church had remained in turmoil ever since its encyclical on the fey. The Pope found nothing inherently wrong with being fey, just as long as they didn't act fey. Oh, and became Catholic. Other than that, he had no problem. I figured as long as Murdock didn't act Catholic around me, I had no problem with him either. He obliged me most of the time.

The thing I liked about Murdock's interest in the fey was that he sincerely wanted to understand. He wasn't content just to be handed answers to questions on specific cases. He wanted to accumulate enough knowledge to bring his own thoughts to bear on a given situation. So, every Sunday morning unless one or both of us had a hangover, we would get together for a little tutorial. The Artifactory was one of our usual classrooms.

We crossed the street and entered the grand side door of the building. As we descended into the basement, the intense odor of smoldering lavender slammed into our noses. The staircase bottomed at one end of the building, which stretched out before us for what seemed an entire city block. People milled about the brightly lit main aisle, wandering in and out of the stalls that lined the way. To either side were two secondary aisles, not as well lit, where much of the hard-core business tended to take place away from prying eyes. An herbalist's booth sat right near the entrance, hence the smell.

We slowly made our way among the booths, browsing casually. The vendors along the main aisle tended to have a mix of quality and kitsch. It seemed that for every apothecary, there were two T-shirt hawkers for the occasional tourist that wandered in. Potions had been experiencing renewed interest, and a number of people were offering ways to attract a lover or repel an unwanted suitor. My favorite find was an elixir marketed as a way to cause your boss to forget why he had come into your office. Cloak-makers busied themselves with last-minute orders for the Midsummer festival events. Costumes for the upcoming parade hung from the rafters. Rank upon rank of gem and stone dealers competed loudly with each other to sell the same merchandise.

"So how'd the date go?" I asked.

Murdock shrugged. "It was drinks."

"And?"

He smirked. "And that's it. Maybe it'll go somewhere, maybe it won't."

And that was that. Murdock is, as the old phrase goes, a ladies' man. As in plural. He's got a look that most women find attractive, and he definitely uses it. He doesn't talk much about that aspect of his social life, but I know enough that most of his dates are barely that, and it suits him fine.

Near the center of the room, we found a wand dealer. I picked up a wand of milled pine from a box of several dozen duplicates. It was about a foot and half long, tapering from about a quarter-inch in diameter to a blunt end. Under the watchful eye of the vendor, I leaned over and withdrew another shorter wand from a tangled bundle at the next seller's table, an old piece of warped yew worn smooth along one end, small knots making irregular bumps along its length. I handed them both to Murdock.

"Okay, which one has any practical use?" I asked.

He weighed them in his hands. "Obviously, I'm supposed to say the nicer-looking one is better, but I think the real question is why isn't it better?"

I smiled. "Very good. The answer is because it's tooled, in this case by a machine. Even if it were done with a knife, it would still not be as effective. Either way, it's unnatural. The act of cutting destroys the natural pathways of the growth of the wood, interrupting the flow of energy. In and of themselves, wands are powerless. They have their own essence, of course, but they don't have any will to use what little they have. Most people use them as focal points for the concentration of energy, and they can even be used as conduits for that energy."

I took the older one from him. It felt quite nice to the hand, its sides worn to a buttery smoothness. I gave it a quick little flick, feeling how it responded to the motion of my hand. "Now this old boy has seen some use. The shape of it has been worn into it with handling. It has had time to adapt its flow to the change in configuration, which an abrupt shaving would never allow."

Murdock took it back and examined it more closely. He even accurately imitated the hand motion I had used. "But what about the nubs? Why doesn't breaking off side branches interrupt the flow?"

I crossed my arms and nodded appreciatively. "You're getting pretty good at this. The little side branches are natural interruptions to the flow of the main piece. It's important to strip them off by hand because, unless you're unbelievably strong, they'll come off in the path of least resistance. In effect, you interrupt the interruption, and the natural essence of the main piece resumes its course."

He performed the same motion with the pine wand. "So is this useless?"

I shrugged. "It's not great. Someone who needs it might make do in a pinch. Personally, I just use my hands unless I'm doing something very delicate." I took the wand from him and tossed it back in the box with the rest. "I suppose if you bought two, they'd make pretty good chopsticks." The vendor heard me and favored me with an annoyed glare.

Murdock put the other wand back. I led him to a table of stones, a range of semiprecious, minerals, and just plain old rocks. "Now, stones are another matter entirely. Using tools is practically required, and you can shape stones any way you want. Most stones have very little essence, and it's spread uniformly throughout. That makes them excellent conductors, resonators, inductors, and condensers."

"Like electricity?" he said.

"Exactly. The only difference is that electricity behaves predictably. When stones have essence applied to them, there's a will behind it. The stones treat the essence predictably, but the effect depends on the intent of the user."

Murdock shuffled his fingers through a box of flat stone rings about the diameter of a walnut. I picked one up, glancing at the vendor, a small harried-looking dwarf busy with a group of elves. Not wanting to insult him, I discreetly turned away and peered through the stone at the crowd. "These are supposed to be self-bored stones. Their centers are worn away by tumbling in streams and rivers. They're rare enough that you won't find a box of them lying on a table. If they're real, you can use them to see through a glamour."

I tossed mine back. Murdock picked one up and looked through it. He scanned the crowd, smiling. "This is pretty neat," he said.

Startled, I plucked the stone out of his hand and looked. Sure enough, the hidden wings of several nearby fairies came into view. A tall, thin, cloaked figure at a table of swords resolved itself into a very ugly ogre of some kind. All along the aisle, I could see several more people who were using various levels of glamour. Laughing, I turned and waved at the vendor. "This one's real," I said, tossing him the stone.

He caught it with one hand, a dubious frown on his face. When he put it up to his eye, his jaw dropped. Giving me a wink, he slipped the stone into his pocket. "Take your pick of the first row of boxes," he said, waving at the useless small wards they contained.

"Not necessary," I said. I paused and turned to Murdock. "Follow me. I have an idea."

I led him between two booths to one of the side aisles. The crowd was thinner here, the prices higher, and the wares more refined. Searching among the stalls, I spotted what appeared to be a jeweler. Several gemstones of different quality set in chains and cords hung from a string across the front. The counter beneath had an assortment of rings, bracelets, anklets, and belts. I felt a buzz in the base of my skull just standing there. I flipped through the hanging chains and slipped one over my head.

Murdock's eyebrows shot up. "You look bigger. Like you've been working out as much as you claim."

"Very funny. These are glamour stones. I'm thinking we should try to bait the killer with an undercover officer wearing one of these to look like the victim profile."

Murdock tilted his head in consideration. "That stuff's always risky."

"We only have two days until Tuesday, Murdock. If the artist sketch doesn't turn up anything, we're in trouble."

Considering, he stared at the line of necklaces. "I'll have to pass it by Ruiz." Ruiz was Murdock's immediate supervisor. I'd met him a couple of times; nice enough guy for someone who was in charge of one of the worst police districts in the city.

I got the attention of the vendor, another dwarf, and asked

him in Gaelic for a fairy glamour. Sometimes speaking the language helped ease the negotiations. He produced an array of stones from beneath the counter. After much searching, he found a couple that had the ability to produce the image of a tall blond fairy and named his price. I shuddered, knowing it was beyond Murdock's budget. The dwarf was in no mood to discuss credit. He didn't want to risk the stones losing their charge, then not being able to collect the debt. I stalked up and down the aisle looking for something more modest, but predictably, the stones were uniformly out of our range.

Frustrated, I stood in the aisle trying not to think of grabbing a stone and running. "Do you know any tall blonds on the force that might pass as a fairy? I'm thinking we just get an enhancer stone, something like the first one I tried on. It'll produce a fairy aura on a human and give him wings, but it won't be strong enough to change his physical looks completely."

He shrugged. "I'll ask around."

As a courtesy, I went back to the first vendor. He'd been extremely civil throughout our earlier failed bargaining and showed no sign of annoyance that we were now looking for cheap. I figured I should encourage that kind of behavior whenever possible. In a matter of moments we had a stone that would do the trick. He even put it in a protective case to keep the glamour from activating prematurely or its essence from dissipating. We left the building and walked toward Copley Square.

"Do you want to come for dinner?" Murdock asked as he unlocked his car door.

Sunday dinner at the Murdocks happened every week at two o'clock in the afternoon. The offer was tempting, but if I went, I'd be committed to several hours. "Can I take a rain check? I'm hoping to see Briallen tonight and need to get some reading done."

"Sure. Maybe it's just as well. It's Bar's turn to cook," he said, referring to his younger brother Barnard. He couldn't help the mischievous smile from creeping onto his face. Bar had a reputation for going heavy on every seasoning he could get his hands on. While all the Murdocks complained about it, no one disliked it enough to take an extra cooking duty for the army that tended to show up.

Shoving a pile of magazines to the floor, I dropped into the passenger seat. Murdock started the car and just pulled into traffic without looking. It must be nice to have a badge.

"So anyone can use this glamour stone? Even non-fey?" he asked.

"Sure. Someone fey needs to make it, but once it's charged, it's charged. It should work for anyone, even a human."

"I thought you needed essence to make it work." He cut across two lanes of moving traffic to make a right-hand turn.

"The essence is in the glamour, which then interacts with the essence of the user."

"So what happens if this enhancer one we just bought is worn by someone who already is a fairy?"

"It'll work like the first one I tried on. It'll just make him look more powerful."

"Is that why I was able to use the self-bored stone?"

"Right. They're just tools. They only don't work if applying essence is necessary to make them work. Like the wand. It won't do anything for a human no matter how much he waves it around because it retains no active essence in and of itself. There's no danger in wearing one."

"Good. Ruiz isn't too fond of the fey. He'll want to know there's no danger." I suppressed a sigh. A cop who didn't like the fey was becoming a cliché. Sure the fey caused trouble, but so did everyone on the wrong side of the law. I didn't think it helped race relations if law enforcement was part of the problem.

Murdock dropped me at my place and pulled away without a word, like he usually did. I phoned Briallen, and her answering machine said, "I know what you're going to say, but leave a message anyway." I left a message. As I waited for her call, I went on the roof above my apartment to read in the sun. In no time, I dozed off.

A cool breeze across my skin woke me with a shiver, and the shiver immediately turned into a wince of pain. I had been out for a couple of hours. A bright tinge of red covered the entire front of my body.

Briallen had not called back. I decided I would just show up at her place. At best, she'd be pleased to see me. At worst, she wouldn't be home.

I hopped a cab for the short ride over to Beacon Hill. I paid the driver and stood on the sidewalk in front of Briallen's house on Louisburg Square in the heart of the old Brahmin neighborhood. She's lived in the townhouse for decades. A double-wide, five-story structure in the classic brick bay window style with mullioned windows of purple glass panes. Large green double doors flanked by old gas lamps that still worked marked the entrance. A new growth of ivy was slowly making its way up the first two floors.

I rang the bell. After several moments, I rang again. When no answer came, I tried the doorknob and was surprised to find it open. I let myself in. The empty entry hall greeted me. I had rarely been in Briallen's house alone. The scent of history hung over the silence, not musty, but the rich odor of timelessness. Mahogany gleamed on the floor and stairs, and brass doorknobs shone with polish. A great clock to the left measured time with its steady tick. Briallen invariably liked to entertain in the rear second-floor parlor, so I went up the stairs in the entry hall.

In the middle of the staircase, where it turned around the back of the house, a landing window looked out over the back garden. A movement there caught my eye. A tree blocked the view, but I could distinctly see someone moving beneath it. I quickly descended and made my way through the back of the house, passing through the long kitchen, with its rich cooking aromas.

As I opened the rear door, I saw lights flickering in many colors and the sound of hushed voices. I stopped on the steps, amazed. Briallen sat on the ground amid a whirl of flits, most of them talking at once, vying for her attention. There had to be a couple dozen of the little guys. I'd never seen more than four or five of them together before. As I shifted for a clear view, my boot heel scraped loudly against the stone step. Amid a series of soft gasps, the flits disappeared. I moved around the tree just in time to see Briallen rise from the ground, turning angrily to face me.

"Who . . . ?" she demanded, only to check her anger when she recognized me. At that moment, a flit materialized in front of her. The blue-winged fey gave me a long, hard look, glanced at Briallen and spoke softly, then disappeared.

"Connor! I thought you might turn up tonight, but not for another hour," Briallen said, striding toward me across the short lawn with her arms outstretched. She wore a long robe of white silk embroidered in gaudy flashes of orange and red that flowed sensually around her when she moved. She had cut her hair since I'd last seen her. It was short now, almost above the ears and falling in loose chestnut waves. She looked stunning as always. Briallen Gwyll had been my first crush and longest-lasting love. I had met her at the age of twelve, brought before her to judge my ability. The first thing she did that night was step naked out of her robe and perform a moon invocation rite. The image so excited me, I had to cross my legs every time I saw her after that for a year.

"I didn't mean to interrupt. Do you know you left the door unlocked?" I said, as we hugged.

She slipped her arm through mine and pulled me out into the garden. "I was distracted. It's always unlocked. It's just not warded against you. Come sit down."

She pressed me onto a stone garden bench that was uncomfortably hard and cold. Silently, she cradled my head in her hands and closed her eyes. For a moment I felt a vague pressure, as though I were wearing a hat too tightly, then it was gone. It had become a ritual whenever we met and no one was around to watch. Briallen dropped her hands and sat beside me on the bench.

"No change," she said.

In a way I didn't understand, Briallen could feel the thing in my head. She seemed more vexed by it than I, if that were possible. She hates not understanding something. Every time we meet, she tests it, to feel it, to see if it's changed, and, with no real sense of hope, to see if it is gone.

"What are you doing out here?" I asked.

Her hazel eyes caught a gleam of moonlight. "I've persuaded almost an entire family of Welsh flits to let me study them! Thirty-two! Have you ever seen thirty-two flits at once? Wasn't it marvelous?"

"Yes, it was. What are you studying?"

"I guess you'd have to say their sociology. And anthropology. And biology if they'll let me." She stood abruptly. "Come, let me show you something."

She walked away without checking if I was following, as though the idea of me not doing so never occurred to her. She was right, of course. We went back through the kitchen, passing through the wonderful smells, and up the stairs to a small study on the third floor. Floor-to-ceiling bookcases lined the walls, filled with just as much an assortment of odds and ends as books. Dusty crystal orbs held art portfolios in place; little boxes with colorful Chinese silk covers were wedged in between old leather bindings. An old computer monitor stared moonily out from a bottom shelf, not used, I was sure, since Pong was a best seller. And everywhere papers splayed out in a spectrum of color from nearly brown parchments to brilliant white photocopy. A large table dominated the cluttered room, piled high with more books and papers, a broken celestial sphere, a teacup, various pens including a handmade quill, a box of pebbles, the fourteenth edition of *Bartlett's Familiar*

Quotations, and a kitchen sponge. And in the cleared center space, a glass cube with what looked like a dried-out milkweed pod.

Briallen lifted the cube gently and handed it to me, her eyes shining.

As I held it, I could feel a strong warding surrounding it. I peered at the object, trying to understand what it was. A chill went through me. What I had taken to be the dried husk of the milkweed were actually the gray, lifeless wings of a flit. They bent unnaturally forward, cradling the still, crouched corpse, whose impassive face was barely visible through the small opening where the wings met. Wordlessly, Briallen retrieved the cube and replaced it on the table.

I followed her out of the study down to the kitchen, where she proceeded to prepare a salad.

"I've never seen a dead flit," I said.

She began chopping greens. "Very few people have. I was talking with one of my subjects about flit funeral processions—which I've seen a number of times—and mentioned that I'd never seen the final disposition of the body. He showed up with that body early this evening. He told me they just leave the body on a suitable hill and the first light of day takes it away."

"But why did he give it to you?"

Briallen began rummaging under a counter, eventually withdrawing a huge earthenware bowl that was too big for the salad. She used it anyway. "He didn't give it to me. He just thought I'd like to see it. I promised I'd put it outside before dawn."

"But you put a preserving ward on it," I said.

She shrugged. "It's only temporary. I noticed it had faded considerably in the short time I had it inside. I suspect any light will do the job; the sun just does it quickly. I think it has something do with essence leaving the body. It's almost unbelievable that something as small as a flit exists on any sentient level. I've been wondering if they're made up of more essence than physical matter."

I leaned over the salad as casually as I could. "Speaking of essence . . ."

Briallen held up her hand before I could continue, a knowing smile dancing on her face. "First, we socialize like the old friends that we are. We can talk business later. Grab a plate."

I ducked my head with a chagrined smile. Briallen is rarely taken unaware. She pulled a huge roast out of the oven, much more than the two of us could eat, and set out more bowls with vegetables and potatoes. We perched on kitchen stools at the counter island and proceeded to catch up. I, of course, had little to say that didn't lead to business. Briallen, on the other hand, had enough things going for both of us.

She had recently taken a yearlong sabbatical from Harvard, where she taught the history of what she liked to refer to as the "Not-So-Dark Ages." She was continuing research into more recent history. In the meantime, she was also beginning her work with the flit clan, trying to cultivate certain plants in the harsh New England climate, and learning how to cook Thai food. I had a feeling the latter was preparation for another trip later on.

She had participated in the early talks of the Fey Summit and was thinking about visiting Germany to assess the political situation there. Briallen had been instrumental in the founding of the Ward Guild, and though she didn't answer to the High Queen, her sympathies lay with the Seelie Court. She had diplomatic status in most European countries as a leader of the Druidic College and was often an advisor to world leaders. It was years before I realized how important she is. I thought she was just a nice lady who taught me spells.

She began clearing away the dishes. "You've been so quiet, Connor. Tell me something you've been doing other than work."

I knew what she was asking. Briallen felt I needed to devote myself full-time to regaining my abilities. I made some efforts, but never enough to please her, or so it seemed. Sometimes I wondered if she was frustrated more by me or by her own inability to find an answer for what's wrong with me.

"Well, for one thing, I'm in the best physical condition I've ever been in."

"That's a good start." She poured two small glasses of port. She handed me a glass, lifted the bottle, and sailed out of the kitchen. I followed her to the upstairs parlor. A fire always burned in the room, even in summer, yet the temperature was never uncomfortable. With the entire house at her disposal, I knew she liked this room the best. It held several welcoming overstuffed chairs, more books, and a view of the garden. I imagined she spent many an evening reading in it until dawn sent her to bed.

"And . . . ?" she prompted.

I settled into a deep-tufted armchair by the fire. "My protective wards seem to activate instinctually. My sensing abilities feel like they're in overdrive sometimes. I still can't do a sending that goes true. Scrying is out of the question. And I seem to forget incantations as soon as I start them."

She pursed her lips. "I know all that. What have you done lately?"

"I tried to light a candle the other day and set my desk on fire," I said, trying not to smirk.

She sharply let a breath out. "Have you tried to listen to your own heartbeat?"

I felt a flush of annoyance. "Briallen, I know my ABCs."

It was her turn to be irritated. "I'm sincerely beginning to doubt that. You want to ignite a precision fire. You want to scry. You want to speak spells. Yet, you don't even bother to build toward them. If you broke both your legs, you'd probably sit and mope until you could get up and run a marathon. And you'd have just as much success as you're having now."

"That's not fair," I said. Her words stung a little too deeply.

"So what? I'm not your mother. I'm not here to make it all go away. You have an extraordinary talent and refuse to use it."

"I don't have those talents anymore." I surprised myself. I never raised my voice to Briallen.

She compounded my horror by laughing at me. "Is that all you are, Connor? A body without talent? I'm talking about your mind. You need to reason your way through this. You need to learn your way through this. But above all, you need to act your way through this. You received a bunch of answers that didn't solve your problem, and now you want me to sympathize with you. I think you know me well enough by now, Connor, to know I have no sympathy for surrender."

I could feel heat suffuse my face. "I came here tonight for help," I said tightly.

A concerned and sincere look came over her face. "And you're getting it. Connor, you have to want to help yourself, too. It's not my job to drop everything and figure out what's wrong with you. I'll help you. I've said that. But I won't do it *for* you."

As I stared into the fire, I could feel my anger slipping away. She was right. Harsh, but right. I wasn't angry at Briallen. I was angry that she was right. For a long time, I had coasted along. The direction of my life had taken a turn I hadn't wanted, and I was letting it control me, pretending that I would simply wake up one day, and things would be back the way they had been.

I focused on the fire, letting the emotions drain out of me. I had to know I could do it, but more importantly, show Briallen I could. No sound came from her, though I could feel her attention. I slowed my breathing, shutting out the sounds around me. Reluctantly, the flames became sound-less flickers of light. I continued focusing on the hearth, my eyes half-closed, as I exhaled into silence. I didn't move, dropping my breathing even more, until I could barely feel the rise and fall of my chest. I pulled myself inward. I could hear nothing, nothing at all for a moment, then finally, the soothing shushing noise that I recognized. I could hear my heart beating. I hung on to the moment, remembering when I first learned how to do this, remembering the promise of my childhood. Taking a deep breath, I opened my eyes. It felt like coming to the surface of a very deep pool.

Briallen took a small sip from her glass. "Harder than you thought, wasn't it?"

I nodded. I could feel a thin sheen of perspiration on my lip. "I'm sorry."

"I take no offense. Now, bring me up to date on the murders."

I brought her through my most recent interviews, including my suspicions about Shay. She took unconscionable delight in Stinkwort's comments about Tansy, and I gave her an embarrassing imitation of the little flit's speech pattern.

"Your accent needs work," she said with a chuckle. Tapping the edge of her glass, she lost herself in thought a moment. " 'Ska.' An interesting word."

"I've never heard it. Joe translated it as 'bad,' " I said.

Briallen tipped her head from side to side. "That's simple at best. Its meaning has broadened in more rustic areas to mean something that's annoying or unsettling, but its true sense is more a physical description. One of the many oddities about flits is that they breed like bunnies, but you rarely see them in groups. They can be indifferent to their selection of mates and, coupled with their clan pride, tend to enter unions too close in the bloodline. The result is invariably a stillbirth and is called *ska,* meaning 'that-which-is-not-to-be' in the sense that the world has rejected the birth. There's a connotation of 'unbelonging' to the word, meaning the child not only doesn't belong to the clan but doesn't belong anywhere."

I looked back at the flames. The Tuesday Killer made everyone who encountered him uncomfortable. Assuming even Belgor's stone customer was the same guy, he had a troubling essence that upset people because they couldn't place it. Maybe they couldn't place it because it had no place. Maybe prostitutes were perfect victims because they accepted people out of the ordinary. And maybe such a person had found a ritual to make himself feel less out of place.

"I'm wondering if the killer is a *ska* birth that lived," I said.

"That would be a bit of a contradiction, etymologically," Briallen said. "Given that he lived, maybe he was meant to live. '*Ska*' inherently means he shouldn't have lived, never mind grown up to kill three people."

"Then maybe '*ska*' is only the closest word to describe him. Maybe he's unique."

"And for that we can be thankful," Briallen said, raising her glass.

"I've been thinking about the point of the murders," I said. I detailed my idea about the heart essence. Briallen became very quiet. Too quiet. "So, tell me, is this a teaching level I've stumbled across?"

She stared into her glass before answering, then looked at me directly. "To a point, yes. Such knowledge exists for the adept. It's forbidden to use."

I took a deep breath to calm my excitement. "Stinkwort said essentially the same thing. Could you teach me?"

She swirled the port in her glass for a long moment, the ruby color catching small flashes of light. Carefully, she placed it on the small table beside her chair. Standing slowly, she walked to the window and gazed out into her garden. "No."

A cold wave of disbelief swept over me. I hadn't expected her to be so direct.

She turned to look at me, her eyes a cool measure of deliberation. "To be blunt, Connor, you're not worthy of the knowledge. You stepped off the druidic path years ago, striking out on your own to further your own personal needs. That's just not how it works."

I could feel heat flushing my cheeks again. "Are you saying you don't trust me?"

She shook her head. "It's not about my personal feelings. These are matters greater than anything so minor as a personal relationship. These are dangerous things, knowledge that should have died as soon as it was thought."

"*Ska,*" I said with a slightly derisive tinge.

Briallen nodded. "In effect, yes. If I can, I will tell you what you need to know to stop this maniac. If I can't, I will step in myself to stop him. Either way, I won't teach you. I can't. Not now. Not in your current condition."

I rubbed my hands over my face. I tried to sigh against the great weight sitting on my chest. "This has to be the most uncomfortable night I've spent with you," I said.

"It's been no easier for me. The big issues rarely are," she said.

"I should go," I said.

Briallen walked from the window and left the room. I followed her down to the front hall, where she stood with the door open.

"You'll look into my idea?" I asked.

"Yes. I think it's a very good idea," she said. She took my head in both her hands and pulled me down to kiss me on the forehead. "We'll get through this, Connor. All of it."

I gave her a hug. "It's so hard to be angry with you."

She squeezed my shoulder. "Maybe you're not trying hard enough. Oh, wait a moment, I have something for you." She hurried off into the kitchen and returned in a moment with a small plastic bottle. "Here, it's for your sunburn. Use it liberally."

I held the bottle up to the light. I could just make out a gel-like substance through the opaque plastic. "You made an unguent for sunburn?" I asked, surprised that she would even take the time to think of such a thing.

She laughed. "No, love. It's aloe vera. Some things work just fine the way they are."

6

In the dim light of predawn I woke with a start, my heart racing, my forehead damp. The entire night after leaving Briallen had been broken by troubled dreams. I ran from an unseen terror. I fell off buildings. I struggled up from deep chasms of water. Futilely, I would raise my arms to ward something off, or raise my voice in a broken chant, only to feel the breath leave my body. And then I would wake, my pulse pounding.

I rolled over toward the window, kicking the sweat-damp sheets down around my feet. Outside on the harbor, a lone sailboat edged across a muddy pink horizon. The boat moved lazily, its single sail full out as it tried to catch the light wind. A dull shimmer across the water marked the path of the rising sun, the waves swelling sluggishly. I loved the water but not boats. I had learned to sail on the Charles River, but I had never particularly liked it. Sailing relied too much on chance. Even as I watched, the wind died and the sail fluttered slack. Some poor sucker out there had a long wait coming.

The edge of the sun pierced the horizon. As if on cue, a

small breeze rippled the boat's sail, and it started to move. I thought I could just make out the small figure of someone jumping back and forth to manipulate the boom. The sail caught, brilliantly white in the rising sun, and the boat began to cut sharply across the water.

Getting out of bed, I pushed the futon aside and stood naked before the window. As the sun rose, I chanted an invocation of greeting, my arms upraised, my head thrown back. The morning light washed over me, my chant drawing its energy into me, renewing me. It was a minor feat, a most basic exercise. The equivalent of giving my essence a shower. It didn't hurt. In fact, it felt good. Very good. Briallen was right; if regaining what I knew meant starting from scratch, then that was what I had to do. Otherwise, I was just a boat waiting for a breeze.

After I took a shower, I called Avalon Memorial and left a message for Gillen Yor, my healer. I had no sooner replaced the phone on its cradle than it rang. It was Gillen.

I glanced at the clock. "Gillen, you're up early. I was just calling to make an appointment."

"What's wrong?" he asked.

"Nothing. I thought I'd come for another evaluation."

"I was concerned something happened. How's noon?"

"Only if you're not skipping lunch."

"I'm the healer, Connor. You just show up for a change." The line went dead. As I replaced the receiver, I couldn't blame Gillen for his brusqueness. I had bailed out of more than one appointment.

I spent the morning planning a course of study. My pride wouldn't let me seek a teacher, but for the steps I was going to take I didn't need one yet. I would start at the most rudimentary lessons and build from there, studying incantations, exercising my memory and doing small invocation spells to strengthen my core essence.

A true druid never abandons the search for new knowledge. And the true druid can only continue by passing on the knowledge gained. I was qualified to teach, but I had let the world of the Guild seduce me into stepping away. It is possible to stay on the path and be in the Guild, but the choice to take the financial benefits for their own sake had proved too tempting for me.

Ability is inborn, but only intense study brings out its potential. It takes endurance. Most people don't have the stamina or enough ability to walk the true path. They abandon their skills or leave the life of study for more worldly concerns, content to gauge the weather for the local village or give vague warning of coming events. They are no longer considered part of the circle, true druids of the path. If the truth of my condition were to be known, I had to discover the truth of myself first. I had to step back onto the path.

At five minutes before noon, I dutifully sat in Gillen Yor's waiting room. As chief healer at Avalon Memorial, Gillen enjoyed a large office suite on the top floor of the ten-story building overlooking the Charles River and Cambridge. Several other people sat in various levels of anxiety around the room, most of them alone except a woman with a small boy who had a bent horn growing out of the side of his forehead. Looked to me like someone had been messing in his parents' potions cabinet. The phone on the abandoned receptionist's desk rang constantly while glow bees hovered around the empty chair.

At precisely noon, Gillen Yor stalked into the waiting room from the outside corridor. He was a small, bony man, about five-foot-three, shiny bald on top, with a long, white beard. Penetrating dark brown eyes peered out from incredibly long eyebrows. Beneath his standard white lab coat, he wore navy blue pantaloons and brown suede boots that came up to his knees.

"Grey," he barked without even looking around the room, and disappeared into his office.

I got up and followed. He was already behind his desk as I entered, and when I sat down, he flicked his hand at the door. It slammed shut. He folded his hands on the clean desktop and leaned forward. "What's the matter?"

I tried to relax. "I had dinner with Briallen last night, and she convinced me to try again."

His eyes narrowed. "She's been treating you."

"No! She checks me out every time I see her, but she doesn't actually treat me."

"Good. It's bad enough you don't do what I tell you without someone else mucking about in that thick head of yours."

The thing I loved about Gillen Yor was that you could never decide whether to laugh or to be angry at him. He was one of the most irascible people I'd ever met, and the best healer in the Northeast, if not the States. The story goes that when he decided to come to America decades ago, the Seelie Court demanded he remain in Ireland or on the Isle of Man. Gillen politely informed the queen that he was not one of her subjects. When she insisted, he left anyway, then sent her his business card with a note to call first for an appointment.

He placed the palm of his hand on my forehead and muttered under his breath. A surge of heat pulsed through my head. A moment later, he removed his hand and took his seat. Talking to himself, he turned to his computer and began typing. From an angle, I could tell he had pulled up my records. His phone rang. He ignored it. He read the screen, scrolling down several times before turning back to me.

"According to my notes, it hasn't changed," he said. His phone rang again. He glared at it but didn't pick up.

"Briallen thinks I should be retraining myself to see if going through the process will help me regain my skills," I said.

The phone rang again. He grabbed it and yelled into the receiver. "I'm at lunch." He slammed it down and looked back at me. "That's not a bad idea. We haven't really explored the extent of the blockage." The phone rang again. Gillen jumped up and stalked to the door, flinging it open.

A cloud of glow bees swirled around him. I tried not to laugh as he batted them away. He moved out of view for a moment, yelling someone's name. He stuck his head back in. "I'll be right back. I have to go fire someone. Don't leave."

I leaned across the desk to look at my file. Most of the entries were similar, noting the lack of progress. I slouched and looked around the room. My gaze fell back to the computer. I glanced at the door, then went around the desk.

I pulled up the main menu and opened the clinical directory. I typed *"ska"* in the search window and immediately got a dictionary definition, not much different than Briallen's. There were referent links to incest, stillbirth, and cross-species progeny. The incest referent was just another definition linking back to the other two. I hit the jackpot with cross-species progeny. As part of a differential diagnosis link, the text recommended that a healer request the presence of a flit when dealing with patients who exhibit unusual congenital manifestations that could not be accounted for physically. Flits apparently have a unique sensitivity to cross-species progeny and might be able to identify a disruption in a patient's essence.

I glanced anxiously at the door. Exiting the main menu, my patient record popped back up. I backed out of it to Gillen's main page access. Moving quickly, I jumped into various access links until I found case research. With mild misgivings, I punched in "cross-species" and got fourteen hits. Typing rapidly, I scanned abstracts of each file as fast as I could, dumped the information, and put my record back on the screen. I managed to get into my seat just as Gillen returned.

Restless with annoyance, he sat behind his desk. "We'll have to schedule a real appointment, Connor. I thought I could fit you in today, but I can't. In the meantime, write up your plans and email them to me. I expect progress reports."

"That's fine. I understand this was short notice." I rose

and walked to the door. Noting the still-empty receptionist desk, I said, "I'll call at a better time to schedule."

His eyes narrowed again, and he cocked his head toward his PC. "One thing you might practice is not leaving your damned essence all over the place. It's probably not a good thing in your line of work."

Trying not to look guilty, I nodded. "I'll try."

As I started to leave again, he called my name. "Just for the record, if the presence of your essence on my side of the desk is not a result of your condition, I'll make your current problems seem like a mere distraction. Understood?"

Now too guilty to hide it, I looked away. "Yes, Gillen. I'll see you soon."

Outside the emergency exit, I scanned the street for Murdock's car. I had called him for a ride, and he was late. Boston's a small enough city to get around easily without a car, not that I could afford one, and most people walk. Even at a brisk pace though, Avalon Memorial is a good half hour from my place. I was not above scrounging a ride when I could. Just as I was about to give up on him and head to the subway, Murdock pulled into the fire lane. I removed a pizza box from the passenger seat and tossed it in the back.

"Something wrong?" Murdock asked as he pulled onto Storrow Drive.

"Nothing. Just a checkup. Don't talk. I'm trying to remember something," I said. While I could appreciate Murdock's concern for my health, I didn't want to forget what was in my head. As a child, I had received standard training once my druidic abilities presented themselves. By far the bulk of my education was oral, in keeping with tradition. As a result, I have excellent memorization skills. To the average person, they might even be considered extraordinary, but to the average druid, they were commonplace. Whether it was a true ability, or a convenient side effect of ability, I didn't know. Whichever, they're extremely helpful.

He took us up on the elevated highway and coasted off

again for the Summer Street exit. In moments, we were parked in front of my building. As I unlocked the building door, I noticed someone had scratched their initials in ogham letters and a numeric year date into the paint by the lock. I guess I should be grateful. Kids usually just broke the lock. Or the window. The art students constantly lost their keys and thought that was a solution.

Murdock followed me upstairs. I let us in, waved vaguely at the refrigerator, and went into my study. Sitting at my computer, I entered the information from the abstracts. Murdock came up behind me sipping a glass of water. Once I had everything entered, I sat back and stared at the screen. If I told Murdock the whole truth, he'd chastise me and use the information anyway. I filled him in on my evening with Briallen and just told him that I got the information from a hospital source.

"So what did you find?" he asked.

I scrolled through my notes. "Two dwarf/human crosses, five human/fairy, two human/elf, and five fairy/elf."

"Looks like we can toss the dwarf crosses," he said, reading over my shoulder. I nodded. The dwarf/human crosses had resulted in children more dwarf than human. I hadn't sensed any dwarf essence on the victims, either, so they didn't fit the profile.

"Most of these kids didn't live past puberty," I said. I counted silently. "That leaves two human/fairy crosses, one human/elf, and three elf/fairy."

"Why just the mother's names? Were the fathers not listed?"

I shook my head. "Unless property or royalty are involved, the fey rarely maintain formal marriages. Women tend to raise girls alone and foster out boys."

All the children seemed to suffer some kind of physical deformity in addition to diminished mental capacity. Not an unusual attribute, I noted with irony, in someone who butchers people. Particularly, violent tendencies didn't seem indicated in the material I had, but that didn't mean they didn't exist. The rest of the information was sketchy at best, the details of each child laid out in case files I hadn't had time to explore.

"Okay, let's run 'em down," he said. He read over my shoulder. "I'll take Dealle Sidhe and Teri Esposito since they're both in the Boston area. I can call New York for Ann Cody."

I printed out a copy for him. "I know someone in England, so it shouldn't take me too long to track down Cheryl Atworth. Germany might take a little longer—Gerda and Britt Alfheim sound pretty common. How are we doing with our decoy?"

Murdock frowned and shrugged. "This is Boston, Connor, not Nordic country. Most of the force is Irish, Italian, and Hispanic."

"You can't find one skinny blond cop? We only have twenty-four hours. Got a Plan B?"

"I know you hate when I ask this, but is there anything you can do?"

I tapped my fingers on the edge of my desk, suppressing my impatience. Murdock had every right to ask the question, and my usual annoyance with it came back to my conversation with Briallen. My annoyance wasn't about his expectation of easy answers. It was my inability to deliver them. "I'm trying, Murdock."

"Have you called the Guild about the missing stones?" he asked.

"Damn, I completely forgot," I said, grabbing the phone. I dialed the main number and asked for Meryl Dian, an old acquaintance in the Guild archives. Naturally, I was put on hold, the strains of plaintive flute music to soothe me while I waited.

"Grey! Haven't heard that name in quite a while," Meryl said, when she picked up.

"I've been on leave."

"Hmph. Fired's what I heard," she said. Startled, I didn't say anything for a moment. "I'm guessing you need a favor. What is it this time? The complete history of the ritual use of toadstools by tomorrow morning? No wait, you already asked for that. If you lost it, like you usually do, I kept a copy. Or maybe you'd like me to stay late and find the name of the last druid priestess of Ulster and those of her pets? I can rush it, of course."

I could feel blood rushing to my face. The curious look Murdock was giving me told me I probably looked as uncomfortable as I felt. "Meryl, I seem to have caught you at a bad time . . ."

"There's never a good time down here, Grey. It's the same old unreasonableness without any gratitude. What do you need?"

"Really, Meryl, if you'd prefer not to . . ."

She cut me off. "Connor, spare me the reverse psychology. I've been around that particular block plenty of times, and while you may think it's worked in the past, you're wrong. If I didn't want to do something, flattery and concern from obnoxious imps isn't going to change my mind. Now, spit it out."

"I'm looking for some selenite stones that were recently checked in by the Boston P.D. They've gone missing. They're connected to the fairy murders in the Weird," I said as quickly as possible.

"When were they checked in?" I opened my database and gave her the dates. I could hear her shuffling paper on her desk. She sighed heavily. "Okay, my computer's down right now so I can't check the log. Call me in a few days."

"Just so you know, the stones are confidential and being kept from the press."

"Oh, gee, there goes the announcement I was going to make on the public address system," she said.

I forced myself to chuckle. "You're the best, Meryl."

"I know," she said, and disconnected the line.

I set the phone down slowly and looked at Murdock. "Was I that much of a prick when I was at the Guild?"

"I didn't know you then." I frowned. "If it's any consolation, I think you're a prick now." I glowered at him, and he smirked. "Well, not a very big prick."

I gave up and laughed. "Okay, so I've spread a little bad karma around. I'm working on it, I'm working on it."

"I've gotta go." I followed him to the door and let him out. Murdock never says good-bye. When I first met him, the abruptness with which he left bothered me, but I've gotten used to it. It's his way, like mine is to want closure on everything.

I went back into the study, trying to remember how I had offended Meryl Dian. I rarely saw her when I was at the Guild. My office was on the tenth floor, while she maintained one of the archival wings in the subbasement. Most of our contact had been by phone, invariably about research for cases I was working on. She was brilliant, if a bit dark and creepy sometimes, but cute in an as-a-button kind of way. She could recount the politics of tenth-century Britain and digress into the decomposition of bodies on the battlefield without taking a breath. How she knew what body parts crows preferred baffled me.

I remembered the druid priestess question from another murder case I had worked on. That one was actually a human serial killer on Cape Cod who was keeping people as pets before offing them in the bathtub. The toadstool history didn't register with me at all. The more I thought about it, the more I realized I probably hadn't been very considerate of Meryl. In the heat of an investigation, I tended to treat everyone as subordinate staff, and, obviously, I had rubbed her the wrong way on more than one occasion. Which was precisely why I could never take Keeva up on her offer. I wouldn't mind working with Meryl. In fact, I think I'd like it. It's the jerks like me I didn't want to have to deal with.

In less than a week, I had been reminded of my own

arrogance, insensitivity, and complacency. Since my accident, I definitely wasn't the person I was at the Guild. It doesn't take too long on the outside looking in to wake you up to a few facts about life, if not yourself. Not that I was suddenly one with the goodness of humanity. I was all too aware of its underbelly to fool myself into thinking it didn't exist. But I definitely didn't see myself arbitrarily dismissing people out of hand anymore. Even if I hadn't been feeling that way, Briallen had opened my eyes to it quite clearly the night before.

I turned back to my database to review the files again. Despite the tugging allure of self-pity, I could always worry about what people thought of me later. I had less than a day to stop an accident of birth from butchering people.

7

I awoke without moving my body, my eyes fluttering open to stare at the ceiling. Lying in dim gray-white light, I slowly became aware of a subtle desire, like a mild withdrawal. In just a few short days of performing the morning invocation ritual, my body was already becoming synchronized with the dawn. It knew it wanted the pleasant sensation of light washing over it, sparking it awake with renewed energy. When I had first learned the ritual as a young boy, my body's essence took weeks to become attuned to the diurnal rhythm of the sun. Now, it was like resetting an alarm clock.

I rolled out of bed and stood before the window with my head bowed and arms crossed over my chest. As the disc of the sun pierced the horizon, its warm glow touched my forehead. Inhaling deeply, I raised my arms. I had forgotten how soothing the ritual felt, chanting the ancient Gaelic paean, waking my body with the stretching postures. I could not remember why I stopped doing it. I couldn't believe I had gotten to a point in my life where doing something so simple had become so inconsequential to me. As the sun climbed to sit momentarily on the edge of the horizon, I ended the chant in the final stance, head thrown back, arms down and out, with the light centered on my chest, the seat of my essence.

The reality that Tuesday had come again pressed itself upon me while I was under the water in the shower. The word beat at my mind, its innocent sounds colored with dread. Another week had passed since I had stood in a wet alley looking at a chest with a crater in it. Today, the cycle was likely to repeat. I dried myself off, picked up my coffee mug, and went into the study.

My first order of business was to call Murdock to see where we were with our decoy. He hadn't checked into the station house yet. It was still early. Rather than call his beeper or his house, I left a message for him. Thinking about the decoy reminded me that I wanted Tansy to observe the stakeout if she were willing. Pulling a glow bee out of the fridge, I held it tightly in my hand, feeling it come to life. It surprised me how quickly it responded. I sent it off to Joe with a message to find Tansy and meet me later in the day.

Before it got any later, I decided to place my calls to Europe. Working internationally usually meant east, which meant I had to make contact before noon. Otherwise, everyone would be going home for the day. I didn't expect the bad guys to accommodate my schedule.

The Avalon database had listed Cheryl Atworth, a human who had given birth to a boy named William, last reported in England. The father was a fairy. She would have been in the States in 1960, making her around sixty-five years old today. The Ward Guildhouse in London was a little sloppy with its paperwork, but since the fey were welcomed and admired in the British Isles, Atworth wasn't likely to hide her association with a former lover. That made my first call to Rory Dean, an old drinking buddy of mine from poorly remembered bacchanals in the early nineties. He definitely owed me a few favors, if not a few beers. After an interminable time wandering through the voice mail system, I finally got Rory's cheery voice informing me that he had gone to lunch. I left a message with what details I had, a plea to rush it, and a promise to visit.

Germany was another matter. The only people I knew there showed bare disdain for Americans, which is at least nicer than what they thought of the Brits and Irish. In the early part of the century, the dwarves and elves had formed the Teutonic Consortium and caused havoc. At the end of World War II, they cut a deal with Russia not to impede the final push into Berlin in exchange for northeastern Germany. When the Berlin Wall came down, a demilitarized fey zone went up next to the city where it abuts Consortium territory. Even now, one of the big issues of the Fey Summit was the constant skirmishing between the Teutonic Consortium and Maeve's fairy defender warriors. The elves routinely threatened to push the border back to France. Humans might have resolved a lot of their differences with the fall of the Soviets, but the fey still stared at each other, spears at the ready, always in danger of resuming their part of the war.

I really didn't have any contacts, but I had no doubt the Guildhouse would be able to find the two people I sought. Berlin kept careful track of fey folk. The fey folk were allowed a Guildhouse only on the condition of strict government oversight. Before the War, the fey had ignored the edict, but once atomic energy had been harnessed, the playing field had leveled, so they acceded to the more stringent demands.

The only details I had were names and dates. Gerda was in the States in and around 1948 and had a son named Gethin. Britt was here in 1972 and had given birth to a daughter she named Welfrey. Their surnames were given as Alfheim, which was just a general elf clan affiliation. The Berlin Guildhouse used a customer-service center that was derisively referred to as the informant center. Nondescript agents, many of them human and suspicious of everyone, took notes, gave no information, and occasionally actually called back. I knew the officious agent I snagged would complain that clan affiliations were scant detail at best, and he did. Still, as politely as possible, I gave him the names and dates, diplomatically asked for urgency, and supplied him with the case number and Murdock's name and my cell number to assure them it was an official investigation.

Frustrated, I wandered out to the Avenue and gazed at the shops, the pubs, and the stores. They were all familiar but, really, they changed every day. A little more wear or a fresh coat of paint. People frequented them, or never came again, or arrived for the first time. Yet I felt as though they were always the same, especially in the morning when everything was devoid of activity. The long street felt like a stage waiting for a play.

A large old woman sat on the curb wearing a ragged sweatshirt, her gray hair sprouting out from beneath a black woolen cap. She jiggled a worn paper coffee cup, making a meager jingling sound. She eyed me impassively as I came near. "Change for a truth! Change for a truth!" she said in rhythm with her shaking.

I paused, digging in my pocket. I wasn't so much looking for a truth as I was just willing to give her money. Normally, I ignored the pleas of street people. The Weird had too many of them, and if you frequented the neighborhood at all, they remembered and pestered you if you'd even once given them a dime. But it was early and I was feeling helpless over other things, so I dropped a couple of quarters in her cup. She glanced at them for a moment, then looked up at me with a huge gap-toothed smile. "Change," she said.

"Yes," I said.

She shifted her bulk so she could lean against a newspaper box. "Change. There's your truth." She chuckled, then closed her eyes as though asleep.

I chuckled myself and continued on. Vaguely, I wondered if she were a failed druidess, one of those with no more talent than for one small thing, say, articulating simple truths, or if she were merely a beggar with a gimmick. Regardless, I knew from experience that change is not always good. Knowing how to make the best of it was what really mattered.

As I moved along, I came to the main stretch of the Avenue that was preparing for the Midsummer parade. Glittery cellophane suns topped old lampposts, which were bound one to the other with banners of frilly green plastic that was supposed to symbolize the new grass of summer. Any bare surface of building wall was layered with advertisements for parties and sales and the latest import bands that would be playing locally.

My cell phone vibrated gently against my hip, and I was amused at how similar it felt to a glow bee. It was Murdock.

"Have you found someone to use as bait?" I asked.

"Not yet. Don't you know any real fairies we could use?"

The answer to that question was both embarrassing and depressing. You never realize friendships are predicated on things like money and power until you lose them. "I have an idea. Can you meet me on the corner of Pittsburgh and the Avenue?"

"Fifteen minutes," he said, and hung up.

I was close to the corner, so I had to wait a long fifteen minutes before Murdock pulled up and I got in.

"What's your gut instinct—are you going to find someone?"

He frowned. "No."

"How about Robin?"

He shook his head. "No way. He's a civilian."

"He's perfect."

"He's a suspect," Murdock insisted.

"He's a minor suspect at best."

"Connor, I've told you before, minor turns into major."

We sat staring out the windshield. A full minute ticked by. "He's perfect," I repeated.

Murdock half turned in his seat to face me. "And what if he's the killer? What if we end up jeopardizing the case against him?"

"We won't. Perpetrators agree to help all the time. Besides, I don't think it's Robin. Shay's sketch was verified by Tansy."

". . . who's an associate of a victim that Shay and Robin knew," Murdock said.

"Now you're being paranoid. Murdock, think about it. We have nothing else. We're stuck. If it is Robin, what better way to stop a murder than by having him wired and watched? It might even lead him to make a mistake by thinking he's *not* a suspect. And if he's not the killer, we may very well catch the person who is."

"Ruiz won't approve this."

"He doesn't have to know. You've already got the equipment. If nothing happens, just don't make a report. If something does, you're a hero."

"Damn," he muttered under his breath. He clenched his jaw and shook his head a few times while he mentally debated. He swiveled back in his seat and put the car in gear. I let out a sigh of relief when he turned down the alley where Shay and Robin lived. He stopped in front of the boarded-up door, and we got out.

He pulled the door open and strode down the dim hall. "Don't put that fuckin' light on," he shouted. When we reached the end, an angry-looking Robin opened the inside door.

The room was a shambles. Clothes were strewn every-where. One of the beds was shifted away from the wall. A small nightstand lay on its side. Shay knelt on the bed, leaning over a pile of clothes. He wore a blue chenille bathrobe, and his hair hung down to either side of his face, which was smeared with makeup. He plucked at the scat-tered clothing, folding it roughly. Robin leaned against the wall, wearing a pale green T-shirt and ripped baggy jeans. He folded his arms tightly against his chest and glared.

Murdock made a small show of looking around the room. Nonchalantly, he straightened a framed poster that had been knocked askew. "Are we interrupting something?"

Shay glanced up at us, then back to his folding. "Spring cleaning," he said. I could feel the anger radiating off him like the heat of a fire. If I closed my eyes, I would still feel him in the room and know he was there.

Murdock put a chair back on its feet and leaned on the back of it as he looked at Robin. "I have a proposition for you."

Robin shrugged. "I get those a lot."

"How'd you like to help catch the guy who did Gamelyn?"

Shay stopped what he was doing but didn't look up.

"What's in it for me?" Robin said.

"Don't you want to know what we want you to do first?" I asked.

A sneer played across his face. "Do I have a choice?"

"Everyone has a choice," I said.

"Maybe in your world, Connor Grey. Down here life's a little different."

"I live down here," I said.

He walked slowly toward me. In my peripheral vision, I could see Murdock casually move into a more defensive stance. I didn't move. Robin came within inches of me, staring coldly into my eyes. As my warding shields tried to activate, I fought down the autonomic response. I didn't want him to get the impression he was a threat. He brought his hand up and with one finger caressed the air over my cheek. "But does it ever touch you?" he said.

"We want you to act as a decoy," Murdock said, to break the silence.

Robin and I continued to stare into each other's eyes. Finally, he smirked and walked back to lean against the wall. "I thought this guy was into fairies."

"He is. You'll wear a glamour stone to fool him," I said.

"Like I said, what's in it for me?" he asked.

Shay swept up from the bed and stepped toward Robin. "Don't! You could get hurt!"

"Shut up, Shay!" Robin didn't take his eyes off Murdock.

"We'll have a wire on him the whole time, and we'll be right outside if anything happens," said Murdock.

Shay glared at him. "And what? This maniac will wait to stick him with a knife until you get there?"

"Shay, I said shut up," said Robin, moving away from him.

He turned away and began picking up clothes. "No, I won't shut up, Robin. I can't take any more of this. The fights. The fear. The risks. I came here to get away from that. I don't want any part of this." He sat on the bed facing the ransacked closet, his back toward us.

"What's in it for me?" Robin repeated quietly.

"We'll work that out when we need to."

He pursed his lips. "And if I don't do it?"

Murdock shrugged. "Same old, same old."

Robin smiled at me. "You were right. I do have a choice—between nothing and nothing. And no guarantee he won't breathe down my neck if I refuse." He cocked an eyebrow at me, waiting, but I didn't want to rise to his bait. He was too smart to believe any platitudes I could throw at him and too stupid to know he'd gotten to this point by his own choice.

"When do we do this?" he asked.

"Tonight," replied Murdock.

"Fine."

Shay made a strangled sound that could have been a sob or snarl. He bolted into the closet and yanked the curtain closed behind him.

Murdock and I went out into the alley and got in the car.

"I've got a call out to Joe Flit. I thought it'd help if we could get Tansy in on this," I said.

Murdock nodded. "How are we going to protect her?"

"She's a flit. She'll bug out if there's trouble," I said reassuringly.

"This better work, Connor."

I didn't respond. I had enough doubts about what I had started without voicing them to Murdock. He could still pull out.

"Can you do a little more background on Shay?" I asked.

"Yeah, I'm not busy," he said sarcastically.

"No, really. Something's not right. This is the second time I've gotten a funny vibe from him. He's definitely human. His essence is particularly strong. I can actually see the edges of his aura. He comes in regular contact with the fey, so that can heighten the effect on someone with such a strong essence."

"So what's the vibe?"

I shrugged my shoulders. "It's just gut reaction. The first time we talked to them, Shay wanted to help. Now he wants no part of this."

"Connor, you forget we're dealing with people on the wrong side of the law. They flip-flop all the time."

"Maybe you're right. Is he under surveillance?"

He pulled up in front of my building. "Since the day we saw him. Funny thing is, for a prostitute, he doesn't do much business. He's had only two suspected encounters, both at a hotel. The rest of the time, he's gone back home before the bars close."

I got out of the car. "Thanks, Murdock."

"I'll pick you up later," he said, and pulled away.

Back in the apartment, I made another cup of coffee. After sitting in the mild carnage of Murdock's car, I surveyed my living room with fresh eyes. I decided another self-improvement project would be to clean up. At least the living room; the study would be asking too much. I needed all the discipline I could reinforce right now. I made up the futon and pushed it back into its couch position, picked up the magazines off the floor, put five used coffee mugs in the dishwasher, and walked around with the wastebasket, tossing out stray wrappers and junk mail. But the time I got the horizontal surfaces clear and dusted, I was feeling pretty satisfied with myself.

I dropped into the armchair, propped my feet up on the windowsill, and sipped cold coffee. I could not place what it was about Shay that bothered me. It certainly wasn't his androgyny. In a way, that fascinated me. Looking at Shay, I automatically found myself trying to sort him into a physical gender category, but his face and body simply refused. I could not resist the thought that someone less in control of their emotions would be angered by it, especially if they were questioning their own sexuality. He was both beautiful and handsome, feminine and masculine.

He seemed educated, which meant nothing. Even given his line of work, he wouldn't be the first nice, middle-class kid to hit the streets. Maybe Murdock was right. Maybe life in one of those suburbs with green lawns and white fences wasn't so nice to someone who didn't fit the Dick and Jane model. Lots of kids came down to the Weird. It was where the fey hung out, where the cool stuff happened. Most of them just visited though. Shay had stayed and somehow ended up with Robin. That was no mystery. It always helped to have a friend down here, especially someone bigger or stronger.

The fact that Shay didn't tell us he'd spoken to the killer disturbed me. The bartender at the Flitterbug mentioned him without any prompting from me, so I was willing to assume the information was reasonably reliable. I could not reconcile Shay's silence about it with his willingness to provide a police sketch. It didn't make sense. Either he would not tell us anything, or he'd give us everything. Whatever his behavior meant, it clearly indicated something more was happening with him than he was willing to let on. And that was something I was going to find out, whether he wanted me to or not.

Twilight came and left the sallow light of the city reflected in the underbelly of the overcast clouds. The beacons of the airport across the harbor burned smoldering red as planes flitted off into the gloom like metallic insects.

Rousing myself, I popped a frozen taco in the microwave. As I poured myself a glass of water, a voice behind me said, "Make that two."

I nearly dropped the glass as I spun around to find Stinkwort and Tansy hovering in the living room. "We've got to figure out a way for you to knock," I said.

Tansy gasped with delight and flew past me to the microwave. Placing both her hands on the window, she watched avidly as the taco revolved.

"Why? It's not like I'm going to interrupt a date," Joe said.

"Says you," I said, sipping my water. The microwave beeped, and Tansy wheeled back with a squeal of surprise.

I took the taco out and singed my fingers as I unwrapped it clumsily onto a plate. "We're going to lay a trap for the murderer. I'm hoping Tansy will help look for him."

At the sound of her name, she fluttered over to my plate and examined the taco. I offered her a bit of meat on the tip of my finger. She took it curiously, sniffed it several times, then flicked it onto the counter with a look of disgust. As I ate, Joe translated my request.

I could tell immediately Tansy wasn't thrilled with the idea. If possible, her face seemed to become even more pale. After an intense exchange too fast for me to follow,

Joe turned to me, and said, "She'll do it, but only if I go with her."

"I was hoping you would anyway."

"Great. The way you keep throwing us together, we'll end up in bed by the end of the movie." He eyed Tansy speculatively. "Maybe I'll give her the ol' twirly-whirl for the hell of it."

"You're so crass."

He scoffed at me. "Yeah, right, like you're one of those Christian saints. I don't knock, remember?"

I laughed. "Actually, I think you've ruined more of my relationships than I have."

"Not that it keeps me busy," he said.

My door buzzer went off. "There's Murdock."

Murdock was in no better mood than when I had left him earlier. He even looked rumpled, which for him meant creases in his shirt and a slightly loosened tie. Tension flowed off Murdock in waves as Stinkwort and Tansy danced around in the backseat. We didn't speak on the ride over. I knew not to press him when he was that wound up. We parked the car in the alley as Tansy continued an incessant chatter. As far as I could tell, she seemed to have an overwhelming need to identify everything she saw. She managed to spot a car, a truck, and a tree several times.

We opened the boarded-up door and walked in. Shay nervously opened the inner door as we approached. He was dressed in a short red tunic with too many reflective beads and had pulled his hair up in a bun on top of his head. He looked like some kind of geisha flapper.

"You're late," Robin said from the other side of the room. He wore a plain green T-shirt with matching shorts, his hair wavy and falling loosely.

"Let's get the wire on," said Murdock. Wordlessly, Robin lifted his shirt. With practiced ease, Murdock taped the wire to his skin, and Robin slipped his shirt back down. Murdock nodded at me, and I removed the small wooden case that held the glamour.

The smooth hazelwood box almost felt like it was vibrating in my hand. I knew the sensation was the protection ward and not the stone. The whole point of the box was to contain and mask the stone. I snapped back the lid and drew out the glamour. It was a small clear crystal no more than an eighth inch round, set in a cheap gold circle and strung on a brown leather cord. As I held it up, it captured the light in the room and gathered it into a small pinpoint. I could feel fairy essence radiating off it as I handed it to Robin.

He gave it a cursory glance, then slipped it over his head. As he flicked his hair out from beneath the cord, Shay let out a small gasp. Robin seemed taller and more languid in the limbs. His lips, prone to a tight line of annoyance, had a more refined haughtiness. His eyes glittered with steely blue highlights and his hair flowed more luxuriantly over his shoulders. The final payoff, though, was the vague shimmer of silver wings that fanned from his back. He looked like a fairy with a mild ward hiding the full spectacle of his wings.

Tansy flew over to him and clasped a flowing tress of hair. "Pretty, pretty," she exclaimed.

Shay reached out and stroked Robin's hair. "You're beautiful," he whispered.

"I don't feel any different," he said.

"You shouldn't," I said.

Murdock looked at me. "Think it'll work?"

I nodded. "His human essence is there if I look for it, but he feels like a fairy. In a crowded bar, it'll work."

"What about when I leave the bar?" said Robin.

Murdock shook his head. "You won't. We just want you to play him, get us a description, then end it. We'll tail him from there."

"What about later? What if he comes after Robin?" asked Shay.

"I don't think he will. Without the glamour stone, he'll probably take no more notice of Robin again than he would me," I said. Shay looked dubious but said nothing.

We went out to Murdock's car. After much rearranging of the backseat, including a trip to a nearby dumpster, Shay and Robin got in the back. We made a slow circle around the block until we came to the Avenue. Sparse traffic filtered through the intersections, and we found a space about a half a block from the Flitterbug with a decent view of the entrance.

Murdock twisted in his seat to face the back. "Now listen, Robin. I want you to keep a running commentary. When you're alone, tell us what you see without drawing attention to yourself. When someone hits on you, I want you to work a description of them into the conversation without arousing suspicion. If someone other than Shay's description makes a play for you, get rid of him as quickly as possible."

"What do you want me to do?" Shay asked.

"Nothing. You stay right here. I want you to listen to the voices. You said you'd never forget his voice."

I could barely contain a smile at the look of shock on his face.

"No way! I'm your prime witness!"

"If you can identify him, he can identify you, and if he sees you first, he's gone before we know it. End of discussion."

Shay crossed his arms and slouched back in the seat. "This isn't even the right outfit for a backseat," he muttered.

Robin climbed out the back and walked toward the bar, with Stinkwort and Tansy fluttering above his head. As he reached the entrance, he hesitated just slightly, enough to make me surmise he was not as cocky as he seemed.

"Can you hear me?" Robin said. His voice sounded muffled, but audible. Murdock gave the horn a quick toot, short enough for no one to be able to place the source. Robin nodded once and entered the bar. From the sudden loud music, I could picture him making his way across the dance floor. I hoped he had the brains to move away from the speakers. Even as the thought crossed my mind, the music receded into the background.

"Hey, what's up?" he said.

"I know you?" said someone I assumed was the bartender. I couldn't tell if it was the same one I had spoken to.

"That's Bem. He's an asshole," Shay said from the backseat.

"No. I'll just have some springwater," Robin said.

"I don't make no money on springwater," said Bem.

"Then throw some vodka in it," said Robin.

"I'm not reimbursing him for booze," Murdock said.

"Let's deal with it later," I said. Murdock can be too process-oriented sometimes.

We settled into an uncomfortable silence broken only by the filtered noise of the bar. Every time Shay fidgeted in the backseat, the beads on his tunic made little clicking sounds. Outside on the Avenue, a few cars listlessly circled the block as though overcome by the humidity. Having a murderer on the loose finally seemed to be having an impact on the night crowd. That and the fact that it was a weeknight.

"Hey, good-looking, you must be, what, six-two? Three?" Robin said.

"How much?" a rough voice said.

"I said maybe six-two or-three," said Robin.

"That's not what I meant," the voice said.

"I know. You trolls are way too impatient. Where'd you get that scar? Bump your head under a bridge?" said Robin. Murdock actually chuckled.

"Fucking fairies, think you're always better than everyone," the troll said. Then he laughed. "Well, you're getting yours now, ain't ya?" There was a long silence with only bar static.

"Do you recognize the voice, Shay?" I asked.

Beads clinked in the backseat. "No, it definitely wasn't a troll I saw. Don't you think I know what a troll looks like?" As if on cue, the troll swore again and left.

"He smelled like Roquefort cheese, too," Robin muttered.

"Only when they don't wash their hands," I said, knowing he couldn't hear me.

The hours crept by. As the evening wore on, more men hit on Robin with less and less originality. I had forgotten how dull stakeouts can be. The only relief came from Robin's caustic comments to prospective customers. The boy did know how to make people go away. He was also quite adept at getting us descriptions without arousing suspicion. Most of those who approached him were human. Only one elf though, probably looking to get off on a little interspecies animosity.

"This is boring," Shay said.

"I thought you were worried it would be dangerous," I said.

"I am. I just never thought danger could get boring."

"I was wondering, Shay, if you heard this guy's voice so clearly because he might have talked to you."

There was a long silence. "No. I would remember, wouldn't I? I only remember hearing him because I was standing next to Gamelyn when they hooked up."

Something about the sound of his voice made me turn and look at him. He had his head cocked to the side, a faraway look in his eyes as he gazed out the window. "I would remember," he said again, though to me or himself, I couldn't tell.

"Hey, get a load of this," Murdock said, bringing my attention back to the street.

A fairy strode down the sidewalk in full glory, her huge gossamer wings fanning out behind like great silver veils. She wore the traditional green frock of the lower classes, an almost ridiculous costume with the obvious power she had. Her lush red hair swirled around her head as if animate, an illusion made all the more by the tiny flits that hovered around her. Flits love a flashy fairy.

Shay snorted from the backseat. "Now *that* is slumming."

The fairy reached the front of the Flitterbug and stopped. As she turned to enter, I saw her face in the reflected glow of the streetlight. A flush of heat swept over me as I felt instant anger. Keeva.

"What the hell does she think she's doing?" I clawed at the door handle.

Horns blared as I cut across traffic. Even as I hit the sidewalk on the other side, Keeva's presence was having an effect. She'd been made as a Guild agent, or at least someone looking to make trouble. Patrons were practically running out of the bar. I muscled my way through the door and was bombarded with music and more people. Inside, I felt overwhelmed by the reek of essence colored by sex, anger, despair, and a little amusement. More people pushed their way out. I could see Keeva on the far side of the dance floor.

I rushed over to her and grabbed her arm. She spun toward me, pulling her arm away, her eyes glowing with white power. My body shields came up so fast, I felt a knife blade of pain in my forehead. The air crackled with energy. Several people around us stumbled away in fear.

"Knock it off, Keeva," I said.

The light in her eyes dimmed when she recognized me, but they remained bright with anger. She wrenched her arm away. "Don't touch me."

I could see Robin at the end of the bar in a cluster of anxious-looking customers. Stinkwort appeared behind Keeva, his face set with suspicion. The way he held his arm across his waist told me he was grasping the hilt of the sword he occasionally wore hidden by a glamour. I hoped his skills matched his determination.

"What the hell are you doing here?" I said.

"Working. Get out before you ruin everything," she said.

"Or what? I'll blow your cover? You might as well have come in here with a siren on your head."

"Get out of the way now, or I'll have you charged with interfering."

I leaned over to her so no one else could hear. "*You're* interfering. I've got something working in here."

She arched an eyebrow at me, then threw a glance over her shoulder. Stinkwort smiled grimly at her. She returned the smile and looked back at me. "Let's talk," she said. She pushed by me and strode toward the door.

Stinkwort flew in closer. "Everything okay?"

"Yeah. Thanks for the backup." I looked to the end of the bar. Robin was leaning in to hear someone next to him. "How's things back there?"

"Robin's a right fine prick. He's been teasing along some old guy for the last ten minutes."

I scanned the nearly empty bar. "Hang by the door while I talk to Keeva."

He followed me back across the dance floor and paused by the door while I continued out. Keeva stood about thirty feet away, her hands clamped on her hips.

"Were you *trying* to scare everyone off?" I said as I came up to her.

She smiled. "Actually, yes. I told you. I'm working a missing person."

"You have a funny way of doing it. You just wrecked my stakeout."

"How I operate is not your business. And you didn't file a stakeout."

She had me. Murdock was going to kill me if she reported

our surveillance. "How I operate is not your business," I repeated back at her, desperately trying to think around the situation.

We stood glaring at each other.

"So, it looks like both our operations are blown," I said.

She poked me hard in the chest. "Thanks to you."

I took a few breaths to calm down. "Blame isn't the point now."

"You just interfered with a Guild operation," she said.

"And you just checked the morning operations sheet without bothering to see if it was updated. Never mind the fact that the cheapest rent-boy would have spotted me sitting in a darkened car. You didn't even look around." The first part was a bluff. The P.D. didn't always let everyone know an operation was going down. Keeva had little use for the human police, so I hoped she wouldn't know that.

She narrowed her eyes at me. "Your point?"

"We're both going to look bad." I held my breath, hoping she'd take the bait. If I knew anything about Keeva macNeve, it was that she hated to look like she'd failed.

Her face became stony as her cheeks flushed red. "What are you proposing?"

I slowly exhaled and spread my hands in a gesture of reasonability. "We both report that our operations were unsuccessful. Nothing more."

I could almost see her mind whirling with options. "I won't be obligated to you," she said.

"If we both report nothing happened, it's done with. Quid pro quo."

"Fine, but you have to report all your future operations to me directly."

I shook my head with a smile. "Quid pro quo."

"Bastard."

"I miss you, too."

She began to say something, then paused as she looked over my shoulder. Murdock pulled up to the curb. He leaned over and opened the door, then popped the passenger seat forward. Shay angrily climbed out.

Murdock waved me over. "Get in. It just came over the scanner. They've got someone in custody. It might be our man."

I exchanged one brief startled look with Keeva before jumping into the car. Murdock goosed his siren as he pulled a U-turn. Stinkwort popped up in the small space between the dashboard and the rearview mirror. Startled, Murdock hit the brakes. Stinkwort banged against the windshield and fell onto the dash.

"Nice reflexes," he said, rubbing his head.

"Sorry, Joe." He hit the gas again.

Stinkwort stumbled back. "What the hell is going on?"

"Someone was taken into custody," I said.

"Does this mean the babysitting job is over?" he asked.

"Yeah, tell Robin and Shay to call it a night," I said.

"And make sure they understand to go home. I'll be there bright and early," said Murdock.

Stinkwort rolled his eyes and blinked out.

"Who caught him?" I asked as Murdock wove through traffic.

"Don't know." His voice sounded tight. Murdock didn't like getting caught out of the loop, especially on his own case.

We pulled up in front of the district headquarters. Uniforms were all over the sidewalk. Murdock parked in front of a hydrant, and we got out. Rushing up the steps, most of the cops hanging around had that keen look as they tried to scrutinize every movement around them. They wanted to be in the know as much as anyone, even if the victims were people they could care less about.

Inside the vestibule, Murdock stopped short. Keeva held the inside door open for him, a slim smile on her face.

"How the hell'd you get here?" he said.

"You may have noticed I have wings, Detective," she said.

Murdock threw me a dubious glance, but I nodded back at him. Fairy wings may seem too insubstantial to carry someone in flight, and, if it were simply a matter of aerodynamics and muscle, it is impossible. The wings functioned as elaborate airfoils for the manipulation of essence. Fairies can move pretty damn fast when they want to. Flits were even faster.

We entered the dingy foyer, where the desk sergeant sat behind bulletproof glass. He buzzed us through a door to the right of his cage as soon as he recognized Murdock. We proceeded through the door and down a short hall into the relative calm of the back offices. Plainclothes detectives lingered at their desks pretending to work. Given their frequent glances to the closed door at the end of the room, it wasn't hard to tell where the action was. Murdock walked briskly past and knocked and opened the door at the same time.

Inside the narrow darkened room, a number of people stood peering through a two-way glass. In the room beyond, a large disheveled man sat at a cigarette-scarred table, his arms wrapped around his chest as he rocked slowly back and forth. His head was shaved, and several bruises made a mottled dark track along one side of his face. The only other occupant of the room was a uniform standing in a corner as far away as possible. Through the tinny speaker, we could hear muttering. "I didn't mean it. I didn't mean it. I didn't mean it," over and over again.

A strange sensation settled over me. Time felt suspended in the darkened room as the man kept up his rhythmic rocking. His eyes looked unfocused. I could feel his essence, relatively strong, and I could imagine him having the physical ability to overpower a fairy. With appropriate apparatus, he might even be able to overcome a fey's other abilities, assuming he knew what he was doing and wasn't as disoriented as this guy seemed to be. I tried to figure out who in the room was throwing out the vibes, but it was hard to tell in such tight quarters.

"Captain's waiting for you," someone said, breaking the moment. Murdock jerked his head at me to follow. Keeva and I filed out behind him. As we walked back through the squad room, I noticed a fairy sitting by himself in the far corner, his dark blond hair in a tangle, the red tunic he wore rent in several places. Tears stained trails through the thick makeup on his face.

The plainclothes detectives did not even bother pretending to work anymore but watched us with various degrees of bemusement and even contempt. Something was not right. As we neared the captain's office, a powerful wave of essence hit me in the face, one I knew instantly. The door opened as an assistant came out, and we pressed into another small room.

Emilio Ruiz, captain of Area B, needlessly waved us in. By Murdock's account, Ruiz was a stand-up kind of guy, by the book for the most part. He had risen through the ranks to captain and seemed content to leave it at that. Ruiz just did his job, overlooked the occasional transgression, and stayed out of politics. Which is why I felt sorry for him since two of the biggest political players in the city had decided to take up positions around his desk.

Sitting with his back to us, I recognized Commissioner Scott Murdock, Murdock's father. The commissioner cocked his head to see who had entered. He was a big man, easily my height, with the same dark eyes as his son. Age had not softened him, and he could still turn heads, with his high cheekbones and gray-streaked hair swept back from the hairline. As far as I could tell, he didn't like me much.

To the left of the desk stood the person whose essence

I recognized: Lorcan macDuin, the Guild's Community Liaison Officer. He was exceedingly tall, often a sign of royal stock back in the old country. He wore his pale blond hair in an intricate braid that hung straight down to his waist. As was his usual, he wore an impeccably tailored black suit over a black turtleneck that made him seem even thinner than he was. A small ripple in the air about his shoulders indicated the glamour that hid his wings. He nodded once at Keeva and seemed not to have noticed Murdock or me. From experience, there was no question he didn't like me.

The commissioner gestured with his hand. "Continue, Lorcan."

MacDuin had not moved at all. His piercing green eyes shifted to me and Murdock before he spoke. "As I was saying, the Guild would be more than happy to take the suspect into custody. I insist on it. There are many curious aspects to this case that our expertise will no doubt clarify."

"Can someone bring me up to speed here?" Murdock interrupted.

There was a pregnant pause while no one spoke. I felt a little like a kid who had intruded on the adults. It was Ruiz who decided to fill us in. "Director macDuin apprehended the suspect in the act of attempting to murder a prostitute in an alley off Congress and brought him here. We were just deciding jurisdiction."

"If I may, sir, but given that the perpetrator's human, isn't it pretty clear he's ours?" Murdock said.

Ruiz glanced a bit uncomfortably at the commissioner. "On the one hand, yes. On the other, the apprehending agent is a Guild member."

Turning my head slightly to peer past the edge of the window blind that separated Ruiz's office from the squad, I could see the profile of the disheveled victim. He hadn't moved, apparently, except to smooth his hair back over his ears. As I brought my attention back into the office, I noticed Keeva make an amateurish attempt at not looking like she was watching me.

"The Guild generally only takes cases they have officially participated in," Murdock said.

MacDuin looked incredibly bored. "As I was saying to the commissioner, Detective, in the interest of calming the public, the Guild would be pleased to bring this murderer to justice for his crimes against our people." The scorn in his voice practically puddled on the floor.

Murdock looked at him in surprise. "You think this is the guy that's been killing fairies?"

MacDuin pinched his lips together. "He is."

Murdock jutted his chin out, nodding. "An entire department has been on alert for a week looking for this guy, and you happened to be walking by and catch him in the act. Nice move."

"Murdock . . ." Ruiz said warningly. I was mildly surprised at his tone myself. Murdock could be a little needling sometimes, but even I thought he was on thin ice mocking a Guild director in front of his bosses.

Murdock smiled his best apologetic smile. "Sorry, sir. This thing's had me a bit on edge."

"Why do you think this human could possibly have done the murders?" I asked. As soon as I said it, I realized how arrogant it must have sounded. "No offense to present company," I added quickly.

MacDuin gave me a measured look, much like he was trying to decide whether to swat me or not. "That is precisely why the Guild should take over the investigation. I am very curious as to how a person with no abilities has managed to overcome several fey, Mr. Grey."

"Your victim's beaten up. That's out of character for our perpetrator," I said.

MacDuin nodded. "There was a tussle in the apprehension."

"No, I think Connor's right," said Murdock. "This doesn't fit. The only other witness we've had was purely accidental. The perpetrator we're seeking knows how to do his work out of sight. It's no secret we have a composite sketch, so I think he'd be even more careful now. I think we have a copycat here."

MacDuin leaned forward and fished a clear plastic bag off Ruiz's desk. He laid it carefully on a stack of papers. Inside the bag was a black round stone. "Correct me if I'm wrong, but few people outside this room know about this."

We stared at the bag. Murdock looked at me, and I shrugged.

The commissioner stirred in his seat. "I take it by all the silence that this stone has been held back?" Murdock nodded. The commissioner rubbed his eyes. "Let's split the baby for now. Lorcan, you take the victim, interview him, whatever. Just don't lose him. We'll hold the suspect for now while I decide the best course."

"I must protest, Commissioner," macDuin said.

The commissioner stood and offered his hand. "I know you must, Lorcan. But it's late, and I'm tired, and we'll all feel better in the light of day. Perhaps we can continue this discussion before our meeting tomorrow?"

For a moment, it looked like macDuin wasn't going to shake hands. He nodded finally and shook. "We'll speak in the morning then." He waved his hand at the door. "Keeva, if you will help me escort the victim."

She opened the door, and they left. As I turned back to Murdock, I saw the commissioner give him a sly wink.

"Thank you for your help, Connor," the commissioner said, offering his hand to me. The man did know how to dismiss someone graciously.

"It was good to see you again, sir," I said. I gave Murdock a quick glance and closed the door behind me. Everyone looked up as I walked through the squad room, but I ignored them. Pushing open the front door of the building, I caught up with macDuin and Keeva and their charge.

"Good catch, Lorcan," I said.

"Thank you," he said, studiously looking away from me up the street.

I sidled up next to him. "I mean, like Murdock said, it was a lucky thing you came along when you did."

"Yes." He still wouldn't look at me.

"So, Lorcan, what were you doing in the Weird this time of night?"

He finally looked at me. "Since you are a former member of the Guild, Connor, I will do you the courtesy of telling you that I was monitoring an operation. And that's the last question I'll answer this evening."

Keeva stepped between us. "Connor, why don't I call you tomorrow? We can wrap up the file."

A long black limo pulled up to the curb. They stood waiting for the driver to get out and open the door. Lorcan and Keeva slipped into the backseat, the two of them sitting like statues. The prostitute and the driver stood uncertainly facing each other. I touched the victim lightly on the elbow as I guided him toward the door.

I leaned forward so macDuin could see me, barely holding back a smile. "Interesting hair color on your victim, Lorcan. When I was at the Guild, we did this little thing called profiling, Things like all the victims having the same hair color. I'd've noticed all the victims were light blonds. Not dark."

MacDuin shot me a look that could have curdled milk.

The driver trotted back around the car, jumped in, and pulled away. I watched until the taillights disappeared around a corner. I walked back to Murdock's car and dropped into the passenger seat. None of the uniforms bothered me. They were used to seeing me and obviously figured Murdock would be okay with me sitting in his car. Otherwise, you don't touch a cop's car without getting a good poke with a stick. I sat staring through the dirty windshield, trying to figure out what the hell had just happened.

I didn't have to wait long for Murdock. He came flying out of the station house, started the car before he was barely in it, and tore down the street. I didn't say a word as he weaved through traffic. After several startling turns, he pulled up in front of my building and turned off the engine. We sat listening to a small pinging noise from under the hood.

"What was that all about with you and your father's wink?"

He shrugged. "It's a game we play. Whenever the Guild's in the room, he likes to give them a hard time. Only because of his position, he doesn't want to look biased. So, he uses me to rag on them."

"He doesn't like the fey much."

Murdock laughed. "No, he just doesn't like you."

"Thanks."

Murdock smirked. "Look at it from his point of view. The fey cause him more trouble than anything else. The Guild dumps all kinds of cases on an overloaded police department. Then, when it looks like we might actually have a chance of nailing a big fat fey fish, the Guild pulls rank and takes the case away. So, no, the fey aren't his favorite people."

I shifted uncomfortably on the seat. "This guy might be a xeno gang member, but there's simply no way he could have done it. A human might get away with it once, but after the first or second murder, everyone's been on their toes. Between Tansy and the bartender at the Flitterbug, we know our guy's got a strong essence, and it definitely is not that mental case rocking in a cell. And the victim's all wrong. Hair's too dark. I didn't smell any alcohol. I got a good whiff of his essence, too. I'm willing to bet he's never been in the Weird until tonight."

"You can tell that?"

I shrugged. "Sometimes. You spend enough time in one place, you pick up some ambient essence. The Weird has so many fey in it, you can definitely tell if someone lives or works here."

Murdock exhaled loudly. "Why is the Guild suddenly so interested?"

I shook my head. "I've seen Keeva twice in less than a week. That's no coincidence. They're hiding something."

"Do you think it might be a rogue Guild agent?"

"It's a possibility, though I think I would have heard rumor of it by now. Keeva and macDuin are quite keen about reputation. They may hate each other, but they hate looking bad more."

Murdock rubbed his hands roughly over his face. "Well, let's call it a night. There'll be a press conference tomorrow."

I got out of the car and stretched. The sky was beginning to lighten. Murdock was up way past his bedtime. I rested my hand on the roof of the car as he started it. Murdock leaned across the passenger seat and gave me a significant look. "There's only one problem with all this, Connor. It's Tuesday, and we don't have a dead body. So, where's our guy?"

I shook my head. "Maybe we drove him underground. Or maybe we just haven't found the body."

I didn't watch him drive off. I was too exhausted to walk up the stairs, so I took the interminable elevator ride. Once inside the apartment, I stripped down and fell back onto the futon without bothering to open it.

I knew I was missing something. Keeva might have been reading the police reports, but I was handling the evidence, touching it, sleeping with it. Our occasionally friendly competition aside, I couldn't figure how she could have got a jump on me and just appeared at the Flitterbug. And macDuin's being in the neighborhood was too convenient. It was possible he was there with Keeva at some point. Their so-called murderer had to be a frame job. With a pang of depression at the thought, I knew one way I might find out. I settled deeper into the pillows, contemplating how I would handle being back inside the Guildhouse.

8

I woke near dawn, the sun beckoning me to acknowledge it. Feeling exhausted from the night before, I briefly toyed with ignoring the impulse to get up. The urge to urinate reared its head and decided for me. I stumbled to the bathroom and managed to finish and get in front of the window just as the sun crested the horizon. I felt better, but not refreshed. I fell back into bed and let myself drift into sleep again.

No sooner had I closed my eyes than I dreamed of floating spread-eagled on a plain of water, staring up at the night sky, the sound of screaming all around me. The water lapped at my ears, a cold moist texture that threatened to cover my face. An explosion split the air, and stars fell, brilliant red and orange, burning me as they pierced my skin, ripping open the flesh to expose my beating heart. I woke drenched in sweat.

It was well after noon by the time I stepped from the shower. As I settled at the desk with a cup of coffee, I realized my own suggestibility. The computer monitor displayed a scene photo of a naked spread-eagled fairy with a hole in his chest, his body tossed among the cartons, candle stubs, and rotting debris of a trash heap. It must have been weighing on my mind as I drifted into sleep. I closed the image file.

The light on the answering machine blinked at me from the corner of my desk, and I hit the REPLAY button. A long static hiss filled the room, followed by the sound of something being knocked over, a muttered curse, and finally Rory Dean's voice boomed out. "Connor! I'm calling you at the most ungodly hour I could manage, and you're still not there. Well, I'll keep it short and sweet since you're not around to annoy. I rang up the Atworth woman, found her rather easily, actually, and had to assure her everything was all right, which I hope is true. Anyway, she's just the most pleasant woman, a bit deaf actually, and most solicitous. Anyway, she informed me that her boy's been gone these past ten years, apparently some medical complication. I don't know if that's good or bad for you, but it must put him out terribly. Anyway, you were so bloody cryptic. Call a body sometime and let me know what's what and who you're drinking under the table these days."

The machine beeped and logged the call at three-thirty in the morning. I hadn't checked. Not that it mattered now. I updated the files anyway. Murdock would want them complete for the record. He had found Teri Esposito north of Boston, but her daughter was dead. Same went for the New York lead. I still hadn't heard from Germany. I was already discounting Britt Alfheim's kid Welfrey since she was female. That left Gethin, the son of Gerda Alfheim, and Corcan, the male child of Dealle Sidhe.

Thinking of Murdock made me pick up the phone and call. I managed to connect with the department secretary, but, naturally, she wouldn't tell me what was going on other than that he was not available. I didn't envy him the paperwork bullshit he was probably shoveling, nor the endless jerk-around meetings that always accompanied a media spin.

I kept the television on in the background waiting for the press conference as I obsessively reviewed the files. The Fey Summit was still going on, the fairies and elves still arguing after all these years on how to behave with each other. Maeve didn't like being photographed, so reporters were left standing outside the mist wall that surrounded Tara—which made for a surreal backdrop. Not everyone was happy about a treaty between elves and fairies. Violent protests had broken out in London and Berlin.

The press conference came late in the afternoon, timed for live broadcast at the top of the first evening news hour. Commissioner Murdock stood at the podium, calm and self-assured, as though he had been involved with the case from the beginning. Murdock himself stood behind his father, reflexively scanning the crowd as though he expected a surprise criminal to show up for the circus. He never took a break. Off to the side of the cluster of police stood Lorcan macDuin. He didn't speak or move. No mention was made of his involvement in the capture of the accused. They even had the poor taste to parade the still-dazed-looking prisoner out to a wagon to be taken to the city lockup. It was enough to make me feel the world was safe for democracy, only I knew better. I turned the set off. At least now I knew where Murdock was.

I threw a baseball cap on my head and went out the door. The day did not want to cooperate with my mood. A brilliant azure sky, free of humidity, arced overhead. The surface of the harbor swelled placidly, so smoothly that it tricked the eye into thinking the water was a clean blue and not just a reflection of the sky.

District headquarters wasn't too long a cab ride. The mobile news trucks were still parked illegally when I reached the station house. While they finished packing up, I lingered on the sidewalk, debating whether to go look for Murdock. He resolved the issue by pushing out the door past the newspaper reporters who hadn't left yet. He spotted me immediately and jerked his head in the direction of his car. As he opened the door on the driver's side, he plucked a flyer out from under his windshield.

"How are you holding up?" I asked as I slid into the passenger seat.

"Fine." He looked at the flyer, then tossed it on the seat. We pulled onto the street and made our way back into the Weird.

"We're going to lose him," he said, making the turn onto Pittsburgh. He shook his head in annoyance. "My dad's going to spring him to the Guild. We got all the public relations out of it with the press conference, so he wants to dump it."

"Why?"

Murdock rolled his head and looked at me from under his brow. "You know the answer to that."

Unfortunately, I did. The police didn't want him. Or rather, the district attorney probably didn't want him. Most people were afraid of the fey, felt they had too much power, in both influential and real terms. A trial at the taxpayer's expense would go down sideways with a lot of folks. Add the profession of the victims, and even more sympathy vanished. Letting the Guild take him was a win-win solution: The state avoided prosecuting a human for crimes against a disliked minority, and the Guild got to look like it was taking care of its own mess.

He pulled up to Shay and Robin's building. "You're fired, by the way."

I laughed. "I figured that was coming."

He got out of the car. "I didn't have a chance to pick up my equipment this morning. You want to come in?"

"I'm not up for the show right now."

He peeled back the door and disappeared inside.

I picked up the flyer. An ogham glyph was centered on the page with some numbers across the bottom. Ogham writing is essentially a long vertical line with various hash marks to represent sounds. Letters can be ascribed by the relation of the hash marks to the central line, either to the left or right and horizontally or angled across. The flyer had a straight line across the central axis, followed by five lines to the left, two lines angled across, and three lines to the right, which roughly worked out to A, Q, G, F. Old Gaelic could be pretty hard on the ears and tongue, but this did not spell any word I knew.

Across the bottom were the numbers 12432. The glyph rang a small bell, like I'd seen it on a band advertisement recently on a wall somewhere. I let it fall back on the seat.

Murdock returned to the car with a scowl. "They're not here."

"You did say you would be here in the morning."

He shot me an annoyed look. "I was busy. Where do you want me to drop you?"

I looked at my watch. "Just take me home. I'm in the mood to wallow in annoyance."

We drove in silence, both of us scanning the sidewalks of the neighborhood. Sometimes you can gauge the night by seeing who was out and about. Too many known troublemakers, and something stupid is bound to happen. A mix of regular folk and the bad guys, a normal night of nervous scuffles proceeds. Absolutely no one around, and you just know all hell's going to break loose somewhere. Tonight seemed a mix, just a regular weeknight in the Weird. We pulled up in front of my building.

"Look, Connor," Murdock said, "don't go taking all this personally. To be in the game, you have to play the game. We did good work. We just didn't know we weren't supposed to this time."

"That's a load of bull coming from you."

He gave me a lopsided smile. "It's all part of the game. We're still playing it. The rules have just been changed. Now we have to figure out why."

I let myself out of the car. "I'm still going upstairs to wallow."

He shook his head at me and put the car in gear. "I'm getting some sleep."

I watched the car disappear around the corner. Murdock didn't fool me. He was angrier than he was letting on. I recognized the signs: the nonchalance about losing the case, the rationalizations of you-win-some-you-lose-some. I pitied the next person to get in his face. All that pent-up frustration letting loose is not a pretty sight. He was lucky he had a badge, or he'd've been up on assault charges long ago.

As I turned the key in the outside lock, I froze. The ogham glyph on the flyer in Murdock's car wasn't familiar because I'd seen a band advertisement. It was familiar because it had been staring me right in the face the last two days, gouged into the paint on my building's door. I touched the scratch, hoping for an echo of essence. I recognized the vague residue of some of my neighbors, but nothing distinctly around the glyph. It had been too long.

I let myself in, took the steps two at a time, and was running a CD-ROM dictionary before I'd even sat down. Nothing came up, so I tried a couple of online resources with no results either. I knew it wasn't a word, but just needed to confirm it. I had an ogham font for word processing, so I made a copy for the miscellaneous file and a note to show it to Murdock. It had to mean something. And who had left it was an interesting question.

A loud pounding on the door came from the living room. Out of paranoid habit, I checked through the peephole, but no one was visible. The pounding came again, startling me back. I frowned when I realized the sound was emanating from near the floor. I opened the door. Stinkwort stood in the hall, a smug look on his face.

"You put dents in the door!" I said, as he strutted in.

"You're never satisfied." He sighed and flitted up to the kitchen counter. He opened a cabinet, rummaged around, and came out with a box of raisins.

I dropped into the armchair. "Have you come to cheer me up?"

He made himself comfortable on the edge of the counter and started eating a raisin almost as big as his head. "Why do you need cheering up?"

"Weren't you listening last night? They took someone into custody."

Stinkwort paused in midbite. "I'm lost. Why is that a bad thing?"

"Because they've got the wrong guy."

He plunged into another raisin. "Are you sure?"

"He's human, for one thing."

Stinkwort dropped the raisin. "What! Who in their right mind thinks a human could take down three Dananns?"

"Lorcan macDuin."

Stinkwort laughed. "Now you're blowin' my wings."

I shook my head. "He brought the guy in. Says he caught him in the act."

Stinkwort shrugged. "Let them take it, Connor. You're always saying they don't do enough."

"But I'm not sure they're doing the right thing this time either. How are your contacts there?"

He laughed and flitted into the living room. "None at all. Flits take care of their own. Let's go drinking. We haven't been on a tear together in a long time."

I watched him hover around the window a few moments. There are worse things to do in a bad mood than drink with a friend who's mostly pink to begin with. I could tell Stinkwort was in too good a mood to let me spoil it. I became aware that he was humming to himself.

"You slept with someone!" I said.

He laughed and did a midair somersault. "I told you I would."

"Tansy?"

He spiraled down behind the couch, laughing all the way, and reappeared from underneath with a huge grin on his face. "It's amazing how impressed these rustic types can be when you show them your sword."

"I've seen your sword. It's not that impressive," I said.

He tapped a finger on his chin. "Hmmm, let me see. When was the last time anyone wanted to see yours?"

"All right, all right, if I go out for drinks, can we drop the bad double entendres?"

"Do I get to tell you all the salacious details?" he asked, racing for the door.

"Only after we're drunk." Which I had already decided meant yes. There was no stopping Stinkwort when he was boasting anyway. If the truth be known, he did get to tell more stories than I did, even if you counted my early twenties. Flits are nonchalant about sex, from the doing to the telling. It wouldn't surprise me if Tansy were somewhere oh-ing and ah-ing with a bunch of her friends.

We trailed into one crowded bar after another. News of the capture had spread. More than a few fairies who had kept a low profile were out and about celebrating their return to walking the streets. The unofficial weeklong party for Midsummer had begun a day early. Stinkwort was in high spirits, and his mood began to rub off on me.

We stumbled out of a nameless bar onto Stillings Street. Stinkwort flew ahead of me in a not particularly straight line. "Wait a minute, Joe, what if Lorcan's involved?" I said in a moment of alcoholic inspiration.

"You're drunk. Lorcan's too much of a coward." He pinged against the edge of a stop sign and almost hit the pavement before recovering his balance.

"I don't know . . . I've heard some stuff about his time during the War. He sided with the elves. He can't be too happy about the Fey Summit."

"All those stories are about who he knew. There's no blood under his nails."

"Yeah, but first he's not interested in the case. Now he is and obviously wants to bury it. He's only gotten on the good side of the Guild in the last couple of decades. Maybe he's still a bad guy."

"And maybe he's just a jerk. You told me once he liked to screw up your cases."

"Gimme a sec." I faced a warehouse wall and relieved myself in violation of city ordinance and my usual modesty.

Stinkwort waited a few yards off as I finished my business. I paused as I approached him. He hovered about ten feet in the air, the edges of his wings vibrating so fast they hummed. Cocking his head to the left and right, he had a tight, strained look on his face as though he were trying hard to hear something.

"Joe?"

His breath came in short gasps as he revolved slowly in the air intently scanning the street. He went very pale, and his eyes began to bulge.

I had never seen him like this before. "Stinkwort, talk to me!"

He gave me a wild look as a nimbus of ghostly light surrounded him. His hair unfurled in a static halo. Opening his mouth impossibly wide, he screamed, an earsplitting thunderous wail. I clamped my hands over my ears to block the sound as a spasm of grief overwhelmed me. The sound welled up higher in different pitches, and I realized that other flits nearby were screaming.

As the guttural cry ended, Stinkwort's sword materialized in his hand as he withdrew it from its glamoured scabbard. It glowed like a sliver of white fire encased in icy blue flame. He pointed it up the street, flew forward a few feet, and vanished. Instant silence surrounded me as I staggered against the wall. All around me, people wandered into the street, muttering in confusion.

Taking a deep breath to recover myself, I began to run in the direction he had pointed. Adrenaline began to eat up the alcohol in my system as I ran. I just kept going, not knowing what to do, just wanting to move. Cars streamed down the street past me, their horns blowing as people scrambled out of the way. The Avenue was a block and a half away, jammed with people running in every direction and forcing traffic to a standstill.

Stinkwort reappeared right in front of me. He still held the sword, and I could see dark smudges on it. "The alley!" he yelled, and vanished again.

I swerved to the left and pelted down a dark narrow confine between two buildings. Someone ran by me, hitting me in the shoulder. I felt a strange sensation sweep past, a sense of wrongness, like a discharge of negative energy. And I could smell blood. As I came to the end of the buildings, the stench was overpowering. I rounded the corner and skidded to a halt.

A human boy lay flung on his back with his legs twisted under him and his head to the side. Stinkwort sat crouched on the ground beyond him, cradling something and crooning quietly. I looked down at the boy. There was no question he was dead. The front of his green tunic was flayed open, dark and wet with blood. His torso had been savaged, as though the killer had slashed and stabbed in a maniacal frenzy. Blood splattered for yards in several directions. There was none of the methodical gutting I had come to expect. Light glittered off a small necklace twisted in his hair, and I fought down the urge to be sick with the realization. I moved the long blond hair away from his face, and I inhaled sharply.

"Fuck," I said as I backed away. It was Robin.

I circled around him to stand over Stinkwort. I realized now that he held a small flit in his arms. A chill ran over me as I recognized the fading yellow-white of her wings. As Stinkwort gently rocked her, the light of Tansy's essence flickered and faded to gray. He held her a moment in silence, stroking her fine pale hair. Then, he placed her delicately on the ground and picked up his sword. His eyes gleamed with red light. "I have his spoor," he shouted, and vanished.

I spun around and looked up the alley. I had it, too. My awareness was so heightened by the excitement, I could almost see the essence that twisted away from the scene. I could smell it on my own shoulder where the murderer had jostled me as he passed. Stinkwort flashed into sight at the street and was gone again. I ran after him.

The trail led out of the alley and up toward the Avenue. Of course. More people had ventured into the street, their voices loud with the excitement of the flit scream. As I drew near the corner, I could feel the killer's essence begin to mingle with others. I pushed through a crowd of by-standers who were following the debate over a fender-bender. On the far side of the Avenue, the scent became stronger again. I ducked down yet another alley and paused. The scent had vanished. Indecisively, I looked back to the busy street behind me.

Taking a deep breath, I concentrated my own essence into my head, toward the only true ability I had left. A pulse of pain instantly burned in my forehead as I felt the scent of the killer's essence whisper in my face. It hadn't vanished. The murderer had put on a burst of speed as only the fey can and had moved so fast, he'd barely left any trace.

I allowed my essence to flow back and ran down the alley. At the end, I came out to crumbling warehouse docks. The foul-smelling essence reasserted itself as the killer slowed down again. Moving that fast used a lot of energy, and he'd already expended a lot in killing Tansy, if not Robin. He was conserving what he had left. I followed him, keeping an eye out for visual contact. The ache in my head had been reduced to a dull throb, but it was starting to build again. The sooner I stopped pushing what little ability I had, the better off I'd be.

I moved in and out of shipping containers and around loading equipment. The scent would thin, pool up in hidden spots, then thin out again in the open. It didn't feel like he was hiding from me, though, or even knew I was behind him somewhere. It felt like he was hunting. Twice I caught a good whiff of Stinkwort, but I was still catching up. It must be nice to have wings and the ability to teleport.

A breeze began blowing in from the harbor, ruffling the lazily swelling surface of the water. I moved faster as the trail started to dissipate. It bent back into another alley and led to the closed door of an old warehouse. As I reached up my hand to open it, a fuzziness descended on my face as though I had stepped into a spiderweb. I felt the prickling sensation of my defense shields activating on their own. The fuzziness diminished a bit, but still hovered around me. I pushed open the door and stepped inside.

I felt an overwhelming desire to lie down. A ward vibrated somewhere nearby, and I didn't have the ability to counteract it. Against the screaming protest of my brain, I filtered more of my essence into my shields. It didn't stop the ward spell, but it prevented me from surrendering to its command to sleep. If I didn't find it quickly, I was going to pass out from the pain anyway.

I stood in what appeared to be a large office. To the right, light from the waning moon filtered through dirt-smeared windows to reveal rows of desks facing each other. With each step I took, I felt the ward spell grow stronger. As I came around the first desk, I found a dark-haired fairy crumpled on the floor, wings dully flickering in the dark. I leaned down and touched his shoulder, and he rolled languidly onto his back. He was still alive.

Cautiously, I continued forward, the killer's essence all around me. At the third desk down, I sensed Stinkwort. The two essences scattered about the middle of the room. Several of the desks were askew, the contents of their surfaces swept to the floor. Stinkwort had fought with him.

I could sense a third essence now, another fairy. Just past the disturbed desks, I no longer sensed Stinkwort, just the killer and the new fairy. Even as I smelled fairy blood,

I could feel the lethargy of the ward-spell taking its toll. Ever slower, I moved farther into the room. At the end of the desks, in an open space by a photocopy machine, I found the victim.

He was young, blond, and well dressed except for the torn front of his shirt revealing his gaping chest cavity. Like the others, he lay on his back, his wings pinned to the floor with two cheap ward stones. I could feel the spell already weakening on one of the stones. I slumped to the floor, staring at the dark hole in the boy's chest and desperately wanting to sleep.

The two wards were working together. The more stones involved in a warding, the greater their effect and the more efficient their energy use. The downside was that they were easier to disrupt than single stones. If I touched one of them directly, though, I risked an energy feedback that would not only knock me out but probably cause physical damage as well.

I looked around groggily for something to knock one of them out of the way. Picking up a stapler, I decided against it. With all the base metals in it, it would just act as a conductor. I moved some papers around on the floor next to me and found a wooden ruler. Thanking whatever gods might be listening, I crawled closer to the body. Straining against my protesting head, I shot some of my essence into the ruler as I batted it at a ward, hoping that the momentary burst would block the feedback. I shouted as something convulsed in my head.

Squeezing my eyes shut, I tried to breathe past the pain. Without needing to look, I knew the spell was broken. I no longer felt the compulsion to sleep though I had the desire to for a different reason. My arm tingled a bit where some of the ward energy had filtered through the ruler, but I could still move my fingers.

I opened my eyes and stared at the corpse. My nerves were so jagged, I could feel the faint whisper of old human essences all around me now. What really intrigued was the pulse of elf essence coming off the victim. I leaned forward to peer into his chest, but it was too dark to see inside. Fighting a wave of nausea I reached my hand into the wet, slippery cavity and touched something hard. I jerked my hand back at the sensation of wrongness. Whatever it was, it felt like an elf had powered it. Touching it hadn't seemed to do anything other than startle me, so I reached back in. I could feel a sandy grittiness in the boy's chest, then the stone that had become the killer's calling card. This time it had some kind of charge on it. I grimaced at the squelching sound my hand made as I withdrew.

My hand glistened in the moonlight as I held the stone up. It appeared gray and no more remarkable than the others. The essence radiating from it made no sense. It would seem most like elf, then shift to a subtle fairy, then back again. As I tried to place the feeling, I thought of Shay. It was like looking at Shay, the pretty-beautiful boy, and trying to decide quickly if he were male or female.

The surviving fairy groaned again, and I went to him. Feebly, he curled away from me in fear.

"It's okay," I said, but he wasn't reassured. I pulled out my cell phone and called 911. As the operator took the address and asked me to stay on the line, a flutter in the stone caught my attention. The energy was dissipating. I glanced down at the kid, who was cowering half under the desk. He looked no worse for wear. He probably wouldn't appreciate my telling him that the vagaries of fate that gave him dark hair had saved his life tonight.

I made a decision and disconnected the call. I had already contaminated the crime scene by removing the stone, and whatever charge was on it was fading. I hoped Murdock wouldn't be too mad at me when he found out. Like they say: In for a penny, in for a pound.

"Help's on the way," I said to the kid. "Stay here. Don't touch anything."

I went into the alley and ran the block or so back to the Avenue. With all the weaving in and out of the warehouses, I had ended up all the way at the far end of the Weird. To my right, traffic was a barrage of light and sound and backing up toward me. Cars coming in from my left were turning onto the Eastern Service Road to avoid the mess. I cursed my lack of ability to do a sending.

A cab turned the corner slowly as the driver tried to see what all the commotion was about. I jumped in the back before he could pull away. Only in the Weird can a man with obvious blood on his hands get a taxi. I gave him Briallen's address. He immediately made an illegal turn and drove quickly along the edge of Southie. I held the stone gingerly between my index finger and thumb with just enough tension to keep from dropping it. The essence on it was definitely fading. We pulled up onto Louisburg Square in an impressive ten minutes. I was surprised to find Briallen's house alive with light, the front door wide open, and Briallen herself standing on the threshold. I paid the driver and hurried up the walk.

"How did you know?" I asked.

"I didn't, really," she said, closing the door behind us. "It was odd. Not like a sending, but more like an impression of your need. What's happened? What is that?" She gestured at the stone.

"Let's go up to the study," I said. Without waiting for an answer, I rushed up the stairs. Briallen was right behind me with a grace and speed I always found surprising. Not for the first time did I wonder about her age. I entered the study and placed the stone on a clear space on the center table. "Hurry! What is the essence on this?" I said.

Briallen peered down at it for a second, then picked it up. She dropped it and recoiled. "It's saturated in fairy blood!"

"Sorry, I should have warned you."

"Blood of a murder," she murmured, picking up the stone

again. Slowly, she rolled it in her palm, staring at it, her lips compressed into a discomforted line. "It's elfin, but twisted somehow. There's a sense of fairy about it, but that feels almost like an afterthought."

"That's what I thought, too. But what does it mean?"

She placed the stone back on the table with a look of relief. "It just feels wrong. What's stranger still is that the stone has been purposefully and intensely infused with it, almost like making a ward. It's almost gone now."

"I'm guessing the other stones were all like this, but I didn't see them until after the essence had dissipated," I said.

"Is this the same type of stone?"

I nodded. "One's white, one's black, and one's gray like this. I'm sure they are all the same crystal, selenite, but they disappeared before tests could be run."

She smiled and arched an eyebrow. "Oh, it's selenite, all right. It's also pre-Convergence."

Impressed, I looked back at the stone. When the fey found themselves bodily transported here after Convergence, pieces of the physical realm of Faerie came with them, sometimes just a house or even less. Those places were very few and are closely guarded. Organic and inorganic material from them is highly sought after because the fey's abilities work best through them. Something pre-Convergence, something actually from the true Faerie, is extremely rare.

"This must be worth a fortune," I said.

Briallen lifted her chin to speak but gasped instead. "Connor, you're bleeding."

Even as she said it, I felt the trickle of blood coming out of my nose. She handed me a tissue, then pressed her hand against my head. "What the hell happened tonight?"

"I think I pushed myself to the limit."

"Go sit in the study. Now."

I took another tissue and did as I was told. Now that my adrenaline rush was over, I felt tired down to my bones, not to mention the pounding headache that threatened to split my forehead open. The usual fire glowed on the hearth, comfortable even though summer heat sweltered outside the windows. I fell exhausted into an armchair.

Briallen came in and wordlessly handed me a cup. I drank it without question, an earthy concoction with the smoothness of honey that permeated my chest with a soothing warmth. Closing her eyes, Briallen held her hands just over my face. They became pale, glowing phosphorescently. I felt the soft force of her essence begin to emanate from her fingers. It molded itself to the contours of my face. I closed my own eyes as the feeling intensified, a sweetly painful sensation that vibrated through my head down to my groin. After a few moments, the feeling vanished, like a warm compress had been taken away.

I opened my eyes. Briallen stood over me, her arms crossed, a pale white light flickering behind her eyes. "Are you trying to kill yourself?"

"I was trying to stop a murder."

"And almost got yourself killed. You don't even have a weapon on you, do you?"

"I have a knife," I said weakly. The pain in my head was receding to a dull thudding at the base of my skull.

She snorted and took a seat. "Fat lot of good that would have done you. What exactly happened tonight?"

I gave her the rundown, starting with Keeva at the Flitterbug so she could understand how the whole disaster happened. "I just don't get what I missed. We were obviously in a seven-day cycle. Why tonight instead of last night?"

Briallen leaned back in her chair and stared at the ceiling. "I've been scouring books for days. Now that . . ." She jumped up and let out a strangled cry of anger. "What a fool! What an idiot! It's a lunar cycle, Connor."

"Are you sure?"

She frowned at me. "I'm dead sure. The calendar is just a feeble tracking mechanism for the moon, not the other way around. The first murder occurred during the new moon, three weeks ago yesterday, the second followed a week later on the quarter moon, the third a week after that on the full, and now tonight, eight days later on the last quarter."

My mind raced as I tried to reconcile the dates in my head. "Are you sure?"

"Why do you keep saying that?" she snapped. "Trust me, boy. I'm a woman *and* a druidess. I think I know the cycles of the moon. It never occurred to me that I was doing invocations in the garden every night a murder's occurred. I'm out there so much, I never made the connection."

We both started at the sound of something falling out in the hall. In the tense moment that followed, a loud moan broke the silence. Briallen was out of the room and halfway down the stairs before I even reached the landing. Down in the vestibule, a flit lay on the floor groaning. I'd recognize the pink wings anywhere.

"Stinkwort!" I leaped down the stairs after Briallen.

As she crouched on the floor next to him, he pulled himself into a sitting position. He held his left arm close to his waist. "Call me Joe, dammit." His voice was weak. His eyes flickered to Briallen. "Sorry, m'lady."

"Don't mention it, Joe," Briallen muttered as she reached out her hand. Amazingly, he sidled onto her palm, something he'd normally considered beneath his dignity. Without dropping his arm, he rolled it slightly away from his body to display a wound. A deep gash ran the length of his forearm to the base of his palm. Thick blood welled up, and he clenched the arm against himself again.

"This night is cursed," Briallen muttered again.

Cradling Stinkwort in her palms, she rose, and I trailed after her up the stairs into the study. She placed him carefully on the table and began searching in boxes beneath it.

"He got another one," said Stinkwort through clenched teeth. "I followed him to a warehouse but got there too late. Chased the bastard all the way to Charlestown before he turned to fight. I almost had him, too. He used some kind of incantation I've never encountered before. It slowed me down, and he stuck me. The damned freak stuck me."

Briallen poured something foul-smelling onto a cloth and held it close to Stinkwort's arm. "This will sting." It always stings, I thought. She pulled his arm and swiftly draped the cloth over the wound before it could ooze again. He yelped, but she held on. Light welled up from her hands, a white nimbus that fluttered like a candle in the fog. A pink aura sprang up around Stinkwort. It twined within the white light, pulling it into his arm in an incandescent swirl. He growled in pain.

Briallen clutched my arm with her free hand. "Sorry, Connor, I need some of that back."

I could feel a tug in my chest, and my mind went fuzzy. It seemed a long moment later that she released me. I swayed on my feet, shaking the dizziness from my head. Stinkwort had his eyes squeezed shut as the brightness of Briallen's essence sheathed his entire arm. All at once, the light went out as though a switch had been thrown. Stinkwort sat breathing heavily, his arm draped across his lap. A thick ugly crevasse of scar tissue ran the length of where the wound had been.

My joints felt like they were held together with string. I stumbled out of the room, back to the parlor, and collapsed in a chair. Briallen came in a few moments later and sat down, too. She was very pale as she stared into the fire.

"Is he all right?" I asked.

She stirred up from her reverie. "He'll live now. He almost died. He lost a lot of blood, and his essence was severely weakened trying to compensate. That's why I had to tap you."

The soberness with which she said it took me off guard. "Well, that's one less person on my conscience tonight."

"You didn't kill anyone, Connor."

"Didn't I? I turned an arrogant little boy and a simple country flit into bait with a glamour stone I gave them."

"Stop being so self-centered. This is not about you. Shit happens."

"I don't see how you can be so indifferent," I said, trying to quell my anger.

"I'm not. I'm just not taking it personally. There's wisdom in knowing the difference between your sensibilities being challenged and your heart being threatened. I'm just telling you not to lose perspective."

I slouched farther into my chair. "How do you manage to make me want to apologize when you piss me off?"

She smiled. "By being right all the time. How are you feeling? Are you up for a short walk?"

"I'm exhausted, but I'll go if you want me to."

She stood. "The invitation is equal parts honor and obligation."

She took my hand and let me pull myself up. I felt lightheaded for a moment, but it passed quickly. She led me out of the house into the street.

"Where are we going?"

"To pay our respects."

We walked up the street in the cool predawn air. Very little noise disturbed this end of town at that time of night. The sky began lightening in the east as we came out on Beacon Street. We crossed over to the Common through an old iron gate and proceeded down a brick lane. At the bottom, a small empty concrete pond basin shone a dull cream color in the light of the streetlamps. Small stones and broken glass crunched under our feet as we crossed that to a hill on the other side. Briallen took my hand, and we climbed the shoulder of the hill. At the top, a circle of trees enclosed an empty grassy space, and we stopped at the verge.

The sound of singing broke the early-morning silence. Its low cadence rose and fell in a mournful chant that grew subtly louder. A group of six or seven flits came out of the underbrush nearby, their wings dimmed of light as they walked. I realized one of them was Stinkwort. They wore simple red caps on their heads and held sprigs of myrtle leaves in one hand. With the other hand, they carried a bier of grass and twigs, on which the dark form of Tansy lay facing the sky. Her face was gracefully calm in repose, her wings already curving around her body like a brittle gray shroud.

The procession moved solemnly to the very top of the hill and lowered Tansy to the ground. The flits slowly circled the body, dropping the leaves around her until she was wreathed in myrtle. One by one they winked out until only Stinkwort remained. He produced a small tea rose from the sleeve of his tunic and reverently placed it on Tansy's chest. Then he, too, disappeared.

Without speaking, Briallen touched my arm, and we descended the hill. Neither of us spoke the entire way back. I couldn't help feeling responsible for the scene I had witnessed no matter what Briallen said. We reached the front door of the house when Stinkwort suddenly appeared in front of us.

"Thank you for attending," he said, with a small bow.

Briallen returned the bow. "The honor was ours."

"I'm sorry, Joe. I know what she meant to you," I said.

He shrugged listlessly. "I honor her life and her spirit and mourn a passing that was not meant to be, nothing more. The People don't die often, and they certainly don't die of senseless murder. A line has been crossed."

I had never seen Stinkwort so solemn and formal. He was unlike the capricious joker I'd come to know over the years, and it made me uncomfortable. I shifted my feet in place, almost embarrassed to form my question at the moment. "Did you get a good look at him?" I asked quietly.

His face remained unexpressive as he spoke. "He fits the description you have. He's also very strong."

"Come back inside, Joe. You need to rest," said Briallen.

A surge of energy seemed to run through him, his eyes glinting with a fey white light. His wings beat in agitation as he hovered back from us and drew his sword. He held the weapon at the ready, his face set with determination. "No, m'lady. There'll be no resting. This *ska* bastard is mine."

He vanished.

9

Hot anger lanced through me. "Call him back, Briallen. Call him back now."

For a moment, as she stared off into the lightening sky, I thought she was calling him. Then she calmly took my arm and firmly escorted me inside. "Let it go, Connor. There's been enough high emotion for one night."

I pulled away from her. "He pulled a sword on your threshold!"

She looked directly at me. The fine lines around her eyes were etched deeper than usual. "Connor, I'm in no mood to quibble about old guest rules. He's hurt. He's angry. And above all, he's appalled at a strike against a fellow flit. It will do no good to embarrass him right now."

"Embarrass? He knows the insult he's given. He violated your hospitality by pulling a weapon on your threshold."

She pursed her lips. "First, he wasn't on my threshold, he was in front of it; secondly, he did not accept my invitation to enter before he did it; and besides, I was not inside the house when it happened, so technically there was no hospitality to violate. Let. It. Go."

"You're stretching to let him off."

She shook her head and walked past me. "Connor, I didn't exhaust myself saving him and healing you tonight so you could annoy me to death. You need sleep more than he does, I think. I've more important things to deal with than a violation of etiquette rules."

I folded my arms triumphantly. "Ha! You just said a violation!"

I felt like an idiot as soon as I said it. Briallen compounded the feeling by chuckling exasperatedly at me. "Come out back before the dawn is gone."

I sheepishly followed her through the kitchen and into the backyard. Even in the dim light of predawn, Briallen's garden was an amazing place. Not far from the kitchen door stood a gnarled oak tree that had embedded itself into the brick wall that separated her yard from the garden next door. A small gravel path wound around the tree and meandered through clusters of flowers and plants that all seemed to be shades of gray in the dimness. On the far side of the garden was a small crescent of grass surrounding a shallow pond that bordered the back of the property.

Briallen led me to the grass and took up a position to one side of the fountain, gesturing for me to take my place on the other side. "I don't get the direct sunrise here, but enough light makes it through for the invocation to be worthwhile." She raised her arms in the starting position, and I did the same. I could feel the sun coming, its nourishing light sweeping toward us. The start of the invocation was almost upon us when Briallen said, "Don't worry, I don't drop trou' for sun rituals." I smothered a laugh as we began chanting.

When we were finished, the garden had come alive with color. Purple foxgloves jutted up among lavenders and heathers. The stone bedding borders overflowed with clover and cowslip. White climbing roses draped the northern wall in a curtain. It smelled exquisite. I felt better—physically and emotionally. My body still ached, but the high-pitched bell in my head was almost gone. Not to mention my anger. I would have a word with Stinkwort when I found him, even if Briallen wouldn't. But I probably wouldn't slap him silly.

Returning to the kitchen, Briallen filled a kettle and placed it on the stove. She leaned against the counter. "You should sleep."

"I know. I'm exhausted."

We did not speak as the kettle groaned with heat expansion. In moments, it whistled. Briallen poured the water into mugs and handed me one. Tentatively, I sipped the hot liquid. It tasted minty and earthy, with just a touch of what actually might have been some kind of tea. Briallen preferred decocting her own blends to dipping a bag. I felt a sudden sense of euphoria that settled quickly into a nice warm feeling. I wondered how the FDA would feel about some of the things she served guests.

"Do you have something like a plastic sandwich bag?" I asked.

"Something like that," she said sarcastically as she opened a drawer and pulled out a box. "Here. I use these strange plastic things when all my burlap wraps are in the wash."

"Very funny. I just need one. It's for the stone."

I set down the mug and went back up to Briallen's workroom. Even though I thought it a little irrelevant at that point, I used the bag like a glove to gather the stone without touching it and pulled the bag closed around it. The strange essence had dissipated, leaving a faint echo behind. A few grains of debris settled in the bottom of the bag, and I remembered the odd grittiness in the victim's chest. I held the bag up to the morning light. It looked like sand. The first victim had had debris in his chest wall if I remembered correctly. I hadn't seen it directly but was sure none of it was sand.

I joined Briallen back in the kitchen.

"Do you want to sleep here?" She lifted the kettle from the stove and refilled it.

"I should just go home."

As I reached for my cell phone to call a cab, it rang. I stared dumbly at it for a moment. No one in their right mind called me at dawn. It was Murdock.

"Where are you?" he said.

"Briallen's. We need to talk."

"No shit. Don't move." He disconnected.

Briallen crossed her arms and shook her head. "You should rest, you know."

"I will," I said, though neither of us believed it.

The doorbell rang. As I gulped the rest of my tea, Briallen preceded me to the door and opened it. Murdock stood on the threshold in a finely pressed shirt, not a hint of the early hour on his face. He gave Briallen a slight bow. "Good morning, Ms. Gwyll."

"Good morning, Leonard. It's so nice of you to ring my bell," she said with a broad grin. I had a hard time burying my own smile. The last time Murdock had picked me up at Briallen's, he made the mistake of sitting in the car and blowing the horn. Not only is that just not done on Louisburg Square, it's never done at Briallen's house. The horn blew for an hour after that no matter how many wires Murdock yanked out.

"I apologize for the time," he said, and raised his eyes to meet mine. "Do you mind if I take Connor with me?"

"Not at all. He has a tendency to overstay his welcome, then ask for cab fare." She took my mug and pushed me out the door. Murdock chuckled politely as he stepped aside to let me pass.

I shook my head. "You are not going to believe the night I've had," I said, as we walked to where Murdock had illegally parked by a fire hydrant.

"You're not going to have a very good day, either."

I tossed some magazines from the passenger seat into the back and sat down.

"What's that supposed to mean?" I asked.

Murdock started the car and backed up the wrong way until we were on Mt. Vernon Street. "Two corpses and one familiar description. You do the math."

"Three corpses." I told him about Tansy.

"Damn," he muttered. "Two fey and one human. It's going to be tough to pry you loose."

"Me!"

"Yes, you, you freakin' idiot. Who'd you think I was talking about?"

"The suspect! You know, big guy, smells bad?"

"I've got the same description from multiple witnesses and a cab driver who had a fare last night with blood on his hands. Guess who it sounds like?"

I slouched in my seat. "This has got to be a joke."

Murdock parked the car in an alley behind Downtown Crossing. "No. It's not. Now tell me everything that happened."

So I told him. When I got to the part about pulling the stone out of the chest cavity, he groaned. I handed him the stone in the bag. He looked at it briefly before slipping it into his shirt pocket. He leaned his head back against the seat and stared at the ceiling.

I finished as quickly as possible. Murdock just sat, not saying a word. He sighed, started the car, and began driving again. "Okay, I can probably get you off the tampering with evidence charge because of the whole essence thing, but it won't be easy. The hard part's going to be keeping you out of a cell for suspicion."

"This is crazy. I'm working this damned case."

"No, you're not. You were fired, remember?"

Exasperated, I shook my head. Murdock crossed the Broadway Bridge into South Boston and immediately slowed down. Even from a distance we could see the cars double-parked in front of the station. You couldn't miss the news vans with their giant antennas pointing skyward and ready for action.

He brought the car down a side street and into the small lot where suspects were normally loaded into vans for transport to the city lockup. Murdock backed into a tight space that didn't block anyone in. Station lots were probably the only place in the city the police parked with courtesy. The fear that they might block someone who could give them a promotion someday was enough for them to remember how to parallel park.

As we got out, I spotted Commissioner Murdock's black sedan. I shouldn't have been surprised considering the situation, but it was still barely seven o'clock in the morning.

Murdock passed me in through the security door. He glanced over his shoulder as we made our way down the hall. "I didn't tell you. The murdered kid in the warehouse? His father's some bigwig from New York."

"Why don't you just put a bullet in my head?" I snapped.

We took the stairs one flight up and were back in the squad room again. More people were crowding around than last time, since it was a shift change on top of everything else. Murdock went straight to Ruiz's office, knocked once, then let himself in. He closed the door in my face, but not before I felt the essences on the other side of the door. My gut clenched in irritation. MacDuin was in there. Murdock wasn't kidding when he said I wasn't going to have a good day.

I tried my best to turn around nonchalantly to face the room. Most of the faces quickly slipped away, not a few with small smiles on them. After several excruciating minutes, Murdock came back out. "Keep it simple and don't piss anyone off," he said. I was feeling too tired to take offense.

Entering Ruiz's office felt different than last time. I didn't like being that kind of center of attention. The commissioner sat in the same seat, macDuin stood again to the left, and poor Ruiz perched on his chair behind the desk like he was ready to bolt at the first opportunity. Murdock sidled along the side of the office to stand next to Ruiz, leaving room for me between him and his father. Standing between two annoyed Murdocks was not my idea of a good time. MacDuin stood ramrod-straight and glowered at me, doing his best to look intimidating.

The commissioner cocked his head up at me, his dark eyes examining my face for a long moment. I would not want to be his kid when a window got broken. "Detective Murdock tells us you had a busy night, Connor."

I decided to go formal. "I can explain what happened, sir." He nodded, not taking his gaze from my face.

"Yes, do," said macDuin. "I would be very interested to know how you just happened to stumble upon not one but two murders."

I ignored him and kept my attention on the commissioner. "I didn't exactly stumble onto the murder. I was with a friend, a flit who goes by the name Joe. What you may not know is that a third person was killed last night, another flit by the name of Tansy. When Tansy was dying, Joe sensed it and led me to the scene."

"What do you mean, sensed it?" asked the commissioner.

"Apparently, it's an ability. All the flits nearby sensed it and screamed."

"I heard about that," said Ruiz. "I didn't realize it was connected to this."

"It was a direct result, Captain. As I came on the scene, the perpetrator ran past me, inadvertently allowing me to catch the trace of his essence. By that, I was able to follow him. Unfortunately, I arrived at the second murder scene too late. He was already gone."

"Yes," said the commissioner, "Detective Murdock has described this ability of yours to me."

"I wasn't aware you had any abilities," said macDuin.

I gave him the barest hint of a smile. "I have many, Lorcan."

"No one else saw this so-called murderer. They only saw you," said macDuin.

"He was moving fast. In my present condition, I could not match his speed."

"You were removed from this case, were you not?" asked the commissioner.

"Yes, sir. But, again, let me point out that I was out for a social evening. I didn't go looking for this."

MacDuin smiled and shook his head. "I believe in your own mind this was some kind of social evening, Mr. Grey. Commissioner, this man suffered a debilitating head injury in service to the Guild. From what I understand, it's incurable and clearly has begun to affect his mental faculties."

"What are you driving at, macDuin?" I said.

He looked at me with feigned pity. "Connor, we have a suspect in custody. I know we don't agree, but this is taking things too far."

I rested my hands on the edge of the desk and leaned forward. "What exactly are you implying?"

MacDuin shrugged. "I am implying nothing. I am saying you killed two, excuse me, *three* people last night in a vain attempt to keep this case open to foster the delusion that your abilities still exist."

Murdock had the presence of mind to place his hand lightly on my arm. It was enough to keep me from lunging across the desk. I took a few breaths. "I didn't kill anyone."

MacDuin turned his attention to the commissioner. "Surely, sir, you find it odd that not one witness saw Grey's mysterious assailant? Where is this flit who helped him? And this other body?"

"Flits take care of their own, and you know it," I said. MacDuin stared impassively at me. I was walking right into his trap. I struggled to calm down. Exhaustion definitely was catching up on me.

The commissioner broke the silence. "Why did you flee the scene?"

"I wasn't fleeing the scene. I was preserving evidence."

Murdock pulled the stone from his pocket and placed it

on the desk. I knew then how macDuin must have felt two days earlier when he played the same move. The look on his face was priceless. Obviously, he already knew no stone had been found on the victim and was going to use that against me, too.

"I found that on the victim. It had a strange essence on it that was dissipating, so I took it to be examined before it was gone."

The commissioner leaned forward and picked up the bag. He held it up to see more clearly. "An awful lot of stones seem to land on your desk, Captain Ruiz."

"Um . . . yes, sir," he replied. Poor Ruiz. Sweat poured off his forehead as he tried to look involved. I had never seen a police captain so marginalized. Of course, with the level of power and animosity in the room, no other captain had ever been in such a situation.

The commissioner handed the bag to macDuin, who took it like someone had given him a dead mouse. While macDuin made a small show of examining the stone, a soft chirping sound filled the silence. Murdock glanced at his beeper and turned it off. MacDuin tossed the bag on the desk. "Another convenient coincidence. No one saw this at the murder scene."

"Perhaps you'd like to discuss the coincidence with Bri-allen ab Gwyll. I took it to her for examination."

To his credit, macDuin didn't quite blanch. He retained his composure fairly well, but obviously he hadn't expected me to bring up Briallen. The commissioner chuckled. "Curiouser and curiouser someone once said. I think, Lor-can, that we should reward this young man. I haven't seen someone slip out of so tight a web of yours in ages."

"I don't know what you mean," said macDuin.

"I mean I think his story is exactly what he says it is. Un-less, of course, you care to dance with the old witch on this."

I hadn't realized Murdock still had his hand on me until he squeezed my arm in warning. He needn't have worried, though. I'm sure Briallen had been called worse things in her time. Besides, I knew a glimmer of light when I saw one, and at least the commissioner's tone held some respect.

MacDuin's eyes burned coldly as he looked at me. The image of his wings appeared faintly in the air behind him, challenging the glamour to its limit. "Assuming for the moment your story is true, what did you find?"

"I'm . . . not sure. I think it's confirmation of a theory I have that the killer has some kind of birth defect. There was some essence on the stone that didn't feel right. These murders might be related to the defect in some way."

"In other words, you have nothing," said macDuin.

I shook my head, then tapped my nose. "I have his scent. I can find him. I just have to figure out where he'll be next. But not if I'm in a jail cell."

The commissioner frowned in annoyance and flicked his hand. "You're not under arrest."

"Commissioner, I must insist . . ." macDuin began, but the commissioner cut him off.

"Let it go, Lorcan. We're wasting time. You're not the only one who has to worry about politics. I am not going to embarrass myself by having yet another person in custody if yet another murder is committed. As it is, the press is going to have a field day with this. I want hard evidence, and I want it yesterday." He glanced up at Murdock. "Am I clear, Detective?"

"Yes, sir," Murdock said.

"Then get moving," the commissioner said.

He didn't have to tell me twice. I opened the door and was into the squad room before he had a moment to reconsider. Murdock was right behind me, his face grim. We retraced our steps through the building and got back in his car.

"Not that I'm not grateful, but why did your father help me?"

Murdock started the car and eased onto West Broadway.

"Maybe he doesn't like macDuin more than he doesn't like you."

He took a left turn from the right lane and drove up Pittsburgh Street. We drove slowly down the alley. A small Honda that had seen better days was parked next to a dumpster. Murdock pulled up beside it. The dirty driver's window rolled down, and Barnard Murdock smiled into my face.

"Hey, Bar," I said. Murdock's younger brother looked exactly like he was his younger brother. Same dark hair. Same dark eyes set off by that same hawk nose. Only everything looked slightly smaller. Everyone called him Bar. No one dared called him Barney.

"Connor! The man of the hour. Can you step in it any deeper?"

I smiled modestly. "Nice to see you, too, Bar."

He cocked his head forward to look around me at Murdock. "You didn't answer your beeper."

"I am answering it. He in there?" said Murdock.

"Yep. You want backup?"

"Nah. We can handle him."

Bar shrugged. "Suit yourself. You coming to dinner on Sunday, Connor?"

"I'm the last person your father wants to see at the table right now."

Bar laughed in appreciation. "Yeah, I just got off the line with someone who filled me in. After you guys left, the Guild guy tore out in a rage. Nice going."

Murdock drove the rest of the way into the alley and parked by Shay's door. My knees ached as I stretched outside the car. I needed sleep badly. Murdock came around the car with his gun drawn but held down at his side.

"Is that necessary?" I asked.

He gave me an annoyed look. "We lost Robin last night. You want to confess to the murders, I'll put it away."

I held my hands up. "All right, all right. I just think it's a little heavy-handed."

"Fine. You go in first."

I hesitated, and Murdock brushed past me with a smug look on his face. Just because I didn't think Shay was capable of murder didn't mean I was stupid. Murdock pulled open the door. The bright hall light was on. We moved slowly along one side of the hall, not quite touching the wall. When we reached the inside door, Murdock paused. We could hear movement on the other side of the door.

We kept back. "Shay?" Murdock called out. The movements inside stopped. "Police, Shay, open up." He didn't answer. Murdock looked at me, and I nodded. Murdock aimed his gun at the door as I crossed to the opposite side of the hall. The prickly sensation of my body shield activating swept over my head. Just as I tensed myself to kick open the door, it opened.

Shay stood on the threshold. He froze when he saw the gun just as Murdock lifted the muzzle away. "Jesus, Shay. You could have answered."

"Sorry," he said. He turned away and went back in the room. At first glance, the room looked like it hadn't been straightened up since the last time we were there. Clothes were still everywhere, mostly piled on the beds. Then I noticed the open suitcases on the floor. "What do you want this time?" Shay asked. He bent over and folded a pair of jeans.

"Are you going somewhere?" Murdock said. He hadn't put the gun away.

"Like I said the other day. I've had it. I'm getting out." He continued packing clothes as he spoke.

"I don't think you should leave right now," said Murdock.

Shay stopped and looked up. "Is this about the sketch? If you need a witness, you don't need me. Ask Robin. He lied. He saw him, too."

"Where were you last night, Shay?" Murdock asked.

Shay's cheeks colored as he nervously brushed his hair back over his shoulder. "I was working."

"Were you with Robin last night?" I asked.

"Yes. For a while. We argued about that stupid glamour stone. I realized you guys just forgot it in the confusion, but Robin wanted to play with it anyway. I told him it was dangerous to pretend he was fey when he isn't."

"Why did you think it was dangerous? We had someone in custody," said Murdock.

He shrugged. "I heard that guy was human. I don't know what the guy I saw was, but he definitely was not human."

"When did you see Robin last?"

His eyes narrowed. "Why?"

"Just answer the question," said Murdock.

"About midnight." Shay sank slowly to the bed, not taking his eyes off us. "I left him at some dive on Congress. Why do you keep asking me about Robin? Where is he?" His voice grew calmer the more agitated he looked. Neither of us answered him. His face dropped a little.

He was neither in complete control nor overwrought, but had the barely contained hysteria of someone trying very hard not to believe what he was thinking. I'd worked enough cases to have seen it before. I looked at Murdock, and he nodded. "We found him in an alley last night, Shay."

Shay closed his eyes and slumped forward, clutching his waist. He sobbed quietly as we watched awkwardly. I didn't think he was faking. I stepped over to him and gently placed my hand on his back. Murdock frowned and shook his head, but I ignored him. I looked around for some tissue and found a box on the nightstand. I handed several to Shay, and he wiped his face roughly before lifting his head.

"He was murdered. The killer got Tansy, too," I said.

Anger fluttered across his face. "And the killer got away, didn't he?"

It felt like an accusation. I nodded.

"Why did you leave him?" Murdock asked.

"I had an appointment," said Shay.

"With?"

"He didn't show me his ID."

"I think that's a convenient way of telling me you recognized him anyway."

"Murdock . . ." I said. I didn't see the point of his pursuing this.

"Even if I did know his name, do you think he'd admit being with me?" Shay glared at Murdock like he was an idiot. Frankly, I thought he was pretty damned close to it.

"Did you see the guy from your sketch last night?" I asked.

"No." He hesitated the slightest moment, just enough to make me uneasy. I still didn't see how Shay could be involved. All along, his stories had been plausible, if uncomfortably coincidental, and his involvement made no sense. He wasn't fey. He wasn't strong. And he wasn't trying to hide anything, or seemed not to be. Maybe it was that he was the least likely suspect that kept Murdock skeptical. No one really has so much bad luck. Except me, maybe.

"Where's my equipment?" Murdock said.

Shay rose from the bed and fished around in the pile of clothes on the bed opposite. He found the wire and handed it to Murdock.

"You're not going anywhere, Shay. Understood?"

He nodded.

Murdock walked out of the room, and I followed him. I turned at the door to see Shay staring forlornly at the floor. He really did look too young to have survived as long as he had, but then all the kids like him in the Weird did. "I'm sorry, Shay."

He gave the barest hint of a smile. "Thank you, Connor. It's nice to know someone else is."

Murdock was already in the car when I came out. As we drove back past Bar, we all waved halfheartedly.

"You were pretty hard on him," I said.

"What did you expect? He's the only real lead I have, and he has no alibi."

"I thought you had surveillance on him."

"We did. He went out an exit of the bar last night we didn't know about."

"It's not him, Murdock. He wasn't at the scene last night."

"How do you know he wasn't?"

"Because I would have sensed his essence."

Murdock pulled in front of my building. He put the car in park and turned to me. "How do you know you didn't?"

I looked at him in confusion for a moment, but he just sat patiently staring back.

"Connor, you said you get a funny vibe from him. Your words."

I still didn't say anything.

"And the killer has a weird essence you've never encountered before . . ."

I fell back against the seat. "Ha!" I said.

"Thank you," said Murdock.

"Let me think a minute." I didn't know if it were possible. Shay definitely had a strong essence, but he was also definitely human. He obviously had a lot of fey paraphernalia in his apartment. I suppose it was possible he had stumbled on something that could alter his essence and even give him strength out of proportion to his actual ability. It would have to be something pretty potent. I doubted a human could sustain it.

"Why kill Robin?" I asked.

"Maybe he found out," Murdock suggested.

"Even if it's him—and that's a big 'if '—what's the motive?"

Murdock shrugged. "Revenge? Jealousy? Thrill? Pick one."

I let out a sigh. "It's a stretch, but at this point, I won't discount it. I'm so exhausted, I can't think anymore, Murdock." I got out of the car.

"You look like hell." He smiled and drove off. I love his social skills.

I lifted my face to a sky white with haze. Already I could

feel dense humidity descending. I needed a shower and my bed. I could feel weariness in every bone of my body. I yawned deeply as I let the elevator slowly pull me up through the building.

Maybe Briallen was right. Maybe I was taking it all too personally. Robin in all likelihood would have ended up dead one way or the other. And Tansy was too naïve to stay away from the wrong elements. As I let myself into the apartment, I thought maybe things might not have turned out differently. And I also thought that maybe, just maybe, Briallen was wrong.

10

I've always been fascinated that when I wake up wearing the same clothes from the previous night, they smell a lot worse than I thought they did when I went to bed. Of course, managing to sleep over fifteen hours before waking at four in the morning doesn't help either. I couldn't stand my own stench, so I hauled myself out of a nest of sheets and took a shower. Dried sweat and not a little blood sloughed off like a layer of dead skin. When I came out of the bathroom, I was too awake to go back to bed. I made myself some coffee, slipped on a pair of shorts, and went up to the roof.

Even though I was practically naked and it was still technically nighttime, the air felt hot on my skin. The humidity of the previous day had never fully dissipated, promising an even muggier day to come. I settled into the lawn chair and sipped from my mug. Regardless of the temperature, I always drink my coffee. A day with no caffeine is like a day with no meaning whatsoever.

Across the channel, a muddy haze hung around the docks like a dirty skirt. Lighted windows dotted the office towers where no one would be working for hours to come, empty offices vibrating with stillness. The taillights of cabs silently slipped in and out of sight on mysterious nightly errands. The only sounds were the hollow white noise of the city and the occasional siren off in the distance. After the bars have closed and even the drunks have made it home, the city still rustles like an insomniac. Complete rest hovers just out of reach until dawn arrives, then there's no time left. The city doesn't sleep, but it dreams. It dreams of regrets and promises.

I felt that way too damned much of the time. Ever since my accident, I'd been poised between future hope and past glory. I hated it, hated the unknown state in which I found myself. If I could never regain my abilities, what would I become? Briallen's words kept cycling through my head. What did it mean to be a body without talent? I know she meant that there's no such thing, but that didn't really answer the question.

For the longest time, I'd beaten myself up over my arrogance. How I didn't appreciate what I had until I lost it. How I'd looked down on everyone else who couldn't compete with me. But now I needed to get past the self-flagellation. I had to find my way back to the path, and the only way to do that was to act. Otherwise, I'd end up with nothing better to do but collect disability checks and sit half-naked sipping coffee in the middle of the night.

As the sky began to lighten, I sat in front of the computer. Methodically, I recorded everything that had occurred in the past forty-eight hours. It was the longest single entry in the file. Nothing is harder for an investigator than to become part of his own case. Even though Briallen and Murdock came at me from different angles, they had made the same point: Don't make it personal. It was hard not to. They were right, but it was hard.

The first thing I did was to retire the Tuesday Killer moniker. It had forced me into a mind-set that left me unprepared for what had happened. I had forgotten that

Occam's razor is a process, not a solution. By focusing on the obvious weekly cycle, it never occurred to me to look for something else. A cheap bank calendar would have spelled out the phases of the moon for me had I bothered to look.

I had the urge to toss all my analysis for fear that I had constrained myself too much. After Murdock's comment in the car, the whole *ska* thing was starting to bother me. Did Tansy, with her limited vocabulary, have only a word for wrong birth to describe the nasty essence she felt, or was she on the money? Was I congratulating myself a little too much for connecting the cross-species cases in Gillen's files? Avalon Memorial was the only fey hospital in the Northeast outside of New York. It would have been unusual if I hadn't found any. On top of that, I'd only found the connection by following other links. Computer search engines are notorious for linking completely disparate information because they're set up by people who don't think exactly like you do. I was surprised some pornography hadn't popped up. It usually does, no matter what gets searched.

I called up Murdock's notes on Shay. As far as I could tell, he was born of human parents. The only people from Faerie to appear after Convergence were fey—always some type of druid, fairy, elf, or dwarf—never a normal human without so-called fantastic abilities. According to the stories, humans certainly played a part in Faerie, but they didn't seem to come through in the unexplained merging of the two worlds. Without a distinct connection to Faerie, I could not see how to link Shay into the killer's profile.

It came down to essence. Essence is like an energy that can be manipulated in different ways. That's one of the things that make the fey races vary from each other. Druids actually join their personal essence to whatever other essence they're working with. It's why we're very good at it, but also why we get tired. Fairies don't have to do that. They can literally pluck essence out of anything with no depletion of their own essence, unless they want to use it. It makes them very powerful, but the trade-off is a lower level of skill in use. And elves manipulate essence only through chanting. They didn't seem to have any direct control of any essence except their own, which they use only in dire circumstances. Humans can activate essence, but only if someone fey has set things up for them. Someone like Shay couldn't do it on his own.

I jumped as my answering machine beeped loudly to indicate it was full. I had turned off the volume and the ringer before passing out the day before. I raised the volume in time to hear Murdock say, "You idiot." He disconnected. I hit playback. The first message was from Murdock telling me he was sending a case file update via email. The next four were also Murdock, all with the same message to call. The last one was the one that had just come in. An annoyed Murdock said, "Call me. Your cell phone's dead, you idiot."

I called, and he picked up immediately.

"The Guild took the case," he said. Good old Murdock, right to the point. I felt like I'd been sucker-punched. "The last victim's father kicked up a stink. I told you he was someone big in New York. I don't think macDuin had a choice."

"That's too easy. MacDuin knows something. I think he's wanted this buried all along," I said.

"Well, it's his case now," said Murdock. "Wrap up your notes and email them to me. I have to turn everything over to the Guildhouse this afternoon."

I could hear in his voice that he was already thinking of something else. "That's it? You're just going to let it go?"

Murdock chuckled dryly. "Welcome to the Boston P.D., Connor. Once the Guild asserts its right, we're out of it. You probably did it to us a couple of times yourself."

He was right. The rules of the game proscribed it. If a crime were fey-related, the Guild could take the case without question. I'd been pissing and moaning that the Guild took only cases it had a political benefit in taking, and they had just proved my point.

"Come by for dinner on Sunday," Murdock said into the silence.

"I'll think about it." Personally, I still didn't think the commissioner wanted to see me at his table. I put the phone back on the cradle and stared out the window. Daylight had returned the city to its waking state. Traffic backed up along the elevated highway; planes took off and landed; and people moved lethargically along the streets in the heat. The Guild had taken the case, and the world hadn't ended. I was mildly surprised.

In the past, I would have taken the opportunity to sweep the desktop clear, perhaps throw a book or two or knock a hole in the wall. After a while though, it began to sink in that I didn't have a maid anymore and would have to clean the mess up myself. Instead, I gripped the edge of my desk and counted to ten. It's not as satisfying, but it is tidier.

MacDuin probably was forced to take the case officially if the last victim's father had any pull. That much I could believe. I just had no faith the other victims would have any justice. They were important to no one but themselves and maybe a small circle of friends. All macDuin had to do was find the killer, or at least set up another sucker and connect him to the last case, and that would be the end of it. The Guild would focus on the one case and nothing else would matter. The denizens of the Weird wouldn't matter. And whatever macDuin was trying to pull with the fake perpetrator would get buried.

I checked my records to see which files hadn't been sent to Murdock yet, then checked them again. While I didn't particularly like helping macDuin, I hated not finishing a job more. I dropped everything into an e-mail and sent it off. No sense causing Murdock grief by not closing up the files.

I wandered about the apartment at loose ends, with nothing to do unless Murdock came up with another case. It was an odd feeling—hoping something bad would happen to someone so that you could get work. Frustration gnawed at me. As a general rule, when all else fails, sublimate. Grabbing a sponge, I cleaned the kitchen and bathroom to occupy my mind. As I tossed the remnants of Chinese takeout from the fridge, I jostled the box of glow bees. I decided to warm one up and send it to Stinkwort. I could at least let off steam by yelling at him for his bad behavior at Briallen's. I didn't know how long it would take for him to get the message.

As I found myself crouched on the floor hunting dust bunnies from under the couch, I sat back on my haunches. "Okay, this is getting out of hand," I said aloud. I could care less if there were dust bunnies under my couch. I wiped my hands, grabbed my keys, and left the building. I couldn't let it go. I had to go to the Guildhouse and find out what macDuin was up to.

While I liked living in the Weird, its one drawback was inconvenient public transportation. Nothing goes anywhere in the middle of the day except downtown, then you have to make a connection to get anywhere else. For a small city, it can take way too long to get to where you're going. More often than not, it's easier to walk. I got lucky and caught the number seven bus on Congress Street, which got me to the Orange Line station in fifteen minutes. As I stood at Downtown Crossing, I opted to walk up Washington Street the rest of the way instead of taking the sweltering subway.

Washington Street used to run right through the old Combat Zone, some urban planner's brilliant idea of a legal human sewer. Now the area consisted of boarded-up buildings and the occasional social service office. Prostitutes still prowled the area at night, which infuriated the residents of nearby Chinatown. Their only consolation was that one of the remaining theaters ran decent chop-socky movies. The other two theaters still catered to the raincoat crowd. During the day the businessmen from the Financial District spent their lunch hours looking for a quick thrill in the peep booths while trying not to soil their suits. It was like the Weird, only for humans. It was an entertaining walk if you didn't think about it too much.

I turned toward Park Square and paused at the corner of Charles Street. The noonday traffic flowed briskly past me. Even with my sunglasses on, the bright sunlight felt like knives in my eyes. All the sleep I had gotten helped, but I still felt like I'd been run over by a truck. I couldn't imagine how I would have felt if Briallen hadn't propped me up a little.

Across the way, the Park Plaza Hotel retained the air of an old Brahmin stronghold, with its prim cornice and orderly tan blocks of hewn granite. Like so many city buildings situated at the intersection of six or seven streets, it pointed into the square like a ship coming into port. As the traffic slowed for the light, I craned my head up at the building next to me.

The Guildhouse looked like anything but an old Boston building. Slab upon slab of Portland brownstone towered up haphazardly into crenellated towers that reached heights unheard of back in Faerie. A little fey ability and modern structural engineering knowledge will do that to an architect. Gargoyles perched on every conceivable surface. They weren't part of the original design, but had accumulated over the years, attracted by the levels of power emanating from the building.

I made my way to the arched main entry facing the square. The sharp end of a portcullis hung suspended over the huge glass doors. I didn't know if it was operational or just kitsch. Directly over the main doors, a stone dragon's head jutted out, its mouth agape, long sinuous tongue curling over needlelike teeth. Unlike the other gargoyles, the dragon was part of the original design of the building but never seemed to attract a resident spirit. Too stressful a position, I guessed.

I felt a flutter across my mind, like a cool dry puff of wind. The feeling was familiar but one I hadn't experienced in a long time. It came again, followed by a sound like stone grating against sand.

You return, whispered the dull dry voice in my head. I leaned back, scanning the upper vault of the entryway. Hundreds of gargoyles clustered in the recesses of the arch—demons, animals, reptiles, and the occasional human joke all staring back at me.

Here, said the voice. I stepped back from the building and examined the pillars near the front. After a moment, I spotted him—a squat little man, no bigger than a house cat, nestled in among the acanthus leaves of a capital. He was chubby, naked, and enormously endowed for his size. A single eye stared out from the center of his forehead, right under a small spiraled horn, and his ash gray face bore a noncommittal expression. As gargoyles went, he was a nice guy.

I relaxed my mind and thought, *Hello, Virgil.* It wasn't quite a sending. You didn't so much send your thoughts to gargoyles. They just listened if they chose to. Virgil was an old friend of sorts. At one time, he sat on the ledge outside my office window in the Guildhouse. The first time he spoke to me, I was rereading Dante, hence the name. I have no idea what his real name is or even if he has one. I was surprised to find him in such a conspicuous place.

Have waited, he said.

For me? I asked.

Yes.

Gargoyles are the damnedest things. They come from their own tradition out of Europe, but you can find them most anywhere. It's not clear if the animated ones became animated post-Convergence, but they definitely went on the move at about the same time. They love Guildhouses especially. The first Guildhouse in New York collapsed from their weight, so later Guildhouses were all built with the eventuality of a couple tons of stones sitting on them.

They almost never speak. I don't know if all of them can, but the ones that do, do so rarely. They move only at night, very slowly unless under extreme duress, and never when anyone is watching. I once monitored the progress of a winged frog from my window ledge to the floor below. It took him a month and a half. He stayed there a day or two, then disappeared. I still don't know why.

Can I help you with something? I asked. I couldn't imagine how I could help a spirit-inhabited lump of stone that had been around for centuries. Gargoyles didn't need a lot of taking care of. A dry, rasping sound answered me, which I think might have been laughter.

Not your moon, Virgil said.

I don't understand, I thought.

Do not know. Will.

Will? Do you mean you will or I will? I thought as loudly as I could. Even though none moved, I felt the attention of several other gargoyles. Virgil didn't respond. I stood patiently, waiting for him to say more, but he just stared resolutely down at me. When it became clear he wasn't going to speak again, I nodded courteously. *Thank you.*

A cold knot formed in my stomach. Had I leaped to yet another wrong conclusion? Was the lunar cycle yet another too-convenient theory? I had never quite figured out why Virgil spoke to me at all and whether it was supposed to help. His words only made sense after the fact and usually referred to something incredibly obvious I had missed. I knew I would end up kicking myself when I finally understood.

For the first time in almost a year, I walked into the Guildhouse. The vaulted marble foyer rose two stories, lit by wall sconces resembling torches. A tour group huddled to one side while their guide pointed out the nondescript space. The Guildhouse is a working building, not a museum, but that doesn't stop people from wondering what it looks like. They don't get any farther than the foyer most of the time unless they're lucky.

To the left of the entrance, a long curving line of fey and humans waited, their faces in various stages of desperation or fear or hope. I used to call them suppliants. Some were looking for lost loved ones, others had a grievance against a fey, and still others had nowhere else to turn for help in whatever dire circumstances they found themselves. They came every day to wait in line to fill out audience requests that were rarely granted. What most people don't realize is that they have better odds of getting into Harvard than getting an appointment with a Guild member. When I bothered to notice them before, they annoyed me. I was like everyone else who worked upstairs; I couldn't care less if it didn't help my career. Now I just saw them as people who could probably use some help.

I moved around the line to get to main reception. Two women, both elves, worked the desk. I didn't recognize either of them. As I approached, the one with the ponytail and too much blue eye shadow held out a clipboard. "Fill out the application and deposit it in the bin on the end of the desk."

"Connor Grey to see Keeva macNeve."

"Do you have an appointment card?"

"No."

"We don't just call up without a card, sir. You can fill out an application if you like." She turned back to her paperwork.

I glanced at the people waiting. I was breaking the monotony, and some were paying particular attention. Leaning over the desk, I grabbed a pen and wrote Keeva's phone number on the form. She'd kill me if anyone overheard it. "This is Keeva's direct line. If I didn't know her, I wouldn't have it. Call her please."

She looked at the number dubiously, but I could tell she knew it was an internal line. With several shades of annoyance, she picked up the phone and dialed. "Her voice mail's picking up. Do you want to leave a message?"

"No. Can I just go up to her office and see if she's in?" I said.

"No." She hung up the phone and turned back to her paperwork again. Once I'd had a sweet office in an end turret overlooking the Common. Now I couldn't get past the first floor without an appointment.

As I debated what to say next, a familiar figure pushed through the front door with double slices of pizza. She glared at someone who came too near as she passed. She wore a black lacy shawl draped over one shoulder, a black sundress, and combat boots. Her skin had the white pallor of someone who rarely went outside. The only real color about her was her hair. I'd seen it black, red, plum, and one entire week it was blue. Today it was orange and clipped in a spiky bowl that set off her pleasantly round features.

Meryl stopped short when she saw me. Wary eyes looked up at me from under her bangs. She only came up to my shoulder, but she had enough attitude for someone twice her height. She bit the tips off both slices of pizza simultaneously. "Grey. Need another favor?"

I could feel heat rise on my cheeks. "As a matter of fact . . ." I gestured at the desk. "They're being officious and won't let me in."

The receptionist overheard and glared at me.

Meryl looked me up and down. "Are you armed?"

"I have a knife."

She nodded once. "Good. I can claim self-defense if I have to kill you." She walked past the reception desk. "He's with me," she said over her shoulder.

"I need to see your pass," said the receptionist.

Meryl turned slowly. "On average, I pass you four times a day. I think you're a twit. You think I'm a bitch. Ring a bell?" She resumed walking. I trailed along behind her.

"Did you find the stones you lost?" she asked.

We arrived at the elevator bank just as the doors opened, and I followed her in. "I didn't lose them. This place did."

The elevator descended. "Whatever," she said around a mouthful of pizza. "They got checked in. Made it to macDuin's department. No one remembers seeing them after that."

Three levels below the street, the doors opened onto a

long, brick-lined, vaulted hallway. Closed doors were set in the walls at regular intervals, and every other light in the ceiling was out. A dry musty smell hung in the air.

Meryl walked out of the elevator. "Are you following me?"

"Well, I did want to talk to you."

We stopped at an old oaken door with ornate iron hinges and a huge old lock. "Oh, I thought you just wanted to run loose in the building. Did you know no one can hear you scream down here?"

She screamed.

The lock jiggled and popped open as the hair on my head stood on end. No one came running. She giggled and opened the door. "I've been playing with sonic cantrips. They work pretty well, except last week I had sinus congestion, and it took me twenty minutes to get the pitch right."

After the dimness of the hall, I blinked at the bright white walls in her office. Blue lateral file cabinets lined the right side of the room, while boxes of various sizes leaned against the left. The center of the room was dominated by an old gray army desk on which sat a computer that looked like its guts had blown out the side of the hard drive. Wires and cables snaked from it to a credenza on the back wall, where another computer sat. Something told me she had a nice little black box operation working into the building mainframe.

"Sit down and don't touch anything," she said. She scooted sideways around the desk to her chair, tossing her empty pizza plate into the wastebasket.

I picked up a stack of papers on her guest chair and lowered them to the floor. As I leaned back in the chair, I noticed the bulletin board on the wall over her head. Magazine photos and news articles covered almost the entire surface. Dumbfounded, I realized notes tucked in here and there had ogham writing on them with numbers scrawled along the bottom. More of the same littered her desk.

"Damn. Meryl, what are these?"

Annoyance crossed her face. "If you had occasionally done your own research instead of sending one of your minions down here, you'd know."

I smiled playfully at her. "I have a knife, remember."

She smiled right back. "And there's a stick of dynamite taped under your chair and *my* body shields work."

"That's a low blow," I said. It was such a bad pun, I could taste it.

She laughed. "It's my filing system. The Dewey Decimal system doesn't quite work in a place where putting the wrong things next to each other can cause hair to grow in unsightly places. You have to balance the energies to keep everything flowing peacefully. I've tried to get the other 'Houses to adopt it, but they're waiting for a full chthonic breakdown before they'll admit it works."

I grabbed a pen and drew the ogham script from the flyer in Murdock's car. "Does this mean anything?"

She looked at the paper, then back at me. "What? Are you becoming a mineralogist in your old age? Those stones went missing last winter."

"What stones?"

She tossed the paper on her desk and gestured at the glyph. "Those stones. Five of them. High-quality selenite. Pre-Convergence. Seized in an illegal container shipment a few years back."

"You know that just by looking at the glyph?"

She nodded. "That's where they were filed. I found them missing. I was using them to anchor a couple of wards. When I walked in the room, there was a hum that told me the wards weren't working anymore. I checked. They were gone. I had to file a cartload of forms over it. You think you found them and lost them again?"

"I didn't lose them," I said.

"Whatever."

"Can you show me?"

We left the office. Meryl led me farther down the hall to

a spiral staircase. We went down another level to a hallway identical to the one upstairs and walked deeper into the building. All kinds of resonant essences bounced through the air. My head began to buzz.

"Man, what the hell do you have down here?"

"Just about everything: weapons, armor, crystals, books. You name it, we got it. Some of it's evidence for on-going investigations; some of it's archives for research. A lot of it's crap. Did I mention you'd know that if you bothered to do your own research occasionally?"

"Not that you're bitter about it or anything," I said.

She held up her hands in a warding gesture. "Touchy-touchy. I'm sorry I mentioned it."

We stopped in front of a door. Meryl positioned her palm outward on the wall near the lock. She muttered something in what sounded like Middle English. A momentary shimmer of light bounced from her hand to the wall, and a keypad appeared. I turned my back and out of habit automatically memorized the sound of the tones. "Don't waste the brain cells. I'm changing the code after you leave," she said.

We entered a high, dimly lit storeroom. I whistled in appreciation. Rack upon rack of steel shelving marched to the right and left and up twenty feet. The lower levels held cabinets and drawers. Judging from the length of the aisles branching out to either side and in front of me, the room had to cover an acre. It had to be deep under the subway system even to exist in that much space.

My head still buzzed, but I had a cottony feeling as well, which told me dampening wards were in place. "Now I know why you like your job," I said.

She grinned. "I don't like my job. I just like where it is."

Weaving our way around boxes on the floor, we walked down an aisle of meticulously labeled drawers. My foot connected with something, and it skittered across the floor with a clunking sound.

I leaned down and picked up a small bowl. It was carved

from a single piece of wood and fit perfectly cupped in my hands. "This is nice. Olive wood, isn't it?"

Meryl sighed loudly. "That damned Parker. He's a new temp who can't file his own fingernails. You'd think he'd be a little more careful, considering."

"Considering?"

She pointed at the bowl. "That's the Holy Grail."

Shocked, I held it away from me as though it were ready to bite. "The Holy Grail!"

Laughing, she plucked it out of my hands. She pulled open a drawer, revealing several more bowls, and dropped it inside. "And so are these. Can you believe some dope managed to sell a few of them? I mean, really, anyone can see the wood's not even two hundred years old. If we ever have another clearance auction, I might take them home for salad bowls." She hip-checked the drawer closed and walked away humming. I have to admit her attitude was growing on me.

I joined her at a bank of drawers. She pulled open a small one and hopped back, looking at me in surprise. "Did you feel that? Something just went off."

I shook my head. "My abilities aren't great under the best of circumstances, and you've got this place heavily warded."

We peered into the drawer. An inset of black velvet filled the entire space with five cupped indentations. Two of them were occupied. A white stone and a black one. I recognized both. "Are these the same stones that went missing last year?"

She nodded. "I've stared at their photos enough."

"Mine, too."

"But why put them back?" said Meryl.

I smiled. "The best place to hide something is where they're missing from. No one looks once they're gone."

"So where are the rest of them, smart guy?"

"A gray one's upstairs with macDuin in the case file for

the bogus killer; another gray one's at Boston P.D., probably on its way to macDuin as we speak. And the last one's with the killer."

"It's black," Meryl said.

"I know. I thought the killings were a weekly cycle until I realized that they're keyed to the phases of the moon. White for the full, gray for the quarters, and black for the new."

"We just had a quarter moon two nights ago."

"And I found a gray stone in a dead fairy's chest."

Meryl shook her head. "Damn! Who'd've thought my stones would turn up this way."

As she finished speaking, I heard the distinctive sound of a door closing. Judging from Meryl's reaction, she heard it, too. I held my finger to my lips.

She frowned at me. "Bob? Parker, is that you?" she called out.

"Shhh!" I hissed.

"You shhh. I'm supposed to be here," she said. "Don't move." She went quickly back down the aisle and out of sight. Moments later, I heard her call Parker's name again, but no one answered. I could hear her footsteps fading away and a door latch opening. She called out a few more times, her voice becoming more and more faint. After a long stretch, I realized I didn't hear anything anymore.

It occurred to me that Meryl might have set off an alarm spell when she opened the drawer. Whoever had cast it would eventually make their way to the aisle I was standing in. I looked around, but that end of the room was too neat, and there was nothing to hide behind. Quietly, I closed the drawer that contained the stones and opened another one enough to get my foot on the edge. As silently as possible, I boosted myself up to the first set of shelves. From there I climbed the remaining shelves like a ladder until I reached the top. I lay flat in the thick dust and peered over.

Seconds stretched into minutes which stretched into eons. I could almost hear my own heartbeat without trying. A cool waft of air washed over me. With all the wardings in the room, I couldn't tell if it had essence tangled in it or if it was just the ventilation system. Moments later I could hear footsteps coming down the aisle, and I slid back. They came closer, a steady gait with a firm destination. They stopped right below me.

I startled as a voice whispered in my ear. "Do you want to come down from there?"

I raised my head and looked below. With her hands on her hips and clearly amused, Meryl looked back at me. I swung my legs over, clambered down the shelves, and dropped the last ten feet to the floor. I brushed at the dust and cobwebs that completely covered me.

"Nothing," she said. "Someone was definitely there, but I couldn't make heads or tails of the essence."

We stood in silence for a moment. "It was Bob," Meryl decided.

"Why didn't he answer?"

"Because he's a temp, and he thinks he's being paid to sleep in the storeroom when I'm not looking."

"Someone who wanted to lead me to that drawer left me those ogham runes, Meryl, and they set an alarm on it to see if I figured it out."

"I led you to the drawer, Grey. Someone who didn't want to get involved remembered the burglary and slipped you a tip that panned out."

I retrieved the stones. Pointedly, Meryl held out her hand. After a moment's hesitation, I dropped them into her palm. I had no authority to keep them, and if she wanted to be a bitch about it, Meryl could have me detained before I even got to the elevator.

"We can't tell anyone about this," I said.

"Are you kidding? Do you have any idea of the hell I caught over these babies?"

"Meryl, someone didn't want those stones found, and

someone else did. We can't tell anyone until I figure out who and why."

She considered for a long moment. "I'll give you until Monday."

"Only if I find the killer. Otherwise, I'll need until the new moon on Wednesday."

An exasperated look came over her face. "Haven't you learned anything, Grey? The phases don't care about the calendar. The new moon's next Thursday."

A cold feeling of dread settled over me. Next Thursday. Midsummer's Eve. And thousands of people would be filling the Weird for the festivities.

Meryl escorted me back to the elevator. "Before you go, I have to tell you about a dream I had about you."

Great, I thought. This could be awkward. Intriguing, but awkward. "You had a dream about me?" I said as neutrally as possible.

"Not just a dream. I'm a Dreamer. I have a geas on me to share my True dreams," she said.

That startled me. Most of the fey had some kind of geas. It's an obligation placed on you that you can't ignore. If you do, really bad things can happen. You end up with a geas all kinds of ways. Some people get them when a vision comes upon someone present at their birth. Some people get them like a curse, when they've wronged someone. They're not given lightly and have a bit of fate bound up in them. What surprised me was that Meryl just out and told me hers. Given the compelling obligation, most people keep them secret so that they can't be manipulated. I have a couple on me myself, and only a handful of people know some of them, and no one knows all of them. "I can't believe you just told me your geas."

She shrugged. "It's hardly a secret when the geas is to tell." She smiled wickedly. "Don't worry. I doubt you'll ever figure out my secret ones."

"So what did you Dream?"

"I dream in metaphors. I've seen you bound in chains, but you break free. I've seen you sinking in a pool of ogham runes—I think we just figured that part out. I've seen you surrounded by knives and stars and hearts. You enter the Guildhouse through a black hole and roam empty corridors. And I saw you broken and alone, surrounded by dead bodies. And I'll tell you this, even though it's not part of the Dream: I haven't Dreamed a single thing since. Every Dream I have these days ends with you crushed on the ground."

"Shit," I said.

The elevator bell toned, and the doors opened.

Meryl smiled. "Yeah. Anyway, nice seeing you."

11

Sweat poured off me as I ran. I had hoped that jogging right after greeting the sun would be cooler than waiting until later in the day. I was wrong. After slacking off all week and skipping a gym date with Murdock, I was paying for it. Of course, I could count chasing a murderer at a full sprint and almost going into a coma as exercise, but I really hadn't been wearing the right shoes then. My hamstrings sang as my feet hit the pavement.

I didn't care that I was no longer "officially" on the case. "Officially" didn't mean anything to me anymore. Not being on the case didn't stop me from being involved when Robin and Tansy died. After all that had happened, I couldn't just let it go. My record back at the Guild was perfect. Except for Bergen Vize, I had closed every case I'd ever worked on and even that case was still open. Vize had gone into hiding after what he did to me, so at least he wasn't pursuing his usual extremist environmental agenda. For the moment, I had time to get him. I didn't have time with this case, and I was going to finish it one way or another.

In five days, the Weird would be teeming with Midsummer celebrants. On a normal holiday, the police and the Guild are stretched to their limits. With the Guild taking the case, the P.D. would be more than happy to disband their task force to increase their street presence. And even given its usual penchant for silence, I hadn't heard the slightest whisper that the Guild was forming its own task force. Maybe macDuin thought he would do it on his own.

The sound of thunder rolled overhead. A dull white haze had settled in overnight, the clouds laced with sheet lightning that had been flickering since the earlier-morning hours. It looked like it would continue throughout the day. I quickened my pace through the empty streets in case it actually rained. By the time I reached Sleeper Street, it hadn't and probably wouldn't. I ended my run with a warm-down in front of my building. As I lingered on the sidewalk, a familiar old Chevy that screamed "undercover cop" pulled up.

"You're out early," Murdock said when he rolled down the window. The refreshing breeze of air-conditioning radiated out of the car. Though his shirt and tie were as neat as usual, the stress of dealing with the politics of the case showed in the tightness around his eyes. Being on an unsolved case could be a pressure-cooker in the station house. Watching it slip away without a conclusion can be even worse.

"Just working off some steam."

Murdock raised his eyebrows. "Anything you'd like to share?"

I nonchalantly stared up the street as I stretched my legs. "Depends. If I came into certain information that macDuin might find interesting, would you feel obligated as an officer of the law to pass it on?"

Murdock gave me an amused, measured look. "Well, naturally, I support open communications between law enforcement agencies, though I do admit that when things get busy, communications sometimes break down."

I studied him for a moment. Murdock was a relatively by-the-book kind of guy, but he was also a friend. I'd never had cause not to trust him. "So are things busy?"

He grinned. "Actually, they're extremely busy right now, and I don't see that changing for the foreseeable future."

"I found the stones." I filled him in on the details but left Meryl's name out of it. While she had shared information with me fairly easily, she wasn't a paid informant. Even Murdock could understand that. Everybody had a source they liked to keep quiet about. Being too free with people's names tended to dry up information pretty quickly. Besides, if I gave her name without her permission, Meryl would probably gut me.

Murdock didn't say anything for the longest time. "Why are you pursuing this?" he said at last.

"Because I have to."

"It's too hot to talk with the window open. Get in."

I opened the door, nudged a McDonald's bag to the floor, and sat down. The air-conditioning cooled off my damp T-shirt more quickly than the rest of me, and I shivered.

"Connor, no one is paying you to solve this case anymore. You need to be realistic."

"Hey, Officer, whatever happened to truth, justice, and the American way?"

Murdock rolled his eyes. "Capitalism is the American way. Cost-benefit analysis is the American way."

"That's pretty cynical coming from a diehard like you."

"You know as well as I do, Connor, that you have to care about the job to do the job. But if you make it personal, you burn yourself out in no time. You can't care too much, or you're dead."

"Maybe I can. For the last year, Murdock, I've worked with you on lots of cases, but they've been advisory. This is the first real case I've had to deal with since I got out of the hospital. It feels good. It feels important. It's about murdered people whom no one else cares about, people who needed the overworked police department and the indifferent Guild to do something about it. We both know that hope might be misplaced. Look, the Guild took the case, and it's barely in the news. You lost the case, and you're ready to move on. And, yes, it's about me. It's about the fact that I don't like it. I don't like that not enough can be done. I don't like that someone twisted enough to commit murder is smart enough to escape me. I don't like that shit happens. Not anymore."

Murdock nodded slowly. "Just don't let it control you."

I shrugged. "Besides, it's not like I have anything better to do."

He just looked at me from beneath his eyebrows. After that little speech, I wouldn't have believed the cavalier attitude either.

"So what do you think about the stones?" I asked.

Murdock sighed heavily and tapped his fingers against the steering wheel. "Someone at the Guild has a secret. The stones lead to the secret. Figure out the stones, and you figure out the secret."

"Well, we know the stones are being used in a ritual. I've been trying to track that down from day one."

Murdock shook his head. "That's not the secret. Take yourself out of the box. The stones were stolen long before these murders."

I sighed. "So I'll keep looking into the stones. Belgor had a customer looking for selenite last fall when the Guild got robbed. I don't think that's a coincidence." I let myself out of the car. "So what brings you down here?"

"Two things. One, I wanted to make sure you sent all your files in. And two, I'm back on another case that I've had on hold since this whole serial killer mess started."

"Yes, I sent the files. Anything I can help with on the new

case?" It was the most polite way I could think of asking for work.

"Not right now. I've got a dead drug dealer. I doubt it'll go anywhere. Call me if I can help you though." I nodded and closed the door. As I watched him drive away, I realized our roles had reversed. His case had somehow become mine. At least I didn't have to pay him for help if I needed it.

Once upstairs, I reviewed the update Murdock had sent me before he lost the case. The fourth fairy victim was a young Danann named Galvin macTiarnach. In town for Midsummer. I actually knew his father from my early days at the Guildhouse in New York. Tiarnach Ruadan was an Old One, born of Faerie, and all around nice guy. When I knew him, he had no children. A mild depression settled over me as I looked at the scene photos. It must be a special hell to wait centuries to have a child only to lose him so senselessly. I hoped he would give some of that hell to macDuin.

The rest of the file gave a routine catalog of phone calls and informant contacts that had led nowhere, followed by Murdock's description of the day before. It's odd reading someone else's version of the same events. Murdock made it clear that he held strong suspicions about Shay. He was nicely dismissive of macDuin's charges against me, though.

At the bottom of the last page was a brief entry note. He had tracked down two of the women from our *ska* list. Both of their children were dead of natural causes. He had found the third woman as well, a fairy named Dealla Sidhe. Next to her name he had simply written an address right in South Boston with the notation 'No phone. Not home again.' Flipping back through previous reports, I realized he had stopped by her house several times. I made a note to ask Meryl if she would check the Guild records on her.

I toyed with the idea of calling Germany. They still hadn't returned my call. The Germans liked doing things their own way in their own time. They didn't take kindly to pressure, especially from someone asking a favor. If I called, I risked being perceived as a nuisance and they could very well not give me the information I needed for even longer out of spite. I decided to exercise caution for the moment, if only because it was a Saturday.

I spent the remainder of the day ensconced in my study, poring over stone rituals. Most druids fall into two groups: sticks or stones. Wood has some wonderful properties, but it has a tendency to react too much with the user for my particular taste. Because they retain some of their own innate essence, using wands becomes almost a partnership. You have to be very nature-oriented to use them to their best advantage.

I have to admit a certain affection for stone work. They do what you want them to, when you want them to, regardless of whether you are tired or it is raining. They always give out exactly what you put into them. And you can start them going and leave them to finish your work, something you can't do with wands.

Personally, when I was well, I tried not to rely on either. No ego about it—the stronger your ability, the less likely you are to use any type of auxiliary apparatus. The tough stuff you do with your hands or your voice or your mind. Actually, that's not quite true. The more power you have, the more likely you are to use wands and wards incidentally. That, in fact, is about ego. In some quarters, nothing demonstrates your ability more than how casually you used it. When I was cleaning the apartment the day before, I noticed the protection wards around the window had been recharged, and so had the ones on the roof. Keeva had probably done it while she sat talking to me without showing any effort whatsoever.

Stones are useful things for people without any ability. You can buy them and pay someone to charge them. Of course, depending on the quality of stone and the strength of the charger, the price can go up considerably. Plenty of the fey make a decent living servicing wards for humans. For someone with no other skills and a dislike of manual labor, it has quite an upside. No overhead, and all it takes to replenish one's essence is a good nap.

Most stone-charging has a purpose. You can set up alarms like I had done in my apartment. Wards can be used to keep someone awake or put them to sleep. They can even be the catalyst for killing someone, though that takes some doing and is extremely illegal. The wards placed on the wings of the murder victims simply immobilized the victims. That was their only point as far as I could tell.

Which is why I was having such a hard time figuring out the selenite stones. The point of charging them with essence escaped me. It didn't seem to do anything to the corpses. It just dissipated.

The stones weren't catalysts, at least not in any sense I could understand. The cause of death was not fey ability-related. Cutting out someone's heart takes only a knife, physical strength, and at least a little psychosis.

The missing hearts were another matter. As the seat of essence, they were powerful organs. Taking them was obviously about taking their power. The essence the hearts contained could be stabilized and held for periods of time, the same way Briallen had held the flit body in a kind of chrysalis to prevent it from disappearing. Just because I didn't know how to do it didn't mean it couldn't be done.

I sat up so sharply, my desk chair squealed in protest. Essence was the connection. The hearts and the stones both held it. The killer wasn't just leaving stones as tokens for the hearts. He was leaving a vessel of essence for the vessel of essence he took.

I tried to go through the idea step by step. It was an exchange, but it wasn't equal. He took more than he left. He needed more. But for what? So far, all the other *ska* births had turned up dead. Was he dying? Were the murders some kind of twisted revenge? Had he somehow discovered a way to make himself well? I shook my head in frustration. Only someone with access to secret knowledge and the will to use it would take someone's essence, like Briallen had taken mine to keep Stinkwort from dying. Only she wasn't about to hand the knowledge over to me on a silver platter. I had to find it some other way.

I paced into the living room. My mind felt numb from the circles it was running in. Outside, orange light smeared across the hazy sky as the sun set. Lightning flickered as it had all day, followed by a lethargic rumble of thunder. My stomach grumbled back. I hadn't eaten, and I needed food. I debated ordering something for delivery but didn't have enough cash for a tip. Murdock was still processing my fee, and my disability check wasn't due for another week. I slipped on an old pair of boots and left the apartment.

Down in the vestibule, mail was scattered on the floor. As I picked it up, a prickling ran along the back of my neck, and my defense shields triggered. Dropping the mail, I spun toward the door in a crouch. The slab of steel was propped open with a newspaper. Flattening my back against the wall, I pushed the door open with my foot. A wave of humid air rolled in, rank with the smell of the channel. The street was dark and empty. The lamppost was out again, a fairly common phenomenon. I could sense no one nearby, though the whispering remains of essence hung in the air above the sidewalk. Some of them felt vaguely menacing, and quite a few trailed into the building.

Behind and above me, I could hear a door open for a moment, releasing a dull roar of music and voices before it closed again. My shields let go as I began to relax. A party was just getting into swing, and some idiot had propped the door open. Shaking my head, I let the door close firmly behind me and walked up the street.

Reaching the corner of Sleeper and Summer, I turned

left. Three doors up, the lights of the Nameless Deli washed out onto the street, an oasis of activity on an otherwise dead block. I paused at the door. Druids can sense the essence people leave behind like perfume. Someone who had been hanging around the front of the deli had also been in front of my apartment building. The person's essence was elfin in nature, but otherwise unremarkable. The coincidence made me pause, especially since I hadn't sensed it between the two places. Looking up and down the street, I saw no one. I pushed open the door.

Walking into the Nameless is always a bit of a shock. The harsh fluorescent lights flare so bright, they make one squint even on a sunny day. At three in the morning, they can be excruciating. Very few people know it is the side effect of a protection spell that makes people less inclined to be aggressive. It is a shoddy spell, but potent enough. For such a bad neighborhood, the Nameless is rarely robbed, and even then only by someone so hopped up on drugs that they end up being arrested right outside the door.

Dmitri leaned on the counter in the empty store, reading a car magazine. He was a dark-skinned Greek with honey-colored hair who'd probably been charming his way into beds since he was twelve. He'd been working for his grandparents since he was a kid and still filled in on the occasional weekend when he didn't have too heavy a class load at UMass/Boston. He glanced up at me with a brief smile, closed the magazine, and trailed along with me to the deli case. I ordered a sub with everything on it.

A bell rang as the door opened, and I tensed. Without turning, I sensed an elf come in behind me, the same one who had been in front of my building. In my peripheral vision, I saw him step up to the register and toss a pack of gum on the counter. Dmitri looked up, grabbed a towel, and wiped his hands. He went behind the register and rang up the sale.

Casually, I looked over. The elf was not quite my height,

decently built, and dressed in old jeans and a white T-shirt. Two little earrings hooped around the point of his right ear, and dark sunglasses covered most of his face. I hate people who wear sunglasses at night. He nonchalantly looked over at me as he collected his change and gum, then strolled out.

Dmitri came back and finished making my sandwich. He wrapped it up, and we went to the register. I handed him a few bills. "Ever see that guy before?"

Dmitri shook his head and gave me change. "Not really. He was in about an hour ago."

"Thanks." He picked up his car magazine again.

I stood in front of the deli for a long moment. The street was empty again, but I could sense the elf's essence trailing to the right—toward my apartment building. Shaking off my apprehension, I walked home. The elf was probably just a party guest, and I wasn't about to go a block out of my way just to satisfy a little prickling paranoia. As I turned the corner, I realized that this would be the scene in a movie where I would think, "Why would that idiot walk around that corner?"

Sleeper Street was quiet. Too quiet, I thought with delicious omen. I mentally chuckled at my own melodrama. Sleeper Street was always quiet; that's why I liked it. A few cars were parked haphazardly along the curb, sharing space with an old refrigerator, mildewed cartons, and glass fragments. No one ever parked in the loading lane of the warehouse across the street. Delivery trucks showed up way too early in the morning for most of my neighbors to get up and move their cars.

In the dimness ahead, I saw movement near my building. A bit of sheet lightning flashed against the overcast and in the brief instant of light, I could see it was an elf with a crew cut. Dressed in a tank top and shorts, he was leaning against the building. He pushed himself away from the wall and moved toward me slowly. I purposely activated my shields. He wasn't the guy from the deli, but that guy was nowhere to be seen. I gauged how far ahead of me he could have gotten before I left the deli and came up with a very short distance. Without breaking stride, I cut into the street. If the guy coming toward me were innocent, he would probably think I was an overly cautious wimp.

In the light of a loading dock, I stopped and made a show of tying my boot-laces. As I came up from the crouch, I discreetly pulled my knife out of my boot, using the sandwich to hide the motion. I held the shaft against the bag, the six-inch blade pressed between it and my forearm. As I started walking again, I heard footsteps behind me. Looking over my shoulder, I saw the elf from the deli about thirty feet behind me. He had doubled back somehow. Not a good sign. Turning away, I felt a rush of adrenaline. The other elf had stepped into the street as well. Definitely not a good sign.

I kept moving at my normal pace, closing the distance between us, pretending I noticed nothing amiss. I could hear the one behind me pick up his pace. The one ahead of me made no pretense of nonchalance. He came directly toward me. When he was ten feet away, I put on a sudden burst of speed and gave him a flying kick to the chest. Before turning away, I had only a brief moment of satisfaction at the startled look on his face as he fell over backwards.

I moved into a fighting stance, flipping the knife forward in my hand as I dropped the sandwich. The other elf ran toward me, shouting in German. A momentary wave of paralysis hit me. The little punk was trying to immobilize me with a grade school spell. His research obviously hadn't revealed that some of my defense shields still worked. They were good enough to blunt the thrust of a simple spell, but not anything stronger. Instinctively, I muttered my own

warding spell, forgetting that no ability had responded to
my command in months. A spasm of pain flickered in my
head, and my knees went weak.

He was chanting again, a more focused immobilizer. I
lunged at him with the knife. He smiled cockily at me as he
easily avoided the blade. The move was enough to let me
know I wasn't dealing with a professional. I hadn't meant
to connect. I wanted to distract him from chanting, and
he'd amateurishly obliged. With a quick roll to the left, he
lost the physical advantage of pinning me between himself
and his accomplice. I came up on my feet at a run. If I
could make it to my building, I'd be safe. The front door
had been keyed to my voice for just that sort of situation. If
I could get through it and into the vestibule, no one would
be able to open it again until I released it—or someone
from the Guild showed up.

Something hit me hard in the back of the knees, and I
fell. As I rolled onto my back, the elf in the shorts grabbed
me by the shirt and hit me in the face. The blow glanced
off my cheekbone, but still hurt. The other elf was chanting
again from a safe distance. As the one who held me hauled
his fist back for another blow, I could feel my limbs starting to compress against my sides. Before I lost all mobility,
I heaved up and grabbed him in a hug. We fell to the
ground together in a tangled knot of arms and legs. I would
have laughed if my situation hadn't been so precarious.
I had broken the spell by using the puncher as a shield.
Whoever the guy in the jeans was, he wasn't adept at spellcasting if he needed a clear line of sight and an isolated tar-
get to succeed. Score one for me.

Before short pants could get his bearings, I bit him on
the shoulder. No one ever expects a guy to bite. It's dirty
fighting, but so's two on one. He made an odd barking
sound and wrenched himself away. I scrambled to my feet.
The apartment building door was still too far away to make

a run for it fully exposed like I was, so I turned toward the spellcaster and ran right at him, my knife held ridiculously out in front of me like a spear. He tried his damnedest to keep chanting this time, but he still didn't get that the knife was just a feint. I didn't want to kill him, just shut him up. He backpedaled away in fear and never noticed my fist making for his throat until the last second. With a pained choking sound, he grabbed his neck. I gave him a knee in the stomach for good measure, and down he went.

Before I could step back, short pants sucker punched me in the kidneys, and I clumsily fell over the caster. He recovered enough to grab my legs. This time I slashed at him for real. He gasped as the cloth and skin split open on his chest but held on to me. The other one kicked the knife out of my hand and hit me in the ribs. As he leaned over to punch me again, a blaze of white lightning shot over our heads. I could feel the electric charge dance through my hair.

"Leave off!" someone shouted.

We all froze. At the end of the street, the black silhouette of a woman strode toward us, her hand raised palm out and glowing white. Short pants chose to ignore her and hit me in the face again. Blood shot out my nose. Another bolt of light blazed at us and knocked him off his feet.

She came nearer. "I said leave off!"

The spellcaster released my legs and crawled away a few feet.

"Face me or flee!" she shouted, boosting a little power to her hand to make her point. They didn't need any more time to consider. In seconds, they were on their feet and running.

I sat up and cradled my nose with my hand. With all the blood pouring out, I couldn't sense who my savior was. She moved out of the light from the end of the street and leaned over me, and I saw her face more clearly.

"Hi, Keeva."

She knelt on one knee beside me with a concerned look on her face. "Is it broken?"

I shook my head. "Looks worse than it is."

She stretched her hand toward my face. "Here, let me. I'm not much of a healer, but I can mute the pain." I felt a brief surge of warmth, and the pain did lessen. The blood still flowed copiously though.

I let her help me to my feet. "Don't waste time here. Go get them."

"It's over, Connor."

"They were trying to kill me!"

She sighed and shook those long red tresses. "Only you can turn a mugging into a murder conspiracy."

I peeled off my T-shirt and wadded it up. Gingerly, I pressed it to my nose. "What are you doing here?"

"Saving your ass, as usual."

"I want to know what you're doing on my street."

"I don't need this." She started to walk away, and I grabbed her arm. She glared at me with her best imperious haughtiness. "You dare!"

I dropped my hand. "Can the more-royal-than-thou crap. You know I couldn't care less. I want to know what you're doing here, and you're going to tell me or I will make your life miserable until you do."

She compressed her lips into a very thin line. I didn't have much concrete to hold over her except for the same petty stuff everyone has. But I had gotten hints of bigger stuff here and there when we were working together. Nothing I couldn't follow up on if need be. I could see Keeva's mind working through the same chain of thought.

"I'm working on an investigation that macDuin wants kept quiet."

"And how does following me fit into it?"

She folded her arms across her chest. "I am not following

you. I had no idea I'd end up talking to you tonight. If I see you getting beat up again, I promise I won't interfere."

I dabbed at my nose. The bleeding had slowed, but some swelling had begun. I knew Keeva well enough to know that would be the end of her explanation. I couldn't force her to tell me any more than she had. I leaned down and picked up my knife. "Who's working the serial killer case?"

She smiled smugly. "I am, like I told you I would. MacDuin spent today reviewing the files. I'm getting it tomorrow."

"Want some help?"

She laughed, like I knew she would. "You are priceless, Connor. The last thing macDuin wants is you anywhere near this case."

I shrugged. "He doesn't have to know."

"But he would. He probably has someone watching us right now."

Looking for a clean spot, I refolded the bloody T-shirt and pressed it against my nose again. "And you like working under those conditions?"

She found something fascinating to stare at on the ground. "It suits my purposes for the moment. Stay out of it or he'll force me to bring you in on interference charges. We've already got you for tampering with a murder scene."

"You forget, Keeva. I was born here. I may be fey, but I'm also an American citizen. He only has free rein with non-citizen fey. He'd need the Commissioner's approval—which I'm betting he won't get—*and* a federal court order—which won't happen quickly on such a minor charge."

"Just stay out of it," she said.

"Suit yourself. I'm not backing off." I walked angrily away from her toward Summer Street.

Scanning the sidewalk, I found my sandwich and picked it up. Thankfully, the bag was still intact and closed. I walked back to Keeva and passed her without a word.

"I can make your life miserable, too, you know," she called out.

I looked back at her, but kept walking. "Keeva, I just picked my dinner out of the gutter. I doubt you can make my life any worse."

12

The Murdock residence on K Street in South Boston had the kind of silent repose that buildings have on Sunday mornings. The well-kept row house had stern black shutters and double-mullioned windows in a brick facade, the forest green door firmly shut. A cement urn on the top step overflowed with white petunias. It was all very respectable. I felt awkward hesitating on the sidewalk, praying that I had arrived after Mass. The Murdocks were church-going Catholics, and I had a vague recollection that services ended about noon. Dinner followed at two, so I had planned on arriving about an hour before. Whenever I had visited in the past, the door had stood ajar, and someone was either coming or going. Most people seemed to just walk in without knocking, a custom I had not grown up with just a few blocks away. That kind of familiarity meant family or very close friends. As I debated whether to knock or ring the bell, someone called my name, and I turned.

I breathed a small sigh of relief at the sight of Kevin Murdock. I had debated how casually to dress for dinner and gambled that even the commissioner would not mind shorts in such unbearable heat. To hedge the bet, I wore a polo shirt so I would at least have a collar. Kevin strode toward me wearing cargo shorts and a T-shirt. Cradling several loaves of bread in one arm, he extended the other to shake my hand.

"Nice eye. What's the other guy look like?" he said, as we walked up the steps.

My hand went up to my cheekbone, and I winced. It was still tender, a little dark under the left eye, with a nice red-black smear near the bridge of my nose. "I think I broke his sunglasses."

Kevin mock-cringed, sucking in air between his teeth. "Damn. Oakley's, I hope?"

I followed him into the oddly quiet house. "Um, a drugstore brand, I think."

He led me through the front hall, past the formal parlor, and into a kitchen rich with the smell of pot roast. He dropped the bread on a pink Formica counter and opened the refrigerator. He handed me a beer and started pulling plates out of a cabinet. Checking the stove, he sipped broth out of a pot and adjusted the spice. I couldn't help thinking of him as a kid. He was still in his early twenties, the last of seven children, and given that the next oldest sibling was pushing thirty, probably a surprise baby. He didn't even look like a Murdock, with his almost black hair and deep blue eyes, but then I'd never met Mrs. Murdock. All I knew about her was that she was gone some fifteen years and not a topic for conversation with anyone.

"Your turn to cook, I see."

He went back into the fridge and rummaged around. "Oh, we *always* follow the schedule around here. Everyone's up on the roof. Go on up. I'll call everyone down in a bit."

I had never been beyond the first floor of the Murdock house. As I climbed the stairs, I passed two men in deep conversation on the first-floor landing. I recognized one of them as a city councilor. They nodded courteously as I passed but continued talking. On the next floor, Grace Murdock sat in one of the bedrooms talking with her sister Faith and two other women. They waved at me in a way that said join us or not, either way's fine. I didn't know them more than to say hello, so I waved back and kept going. I always had to make a conscious effort not to make fun of their names in front of Murdock. Whatever his religious convictions were, his father's were definitely enough for the whole family. The next two floors held more bedrooms and a closed door that, by the look of the other rooms, probably was the commissioner's bedroom. To the left of the door, a last flight of stairs was a little steeper, added on well after the townhouse was built, when homeowners finally shed the old Brahmin decorum and started hanging out on the roof.

A burst of conversation surrounded me as I stepped out of a skylight and onto the deck. My eyes picked out faces I knew: Murdock, of course, his brother Bar, the commissioner, a couple of obvious cop-types, a neighborhood activist whose name I didn't think I knew, several more people whose identities I couldn't begin to guess.

"Glad you came," Murdock said from behind me. When I turned, he pulled back in mild surprise. "Whoa! Do I want to know what happened?"

"Let's just say it was a mugging that went bad."

He grinned. "You should have called the cops."

"I had some unexpected backup."

Murdock looked at me with curiosity, then smiled. "House rules: no business discussions on Sunday. Let me introduce you around." He ran through the guests, giving me brief bios under his breath. Nearly everyone had some political agenda, which was no surprise given whose house we were in.

"I never realized you can see the harbor from here," I said, changing the subject. The Murdocks' home sat in the middle of Southie, with the Weird and the downtown skyline beyond it to the north and the harbor directly east. West and south, the low-rise neighborhoods of Dorchester and the South End out to Roxbury spread out. If the neighborhood ever got discovered, they could make a mint selling the place.

"It's going to ruin the whole damn game!" said the man standing next to me and talking to the commissioner. Murdock had said he was a local political fund-raiser. I groaned inwardly because I knew what was coming. A fairy had just won a case before the Supreme Court, allowing him to play for the Red Sox. Always a place where baseball ruled the hearts, if not the minds, of its fans, most of Boston was in an uproar over it.

"I think we'll have to wait and see," the commissioner said diplomatically.

The man looked at him in horror. "Wait and see? Come on, these guys got powers the average Joe can't compete with. How are we going to keep 'em from flying from base to base? The only way to compete will be to just hire more of them until there ain't any normal people playing."

The commissioner seemed to look around to see who was listening. He glanced once at me before saying, "I agree that will probably happen eventually. The only way to fight fire is with fire sometimes." The fund-raiser nodded vigorously. The commissioner placed a companionable hand on his shoulder. "The fey may intrude in areas they don't belong, but God knows we need a better outfield."

"What!" the fund-raiser said, then almost choked on his own laughter. "You're too much, Commissioner."

He smiled indulgently. "Yes, well, I believe dinner should be about ready." The fund-raiser laughed again and followed the commissioner downstairs.

I arrived in the blessedly cool dining room just as everyone was jostling for chairs and ended up sitting between the fund-raiser and a young black woman from a nonprofit arts council. The dinner was served family style, and dishes were passed with the overt politeness of people who did not normally share food. That is, until the banal pleasantries became exhausted, and someone said something more pointed.

I had only half an ear to an arts funding lament, when the woman next to me said, "And, of course, the fey don't help."

"How do you mean?" I asked.

She shrugged as she moved steamed potatoes around on her plate. "It's trendy to be associated with fey art, so fey artists attract money that should rightly be going to struggling organizations."

"But is that the fault of the fey or the people who buy their art?"

"Of course, it's the fey," the fund-raiser interrupted, as he took an oversize bite of pot roast. "They push in everywhere—sports, politics, the arts."

A quick glance around the table made me realize there were no other fey present, unless someone was a druid I couldn't sense. "Isn't that generalizing a bit?" I tried to maintain a neutral tone.

"It's hard not to be annoyed by someone who smears some paint on pointed ears, then rolls on the canvas. That idea is decades old, but it sells simply because a fey is doing it now," said the woman.

"And now they want to be categorized as a minority so that they can force themselves into other neighborhoods and destroy them like that Weird place," said the fund-raiser.

I sipped water from my glass to remain calm. I had grown up not two blocks from the table we were sitting at. "The fey live all over the city, even here in Southie," I said.

"Oh, I don't mean those. They're working folks like you and me. I don't think I've met you before, by the way."

"I'm a friend of Leo's," I said. It always felt odd for me to use Murdock's first name.

"Are you on the force?"

"No. I run an art gallery for druids."

The fund-raiser chuckled. "Everyone's a comedian today."

"I don't think that's funny," the arts woman snapped as she shifted her back to me slightly. That pretty much killed the conversation. As I finished eating, I glanced up at the commissioner. He was nodding as the man on his left spoke, but his eyes were on me. He didn't change his expression for a long moment, then the slightest smile fluttered across his lips. No business on Sunday, my ass, I thought.

After the meal, I lingered in the parlor mentally debating how long I had to remain in the name of politeness. The conversation often veered into complaints about the fey— sometimes subtly, sometimes obviously. I kept quiet, merely nodded at occasional remarks to fend off any actual verbal exchanges. It struck me at how vocal people could be with their animosity when they found themselves in like company. I had done it myself at the Guild, but the level of anger, even hate, in the room surprised me, all the more so considering so many of those in attendance were theoretically civic leaders.

After another hour, I approached the commissioner when he was briefly alone.

"Thank you for dinner. I'm sorry I can't stay longer, but I have an appointment," I said.

"Really?" he said in a way that made me feel instantly guilty. I wanted to say, no, I just can't stand being around your guests anymore, but I refrained. He continued smiling. "Well, it was good to see you under less unfortunate circumstances. Have a good evening."

Maybe from his point of view, I thought. We shook hands, and I made for the door. As I stepped outside, the doorknob pulled out of my hand, and I turned to see Murdock standing on the threshold. "Leaving so soon?"

"Why did you invite me today?"

He glanced over his shoulder, stepped fully out of the house, and closed the door. "What do you mean?"

"You know what I mean. You knew who was going to be here today, but you invited me anyway. I haven't heard so many sophomoric comments about the fey since, well, since I was a sophomore."

He crossed his arms and leaned against the arch of the doorway. "I thought it was important for you to see you're not the only one who dislikes the Guild."

"You could have just told me."

He shrugged. "You wouldn't have heard me."

Annoyed, I looked away up the street. I didn't like being played, but he was right. After a couple of calming breaths, I felt the anger in my chest dissipate. Murdock was one of the few people I knew who could get away with a stunt like this, especially when he was right. "Okay, lesson learned. Happy?"

"Satisfied is more like it. You have a tendency to get incredibly focused, which is a good thing sometimes. But you need to keep it in perspective. The Guild doesn't do what it does just to personally piss you off. It pisses off a lot of people."

"What, so I should ease up on the Guild?"

He gave an exasperated sigh. "No, I'm just trying to tell you that the only way to change the Guild is to work with it, not against it. Though they wouldn't say it quite that way, most of the people inside the house understand that. That's what they work for every day: change everyone can live with."

"Even people who hate me?"

"The way of the world is conflict, Connor. That won't change. You can only change the resolution."

I looked at him curiously. "When'd you become such a philosopher?"

He grinned broadly then. "I keep telling you not to make

things personal. You'll accomplish more and regret less. If that makes me a philosopher, then, hell, kiss my ring."

The air felt slightly damp on my skin and it moved enough to persuade me it would be bearable to walk. I like walking everywhere, but the ongoing heat was getting to be depressing. As I moved northward, the neat, trim row houses of Southie gave way to a section of warehouses that still served as offices and storage. Long blocks empty of even parked cars stretched out, ranks of loading docks closed tightly against the Sunday silence. Crossing over Congress Street and into the Weird proper brought more traffic but no one on the sidewalks. It was like taking a walk from content to depressing.

Murdock's little speech about working with the system got me thinking. It only made sense if both sides were willing. And for the moment, the Guild wasn't playing. So I decided it was time to help them cooperate.

I got on my computer and put in motion a chain of user accounts I had set up on various servers. I watched as one account after another opened and closed, hiding my tracks through the Internet. The accounts jumped from Boston to Texas down into Mexico then over to Japan. From there I traveled to a cybercafe frequented by kids who liked to launch poorly written viruses from Malaysia. The server there was a chaotic mess as a result, but nice camouflage. From there I set a random jump to Morocco, which brought me to the log-in at the Boston Guildhouse. I typed in my user ID and password and hit enter. The screen refreshed and asked me to reenter the password. On the off chance I had mistyped, I entered it again. I got another reenter password and jumped out.

"Damn," I muttered. Rubbing my eyes, I leaned back in my chair. My back door into the system had been closed. Someone had done a sweep and found me, or rather the bogus identity I had set up. Taking a deep breath, I started again, except when I reached the final log-in at the Guild, I used the user ID of a temp account I knew in payroll. It let me in with no problem. No problem except it was a low-level account with no privileges.

I began poking around in the directories but stopped. It would take too long to set up another account. I debated whether to crack macDuin's. The beauty of having worked at the Guild was that I knew the system, how passwords were set, and where to look for them. The downside was that I might be discovered. I had no idea when they had found my account or whether they were monitoring for illegal code more than usual. I knew the folks in the tech department were pretty good. I had taught them a fair amount. I decided to go hunting for a remote access number instead.

Since I was already in, I made my way into the system's password files. It's a lot easier than you would think. I found the file I wanted, then looked for another account with the same dial-up access number. I was only slightly surprised that I didn't find what I was looking for. A little burst of inspiration hit me. I jumped into the system log, scanning for the access number from the first password file. I had to go back a couple of weeks, but I finally found a remote dial-in. There was a routine, obviously permissible, log-in at 1:32 A.M. followed by a logout a little later at 1:48. Two minutes later there was another log-in from a different access number, an access number that was so different, in fact, it didn't belong on the Guildhouse server. But it was there. I smiled broadly. Knowing Meryl, she had wired it herself and was working an untraceable line from the phone company.

"Gotcha" I said softly to the screen. I went back into the password directory, used the illegal phone number as a search criterion, grabbed a copy of Meryl's backdoor password file, and logged out. I then dialed in to a random local university, launched my password cracker program, and set it to work on Meryl's password. Local universities expected extensive CPU activity. They tended to let students mangle the system as long as it didn't slow it down too much or screw up someone's work.

It would take a while for the program to run, so I made coffee. I settled on the futon with Woodbury's *Stone Magic: The Simple Explanation*. It clocked in at over one thousand pages in very tiny type. Despite its density, the author had endeared herself to me with some very simple advice about stones: When all else fails, throw 'em. I made my way through a good chunk of the selenite section. There were an enormous number of uses for the crystal, and it would take some time to follow up on all of them. My computer chimed.

I strolled into the study sipping my coffee and pulled up the chair. The program had cracked the password. It was "HiConnor." I sat stunned as I stared at the screen. Then I laughed so hard, I almost fell out of my chair.

I dialed in to the Guild on Meryl's illicit line. A plain box opened asking for user ID and password, and I typed them in and hit Enter. I knew Meryl's skills well enough to know that once I was in, no one at the Guild would know I was there.

The screen became a black hole, and I was in. A cartoonish white stone gate slowly resolved itself into view with an inscription on the lintel: *Lasciate ogni speranza, voi ch'entrate*. Very cute. The gate faded and a standard Windows desktop appeared. A text box popped up that read "Answer the Phone."

The phone rang, and I jumped. I picked it up.

"You took only slightly less time to get in than I thought you would. I'm impressed," said Meryl.

"Are you enjoying playing with my head?"

"Oh, hold on," she said. I heard what I thought sounded

like a lighter and some muttering. A wave of static welled out of the phone and encased itself around my head. The receiver stuck to my ear, and I couldn't move my hand. Meryl giggled. "*Now* I'm playing with your head. I don't want anyone tracing the call or listening in."

"How did you know I would break in?"

I could hear her take a drag on a cigarette. "Only two kinds of people don't ask about my computer setup when they see it: those that are completely clueless and those that know exactly what it is. They did a cleanup recently, and your account got wiped. I knew it was only a matter of time."

"So now what?"

"So, feel free to come on in. I have a fair idea of where you might want to look, but I've locked down certain areas that are just asking for trouble."

"What if I want to get into those areas?"

"This isn't a negotiation, Connor. I'm protecting my access. You go anywhere I don't want you to, and session ended. Needless to say, this line and the account will disappear after you log out."

"Will the Secretary disavow any knowledge of my activities if I'm caught?" I asked sarcastically.

"The Guild already has," she shot back.

"Why are you doing this?"

I could picture her shrugging. "I like having people in my debt, and this is a big one. If you get caught, I will trash your system so bad, the new box you get to replace it won't work. Have fun and make it quick." She disconnected. The static popped like a soap bubble. I hung up the phone with grudging admiration. I didn't know what game she was playing with me. Whatever it was, I had a feeling she was merrily leading me down the path to hell.

I decided to play by her rules and just get in and get out. She had guessed I'd be interested in macDuin and had left his files wide open. I checked to see what word-processing documents he'd been working on recently and what databases he had accessed. I grabbed copies of anything that looked interesting. He'd also spent a lot of time looking up books in the Guild library. I scooted over to the library log and grabbed whatever searches he had run. Then I entered the open cases database, found the files for the murders and the selenite theft as well, and took those.

I looked for Keeva's files and found them easily. Meryl had locked me out of email, but everything else was open territory. I just skimmed. Keeva was smart enough not to leave a paper or electronic trail, and the slim amount of material in her directories proved it. I didn't even bother opening anything. I was tempted to crack the emails, but truth be told, it was more about ego than a desire to read them. I felt voyeuristic enough already. While I had no compunction about violating macDuin's privacy, I at least owed Keeva some courtesy for her recent intervention. That, plus, I had a sneaking suspicion she was helping more than she wanted me to know.

I sat for a moment, willing myself to think quickly and, if possible, brilliantly. Once I logged out, I'd have a hell of a time getting back in. I would have dearly loved to just sit and do some spell research, but that might show up as a lot of time on the system. Without knowing how well camouflaged Meryl's account was, it might raise questions. I ran a mental checklist like a nervous shopper before leaving the store. Taking a deep breath, I logged out.

I stared for a long moment at the list of files now innocently residing on my hard drive. I'd never stolen files before. I'd used my back door in the system when I occasionally lost access under my regular account or had to go into someone else's files for more information than they were willing to share. But I'd never considered those times as theft. I always had the rationale that I had a right to the information that someone else hadn't quite figured out yet. But I'd never actually taken anything I simply shouldn't have.

Having entered the Guild and wandered around unseen, I wondered if I had realized Meryl's dream and sealed my own fate. If I was going to end up dead, I might as well find out why. I opened the files.

13

I woke to the sound of crunching. Rolling over, I peered into the kitchen through the predawn light. Stinkwort sat on the edge of the counter, an almost empty bag of Oreos lying beside him. I fell back on the bed, rubbing my eyes. "Where the hell have you been?"

"Busy," he said. A moment later, his voice was closer. "I just got a half-dead glow bee about an hour ago."

I opened my eyes again. He hovered over the bed.

"I'm pissed at you, you know, but it's too early to yell."

He shrugged. "Then don't. Come on, get up. The sun's rising."

I swung my feet onto the floor. Stinkwort doffed his tunic and let it flutter to the coffee table. He flew to the window, facing out, his arms and wings spread wide. I stood up and pushed the futon closed. The sun crested the horizon, and I automatically started the greeting ritual. Stinkwort swooped and whirled around me in a complex aerial pattern, his wings occasionally touching my skin as he wound about me. We began to move in our own rhythm, pulling the sun's energy in and reflecting it back and forth between us. A pleasant resonance developed between our bodies, amplified by our movements. It felt very sensual without being sexual. As I relaxed more, I let my body respond, shedding the strictly prescribed motions I normally practiced. My limbs felt fluid, more in tune with the ritual than usual, as Stinkwort swirled and dove, his wings becoming so bright the edges lit white. I lost myself in the sway of the light. I became still, more by feel than any conscious thought. The newly risen sun blazed in my eyes, and it felt glorious.

For a long moment, neither of us spoke. I felt simultaneously exhilarated and spent. I went into the bathroom and came out wearing my bathrobe. Stinkwort had dressed and settled on the coffee table.

"What just happened?" I asked.

He stretched. "Now you know why flits like to greet the sun together."

"I can't believe how good I feel. Even my headache's gone." It was true. The thing in my head caused a chronic low-grade headache. I had become so accustomed to it that I judged my discomfort by its severity instead of whether I was in pain or not.

"It's a flit thing, Connor. We can ride the currents of someone else's essence. When a clan flies together, we generate enormous power. The Danann Sidhe would, too, if they would let it happen, but you can't get two of them to agree on the time of day, never mind surrender to someone else's flow. And, of course, you druids can't fly."

As he spoke, he kept flexing his fingers and stretching his left arm. A sharp white scar wrapped around the forearm vividly displayed the path the knife had taken as he had twisted away from it. "How's the arm?"

He looked down at his hand and waggled his fingers. "It's numb in the morning, and I never seem to have any strength in it. The Lady Briallen did something to my right arm to make it stronger. I'm taking that as a sign the left won't get any better."

"You were foolish to face him alone."

Stinkwort flew away from me and stood on the windowsill looking out. "I don't want to talk about that night. What happened to your eye?"

"I got mugged. Where've you been?"

"I've been looking for that damned belly-crawling *sarf*," he said sharply.

"And?"

He shrugged. "And nothing. I put the word out to the clans, but no one's found anything that feels as *ska* as this bastard. Wherever he is, he's got heavy protection wards. What about you?"

"I stole some files from the Guild."

Stinkwort gave me an indifferent stare over his shoulder. "That's it?"

"It's a failure, Joe. I've resisted doing it because it would mean I couldn't do anything else. I tried to solve this case like I've solved my other cases: by using my abilities. But I couldn't do it, so I stole some files."

He looked back out the window, scanning the docks below. "So, you stole some files from the Guild. What's the big deal?"

"The big deal is I've been reduced to breaking and entering. I can't do anything anymore."

Stinkwort tapped his chin in thought. "Bullshit."

"Don't patronize me, Joe. If I still had my abilities, I would have caught this guy a long time ago. I could have done a scry to find out things. I could have cast a spell to trail him from the first murder scene. I could have chased him the other night and caught him with my bare hands. If I still had my abilities, Tansy would still be alive."

He sat down on the windowsill and crossed his arms. "Connor, I've lived too long to play this game. It's pointless, and you know it. You use what you have. Wishing doesn't make a flit a fairy."

I smiled in spite of myself. It was an old saying mothers used. The obvious implication being, of course, that it's better to be a fairy. I didn't think I'd ever hear a flit say such a thing. I raised my head and saw that Stinkwort had a small, curling sneer on his lip. Some people might think it's better to be something else, but no flit thought it was better to be a fairy.

"That doesn't make me feel any better."

Stinkwort fluttered up. "I have to go, Connor. I've got people waiting."

"I think I know the blood ritual he's using." He hovered for a long moment, just staring at me. I leaned back in the chair and made myself comfortable. "I don't know exactly, but I've found an empowerment spell. The stone used is bloodstone, ironically, and the blood is goat. I imagine fairy blood could be used for greater results."

"Connor, knock it off."

I ignored him. "The spell's only temporary, but it definitely has the ability to increase the strength of the spell-caster's essence. I'm not quite following the substitution of selenite, though. It's mostly used for moon rituals, which we know is related now, and I'm guessing it gives the spell an added boost."

"Connor . . ."

I ignored him and just kept talking. "The problem is the temporary nature. My guess is our guy's dying, and he's trying to save himself. All the other *ska* births have turned up dead. Whatever this guy's doing, he's playing for keeps. He knows he can't keep killing fairies. He's figured out a way to maintain the stolen essence. But from what I've surmised, it takes a lot of power to catalyze the spell and make it permanent. If he had that kind of power, he wouldn't need to do all this in the first place. It's got to be something about the selenite. What do you think?"

"I think you're out of your freakin' skull. You don't guess with blood rituals, Connor. And you don't go off trying to figure them out on your own. I've got enough goin' on without worrying about you."

"Tell me what you know about them."

"Trust me, Connor. You're in no condition to mess with blood rituals. When things go wrong with them, they go seriously wrong. Ask the Lady Briallen. She knows."

"I've already asked. She said no."

Stinkwort flew straight up with his hands held out against me. "If she won't tell you, I sure as hell won't. Keep out of it, Connor. Let the Guild handle it."

"Joe, it's not like I'm going to perform the ritual. I'm just trying to figure it out."

"Then do it the sane way. We both got his scent that night. Help me search that way."

I gestured toward the bruise on my face. "I can't smell a damned thing."

He stared down at me. "Fine. I'm going to find this guy before you get hurt." He vanished.

"Well, that went well," I said to the empty room.

I let my head roll against the back of the armchair and stared at the ceiling. I could understand Stinkwort's concern. Plenty of spells could be done without innate ability. Even humans could activate an enchantment with the proper tools. The four elements of Air, Fire, Water, and Earth could generate a flow of essence from their natural surroundings. Even chanting under the right circumstances could be done with decent results if the environment were prepared. The power of words could bend ambient essence even to a novice's command. Problems cropped up when someone did something beyond their ability, or lack thereof. It's pretty easy to snuff out a candle if you need to. It's another thing entirely if you've accidentally caused a bonfire.

No matter what the ritual, spell, or incantation, blood was like gasoline. One of the first things you learn on the druidic path is don't mess with blood. The injunction is strictly enforced. Even promising students can find themselves shunned by mentors for mild transgressions. After over twenty years of study, I had still not been initiated into the workings of blood. At the rate I was going, I wasn't ever likely to be.

I had found the blood ritual in the late evening in an old poem tucked in among folklore from Eastern Europe. Either the author had thought it inconsequential, or she had missed editing it out. It gave me enough to figure out what it could do. If you read enough spells, you tend to recognize a True one from neopagan chuckles.

But the big payoff of the night came when I went looking at macDuin's files. The name 'Dealle S.' had popped up in a list of contacts relating to the selenite theft the previous fall. MacDuin had made the entry. An 'S' followed by a period was a typical Guild abbreviation for sidhe, and Dealle was the same as the name of the woman Murdock had been trying to contact. In a world where people went by their first names unless they were royalty, the odds of two people having the same name were high. I was willing to bet good money that the odds of two people having the same name connected to two different Guild cases and macDuin were low. I still hadn't heard from Germany about the elf/fairy hybrid named Gethin, but Dealle and her son Corcan were looking pretty interesting now.

I took my time showering and getting dressed. I didn't want to show up at Dealle's house so early she would be angry, but not so late that she would be gone again. I didn't have to check Murdock's file to know he had tried her house at different times of day. He had even done the before-work check like I was about to. If she wasn't home, I had nothing else to do but sit on her porch until she returned.

Dealle Sidhe lived in South Boston, but near enough to the Weird to keep it cheap. I made my way down A Street until I came to Second. The street had a multiple personality disorder. Buildings of every conceivable type had been put up as though the neighborhood couldn't decide what it wanted to be. Blank-faced wooden houses sat next to small warehouses with the odd chunk of row house here and there. Most of them looked abandoned, but the closed-up feel had more to do with protection than emptiness. People did live there, people desperate for a sense of security but without enough money to buy it. It was safer than the Weird, but a far cry from the safer sections of South Boston. Windblown newspapers cluttered doorways instead of white petunias.

Dealle Sidhe's address turned out to be a wooden triple-decker townhouse. A bay window marked the living room, and a small porch fronted on the street. The upper windows were boarded. At one time, the house had been white, but it had long since gone gray, the paint peeling in sheets. A wire fence of windowpane mesh enclosed the five-foot patch of front yard.

As I opened the gate, it scraped against the chipped concrete sidewalk. At the base of the steps sat a business card. I picked it up. Murdock's. I was about to mount the steps when I noticed a second card in the grass just off the walk. A third had blown against the side fence. I looked down at the card again. No surprise she hadn't called. Looking up at the house, I wondered if she even lived here anymore. I decided to try the door, or at least leave the card more securely.

I mounted the steps. No sound came from the house. No one was home. No one at all. Murdock's file had not mentioned if Dealle had a job. It seemed incredible that four visits by two investigators had come up empty. I reached A Street again and turned the corner. In my peripheral vision, I noticed something white flutter into the gutter. I took another step and paused, looking up and down the street. A mild disorientation skittered over me, but A Street looked as it always did. I resumed walking. I went another block before abruptly turning and retracing my steps to where I had first stopped. Stooping, I picked up Murdock's card where I had dropped it. I looked down Second Street and smiled.

I returned to Dealle's house and stood at the gate. I tried to take a deep breath through my nose, but I still had too much congestion to sense anything. I looked at Murdock's card and walked up to the steps again. No sound came from the house. No one was home. No one at all. This time I had gone only a few houses away before I realized I had left the porch. Murdock's card was still in my hand. I went back.

I stared intently at the front of the house. Nothing seemed out of the ordinary. Some fey put small signs for those who could see, a few ogham runes scratched into the doorjamb that could be easily overlooked or perhaps herbs hanging over the door a certain way. I had even seen joke signs planted on lawns that read BEWARE OF THE TROLL. But Dealle's house looked nondescript by any of those measures. It wasn't until my eyes had passed by the woven rush doormat several times that I noticed it didn't sit quite level on the ground. A thin dark line ran along the whole front edge of the mat. I was willing to bet it was a smoothly cut stone, perfect to charge as a ward. Dealle didn't want visitors. Whether it was paranoia or privacy, I was determined to find out.

The spell was elegant and subtle. Rather than bluntly repelling any intrusions, it answered a question anyone approaching would be wondering—was anyone home? Unless someone had been specifically invited, the answer was no, and to avoid any persistent knocking, the ward deflected visitors calmly on their way. Since it responded to the intent of someone approaching, I changed my intent. My question was no longer was anyone home? I assumed that. Now I had to resist the compulsion to leave.

I took a deep breath and strode to the door. I made it all the way to the mat before I felt the urge to run. I pressed forward, reached out my hand, and grasped the handle of the storm door. Over and over, the thought that no one was home beat against my mind. I held on to the door and the knowledge that Dealle was inside. Sweat broke out on my forehead as I lifted my hand to knock. I could feel nausea beginning to well up from the strain of resisting. I desperately wanted to run, but I brought my fist down firmly and banged against the door. It sounded unconscionably loud. No one answered. I shoved the thought that no one was home out of my head. I banged again and again, keeping my eyes focused on my fist around the handle. I stopped wondering if she were home, stopped caring even. The only thing that mattered was that I kept bringing my fist down.

The door opened. I almost stumbled from the release of pressure as the ward deactivated. Inside the dim hall, I could see a small figure through the cloudy glass of the storm door. I let go of the door handle and flexed my fingers to relieve the cramping. The knuckles on my other hand were bright red. At least they weren't bleeding.

"Dealle Sidhe?" I managed to say. I was practically hyperventilating.

"Yes," she said. Her voice had a soft, musical quality.

"My name is Connor Grey. I used to work for the Guild. I'm helping out the police with a case. Can I speak with you for a few minutes?"

I still couldn't see her face clearly. Without speaking, she opened the door and held it for me to enter. I stepped into the front hall. Dealle closed the door and gestured toward the parlor to the left. She was a small woman, dressed in a simple white gown, her long brunette hair tied back loosely. She seemed aged, unusual for a fairy, her face lined with worry. In the dimly lit room, her wings gave off a soft pearlescent glow as they undulated in the small draft of my passing.

"I will bring some refreshments," she said.

"That's not necessary."

She paused. "Please allow me. It will be my apology for the door," she said softly.

Four large armchairs sat in a loose circle before the fireplace. The room had a Victorian air to it, overstuffed and cluttered, but impeccably clean. Little animal figurines crowded onto several tables interspersed with clocks and candlesticks and finely wrought boxes in metal and wood. An old air conditioner labored in the side window, cooling the air enough that if you didn't move too quickly, it was comfortable. I sat in one of the chairs. I could feel a vague buzz across the back of my head. Dealle evidently had lots of spells simmering about the house.

She returned with six small crystal glasses on a tray that she placed on the butler's table in the center of the chair grouping. Primly, she sat opposite me.

"Welcome to my home." She leaned forward and picked up the glass with the water in it.

I couldn't resist smiling as I picked up the matching glass of water. She was treating me like a formal guest in the old tradition. In Boston, it was saved for special occasions. Since Convergence, it denoted a sign of class in better homes.

I downed the water. "Thank you, that was very refreshing."

She returned her own empty glass to the tray and picked up the next one with mead in it. I leaned forward and did the same.

"I hope you didn't have too much trouble finding the house." She sipped the mead more slowly than the water.

"No, it was quite easy." We both took a moment to look around. A little thrill of discovery ran over me when I noticed a picture on the mantel. It was of a man with an oddly angular face, almond-shaped eyes and completely bald. Even though it was just a head shot, he looked big. He also looked a lot like Shay's description. I wished my sinuses were clear so I could sense his essence in the house. "This room is lovely, by the way. You must spend a lot of time here."

"Yes, I do. The streets are not safe." She replaced the empty mead glass and picked up the whiskey. She raised the glass. "*Slainte.*"

"To your health as well," I said and sipped the whiskey. Jameson's. Gods love the Irish.

"How may I help you?" Dealle asked.

"I'd like to ask you about your son."

Her eyes went down to her glass. "Has he caused some trouble?"

Well, that answered whether he was alive. "Is he at home?"

She shook her head. "No, he's at school. Well, we call it school. It's more of an institution."

"Is he ill?"

Her eyes met mine. The old fey make unnerving eye contact. They have a stillness and patience about them that comes with unimaginable age. Dealle's eyes had a flicker of defensiveness behind them as well. "I believe the phrase current these days is 'mentally challenged.' I suppose that's an improvement. A couple of decades ago, they officially called him a moron."

"Is his father here?"

She did look away then. "His father is . . . German. I have not seen or heard from him in years."

"Dealle, I don't mean to embarrass you, but by German, do you mean elfin?"

She nodded. "When I discovered I was with child, I was ecstatic. I had never had a child. I knew there were risks involved for a child of an elf and a fairy, but I was willing to take them. When Corcan was born, the way he is, his father left."

"How long has he been hospitalized?"

"He's not. It's a day program, five days a week at the Children's Institute near Day Boulevard. He's functional, but needs supervision. They teach him basic skills, and he gets to play with other children."

"Children? He's an adult about fifty years old, isn't he?"

She smiled coldly. "What's fifty years to me but a flicker of time? He's a child and has the mind of a child."

"Does he ever go out alone?"

"Just to and from school."

"Never any other time? Not at night, maybe, after you've gone to sleep?"

She hesitated an awfully long time. "No." She gestured toward the front door. "There is more than one ward in this house." Since she was being so forthcoming, I decided not to point out that I had overcome one of her wards. Someone with ability would have an even easier time.

"Has his behavior changed recently?"

"Why are you here, Connor Grey?"

She caught me being sloppy. I hadn't planned the interview out. I was hoping I would show up, recognize the killer's essence, and call Murdock. As it was, I couldn't very well say to this woman I thought her son was a psycho killer with absolutely no evidence. "I'm doing background research into cross-species progeny. It may be connected to a case I'm working. If I could have a better understanding of the behavior of such individuals, it might be predictive of future behavior."

She leaned farther back in her chair. "What kind of behavior?"

"Given my profession, it shouldn't surprise you I'm interested in aggression. Specifically, aggression as it relates to fey abilities."

"My son has hurt no one." I didn't like the harder tone her voice was taking. I was clearly treading on mother-bear territory.

"I didn't say that, Dealle. But since you've brought it up, what can you tell me about Corcan's abilities?"

She shrugged. "I've been told he has a strong essence, but he doesn't understand that. When he's angry or upset, rooms tend to get a little overturned. The Institute is working on that. He's never hurt anyone."

"May I see his room?"

The question startled her, and she didn't immediately respond. "I suppose. Why?"

I shrugged. "It's nothing. I'd just like to see the environment he spends time in."

She rose from her chair and led me back into the hall. Corcan's room was the first bedroom on the left. A large bed took up most of the floor space. It had a bright red comforter with racing cars on it. A straight-backed wooden chair stood against the wall by the door and beneath the window on the opposite side was a small chest of drawers. The walls were vibrant yellow and white painted in Celtic spirals. Centered on each wall, up near the ceiling, pentagrams had been stenciled in blue. They were later additions. The spirals flowed behind them.

I pointed. "Whose pentagrams are those?"

"They help him focus when he's upset. He doesn't understand it has to do with ability. We're teaching him how to channel his aggression into calmness. It didn't seem to work at first, but his caregiver kept adding pentagrams. Now there is one wherever he turns. It seems to help."

I nodded and walked to the chest of drawers. Resting my hand lightly on a handle, I looked at Dealle. "May I?" Annoyance crossed her face, but she nodded. I went through each drawer. The top held some nonsense toys hidden beneath several pairs of underwear. The next drawer held shirts and the bottom, pants. All of it was neatly folded. I made sure not to disturb anything.

I closed the last drawer and opened the closet without asking this time. More clothing hung neatly, and a few pairs of shoes lined up perfectly against the back wall. The shelf across the top held sweaters. Dealle obviously kept close tabs on her son. No hearts in bottles. I didn't think there would be.

"Are there any other places your son might keep things?" I asked.

She shook her head. "He's not allowed in the living room. Mostly he plays in here, watches TV in the kitchen, or plays in the yard."

"May I see the yard?"

She led me farther down the hall to the kitchen and pointed at the back door. I looked out the multi-paned window to see a tiny, blacktopped space with a basketball hoop. A couple of balls sat on the ground, and a bicycle was chained to the back fence. Nothing out of the ordinary. No shed to hide things. No turf to bury things. I could feel another nasty buzz at the base of my skull. Another ward must be hidden under the back doormat.

I looked around the kitchen. Again nothing unusual. The place hadn't seen a remodeling in fifty years. White chunky wooden cabinets with metal drawer pulls. Glass-fronted upper cabinets with plates, cups, and bowls all neatly stacked on the shelves. Next to the hallway entrance was a closed door.

"Do you have a basement?"

"He doesn't go down there. He's afraid of the dark."

We stood uncomfortably in the cool white of the overhead fluorescent light. Nothing fit. Corcan didn't sound like serial killer material, but there had to be a reason Dealle Sidhe's name was in macDuin's files. "Dealle, why did the Guild contact you last fall?"

She looked at me curiously. "They didn't. I contacted them." She pulled out a kitchen chair and sat down. "I thought they could help."

That took me by surprise. "With what?"

She hugged herself as an old anxiety creased her face. "Corky didn't come home from school on time one day. When he didn't show up by nightfall, I went looking for him but couldn't find him. I called the police and the Guild. Neither was particularly helpful. It didn't matter anyway. Corky showed up the next day in front of the house. He was scared and confused. He had taken a wrong turn and got lost."

"Was there any change in his behavior after that?"

She shrugged. "Nothing surprising. He was afraid to go out by himself for a while."

"And when was this exactly?"

"Last September. I don't remember the date. It was the last week of the month."

I nodded. The selenite stones had gone missing shortly before that. Not to mention that Belgor's strange customer had shown up around then, too. The stones aspect of the case was starting to tie together. "You seem quite adept with wards, Dealle. Do you ever work with selenite?"

Her eyes narrowed at me. "It's an old stone to work with. I don't care much for the power of the Moon. It's the work of secrets and sunderings."

Personally, I couldn't argue with her. Moon-work was mostly women's. I never had much success with it myself. Give me the Sun and a sharp edge any day.

"It's just a Power. Its use can be positive or negative depending on the user. You know that."

She smiled thinly. "I'm a bit older than you, Connor Grey. I lived in the True Land before we were thrust into this sickened place. Trust me. The Moon is no friend. The Light of Day reveals all."

Her phrasing gave me pause. The True Land was how elves, not fairies, referred to their lost home. I suppose given her choice of mate, it shouldn't be surprising. I had a hunch Dealle was an elf sympathizer, as in superior to the rest of us, we-should-rule-the-world kind of way. "And the True Land remains the True Land, beneath the Light of Day/Take me back to the True Land, and out of the World of Decay," I recited. It was part of an old ballad from World War II that the fey of Germany sang.

Bingo. Dealle's eyebrows shot up. "I didn't think someone so young would know that song."

I shrugged. "I have an interest in history."

She sighed with resignation. "Yes, it is history. I was happy in a very sad time, but this is the world we live in now. Truths were told, and mistakes were made. And love lost. Some of my old acquaintances still fight for Faerie. I only have time for Corcan now."

"I didn't mean to bring up painful memories." I didn't know what to say. She had that exhausted tone that people have when they've lost their ideals.

"You were born here. You know nothing," she said, her voice bitter. She stood and walked out of the kitchen. I hesitated before following her down the hall to where she held the front door open. I had no authority to insist on staying.

"I'll be the judge of my memories," she said.

I bowed slightly. "Of course. Thank you, Dealle. You've been helpful."

As I walked down the front steps, she called my name, and I turned. "My son's a good boy. You remember that."

I didn't say anything, but smiled and nodded. She closed the door. I could feel a little buffer of air tickle my face as the ward reactivated.

I shoved my hands deep into my pants pockets as I strode up the street. I had gone to the house with the hope of finding a killer, with the added bonus of embarrassing macDuin for overlooking evidence in his own files. Instead, I found a mentally challenged man without the skills to find his way home, never mind slaughter six people.

Corcan "Corky" Sidhe had vanished for a night about when the selenite stones were stolen. Given that the Guild hadn't officially investigated his disappearance, macDuin's note at the time practically confirmed there must be some connection. What I couldn't figure out was why Dealle's name was in the file if no one had bothered to follow up on it. And why macDuin in particular hadn't followed up made that even more interesting.

For all her willingness to answer questions, Dealle made me uncomfortable. Fairies and elves always made a toxic mix, and Dealle obviously hadn't let go of all her political sympathies. And she knew stone work.

An old man walking toward me glanced uncertainly away as I stopped short on the sidewalk. MacDuin had been an elf sympathizer during the War, too. It was possible he knew Dealle from that time. And if he knew Dealle, he probably knew about her son. Stinkwort had said once that there was no blood on macDuin's hands. I wondered if macDuin or someone he knew was somehow controlling Corcan. But the level of Power required was significant, and I didn't think macDuin had it in him. Still, the reduced mental capacity might make it feasible, especially if macDuin had found a way to augment his abilities.

I started walking again. The frustrating part was motive. If macDuin was connected to the murders, what could he hope to gain? A cold thought occurred to me. Tiarnach Ruadan, the father of the latest victim, was a war hero on the front lines for the last push into Berlin. Although the humans had reconciled their differences decades ago, relations between elves and fairies had only begun to approach resolution at the Fey Summit. Could macDuin be seeking some kind of delayed revenge?

If the idea that someone would want to disrupt the peace process weren't so horrible, I would have laughed at myself. But if enough paranoid people believed something, it didn't take too long for them to start their own conspiracy. And if macDuin had come to the conclusion that working within the system wasn't changing anything, maybe he had nothing left to lose.

14

Tuesday morning I returned to my apartment without the usual cleansing feeling I get from my five-mile run. Instead of doing my normal route around the old fort, I had spent much of the time running through the Weird and passing the murder sites. The experience was both frustrating and strange. I tried to find some pattern to the locations, some unifying characteristic that would clue me in to where the killer might pick next. A simple glance at a map demonstrated no pattern other than the general neighborhood and opportunity. All the deaths had occurred in places with only the similarity of isolation. Not much help—most people try to keep out of sight when they are gutting someone.

Running from empty, trash-filled alleys into the brash activity of the Avenue made the whole experience surreal. Midsummer activities were coming into full swing, with all manner of people roaming the main streets, laughing and singing. I had to wonder if they were blissfully unaware of the killer in their midst, coldly indifferent, or merely unconcerned.

As I sat at my computer, I reviewed the evidence again. Contrary to my conversation with Stinkwort, I wasn't all that sure I had the stone ritual nailed. I had a strong hint at best, but the effects of substituting different types of stone remained a mystery, to say nothing of whatever incantation might be involved. Thinking of the stones made me realize I hadn't heard from Meryl. I took that as a sign she was keeping her word not to disclose their mysterious return to the Guild until Thursday.

I looked back at the case files. All the evidence had been consistent until the last death. The killer had left dirt in the chest cavity of the most recent victim. Or, more precisely, sand. Clean, sterile sand according to the analysis. I had an uncomfortable tactile memory of my hand covered with sand grit and blood.

I opened the file on Ragnell, the first victim. The P.D. had taken its time with tests because Ragnell's clothes were so dirty. He had been sleeping on the street. He couldn't have charged much for his services unless the client was into unwashed clothes. I had no delusions that such people didn't exist. Murdock had appended an undated forensics report. It read like a catalog of debris: cat and dog hair, multiple human hairs from different people, food particles, bits of lavender, hawthorn leaves, horehound, cloves, unidentifiable ash, and good old marijuana stems.

The hawthorn leaves didn't surprise me. The tree was sacred to fairies, and many of the fey carried leaves as protection or touchstones. The lavender, clove, and dope didn't surprise me either. Even humans, mostly of the alternative music bent, would have them these days. But the horehound struck me as odd. It was used mainly as a curative for coughs and colds. I skimmed back through the rest of the report, but I didn't see any indication that Ragnell was sick.

A red flag jumped out at me. The medical examiner had made a note that ash had been on the body, not just the clothes, but the body itself. Some of it was near the chest wound. I sent Murdock an email to see if he could find out if any herbs were in the wound. I didn't think I was wrong though. I had no doubt they were on the body, at least in charred remains. Ingested in certain forms, horehound could be used for colds. But burning it in conjunction with hawthorn leaves was a restorative of spirits. That fit neatly with my theory about the killer trying to heal himself.

I scrolled through the forensic reports of the other victims. My momentary elation began to fade. No herbs showed up in the other cases. The only odd thing about Pach, the second victim, besides the gaping hole in his chest, were a couple of fresh minor burn marks. No ash residue. There were no indications of anything like herbs or ashes on the third victim. It had been raining that night, and the body, like all the others, was naked. Some evidence had probably been lost. And then the fourth victim just had the sand.

I made a list of one to four on a piece of scrap paper and wrote the anomalies for each victim: ash, minor burns, nothing, and sand. The first two items obvious were connected by fire, but that left me with two more unrelated items. I looked back at Gamelyn, the third victim, and read through the file again slowly. Nothing. I stared at the crime scene photos.

I remembered that my senses were in overdrive that night. Because of the rain, everything had smelled more intensely. It was how I had caught Tansy's essence even over the stench of the dumpster. That night had been the last time it had rained in two weeks. Weather forecasters, the meteorologist kind, had remarked that every storm front in the last two weeks had skittered south toward Cape Cod without touching the Boston metro area. Strange for the region, especially this time of year. At number three on my list, I wrote the word "rain" next to the nothing.

Some people get goose-bumps when they realize something exciting. Me, I get a rush of adrenaline. As I looked at my list, I got one huge burst. It wasn't about the ash. Ash was just the residue when incense is burned. Incense is burned to invoke the power of Air. Another check of Ragnell's scene photo revealed a candle stub in plain sight. Dripping wax could burn skin. Candles are lit to invoke the power of Fire. Gamelyn was killed on a rainy night. That everything at the scene was wet would have obscured the fact if Water had been present in the ritual. And then there was the sand at the last scene. Earth. I knew now that only one more murder waited to occur in two days' time. A new moon on Midsummer's Eve would complete the lunar cycle of the ritual. While many people work with the four natural elements, a fifth element can be included, and I was sure it was about to be invoked: Spirit, which some call Essence.

Air, Fire, Water, Earth, and Spirit. The five primal elements of Power. The five points of invocation of every ritual invoked with a pentagram. With his surprising room decorations, Corcan Sidhe was back in the picture.

In reviewing macDuin's files, I had come across numerous library searches for old grimoires. I had reprints of some of them in my study, but none made any connection for me. I spun in my chair and called Meryl. She answered on the first ring.

"Hi, Meryl. I'm in my apartment. I feel safe here because the Guild put in protection wards."

I listened to several moments of nonresponse while I hoped Meryl got the message.

"I'm busy now. I'll call you tomorrow." She hung up. I quickly turned off the ringer. Anxiously, I stared at the caller ID on the receiver. The display changed from idle mode to indicate someone was calling from a masked phone number. I put the receiver to my ear and hit the on button. A familiar sensation of static bristled out of the phone and surrounded my head.

"So you think your apartment's bugged?" she said.

"Just a precaution. I'm getting paranoid."

She sighed. "Hang on." I heard her drop her phone, papers rustling, the crash of something falling followed by cursing—the vulgar kind—then some typing, some tapping, a couple of beeping tones and, finally, an ear-piercing wave of static.

Meryl got back on the line. "Oh, okay. You're cool. As far as I can tell, your line's clean."

"I need you to do something for me."

She sighed so heavily, I thought I could feel a ripple in the envelope of static. I was starting to get used to the feeling. "You really don't know when to stop, do you?"

I grinned. "No. I get that a lot. I don't need anything that will jeopardize your position. MacDuin was researching books. Two in particular I know aren't available outside the Guildhouse. One is a collection of manuscript fragments of the writings of the druid Cathbad. The other is something called *The Brown Book of Cenchos*."

She laughed. "That's a joke, Connor. It's a book of nonsensical spells attributed to the Fomorians. They call it the Brown Book because it's supposedly bound with the tanned skin of a Tuatha de Danann king. Cenchos is the mythical bogeyman of the Sidhe. Legend has it that he twisted the de Dananns he captured and founded the Unseelie Court. He was defeated by being spell-bound into the sea with his followers."

"What makes the spells nonsensical?"

"They mix things up, use herbs and stones in ways that make no sense. Plus, they're written in what is supposedly Fomorian, which apparently sounds like a garbage disposal backing up."

"I still need to know if any of its spells have to do with blood, selenite, and pentagrams."

"You're assuming I can read Fomorian."

"I've never underestimated you, Meryl."

She snickered. I read the call numbers off to her. "I'll call your cell phone if I find anything."

"Wait, before you go, I wanted to ask you why mac-Duin's interview about the selenite theft isn't in the file."

"Oh, that's easy. He wasn't here. He was on leave."

"Meryl, he was here. He did these library searches the week of the theft, and if I'm reading these codes right, he entered several storerooms in the Guild basement, including the one where the stones were."

"Hold on." I could hear her typing for several moments, then the sound of a chair being pushed back. Several papers were shuffled around. "Nope. I was right. There are several references to preparing reports for when he came back. He was in Germany. He was gone about a month and mad as hell about the stones when he came back."

I got a cold feeling in the pit of my stomach. "Meryl, listen to me carefully. I think macDuin may be involved in the murders. I'm finding several connections, and if he said he was in Germany, I think he's lying. I need that spell info, but don't let anyone know what you're doing. Don't leave a trail of any kind. And whatever you do, don't tell macDuin you found the stones."

"I'll give you this, Grey, you keep life interesting." The shield around my head evaporated as she disconnected.

MacDuin had firmly moved onto my suspect list. Whatever he was up to, he clearly was intimately involved. I cursed to myself for being an idiot. I should have realized weeks ago that I had a security breach in my own apartment. Someone from macDuin's office routinely recharged my protection wards. Any one of them could be a recording stone. Since I didn't have any ability to test whether any of the wards were actually recorders, I couldn't just

toss them all. I did need the ones that were actually protecting the place.

In a few minutes, I had a knapsack packed with some
clothes, a disc with the Guild files on it, and my cell phone
charger. Standing in the middle of the living room, I tried
to think of anything else that should be tossed. I had blabbed
out loud to Stinkwort about the stolen files. I copied the case
files onto another disc, then deleted them from my hard
drive. I knew they were still on the drive like ghosts in the
machine, but I didn't have time for a deeper scrub. At least
it would slow someone down. The only other necessary
item was my leather jacket—I never traveled without it. I
grabbed the jacket and hit the street.

As I left the building, I found my disability check from
the Guild in the mail. I didn't know whether to take it as a
sign of irony or farce. In either case, I needed the cash. I
stopped at the Nameless to cash it. There wasn't a bank or
an ATM anywhere in the Weird, but the Nameless took
even my personal checks. They wouldn't hesitate to take
the Guild's. I grabbed a sandwich while I was there and
headed out to Congress Street.

I could hole up in some café and plan my course of action, but the Weird was getting a little too chaotic for me to
concentrate. People were already filling the side streets
with Midsummer revelry. Besides, if anyone came looking
for me, that was where they'd expect me to be.

Meeting Corcan Sidhe for myself seemed as good an idea
as any. The Children's Institute in Southie was an easy hike.
I took the same basic route I had taken home from Murdock's the other day. Once I had passed into the more genteel
section of the neighborhood, the only signs of Midsummer
celebration were tasteful wreaths on the doors. Holly and
oak, the emblems of the Wood Kings, graced the doors of
both fey and human alike. Everybody likes a fun holiday.

The Children's Institute had started out life in the last
century as something called the Idiot Asylum. Depending

on how delicate your sensibilities were, you thought that was either quaint or barbaric. Over time, it was abandoned, then reopened years later as the Children's Institute, where once again "mentally challenged" individuals found treatment. Some of its buildings were torn down until what had once taken up the entire block bordered by M and N Streets between Eighth and Ninth was now a small cluster of squat ugly brownstone buildings that huddled on the Ninth Street side. Neighborhood kids still called it the Idiot Asylum.

I cut between two barracks-like buildings into the remnants of an old quad in front of the administration building. Children played on a pathetic patch of lawn, more crabgrass than turf. The trees and shrubs scattered here and there were bedraggled and sad, like someone had stepped on them, and they had desperately tried to upright themselves. A few kids sat in circles on the ground, while others held hands and played running games I didn't recognize. They looked awkward, everyone a bit off-balance and moving in slow-motion. It took me half a moment to realize that staff members were among them, wearing street clothes instead of the traditional whites. I had almost reached the steps to the main building when I heard a deep, distinctly adult, laugh.

To my left, two people stood off by themselves. A woman who apparently was staff tossed a ball back and forth with a large, ungainly man. The woman had her back to me, her dark hair falling loosely and brushing the collar of a simple white T-shirt on her petite frame. The misshapen elf-like man with her wore a sloppy gray sweatshirt and worn cotton workman's pants. His head was as smooth as an eggshell. I recognized him from the photograph in his mother's living room. Corcan Sidhe ran wildly, clutching clumsily after the ball. A huge grin broke on his face when he caught it and threw it back.

The woman laughed as she caught it, turning enough to the side for me to catch a glimpse of her face. I had one of those strange moments when I'm surprised but not surprised at the same time. I strolled over. "Hello, Shay."

Shay looked at me, the smile on his face dying instantly. He tossed the ball hard over Corcan's head, and the big man lumbered after it. Shay crossed his arms across his chest. "Couldn't this wait until I got home?"

"I didn't know you worked here."

"I volunteer. And you could have asked the goon who's been following me all week." He gestured toward the side street visible between two buildings. Bar Murdock's pasty Honda sat at the curb across the street.

I glanced over at Corcan. He rustled through the bushes like some mysterious beast in a jungle film. I could see the ball on the other side, but he had not figured out where it was yet. "Let's talk."

We crossed to a nearby bench and sat down. In the midst of his search, Corcan became distracted by a butterfly and chased after it. "What are you doing here, Shay?"

"I just told you, I volunteer." I could tell by the anger that swept across Shay's face that I was having trouble hiding my skepticism. "What? You think because men pay me to take off my clothes I don't care about things like this?"

"You have to admit, Shay, the hooker with a heart of gold is kind of cliché."

He stared intently at me. "Let me ask you something, Connor. If you met me here first and found out what I do at night later, would you think of me as a charity volunteer who occasionally gets paid to satisfy someone's sexual needs or would you think of me simply as a prostitute?"

I shrugged. "Fine. You're more than a prostitute. I get the point."

"No, you don't. If a civic leader is exposed as a john, would you think of him as simply a john or does he remain a civic leader?"

I sighed and looked over at Corcan. He found the ball and was making his way back to us. "A civic leader."

"Then you can shove your surprise and your clichés."

He did have a point. People who operate on the fringes of society do get perceived as nothing more than what they do. It's easier to forget that a drug dealer has a family or that a prostitute has a life. It doesn't always make them better people, but it reminds you that they are people.

"I really am sorry about Robin, Shay." And I was. We had hardly met under the most congenial circumstances, but he was just a kid.

Shay's anger subsided a bit. "Thanks. He didn't have many friends. I had him cremated on Saturday."

"Shay, I have to ask you, the day Murdock and I came by to ask Robin to help, you two were arguing. Why?"

Shay shifted uncomfortably on the bench. "We had a complicated relationship. Robin thought I was leaving him."

"Were you?"

"No!" he said forcefully. "He only thought that because . . . because there's something wrong with me. I have blackouts. He thinks—thought—I was lying to cover up an affair."

"Have you seen a doctor?"

He gave me an exasperated look. "I don't exactly have insurance, Connor. The episodes started the end of last year and have been worse recently. I'm hoping they'll just go away. I don't have much other choice."

I can imagine how he felt. At least the Guild still picked up the tab on my health care. I couldn't afford it otherwise. "I'm sorry. You have a lot going on."

He shrugged. "Yeah, well, life does that to you."

Corcan came running back. From a few feet away, he tossed the ball, and it dribbled to our feet. Shay picked it up and tossed it again. Corcan didn't turn, but looked at me curiously. "Is this a new friend, Shay-shay?"

Shay took a long moment before deciding to answer him. "Say hello to Connor, Corky."

The big man trotted forward and extended a big meaty

hand. I fought the desire to pull away, not wanting to touch him. I did shake his hand though, inhaling so sharply my nostrils must have closed. I still couldn't smell a damned thing. "Hello, Connor. Are you taking us to the Castle?" He spoke as though his tongue were too thick for his mouth.

"No, Corky," said Shay. "I told you that's the day after tomorrow. Two more days. Go get the ball, honey." He ambled off like a big bald retriever.

"We're going to watch the Midsummer fireworks from Castle Island," Shay said.

"How long have you known him?"

"Since last summer. He's afraid of most people, but he likes me. The staff thinks it's because I'm male but look female. On a certain level, he relates his own condition to me."

"He looks a lot like the police sketch you helped develop."

Shay's chin shrank back in surprise. He watched Corky running around for a moment before answering. "No. He doesn't. Connor, look at that group of kids over there." He pointed over my shoulder to a small group holding hands and dancing. They all had vaguely similar features that marked them with Down's syndrome.

I looked back at Shay. "Your point?"

"Now, without looking back, tell me their ages and how they look different from each other."

I didn't speak. The urge to look again was compelling.

"Let me help you," said Shay. "At a glance, only three of those kids have Down's, though I'm betting you think they all do. Two of them have a different genetic physical retardation. Their ages range over fifteen years. One of the two with thick sideburns is actually female. Now, before I knock you over the head, what the hell do you think you're implying about Corky?"

I'll give this to Shay. I had a foot and half in height and more than fifty pounds in weight on him, and the kid still had the balls to threaten me physically. It didn't mean I was

amused. "Look, Shay, the only thing keeping you out of
jail at this point is the fact that I haven't put in a call to
Murdock, so knock off the attitude. Now, tell me about the
pentagrams." He crossed his arms again and threw himself
back against the bench.

He looked at me suspiciously. "Corky's pentagrams?
They're for meditation." He considered for a moment and
nodded. "I added them one at a time. The first one was
about a month ago." A chalky pallor swept over his face.
"Oh my God, Connor! It's not what you think."

"What do I think?"

"Corky wouldn't hurt anyone. I just showed him how to
calm himself when he was upset. I don't have any fey
ability—I couldn't even get aromatherapy to work on Robin.
Corky doesn't even go out at night! He's afraid of the dark!"

"You might have activated something, Shay. Cross-
species children have all kinds of mutations. You might not
have been calming him."

Shay's hands flew to his mouth as tears sprang to his eyes.
"No. It can't be. Tell me Robin isn't dead because of me!"

I couldn't help myself. I reached out and put my hand
on his shoulder to reassure him. "I'm not going to lie to
you, Shay. I don't know."

"What's the matter, Shay-shay?' Corky said, popping
up in front of us. His face looked stricken.

Shay brushed the tears off his own face. "It's nothing,
Corky. Something got in my eyes."

The big man grabbed his hand. "Let's go to the Castle.
That will make your eyes better."

Shay forced himself to smile. "Thursday. We'll go then.
Okay, Cork?"

Corky pouted. "Okay."

He let Corky pull him off the bench, and as Corky led
him away, Shay looked back at me, hurt and confusion flickering in his eyes.

Back on Ninth Street, I slipped into a cab and asked the driver to take me to Avalon Memorial. Fresh cash in my pocket tended to make me lazy. I had to see Gillen Yor. If anyone knew the effects a mixed essence had on spells, he would. I had to agree with Shay, though. Something as simple as meditation could not possibly go that haywire.

I stared unseeingly out the window. If he hadn't already, I'm sure Murdock's brother Bar would tell him I was at the Institute. He was going to want to know why. With another link to Shay, Murdock would lock him up in a second. He would have every reason to do it. I would have in his shoes.

Shay's continuing involvement had to be more than co-incidence. He'd attempted things he did not have the ability to perform. Given his blackouts, he might not even have known what the hell he was doing. I had to wonder if the whole mess was a result of an accident on his part, an accident he didn't even know he had caused. But I couldn't find any convincing evidence. The sad little room he shared with Robin held no trace of powers being worked. As Shay admitted, even the pathetic parlor tricks he had tried with wards were useless.

I felt a light touch on my forehead, like someone had placed a cool fingertip just above the bridge of my nose. If anyone had been there to see, they would not have noticed any reaction on my part, so subtle was the sensation. I was about to receive a sending, a true sending that no glow bee could hope to imitate. From experience, only one person contacted me so gently. As the cab made its way over the Broadway Bridge, Briallen's voice filled my head with sound.

I need to see you immediately.

I waited to see if there was more, but the cool feeling slipped away. Sendings were wonderfully convenient and precise, but they worked best if kept simple. I tapped on the scarred plastic partition and changed my destination. As I got out on Louisburg Square, I tipped the driver generously to make up for the loss of the longer fare to Avalon Memorial.

I didn't knock. The house felt empty. I paused by the newel post at the foot of the stairs, my skin alive with tension. Just as I set foot on the first step, I heard Briallen call from the back of the house.

With a sigh of relief, I relaxed and made my way through the kitchen to the back door. Briallen sat on the edge of her fountain, wearing a black swaddle of fabric that was too shapeless to call a dress. The fountain's spray was off, giving the backyard an uncommon stillness. Briallen lifted her head and smiled when she saw me, reaching out a beckoning hand.

"That was fast," she said.

"I was halfway here."

I took her hand and sat next to her. She looked much better than the last time I saw her. Placing her hands on my head, she looked directly into my face. I felt the usual pressure. As she released me, her brow creased for just a moment, and she touched me once more briefly.

"What is it?"

She shook her head. "I thought I sensed something, but it's gone now. The darkness felt, I don't know, smoother."

"I did the sun invocation with Joe yesterday. It made the headache go away for a while."

"Yes, he told me."

I raised an eyebrow. "And what else did he tell you?"

"That you're investigating blood rituals and won't listen to reason."

I took a deep breath and released it slowly. "I didn't come here for a lecture."

"You're not getting one."

"Oh. Good. Then maybe you can help me. What do you know about *The Brown Book of Cenchos*?"

She wrinkled her nose. "Not that old thing."

"Why would macDuin be interested in it?"

"I don't know. Why do people collect clown figurines?"

"Briallen, I'm serious."

She shrugged. "Connor, it's apocryphal. It makes no sense. There are spells in it that claim to do things they would never do."

"Like maybe something that looks like a meditation ritual can actually send someone on a murderous rampage?"

"Well . . . not that clear-cut. It's more like explaining gravity by denying its existence."

I thought about it. "I don't get it."

She nodded. "Exactly."

"Okay, let me take it from a different angle. How could a simple meditation ritual have the opposite effect?"

"I don't know. Maybe you need to see something." She twisted slightly on the edge of the fountain and waved her hand gently above the water as though she were caressing it.

"Briallen, scrying splits my head open."

"Yes, yes, I know. I'll take care of it."

She held her other hand up toward me and began to chant. My body shields activated, not from an instinctual response to danger but merely from her command. I shivered. No one had ever done that to me before. With an ache of remembrance, I felt my fragmentary shields pulse with life again as their edges flowed out to meet each other. Seamlessly, they joined over the entire surface of my body as they once had, an invisible layer of armor to defend against unwarranted intrusions. It caused me no pain since it was not of my doing. Except for the small part of my own essence in the fragments, the protections were all of Briallen's power.

All the while, Briallen continued setting up the scry. Even when you were fey and could do things humans couldn't, watching Briallen work was both awe-inspiring and humbling. She needed no accoutrements, only the raw power of her concentration and her knowledge of invocations. Even as she worked my shields, her hand smoothed the water of the fountain to an unnatural stillness. Once I was fully warded, the cadence of her chant shifted into an older Gaelic, its rough sounds oddly soothing from her lips.

She spread both hands over the water. The surface reflected the dull haze of the sky. The image shimmered jarringly as though someone had tapped the edge of the fountain. A curling wisp of gray smoke rippled on the edge, eating at the reflection of the sky until the entire visual surface pulsed with shadows of mists just beneath the still water's surface. With hands spread wide, Briallen did not move at all, her taut form leaning forward. Her eyes shone whitely as she increased the urgency of the chant. Something seemed to roll sensuously beneath the surface, pale green, then silver and white.

I let my gaze flicker to Briallen. Beads of sweat clung to her face. She was pushing hard at the invocation. Even someone with rudimentary ability would have lifted the veil of smoke by then and caught a glimpse of the future. The real skill came in the clarity of the vision. Some could only get the most obscure hints and symbols, while someone like Briallen could see events almost like watching a movie. But after over twenty minutes of intense chanting, still nothing happened. Something was seriously wrong.

A thick unsettling blot of darkness formed in the middle of the fountain. It deepened and spread outward like a giant pupil. Nothing appeared in the inky depths. The blackness enveloped the whole of the fountain, a darkness so deep and complete that not even our reflections marred its surface.

With a gasp of frustration, Briallen pulled herself up and away. She stood with her head bowed, one hand to her face, the other hovering over me like a benediction.

"Briallen . . ."

She lifted her head. "Go inside. I need to close it."

There was no discussion in her voice. I hurried into the kitchen, uneasiness creeping into my gut. As I stepped inside, I could feel her release the protections on me. I flinched at the sudden stab of pain in my forehead and moved away from the door. The pain lessened, but not much. Scrying had the worst effect of anything on me. I kept moving back into the house until I was in the foyer. I could still feel a hot needle-like pinging, but I refused to go out into the street. I sat on the bottom step of the stairs and held my head, trying to will away the pain. After an eternity, it subsided, and I looked up to see Briallen standing over me. She had a solemn, yet wild, look on her face. Her skin was very pale and damp, and her short hair hung in wet strands.

"You're soaked."

"It was necessary. Let's go up." She passed me smoothly onto the stairs, and I followed her into the sitting room on the second floor. She stood before the small blue flames on the hearth, her back straight and arms at her sides. "It's been like that for days," she said without turning.

"What is it?"

She moved to an armchair and sat. "That's the million-dollar question. The Queen asked me to answer it."

"Maeve?" I couldn't help the surprise in my voice.

"Of course, Maeve. She called me this morning."

"She called you? On the phone?"

She frowned. "Yes, on the phone. What's wrong with you?"

I laughed. "I just find it incredibly funny that the High Queen of Tara called you on the phone."

"What did you want her to do, send smoke signals? We've known each other for years. She's calling everyone she can."

I lowered myself into the armchair opposite her. "What's wrong?"

She shifted the damp folds of her dress away from her knees. "The future is closed. No one's been able to pierce the veil. A turning point in time. What we do not know, what we cannot see, we cannot try to change. It must play itself out the way it will."

I'd never heard of the future being "closed" before. "It's a bad thing?"

Briallen looked down into the flames. "That's not the question. It's a question of understanding. We have to prepare, if we can, for what may come. The last time something like this occurred, Convergence happened."

I fell back in the chair, too stunned to say anything. "Are you kidding me? How long has this been going on?"

"I've been hearing rumor of strange happenings for weeks. It's why I haven't been as helpful to you as I could have been."

I leaned forward in the chair. "Don't be ridiculous, Briallen. I'm not that self-involved. I may be bitching about the lack of attention the Guild is giving these murders, but I think you might be a little better recognizing priorities than they are. What do you need me to do?"

She moved her hand from beneath her robe and held out a dagger in an old leather sheath bound with thongs of leather. "I need you to stay alive."

I took the dagger from her. Finely wrought silver wound about the pommel, and the handguards were plated in gold. The whole of it was encrusted with fine rubies and crystals and a large emerald at the base of the hilt. I slid the blade slightly from the sheath. It was double-edged, inscribed with tiny runes, and shone with new silver brightness. The sheath itself was stamped with more runes and symbols and blotched with stains that I just knew were blood. It weighed more than I would have guessed, but still had a nice balance in the hand. And the damned little thing hummed with power.

"I can't accept this, Briallen."

"You must. What's coming is cataclysmic, Connor. I won't have you unprotected."

"But this must be worth a fortune!"

She shrugged. "What's a fortune weighed against a life? It's old, I'll grant you. Several people have possessed it. Now you will."

"I'll take it on one condition."

I meant it conversationally, just as a preface, really, but Briallen sat very still, like she was considering whether she would accept a condition. "What?"

"That you'll take it back when I don't need it anymore."

A mysterious look passed over her face, at once surprised and resigned. "I'll accept that. Put it on."

I gave her an odd look as I removed my right boot. Briallen can be downright pushy sometimes, but it never paid to disobey. I lashed the sheath around my ankle and put the boot back on. After a few wiggling adjustments, I felt I could live with it. I had to take my regular knife out of its boot sheath, though, and slip it bare into my left boot. Not the safest position, but I would figure it out later.

"Use it with care," she said. "It has some powerful wards, and I've put a few of my own niceties on it, too."

"I will. So what exactly does Maeve want you to do?"

"Learn what I can. Scrying obviously isn't working. I'm going to try some dream prophecy."

Not surprised, I nodded. *Imbas forosnai.* The ancient ritual of dream and prophecy was the only logical course when scrying didn't work. Now I knew why Briallen had summoned me. She would be in a deep trance for days. And she would be vulnerable. "You want me to stand guard while you sleep."

"Yes and no. I don't know what may happen, but I doubt you're strong enough to stop it. There are very few people who could protect me better than myself, and they're all busy working on this right now. I need you to awaken me."

"So I'm useful because I'm powerless."

She rolled her eyes. "You're useful because no one would expect I would use you. Unexpectedness has its own power. No one must know about you. I haven't even told Maeve."

Maeve, the Bitch of Tara, Ice Queen and Iron Ruler. Just as many people fear her as love her. Enclosed in a girdle of mist on the hill of Tara in Ireland, no one passes into her keep—or her presence—without consent. And she just phones up friends of mine when she needs help. "What's she like?"

Briallen steepled her hands at her lips. "Strong. Of all the queens, I think she's probably the most beautiful, but I'm sure others would have their own opinion. Her hair is like ebony, and her skin is alabaster. She can be as cold as drawn steel and never lets her guard down. People curse her, but the fey are lucky she was the ascendant queen when Convergence happened. This world would have descended into chaos without her leadership. She may be harsh, but she's kept things from falling apart."

"If only she cared about all the fey as much as the monarchy," I said.

Briallen shrugged. "That's a matter of opinion. If she can finally defuse the German situation and end the Teutonic-Seelie stalemate, the entire world will be better off. Humans may fear nuclear weapons, but I'm more worried about an all-out fey war. Suffice it to say she's got a lot on her plate."

In her usual manner, she stood and walked out of the room. In the outer hall, I found her going upstairs. I followed her firm tread to the third floor, where the guest bedrooms were located. Surprisingly, she led me up to the fourth floor. I knew she slept up there, but had never seen it. When I was a kid and came to the house for lessons, I would sneak away to explore when she was distracted by conversation with someone. The staircase beyond the third floor was blocked by wards, and I couldn't pass. It didn't stop me from trying, but I never got through. Here I was just sailing right along. The fourth floor landing had four closed doors. To my astonishment, Briallen kept going up to the fifth floor. She waited for me on the landing.

The top floor of the house had wooden doors at either end, both closed. Incongruously, a great stone door set in a stone arch stood in the center of the landing. Briallen laid her hand on the door. "You're about to see something I rarely show anyone."

She pushed, and the door opened soundlessly. A dim white glow came from within. Inside was an oval room, its walls paved with slate and curving inward toward the center of the ceiling. Where the tiles met, stones of all kinds glittered in the crevices. Onyx jammed in next to crystals of pink and yellow and blue. Bloodstones lined the baseboards, along with quartz of all kinds mixed in with opals and firestones. Even the floor had a fortune in precious stones, including what could only be true rubies, emeralds, and diamonds. I couldn't possibly catalog them all. The dominant stones were selenite, other moonstones, and sapphire for invoking the powers of the night, only fitting for a druid daughter of the Moon. In the center of the room stood the lone piece of furniture, a white granite slab of a table just the right length for Briallen to stretch out on if she chose. A preternatural light glowed from various places, reflecting back and forth in a myriad of color.

Druids are notoriously guarded about their private sanctums. The one I had before I lost my abilities was much simpler, but I had still shown it to only a handful of people. "I'm honored," I said.

"I've already keyed the door to your essence. Once I close it, only you can open it from the outside. If I'm not out in three days, come get me. With any luck, I'll have figured this all out."

She reached out and hugged me. As I held her, she gripped hard before releasing me. The seriousness of the situation was sinking in. Briallen was always physically and emotionally demonstrative. But that one hard squeeze told me she was scared. She stepped back into the room with a grim smile on her face. The door closed, meeting the jamb with a soft thump that sounded like the sealing of a tomb.

15

I tried calling Gillen Yor several times the next morning but kept getting his answering service. Finally, by midafternoon, I got a real person on the line who informed me that Gillen was unavailable until further notice. As I turned off my phone, I glanced up at the ceiling as though I could see through it to where Briallen lay in deep meditation. I knew she would have helped the queen with just about anything if asked. But if Maeve had gotten Gillen to investigate as well, and he had agreed, it truly was serious.

Waking up in the guest room in Briallen's house had felt like coming home. When my abilities kicked in at twelve, they kicked in hard. I'd spent many weekends in Louisburg Square away from my family. At first it was exciting learning things most kids only dream about. It became frustrating when I began to realize how hard it was going to be. Occasionally, it got lonely—adolescent angst coupled with the stigma of truly being different. The best part was making Briallen smile. Most times I did it with a joke, but often enough it was because I did something right. I began to strive for that.

I let my fingers trail over the bindings of books in Briallen's study, looking for something, anything, to find a way past my dead end. Should I make Shay remove the pentagrams or not? Were they working as part of a meditation exercise or weren't they? I tried randomly pulling books off the shelves in the hope that something would literally fall into my lap, but fate didn't want to play the game. I was beginning to think my best bet might be a coin toss.

My cell phone rang. I picked up, and traffic noises blared in my ear.

"I'm at a pay phone across from the Guildhouse. I didn't want to use any lines inside. They're doing spell sweeps," Meryl said. "Listen, I've been studying the books you asked about the other day. I think I found something a little freaky. It's a spell of binding that unbinds. If I'm reading it right, it's about old powers. The real old ones. Like lock-them-up-and-throw-away-the-key old ones."

I said a silent thank-you to whoever might be listening.

"Can you meet me at the bandstand on the Common in five minutes?"

"Got it." She disconnected.

I went back to the guest room to put on my boots. Briallen's dagger had already started feeling comfortable on my ankle, but I still didn't like being without my old knife. Until I either bought new boots with a left foot sheath or made one of my own, I decided to leave my old blade behind. It wouldn't help if I managed to stab myself in the foot. I left the jacket, too. It was damned hot, and at least at Briallen's I wouldn't worry about it getting stolen.

I paused in the foyer. Briallen lay in a trance trying to find the cause of a blackout on the future, the kind of blackout that had happened when Convergence occurred. Meryl had found a Fomorian spell that unbound old powers with blood and pentagrams. When old powers were spellbound, it was usually behind dimensional barriers, the same kind of barrier that had been pierced during Convergence.

A chill ran up my spine, and I ran up the stairs again. I had a spell that would bring about a cataclysm taken from a book that macDuin had read. I also had a series of ritual murders that fit the spell and that macDuin was trying to suppress. And I had an unexplained connection between macDuin and Corcan Sidhe. If the spell succeeded, it could create a world like old Faerie with the remaining humans as subjects—just like the elves and their fairy sympathizers wanted during World War II. Like macDuin wanted. The connections had to mean one thing. MacDuin was some-how using Corcan Sidhe to pierce a veil into the Fomorian prison and free the most powerful enemy of the Celtic fey. All hell would break loose on the world again. Only this time an enemy would be unleashed that no one had fought in millennia. Humans would have little chance of survival. Just the fey would, leaving a world dominated by the fey. MacDuin had set it all in motion again.

As I was about to press my hand against the door of Briallen's sanctum to wake her, I hesitated. She had scoffed at the possibility of a Fomorian spell. If I were wrong, I could be setting in motion the cataclysm she feared by disturbing her. If I were right, I could be facing certain doom by not waking her.

I rushed back down the stairs. I needed the spell. If it did what Meryl thought it would, Briallen would see it, too. It would be the proof I needed to justify interrupting Maeve's request. I locked the front door as I left. Briallen might have the house warded to the teeth, but it made me feel better. My cell rang again.

"I know, I'm coming," I said, thinking it was Meryl.

A static hollow sound echoed in my ear. For a moment I thought Meryl had called back with her silencing spell.

"This is Gerda Alfheim," a woman's voice said. Even through the bad connection, it had that continental smooth accent you hear in old movies, with just a touch of Nordic to it. They had taken so long, I had given up on the Germans.

"We have a bad connection. Please hold on." I had reached the end of Walnut Street where it dead-ended on Beacon. Loud, heavy traffic moved in both directions. When a brief opening appeared, I rushed across the street to get to the relative quiet of Boston Common.

"You were calling about my son Gethin. Is he all right?" Gerda asked.

"He's here? In the States, I mean?"

"Well, yes. He's in Boston. I thought that was why you were calling."

I skipped down the short flight of stairs into the Common. I held my hand over the speaker of the phone to hear better. Most people cover their open ear to block out intruding noise, not realizing the speaker picking up ambient sound causes more of a hearing problem. I stood looking back and forth for an easy path across the Common, but there wasn't one, so I cut across the grass. "How long has he been here?"

"A few months this time. I was getting concerned because I haven't received a check-in call. What's this about?"

"I was doing some research, and your name came up. I really don't know anything about your son except that he is cross-species."

There was a long pause. "That's some rather personal research."

Her voice had gone cold. I could feel that I needed to tread carefully, or I would lose her. "We have a situation here I hope you can help me with. Has he ever been violent?"

Again there was silence. The moment dragged on. "I am not going to say another word until you tell me what this is about."

"I'm consulting on a criminal case that the Boston Guild-house is working on." It wasn't quite true, but not quite false. She didn't need to know that.

"The Guild?" Her voice was tinged with suspicion now.

"They have primary control of the case. There've been a number of fey-on-fey murders."

Again there was silence. She did not speak for several moments. "Hello?" I said.

"Keep Lorcan macDuin away from my son, Mr. Grey."

Stunned, I skidded to a halt. I was on top of the hill where I had witnessed Tansy's funeral. The bandstand sat downslope a few hundred yards away. Meryl hadn't shown up yet. "How do you know Lorcan macDuin?"

"He's at the Guildhouse there, isn't he? He has an unnatural attraction to Gethin. He even came to Germany last year to contact him. You asked if my son were ever violent. The only time I saw Gethin upset was because of Lorcan macDuin. Please, you must keep him away from him."

"I don't understand. Why did you let him come to Boston if you had concerns about macDuin?"

"What?"

"I said why did Gethin come to Boston?"

"I can't hear you, Mr. Grey," she said. A wave of static crackled in the phone. I spun wildly in a circle hoping the signal problem was on my end. The static grew louder. The call went dead.

"Damn," I said. I jabbed my finger at the phone to turn it off. The caller ID didn't list a return number. I paced across the hilltop, hoping she would call back. I kept glancing over to the bandstand. Meryl hadn't appeared yet. A line of trees obscured the view to the intersection she would be coming from.

My body shields came up and an instant later I felt the tingle of a spell across my skin. Before I could move my head more than a couple of inches, it froze in place. The rest of the spell draped over me like a layer of cool static that might have been refreshing under different circumstances. Someone laughed just behind me. Footsteps came closer and stopped beyond my peripheral vision. A hand snaked around and plucked the phone from my hand.

An elf walked in front of me. He had a cocky grin on his face as he dialed my phone. Even though it had been dark, I recognized him as one of the guys who had jumped me. The one I had bit. He wasn't chanting, so I knew his spellcasting buddy must be behind me.

"We've got him," he said into my phone. He stared at me while he listened, nodded once, and disconnected. He lowered the antenna and slipped the phone into his pocket. With a smirk, he stood beside me and clasped the elbow of my still-bent arm. I felt myself rise an inch or two above the ground. He propelled me forward, walking nonchalantly like we were out for a Sunday stroll.

I tried to open my mouth to yell, but they had me in a pretty tight binding. We moved down the hill toward the city information booth and away from the bandstand. Fighting against the resistance, I managed to move my head to the right, but not far enough to see if Meryl was riding to the rescue. Sweat broke out on my forehead from the effort. We paused on the foot of the hill where a main path through the Common ran, waiting while a young couple walked past, oblivious to the sight of a tall man frozen in position with an elf holding his arm. I felt utterly ridiculous.

The elf pressed me forward, and we proceeded around the information booth. People milled all around us, but absolutely no one gave us a second look. As we neared the curb on the Tremont Street side of the Common, the elf companionably put his arm across my shoulders. A black Lincoln Town Car with black-out windows sat illegally parked, a Guild permit discreetly displayed on the rear windshield. Someone came up behind me, muttering. The other elf, the spellcaster, had made his appearance. He opened the rear door of the car, and before I knew what was happening, they grabbed my shoulders and pitched me headfirst inside. The door slammed roughly against my feet, launching me forward. I banged my head against the opposite door.

My nose pressed against the leather upholstery. Without

anyone holding me, I was able to shift my body weight and roll over. I ended up halfway onto the floor, but at least I was faceup. The front doors opened one after the other, and my abductors sat down. I could see the spellcaster. He wore sunglasses again, but I could feel his eyes on me as he kept muttering in German. The car started and began moving.

Trees passed through my line of sight through the sunroof. We paused at a traffic light. The car had started rolling again when a sharp jolt rocked us. The spellcaster spun away from me in surprise. It took a long, slow moment for the binding to fade. I began to sit up as a second impact hit the car, and I fell back against the seat. The elves yelled at each other, but I couldn't make sense of what they were saying. As I grabbed at the door handle, the spellcaster turned and shouted. A ball of light burst from his hand and hit me squarely in the chest. I hunched forward, gasping for breath, and felt the binding spell descend on me again. The car sped up, pressing me into the seat. A third impact struck, but it felt only like a strong wind buffeting the car compared to the first two.

I could see where we were going now. We careened through traffic on Tremont Street, not bothering to wait for the light at Boylston. The Guildhouse loomed up on the right in the next block, and we circled around to the front. The dragon over the main entrance seemed to be laughing at me frozen in the backseat. We made the next light legally. As we entered the intersection, the driver made a wild right turn back around the other side of the Guildhouse, then another turn down the access alley on Boylston. A garage door opened as we approached, and the car swept under it with inches to spare. An old dwarf woman in the attendant's booth gave a desultory wave as the car passed.

The garage seemed to go on interminably. We circled down into the depths of the building. As with so much of the Guildhouse, it was hard to tell if I were being brought through a series of illusions or if the space were actually this vast. We came down a ramp that ended in a small area barely big enough for three cars.

I heard the pop of the trunk, and the driver got out. I groaned inwardly. There's nothing I hate more than being carted around in the trunk of a car. It's never comfortable. The driver walked out of sight for a moment. I could hear rummaging sounds behind me in the trunk. The back door opened, and he shuffled in on his knees. With quick movements, he wrapped duct tape around me, binding my arms and ankles. The spellcaster stopped chanting. Before the binding could wear off again, the driver backed out of the car.

The spellcaster coughed a couple of times. "I need some water."

I sat still as the spell slipped off me. The driver stood several feet away from the car. I eyed the spellcaster as he got out. He was the one I had to worry about. Even though his binding ability wasn't a very strong one, he had enough to stop me. If I could incapacitate him, I might have a chance against the driver. I had no delusion that that chance was anything other than extremely small.

"Move out of the car slowly," the driver said. I swung my legs out and stood. It wasn't the side of the car I wanted to be on. The spellcaster came around to our side, closing the trunk as he passed it. So, I wasn't going for a ride.

"We can do this the hard way or the easy way," the spellcaster said. "Either we carry you with no problems, or we beat you up the side of the head until you pass out, and then we carry you."

I smiled at him. "What's the matter? All out of juice?" The driver punched me in the stomach. I wasn't ready for it and keeled over like an embarrassed sack of rocks. So much for taking either of them out.

"Okay. Okay. I won't struggle."

It was the driver's turn to chant. I felt my weight dissipate as I almost left the floor. The two elves stood on either side of me and grabbed my arms. I floated up with little effort. They guided me to an old wooden door. "You guys make a great team. I guess you have to, considering neither one of you can stand on your own."

"We could drag you if you prefer," said the driver. He opened the door with his free hand. I could feel the slight tingle of a ward stone as we passed into a long corridor. It had the same look as the old basement corridors, only long disused. Dust and debris lay thickly along the edges and a single, old-style wall torch flickered orange halfway down. Just past the torch, we stopped at an iron door. The driver opened a small viewing panel and peered into blackness. He gave no indication what he was looking for. He closed the panel and opened the door.

As if on cue, they dropped me to the floor. The driver patted me down. His hands seemed to insist on avoiding my right boot. For a moment, I thought he might be an ally after all. But more likely, Briallen had a warding spell on the dagger she gave me. With his own knife, he sliced some of the duct tape to loosen it. They shoved me inside the dark room and closed me in.

The little square panel opened. "Let me know when you've got the tape off," the driver said.

I sneezed. The room had a rank odor of rot and urine. It was so bad, I could smell it even through my sinus congestion. I flexed my arms and heard the gratifying rip of the tape. After several more tries, I managed to free my right hand and remove the rest along with what felt like most of the hair from my arms. The tape around my legs gave way more easily.

"Done," I called.

"Put out your hand," said the driver.

With not a little reluctance, I put my hand through the opening expecting it to be slapped, followed by giggles. Instead, he pressed a kitchen match into my palm. The beam of a flashlight blinded me, and I stepped back.

"You get the one match. Don't ask for another."

The flashlight beam illuminated a small torch a few feet away on the side wall. I felt the wall to make sure it was dry, then raked the match head against it. It flared and before it went out I touched it to the torch. A feeble yellow flame flickered up. I turned back to the door. He slammed the panel closed. I could hear their muffled voices through the door as they settled in to watch.

I took in my surroundings. It was an old storeroom of some kind, forgotten in the depths of the building. A small space near the door remained clear, but the rest was a jumble of boxes and crates and old furniture. And a bad smell. I hoped nothing—or no one—had died. That wouldn't be a very good omen. A coolness permeated the air that the torch would never warm. I knew I should have worn my jacket. A soft sound rustled in the pile of junk. Rats. On top of everything else, I had to contend with rats. At least I understood their motives.

I paced in the dim silence, trying to understand how I ended up in a dark dungeon on a summer's day. I had run too late and hidden too obviously. I wondered if Keeva knew about the recording stone in my apartment, or if she had unknowingly been charging it up for macDuin all this time. I couldn't believe even she would stoop so low. I didn't get it. If she was working against me, why had she bothered saving my ass the last time the two elf goons came around?

I resisted the urge to try the door. Not even these guys would be dumb enough to leave the door unlocked. I had to wait and see what macDuin had planned for me. I just hoped I didn't wait too long. It wasn't exactly cold in the storeroom, but the creeping damp air was already getting uncomfortable. I didn't relish the idea of rummaging around in the pile of junk to find something smelly but warm to wrap myself in.

The fact that Gerda Alfheim's son Gethin was in Boston intrigued me. What were the odds? Too high to be more than coincidence. Was he lured here? I wondered. I thought of Corcan Sidhe, half-elf and half-fairy, just like Gerda's kid. All the other cross-species children had died except these two. Dealle Sidhe had old German connections; that much was clear. Could Gerda have sent Gethin to her? Fostering was far from unusual among the fey. Who better to foster a mentally handicapped child than someone who had one? And macDuin was aware of both of them.

Footsteps sounded out in the corridor, and my guards stopped talking. The gait was long and firm. I didn't need any special ability to recognize it. The bolt on the outside was thrown, and the door opened. MacDuin stood in the doorway flanked by his annoyingly smirky minions.

We faced each other silently. He wore his usual black suit, but here within the confines of the Guildhouse, or maybe just for my benefit, he made no attempt to hide his wings behind a glamour. They rippled up high behind him, their translucent texture reflecting gold and silver pinpoints of light from the torches.

I tried my best to look unimpressed. It wasn't hard. I'd seen it before. "Care to explain why you had me kidnapped, Lorcan?"

He merely smiled. "I came to be sure you were secured. You are fey. I can always say I was holding you for questioning in a case."

"Even the commissioner wouldn't believe that."

If anything, his smile broadened. "I wouldn't expect him to."

That gave me a cold feeling. "What's that supposed to mean?"

He arched a languid eyebrow. "Let's just say that the commissioner and I have come to an agreement, and you are not part of it."

That really didn't sound good. I decided to bluff. "People are going to be looking for me, and you're the first place they'll go. I was on the phone when your goons grabbed me."

"He's lying. He didn't have time to say anything," said the elf who had driven the car. He leaned in toward me with a sneer. "He didn't even know what hit him."

I rolled my eyes toward him. "Don't make me bite you again."

A touch of real amusement came to Lorcan's smile. "You should have stayed out of this, Connor." He turned to the spellcaster. "Keep him here for now. He will prove useful in a day or two." He began to walk away.

"I know about Germany."

Lorcan put a hand up to stop the door. He gave me a measuring look. "What do you know about Germany?"

I had to bluff him. I didn't know if he was lying about having been there. "I know what you did."

"Meaningless. Many people knew I was there last fall." He turned his back and gestured for the driver to close the door.

"I know about Gerda Alfheim."

That got him. He froze in place for a long moment before facing me. With a placid stare, he took several more moments as he seemed to digest what I said. "That does complicate things. I didn't think you had gotten this close. I had hoped when this was all over, your conspiracy theories would look like a desperate alibi. You might provoke a few unwanted questions now."

"You're going to pin this on me? Do you think Gerda Alfheim will keep quiet if I go to jail?"

He shrugged. "I wouldn't place my trust in Gerda if I were you, Connor. She will be taken care of in due course."

I took a step forward. MacDuin raised his eyebrows in response, but otherwise didn't move. "Lorcan, you can't believe what you're doing will help. You won't be able to control it. No one will."

"You are not the first person to underestimate me, Connor.

I haven't worked to convince Maeve of my sincerity only to have your pathetic interference ruin everything now."

He turned to leave again. "How did you do it, Lorcan? Does Dealle Sidhe know what you're doing, or is she just as blinded by her political ambitions as you are?"

He gave me a curious stare, then amusement glittered in his eyes. He gave a long, low chuckle. "As usual, you think you have all the answers, but you're the same arrogant fool you always were. As you sit rotting in a jail cell, you still will have no idea what happened here. And I like that very much." He spun on his heel and swept out of the room. One of the goons slammed the door. I deducted points from both of them for melodrama. I kicked the door to make us all even.

What had I missed? Meryl had said the spell she found would unbind an old power. If it had come out of *The Brown Book of Cenchos*, it had to be a Fomorian power. The only reason macDuin would want to release something like that would be to cause chaos. Just like he wanted during the war. I doubted anyone living would know how to counter Fomorian abilities. Hell, they had ruled over the Tuatha De Danann at one time. They were a race so forgotten even Briallen thought their rituals were nonsense. Mac-Duin had to be insane if he thought he could handle whatever came through the opening the spell would create. I shook my head. With six people dead, I had no business being baffled by macDuin's sanity.

Another rustling sound caught my attention, and the culprit made its appearance. A large brown rat skittered along the edge of the room, lifting its nose to scent the air. It had a thick patch of fur on its head that looked charmingly like a crown. Rearing onto its hind legs, it sniffed in my direction. I looked around for something to throw and picked up a split chair leg. The rat had already turned away, but I took a shot at it anyway. I missed but scared the hell out of it. It plunged into the pile of trash, and I could hear it scratching its way frantically toward the back of the storeroom.

The voices on the other side of the door faded away. I stood listening to the silence, willing myself not to focus on how angry I felt. Anger clouded thinking. Having been in enough locked rooms in my time, I knew that thinking was usually the only way to freedom. Of course, if that failed, I still had the dagger in my boot.

16

A shrill screaming filled the air, punctuated with flashes of color. I huddled close to the ground, my heart racing in what I wanted to think was excitement but really was ordinary fear. Something closed in on me, something dark and huge. I fumbled for the dagger in my boot. As I pulled it from its sheath, it blazed with a white light. A scream rent the air.

I awoke in darkness. Cold air pressed against my skin, and the hard stone floor beneath me felt more unforgiving than ever. The torch had gone out. My breathing seemed louder than it was, fast and ragged from the nightmare. I took deep breaths to slow my heart rate and shake off the dream.

My knees crackled when I stood. I rubbed my arms to bring blood to the surface. Every time I dozed off, I felt colder when I woke up. It wasn't so cold that I would die, but it was damned uncomfortable in the meantime. I windmilled my arms to try to force more blood into my hands. It only helped a little.

When I still had light, I had gone over the room. While I found a fair-sized inventory of old office furniture, a hidden exit did not appear. The only outlets were two small drainage grates in the back, which the rats probably found convenient.

In darkness, boredom set in, followed by sleep. The faintly luminous face of my watch displayed the progression of time with agonizing precision. Every time I awoke from a nap, I was equally surprised whether five minutes or two hours had gone by.

Around four o'clock in the morning, my certainty that they would not be so stupid as to leave the door unlocked lost to my fear that they were that dumb, and I was even dumber for not trying. I tugged at the handle. It was locked. I went back to sleep.

The silence gave me a sick, frustrated feeling in the pit of my stomach. I had never been imprisoned before. I had been trapped under various circumstances but always in the context of moving events. I had known that just on the other side of a door or up on a roof or just a block away in a car, someone knew where I was and was coming to help. Now events were moving, but I had been taken out of the flow. I had no control. Not enough time had gone by for me to lose hope, but outside was a different matter. Outside Midsummer was coming. Night would fall and with it the official new moon of Midsummer's Eve. Someone would die, but this time chaos would break out. I dozed off again.

Breakfast came in a paper bag dropped out of a blaze of light from the corridor that was cut off when the panel slammed shut. I groped around until I found it. The reek of greasy fries plumed out of the bag so strongly I could smell it through my congestion. Burgers, fries, and a water bottle. The food was cold and the water was warm. Not my usual morning fare, but my stomach had given up trying to tell time somewhere around midnight. At least the crinkle of burger wrapper was a new sound.

I still had Briallen's dagger. Before the torch died, I had tested the strength of the door. The wood was old, but by no means rotten. Hacking around the hinges until they fell off would take a while, and the elf goons would stop me before I got very far. I'd only end up losing the dagger. I might be able to take at least one of them out if I tricked them inside. But that was the oldest gimmick in the book.

I didn't relish stabbing one of the guards. They didn't seem to have an agenda other than being macDuin's strong-arms. That didn't mean I liked them any better, but I doubted they had signed on for the job expecting to get killed. Maybe I'd just wound them really, really bad. I stared at the door, willing it to open, and eventually fell asleep again.

Some hours later, I lifted my head from my knees. I had the vague sensation of being awakened by some kind of noise. Voices could be heard out in the corridor, rising and falling in intensity. At least two. A moment later, I realized one of them was a woman's. A third voice chimed in, low and urgent. The guards had company. I couldn't make out what was being said, but the tenor was rising.

The voices grew louder as they approached.

"I don't care. The plans have changed," the woman said.

"He said tomorrow," one of the elves said in German.

"I'm not leaving without him. We don't have time."

The door flew open, and blinding light hit me full in the face. Amplifying the effect was the vision of a fairy in full blaze of anger, her wings flaring up and out. I held up my arm to deflect the glare after so much time in the dark. My eyes ran as I blinked hard to focus.

"Keeva?" I said.

"Come on, Connor. I don't want any trouble from you either."

"I want to call macDuin," said one of the elves.

Keeva spun toward him. "He's busy, you idiot. Why do you think he sent me?"

Something didn't feel right. My sense of perspective seemed to be off as I looked down at her. Keeva was tall enough to look me in the eye, yet I found myself staring at the top of her head.

"Keeva?" I said again.

"Let's go, Connor. I'm on a schedule."

She grabbed my arm and pulled me into the corridor.

She shot a sideways look at the elves. I could see them more clearly then. They were pissed off and confused. Keeva peered into the dark storeroom. Standing so close to her, I could see a mild blurring about her features.

"MacDuin wants you to go to the bookstore in Kenmore Square and wait for us. We'll be there in half an hour," she said to the elves.

The spellcaster stepped forward. "That's not the plan."

She sneered at him. "Oh, I'm sorry. I'll tell Lorcan to check with you next time."

They exchanged glares. Keeva grabbed my arm again and forced me down the corridor. The elves had remained where they were, angry uncertainty on their faces. Keeva straightened up again and stared them down. "Get moving. I'm not going to tell you again."

"We really have to move," she said under her breath as she passed me. We hustled up the corridor away from the garage. Another oaken door blocked the far end, and it took no more mystery than a good hard tug on the metal ring in its center to open it. As we passed out of sight of the corridor, I couldn't resist the urge to smile and wave to my former captors. I had to admire their nerve. They still hadn't moved.

We were in yet another corridor. This one had electricity, but only a few lights. I looked down at my rescuer. "Um, Keeva, your orange roots are showing."

She looked at me from under her brow. For a disconcerting moment, another visage hovered behind Keeva's. Air rippled across the face, and it faded away. So did the wings.

Meryl crossed her arms and tapped her foot. "If you wanted a perfect glamour, I would be more than happy to lock you back up for another couple of hours."

I held up my hands in surrender. "I'm not complaining. It was long enough."

She frowned at me. "I would have been here sooner if someone hadn't thrown something at Muffin and scared him half to death."

"The rat? That was your rat?"

She twirled her hand over her head. "Cute little guy with a tuft of hair on his head that looks like a muffin? Let's just say we're on good terms. Hurry up. Those two idiots might still decide to follow us."

We made our way through a series of twists and turns, the lights becoming brighter with each step. Meryl's knowledge of the lower corridors of the Guildhouse was either the product of careful map study or incredible nosiness.

"How did you know I was here?"

She shot me an annoyed look over her shoulder. "Who do you think tried to peel the roof off their car? I didn't think fast enough. I should have blown out the tires. I was on my way back here when you drove past me again and right into the service alley. I was too exhausted to try anything then." She opened a door and held it for me. "Those are the dumbest elves I've ever met."

We came out in a corridor not far from the storage area Meryl had shown me days ago. She pulled a slip of paper out of her pocket and opened it. "Here's the spell I found. It blasts a hole between dimensional barriers using fey blood and hearts. I translated it into ogham since I knew you were more comfortable with that than Fomorian. Some of it I just put in phonetically. And that asterisk is pronounced like this." She made a thick, throat-clearing sound.

"Where the hell did you learn Fomorian?"

"Let's just say I had an interesting childhood. So, do you need any more favors, or are you deep enough in debt to me as it is?"

"Do you have a cell phone I could borrow?"

She sighed heavily and pulled a cell out of her pocket. "Go. Before I regret getting you out of that hole."

"Thanks, Meryl. I won't forget this." Impulsively, I kissed her on the top of the head and ran down the corridor to the elevator.

"I'm not paying your roaming charges!" she yelled, as the doors closed. Meryl's impersonation had given me an idea. I called Keeva. She picked up on the second ring. She wasn't surprised to hear from me. I breathed a short sigh of relief. I hoped it meant she didn't know I was supposed to be trapped in a dungeon.

"Keeva, I need to know where macDuin is."

"Connor, I don't need you screwing things up for me with macDuin."

"He just kidnapped me and had me locked in a storeroom for the last twenty-four hours. I think he's behind the murders."

She didn't speak for a moment. "Do you know how paranoid you sound right now?"

"Keeva, I can prove it. But right now, we have to find him and stop him. I think he's still loyal to his old politics from the war and wants to establish a dominant fey world here. He's going to open some kind of dimensional rift, and it's going to make Convergence look like a hiccup."

"Okay, I was wrong. *Now* you sound paranoid."

The elevator doors opened as I looked at my watch. It was already almost 8:00 P.M. The sun would be setting soon. The main corridor on the first floor was empty.

Midsummer's Eve was a Guild holiday. The security guard looked startled as I breezed past the reception desk.

"Keeva, trust me. I have the spell he's going to use. If you won't meet me, just tell me where he is."

"You have a spell?"

It didn't seem the time to express any doubts. "Yes."

I paced on the sidewalk under the dragon lintel. It never helped to push Keeva.

"He's home. I'll meet you there." She hung up.

I let out the breath I hadn't realized I was holding.

I debated whether to spend the money for a cab, then laughed. The end of the world was coming, and I was worried about my budget. I flagged down a black-and-white Town Taxi. MacDuin lived in the Charlestown Navy Yard, and the driver was all too happy to take me there. Any destination that forced a route through the winding streets of downtown automatically meant a hefty fare.

I called Murdock. Loud street noise made him difficult to hear.

"Where the hell have you been?" he said.

"Long story. Your brother Bar still has Shay under surveillance, right? If he's with the big elf that acts like a child, pick them both up. And be careful. The elf is dangerous."

"Okay. I'll get the long story?"

"I hope so. Do you have this number on caller ID?"

I heard him fumble with his phone a moment. "No," he said.

So like Meryl to block her number. I gave it to him. "Call me if you get him, Murdock. And call me fast."

"Done," he said.

I put the phone away. Working with Murdock was a hell of a lot easier than with Keeva.

We did a stop-and-go creep around the Common. As we reached the top of Beacon Hill, I steeled myself to start blurting directions. If the driver continued down the other side, we would run into one of the few streets that led into the Weird from downtown. I checked my watch again. The parade on the Avenue would be just reaching its peak, and the streets would be an inescapable traffic jam. He saved me the trouble of being annoying by turning off on a side street. Once off the Hill, we weaved through twisting streets to the Charlestown Bridge.

As we turned into Charlestown, I pulled out the piece of paper Meryl had given me. The spell was simple, but long. As I mentally sounded through the words, I could hear the ancient cadence of the Celts, only darker, more primal-sounding. Meryl had provided a rough translation. It didn't have the rhythm of the Fomorian, but it still read like a paean to the world. It was a calling to forces greater than the individual, deep forces that bound together reality. The verses sang to the ancient elements of life represented in the five cardinal points of a pentagram.

I could see now what Meryl meant by the oddity of the spell. Paradox seemed to run through it, giving an honoring to bindings yet asking for freedom; asking for release within the bounds of flesh. Yet, it had its own logic. Something wanted out, and out badly.

Below the spell and its translation, Meryl had written two more spells. They were formal in the very ancient tradition of the Tuatha de Danann, powerful spells of binding. Next to each of them, she had drawn large question marks. They were spells that did the opposite of the Fomorian one. A layman might call them counterspells, but true counterspells were devised to defend against specific spells. Meryl's notes were informed guesses. Good ones, but guesses nonetheless.

A queasy feeling crept into my stomach. Nothing that powerful had been uttered in over a thousand years, probably longer. No one had a reason to. And I didn't have the ability to give the words the power they needed. I hoped Keeva would have the strength to hold the de Danann spells long enough for them to work. The easiest course was to stop macDuin before he even began the ritual.

The cab pulled into the parking lot of the Charlestown Navy Yard. I gave the driver a tip so big, I left him staring at his palm.

The Navy Yard no longer retained its original function. Shipbuilding had left Boston long ago. The old buildings had gone derelict until someone had the idea of making them residences. Everyone thought the people who moved in were crazy to pay exorbitant prices to live in the middle of a crime-ridden neighborhood. They got the last laugh though. More development had spread around them, and the condos were worth ten times what the original owners had paid for them.

Keeva was nowhere in sight. No one was in the area at all. Across the way, a few cars sat near the edge of the pier. Beyond them, boats of all sizes dotted the harbor. Their slack sails waited in the humidity for a breeze. I moved down the sidewalk to macDuin's unit. The door stood ajar. I didn't need instinct to call up my body shields. The familiar tingle spread over my head and chest. Comforting, but useless. I was tired and had little energy to do them much good.

I slid along the inner wall of the entryway and tilted my head to listen inside. I could see part of the foyer where an area rug lay askew. Without taking my eyes away, I reached down and slipped the dagger from my boot. An open, unattended door is never a good sign.

I tapped the door with my toe, and it fell back against the inside wall. A faint current of air-conditioning radiated against my face. I could see the entire entryway, a mail table with fresh-cut flowers, small oil originals above it, and the archway to the living room beyond. To the left, stairs led to the second floor. I could hear no signs of movement.

I eased into the entryway. Something glistened on the third step. I didn't need to be a hematologist to recognize fairy blood. As I moved closer, I could see another spot on the railing near the top. I leaned forward and closed the front door. Without knowing who had left the trail of blood, I didn't want any surprises coming in behind me.

I darted a look into the stairwell. The landing was empty. Testing each step for noise, I made my way to the second floor. More bloodstains showed on the walls and floor. In a technical sense, I was contaminating a possible crime scene, so I did my best not to disturb anything. The bedrooms on the second floor were empty. The blood trail continued up.

As I crept up the last flight, the top floor came into view. The stairs led to a room that stretched from the front of the building to the back. Great beams crisscrossed the ceiling. As my eyes came level with the floor, I looked under a couch that had been positioned against the railing. Someone lay on the floor, a man by the look of the bare feet facing me. I could see no one else in the room. Unless someone was lying on the couch, the townhouse was empty except for me and the prone figure.

I walked up the last few steps and almost slipped on a broken ward stone on the floor. I picked up a large chunk of it and recognized it as the same material as the wards from the other murders. Whatever purpose it had served had been destroyed with the stone. Coming around the couch, I stopped in surprise.

MacDuin lay on the floor. He had been stripped naked and pinned to the floor like a butterfly. Ward stones held his wings flat, just like the other victims. His chest had been split from collarbone to abdomen and wrenched open. It had been done with such force that his lungs were splayed to the sides, and the heart appeared to have been torn out instead of cut.

I edged around the body to get a closer look. Too late, I felt a tingle across the nape of my neck. Even as I pulled back, the field of another ward stone grabbed me, and I froze in place. I let out an angry sigh, cursing myself for stupidity. I had taken the lack of any sensation of a ward as a sign that there were none.

The wards on the wings were too small and far away to be the culprits. The ones at the other murder scenes had been keyed to each other to hold the wings back. Even given my recent propensity for walking into traps, I didn't think it was too much to assume these stones were any different, but obviously I was wrong. I tried rolling my eyes to the extreme, but couldn't place the offending stone and only hurt my eyes.

I stared into macDuin's face. He hadn't gone easily. An open cut on his cheekbone looked like the result of a punch. It had probably thrown him into the ward field I was in now, and the rest had been by the book for the murderer.

In the dead silence, a familiar sound caught my ear. French doors at the back of the room led to the balcony. The distinctive hum of fairy wings in motion whirred from the same direction. Most fairies dampened the noise unless they didn't care if someone heard them coming. I let out a sigh of relief when Keeva fluttered into view. She brought herself down onto the balcony with long practiced ease. She reached for the door and paused when she caught sight of me. Her lips compressed into the thin line that I had learned long ago meant annoyed condescension. She opened the door.

"Well, well, well, don't we make a pretty picture?" She held her arms loosely at her sides, waiting for me to respond.

"Oh, can't talk?" She paced near the door, making exaggerated thoughtful poses. "Let me see, what could have happened here? Could it be the great Connor Grey is trapped?" She gave me a sideways smirk. I tried to throw as much anger into my eyes as I could under the circumstances.

"Imagine my surprise when I find my dear, beloved boss sliced open and a former, troubled employee poised over him with a dagger. I do wish I had a camera." She stopped moving and faced me again. "You do know how much macDuin would have loved this moment." She leaned forward with just her upper body and peered down at the body. "He doesn't seem to be enjoying it though. Pity."

She looked at me again and shook her head. "I have to hand it to you, Connor. You do know how to be in the right place at the wrong time. MacDuin said you would spoil everything. He wanted to frame you for the other murders, you know. And now here you are, conveniently located next to another body. Maybe I'll pick up on that little aspect of his plan."

She slipped a knife from her belt and hefted it in her hand. Glancing at me once, she paced again without speaking. A bead of sweat slipped down my spine. I watched her move back and forth. She looked down at her knife again. She knew. She knew about Corcan. But macDuin was dead. Someone else had to be controlling Corcan. A new dread gripped me, and I pressed as hard as I could against the ward-spell.

"No," I said. It came out strangled and the spell bore down around me again.

Keeva smiled broadly. "Very impressive. I think it's time to put you out of your misery, don't you?"

She threw the knife. My heart hammered in my chest as I watched the hilt leave her hand. The knife flew at me with nauseating slowness, light catching the blade as it soared across the room. It's been said that the doom of the world can rest on the edge of a knife. For once, I believed it. The knife whistled past my ear and stuck into a beam somewhere above me. A loud report rang out as something fell. I stumbled free and almost landed on macDuin.

I turned in confusion. Another ward lay broken on the floor. I spun back to Keeva. She just stood there with her arms crossed and a smile playing on her lips.

"That . . . wasn't . . . *funny!*"

She shrugged. "Sorry. I couldn't help myself."

I put my dagger back in its sheath and slipped it into my boot. Given my condition, it wouldn't be much help against Keeva anyway. "What the hell happened here?"

She walked over to macDuin and squatted by his side. "He was like this when I got here. Heart's gone." She stood, wiping her hands on her thighs.

"Why did you let me walk into a trap?"

She poked me in the chest. "I didn't *let* you do anything. The front door was open when I got here, and I thought you had done something stupid like go inside. I got rid of the ward at the top of the stairs, but the angle was bad for the other one, so I went around to the balcony. I'm surprised you didn't sense it."

I rubbed my nose. "I've been having trouble smelling anything."

Keeva bit her lower lip and looked away. "Promise you'll let me explain?" I cocked my head to the side in confusion. She reached out and placed her hand on my forehead. I felt an odd shifting of pressure, as though I had ridden in a fast elevator and my sinuses were catching up a second late. I could breathe again. I sneezed and gagged once very hard. Between macDuin's exposed organs and the killer's essence, the stench in the room was overwhelming. I grabbed Keeva's arm.

"What the hell did you do to me the other night?"

She wrenched her arm away with no trouble and stepped away from me. "I saved you a trip to the hospital. When macDuin realized you knew Gethin's essence, he wanted me to block you. I refused, so he sent his henchmen after you. You should thank me. I got them *and* macDuin off your back."

"Gethin? Then he knew Gethin is here?"

She looked at me in confusion. "Of course he did."

"I thought Lorcan was using Corcan to commit the murders."

She shook her head. "Wow. No, Connor. You're way off. Corcan didn't commit the murders. Gethin did. I thought you figured out the ritual? Gethin's dying from genetic defects. MacDuin told me he had a spell to cure himself. He's more fairy than elf and was murdering the prostitutes for their hearts. He needed them to purge his elfin essence. As best we could tell, he needs Corcan as a final purging vessel to accept his elfin essence."

"Then why was macDuin trying to end the police investigation?"

She stared at me in confusion. After a moment, she nodded. "Connor, Gethin's name is macLorcan. MacDuin and Gerda Alfheim had an affair during the war. He's macDuin's son."

Stunned, I lowered myself onto the couch. The image of macDuin laughing at me in the basement of the Guildhouse rose in my mind. He had realized I didn't know. And he didn't tell me. And he had intended to frame me. I looked over at the body and tried to feel bad he was dead.

"I can't believe this. He was willing to let people die to protect his son?"

"MacDuin was trying to stop him, Connor. He didn't want anyone to know. He was afraid the press would find out the killer was a son he had with a radical activist. Connecting him with Gerda Alfheim would bring his old war collaboration ties out again. He really had put all that behind him, but his reputation would never have recovered again. Especially not with Maeve. With the Fey Summit winding down, she can't afford anyone being suspicious of her motives."

"You were helping him."

She smiled. "I did more than help. I caught the bastard. Two days ago. MacDuin was keeping him locked up here until after Midsummer so he couldn't kill anyone else and complete the ritual."

Now I understood the sensation of more wards in the house. A closed door at the back of the room vibrated with blocking wards. I went over to it. "This is where he kept him?" Keeva nodded. I opened the door. Inside was a small alcove room with just a bed. Above it was a window with a shattered frame. Gethin must have gone out that way and set the trap for macDuin. That wasn't what grabbed my attention, though. A pentagram was painted on each of the four walls and centered on the ceiling was a fifth. Gethin had drawn them in his own blood.

Realization swept over me. "We have to leave right now. I know where he's going to do the ritual."

Keeva gestured at MacDuin. "The ritual is over, Connor. Gethin got his last heart from his own father. He's probably fully fairy by now."

"Think, Keeva. The hearts are not here. This is about more than healing Gethin. Didn't you wonder about the pentagrams?"

I handed her the spell Meryl had given me. The color drained from her face as her eyes moved down the page. She gave the paper back. "This isn't the spell macDuin showed me. Where do you think Gethin is?"

"Castle Island. Shay was going to take Corcan there for the fireworks. Gethin must be meeting them."

She strode onto the balcony, shots of light beginning to course into her wings. In the gathering dusk, she glowed above me as she lifted into the air. I stepped beneath her, and she hooked her hands under my arms from behind. My stomach dropped as my feet left the tiled flooring. We soared above the building.

The setting sun smeared streaks of orange and red across the horizon. To the east over the harbor, the sky had faded to a flat gray. Too anxious to wait for full nightfall, people were already shooting off cheap fireworks, little bursts of color to the south over the Weird and South Boston. We made straight for them.

Black clouds sprang up in the east, lightning flickering among them. A gust of wind hit us, and Keeva veered sideways. Reacting to my fear, my body shields materialized. Keeva almost lost her grip on me as the shields made me harder to hold. She dug her fingers painfully into my arms as I tamped the shields back down. We were out over the water, the downtown skyline slipping past. The surface of the harbor shimmered in a haze of white foam. A stronger gust of wind battered us, and we dropped a dozen feet before Keeva recovered. We skimmed near the surface of the water, where fish were running in all directions, sending up a frenzied spray. People on boats scrambled to pull in their sails.

Keeva began chanting, trying to use the wind's energy to work with her. Her flight stabilized as we shot over the Weird. Old Northern Avenue was a blaze of color and movement. People jammed the length of the street, dancing and flying in celebration. Keeva kept us just above the fray, weaving in and out of other fairies. We joined a small convoy of people flying out to Castle Island for the fireworks. Away from the distractions of the Weird, apprehension replaced excitement on faces turned toward the dark cloud bank that had spread rapidly over the harbor.

Castle Island came into view, its shores lined with hundreds of people. Fort Independence spread out below us, its five sides of granite rising thirty feet above the crowd. It was the biggest damn pentagram in the city. A green parade ground should have been visible at its open center, but

a sallow haze of light glowed instead. The essence that radiated off it pulsated with malevolence.

"I can't get through that," Keeva yelled. She banked to
the right and brought me down in the parking lot. On the
opposite side, more people filled the causeway that looped
around Pleasure Bay. Keeva and I pushed our way through
the crowd.

I pulled out the cell phone and called Murdock. "Where
are you?" I said.

"I'm at the front gate of Fort Independence." I closed the
phone. Someone let off firecrackers, and the crowd roared
its approval. I grabbed Keeva's sleeve and pointed at the
fort. I had to yell to be heard. "Front gate!" She nodded
once and grabbed me again. We launched over the crowd
and flew up the hill. Coming around the nearest rampart of
the fort, I could see Murdock scanning the crowd, his hand
resting on his holstered weapon. Keeva dropped me right
next to him.

It says something about the world we live in that Murdock didn't blink an eye at my arrival. "What's going on?"
he asked.

"The end of the world. What happened to Shay and
Corcan?"

Murdock jerked his thumb at the closed gate. It stood
about fifteen feet high with iron hinges. An unlocked chain
dangled from the door rings. Even with all the fey milling
about, I could feel the sealing spell on the door. "They went
in there. Door won't budge."

I turned to Keeva. "It's a spell, not a ward."

She rested her hand on the panel of the door to sense the
level of power. Pulling her hand back, a ball of white shot
from her palm and raced around the edges of both doors.
She tugged one of the rings, and the door opened. I guess
they weren't expecting high-powered company.

Inside, a passage glowed with the same sickly light we
had seen above. A wrongness throbbed on the air that even

Murdock could feel by the look on his face. He unholstered his gun, gave us a nod, and went in. Keeva rolled her eyes and pushed past him. "That gun isn't going to do much good here, big guy."

The far end of the corridor framed the parade ground in a simple arch. In the center, a naked, bone white figure stood, fairy wings undulating out from either side of him. Dark almond-shaped eyes stared from a worn face of ecstatic triumph. Seeing Gethin macLorcan in person made me realize that Shay's police sketch really had looked nothing like Corcan Sidhe. I had been seeing only the superficial similarities.

Shay lay crumpled on the ground just on the edge of the lawn. Ignoring him, Keeva walked onto the grass. Murdock trailed behind her with his gun drawn as I leaned down to check Shay. I couldn't tell if he was breathing. I wondered if he knew how over his head he had been. Pulling my dagger, I stepped up behind Keeva. The blade felt warm and alive in my hand, its runes grabbing the light around it.

Gethin had drawn himself inside another pentagram. Spirit jars sat at the five points, filled with herbs and water and the unmistakable shapes of hearts. Corcan lay at the center, his head near Gethin's feet. His body was rigid, and he stared straight up without seeing.

"You've done enough," said Keeva.

Gethin brought his gaze down, inspecting her with coal black eyes. His ears were not so much rounded as stunted points.

"I've just begun," he said. The voice. At once raspy and clear, like someone who had been smoking all night and talking too loud. It wasn't a voice to forget. Neither was his essence. Stinkwort and I had been so close the other night. We could have saved the last victim and even macDuin if we had been faster. His essence still felt wrong, but it had become muted, more fairy in nature, with a distasteful edge to it.

As I moved closer, the hair on my arms bristled. He had already sealed the circle around the pentagram and erected a protection barrier. Most sane people did that with themselves on the outside.

"You don't have to do this. You got what you wanted," I said.

His eyes shifted to me. "What I wanted? No. What I wanted was to claim my mother's noble heritage. Instead, I must wear the disgusting wings of my traitorous father."

Keeva had circled around the pentagram. She kept one hand near her waist and flexed at the wrist. She was gauging the strength of the shield. When she reached the point opposite me, she shook her head. She hadn't found any weakness.

"You can't do this," Keeva said.

Gethin's face twisted into a sneer. "Only you think in terms of cannot." He spread his arms out. "Look at my power, de Danann. Look at your own. You waste yourself. If more of you had joined my mother's people, we would be ruling this place. Instead, you cower before the humans, content to take the dregs they offer."

"Let Corcan go. You don't need him anymore," I said.

"I need him to open the way. I am keeping my word to my mother, unlike my father. She found me a cure. Now we will cure the world." He began to chant. I recognized the spell. Good ol' Meryl had hit the nail on the head. Gethin was opening a door into chaos. Wind picked up in speed. Outside the fort, someone shot off a roman candle that glimmered red-orange through the hazy light of the protection barrier Gethin had erected. More explosions went off as the first display of fireworks appeared overhead.

"This spell will kill you!" I shouted. He faltered for a moment.

"You're wrong. It opens the door for The Defeated Who Will Conquer. They will ally with us, and we shall rule together." He had the fevered gleam in his eye of the rabidly insane. There wasn't going to be any reasoning with him.

He began chanting again. He raised a hand, and a burst of yellow light tore through the barrier and into the sky. It seemed to fly up forever and scatter among the clouds. A heavy silence spread around us except for Gethin's guttural muttering. Off in the distance, a moaning broke out. The ground vibrated with a deep thrumming. A torrent of air pounded down out of the sky, throwing us off our feet.

I lifted my head against the pressure. A towering wall of water ringed the walls of the fort, a dark, malevolent green surging toward the open sky all around and above us. Gethin had called up the sea. The wind died down. Confused shouting came from outside the walls, and more stray fireworks arced against the darkness.

Keeva flew to my side. "We can't penetrate the pentagram. The shield's stronger than anything I've seen."

"That's not the real problem." I looked up at the wall of water around us. "That's where all hell's going to break loose."

"Will someone please tell me what's going on?" said Murdock. He had not taken his eyes or his gun off Gethin.

I pointed at the seawall. "*That* is the gateway to a dimensional prison. The Dananns spellbound some critters called Fomorians. Gethin's breaching the barrier to let them out. They're big and nasty, and they're not going to be very happy to be here."

"Sorry I asked." He cocked his gun and aimed at Gethin. "So why don't I shoot him?"

"You can't see the barrier around the pentagram, but it will stop a bullet."

Gethin continued chanting, facing each of the points of the pentagram in turn. He picked up a stone blade and crawled around Corcan, inscribing runes into the ground. Pinpoints of light appeared in the spirit jars and raced around the hearts. They pulsed with an eldritch glow. Five columns of red light shot from them and pierced the clouds that capped the ring of water around the fort. A tremendous clap of thunder broke, the force of its vibration almost knocking us to the ground again. Above us, the clouds revolved in a circle like the beginning of a tornado. The center rippled and tore open, widening like the pupil of a dead eye. Oddly, no stars shone in the blanket of black. The surface of the wall of water rustled like a windblown curtain. Figures moved beneath the surface, huge unshapely things, vague and undefined.

"Keeva, use the binding spell to bind us all in here. We have to block Gethin's access to the water."

She closed her eyes in concentration. She shook her head. "I don't have your recall, Connor."

I fumbled in my pocket for Meryl's note and thrust it at her. "Learn quick. I'll try and distract him."

I flung myself at the pentagram. The invisible barrier yielded a few inches, then threw me off. Gethin didn't even notice. My dagger had gone flying when I landed on the ground. As I picked it up, the runes on the hilt glimmered. Bracing for the inevitable pain, I forced some of my own essence down my arm, and they burned brighter. The blade had some ability in it even if I couldn't access most of my own.

I approached the barrier again and slashed at it. A shower of sparks rent the air, pitting my skin with burns. Gethin did not stop chanting, but he glanced at me that time. I slashed again. More sparks cascaded over me, and I stumbled away. Gethin stretched out his arm, and a charge of energy hit me in the chest. I fell on my back.

I sat forward, clutching the hot, sore spot on my chest. It hurt like ten fists had pummeled me.

"Got it," said Keeva. She launched herself into the air above Gethin and began to chant. As she flew above us, a faint trail of blue light began to appear behind her. She had taken the shorter spell by the sound of it. I could sense the weaving of her words bonding to the top of the battlements of the fort. The spell wouldn't take down the seawall, but if she managed to close Gethin inside the spell, his own spell would be trapped.

I hit the barrier again. This time I was prepared for Gethin's countershot and rolled out of the way before it even left his hand. It hit the wall behind me, and Keeva screamed. The power from Gethin's bolt had latched on to her spell. It went wild. She was spinning out of control, her face contorting in pain. I watched helplessly as she spun faster and faster in the air. With a burst of electric blue fire, she vanished from sight.

I screamed for her. No answer came. My senses trembled with the power of the shield capping the parade ground. I could feel her essence permeating it, but I could not feel her physical presence anywhere. In the sudden quiet, I heard laughter. I turned back to the pentagram. Pure joy lit Gethin's face as he raised the stone knife over Corcan's heart.

"No!" Murdock shouted.

I shouted, too, but too late. He fired his gun. The barrier burst into a fury of white light as it absorbed the bullet, folding in at the point of impact. The bullet funneled inward. Just when I thought it would stop, it grazed Gethin's arm as he brought it down. He recoiled and dropped the knife. The funnel of light reversed itself, bouncing back to where the barrier had been.

"Get down!" I yelled to Murdock. He either didn't hear me or didn't understand. The funnel flattened out at the barrier and exploded outward. It took him in the shoulder and flung him off the ground. He sailed limply through the air and landed with a sickening thud. His body tumbled out of sight into the entrance passageway.

Gethin dropped to his knees. The bullet had only grazed him, but clearly it had stunned him a little. As he stretched one hand out for the fallen knife, he rested the other on the ground. Time moved slowly for me as I stared at that hand. The one steadfast rule of any protection barrier around a pentagram is that only the one who casts it can break it. I stared at his hand, fully halfway outside the invisible barrier. I flung my dagger. He screamed as it pierced him between the knuckles, pinning his hand to the ground. Before he could react, I grabbed the hilt of the dagger and yanked him the rest of the way out of the pentagram. The barrier dissipated immediately.

Gethin screamed and launched himself on me. His fist connected with my cheekbone and knocked me to the edge of senselessness. He straddled me and flailed away as I tried to block the blows with my arms. I swung at him with the dagger. He deflected it, and it flew from my hand. He hit me again.

As he brought his fist up for another blow, he paused and looked up. Blood was running into my eyes, but I saw lights in the sky above us, flickers of blue and green, yellow and pink. They were like fireworks, only moving with a purpose. Gethin pulled back onto his feet and shot bolts of white light upward from his palms. The lights swirled and danced away from it, but kept coming.

I shook my head to clear it. I could hear chanting.

The sounds resolved into words, a phrase repeated over and over. *Ny a wrug agas dhestrewy jy.*

It wasn't a chant. It was a war cry. *We will destroy you.*

I laughed in disbelief. It was Cornish. The People had arrived. By the hundreds, flits spiraled into the parade ground screaming for all they were worth. The Power of their dance surrounded me, filling my body with essence, like the day Stinkwort had performed the sun greeting with me. Only this time it was off the scale. The black mass in my head receded. I dragged myself to my feet. The block was gone. I could tap my essence. All of it. I had my ability back.

I picked up my dagger and called out to Gethin. I pointed my dagger at him. "Hey, asshole. Know what happens when you use a knife for a wand? It hurts like hell." Energy coursed down my arm and shot out the blade. It hit him in the head, and he collapsed. The flits swarmed all over him. Gethin struggled and screamed under a fury of color. The flits were screaming right back at him. One broke away and flew toward me, his sword held aloft.

Stinkwort hung in front of me, his body bathed in blood. The flush of battle euphoria suffused his face. "I said we'd get the bastard!"

"You must have called in every clan in the country."

He fluttered back. "Near enough. You okay?"

"It'll hurt more in the morning."

Joe gave me a great big grin. "It always does. I have to stop them before they kill him."

"What are you going to do with him?"

His grin broadened into that impossible smile. "He's a fairy now. We're going to give him fairy justice." With that, he shouted in Cornish, and every single flit vanished. Gethin had disappeared, too. They had taken him. Only one place dispensed fairy justice: Tara, where Maeve ruled with a cold hand.

Corcan had not moved. I bent at his side to check for a pulse. It felt faint, but it was there. I turned his head toward me. Gethin's knife had nicked his cheekbone when it fell. A bead of blood trembled at the edge of the cut. As if in slow motion, it detached itself and dripped. Up. Startled, I stepped back. Before what that meant occurred to me, the droplet floated out of my reach.

It gathered speed as it rose. I watched helplessly as it shot up to the seawall. The sea had not fallen back. The water shimmered where the blood made contact, and a black and sinuous crack appeared. It bulged, turning blacker, and something stepped through. A mass of gray darkness coiled in the air and descended. It touched the ground on the other side of the pentagram and resolved into a mass of quivering flesh. An arm uncoiled, thick and greenly scaled, and then a head no more than a lump attached at the shoulder, with a single bulbous eye and a mass of teeth. I'd seen pictures that I thought were nightmare exaggerations. This was no exaggeration. The Fomorian unfurled, a sickly gray torso supported by thick, black stumps for legs. It smelled like the rot of a thousand fish left in the sun.

It swiveled its body around until its eye found Corcan. It shambled a few steps toward him, and I raised my dagger.

"Back off." I have no idea if it understood me, but it stopped. Its eye rotated up. My body shields activated, the real ones, covering my entire body in a cushion of protection. It felt good to have them back, but I wasn't too thrilled at the cause.

It howled and lifted an arm. A sword appeared, a great length of jagged ebony iron. I couldn't tell whether it had it when it fell or had just conjured it from somewhere. It hefted the sword and eyed my dagger warily. While I held its attention, I used my free hand to work a protection spell over Corcan.

The thing raised its blade and swung at Corcan. In a shower of green sparks, it bounced off the barrier I had made. My protection spell evaporated like a mist. I shot a bolt of energy at the ground, and the Fomorian leaped back. I stepped between it and Corcan and recast the protection.

The blade swung toward me. Dodging away, I clawed my left hand at the air. White lightning crackled from my fingertips. It caught the creature in the chest, and it let loose an unearthly howl. The eye began to glow. My limbs suddenly grew heavy. I could feel some kind of spell draping over me. I tried to shake it off, but I didn't understand how it worked. I crumpled down. The Fomorian came toward me, sword raised. My hands were anchored to the ground. A mistake. I waited until it was ready to bring the sword down, and I tapped into the essence of the earth around me. The ground between us erupted in a shower of mud. The thing lurched sideways, its sword striking my leg with a glancing blow. Red pain lanced through my knee.

I scrambled toward the fallen thing and plunged my dagger into its thigh. It screamed again. A fierce heat blistered up my arm. I jerked the dagger out and fired bolts of pure energy at it. The Fomorian flailed wildly, scrabbling away. It flung the blade at me. My shields absorbed the impact, but the power of the thing knocked me off my feet again. I landed hard on my side and felt ribs crack. Curling into the pain, I crawled away. It thrust a hand out and more heat blazed across my body. I smelled a nasty burning odor and realized my hair was on fire. I rolled again, grunting against the pain in my side as I batted at the flames.

As it reached for its weapon again, I used the simplest of spells to send the sword soaring out of the parade ground. The thing bellowed in fury, dragging itself to its feet. I held the dagger out and shot the same bolt of energy I had used on Gethin. He only hesitated a moment, shrugging it off. With a roar, he surged forward and punched me in the face. Blood gushed out of my nose.

The energy from the flits was wearing off. The darkness in my head gnawed at the edges of my mind. It hadn't gone away, only receded from the essence supplied by the flit clans. I wasn't going to make it. The Fomorian was too strong. I had no idea how to counter his strength, never mind his power. He hit me again. My head snapped back against the ground. He crouched over me and began swinging. Blow after blow struck me, sending me skittering across the ground. The only reason I wasn't dead was that my body shields blunted the force. But they were only blunting the blows. I began to lose consciousness. He hit me again, and I went airborne. I landed hard against the wall and slumped to the ground. A wet sound rattled in my chest. I felt the unmistakable pain of a rib puncturing my lung.

I was burning out. Channeling essence through the body is exhausting under the best of circumstances. I could feel lots of things broken inside me. I didn't have much time left before nature took its course. In desperation, I called up the one thing I had strength for. A deep white fog hissed around me, hiding me from sight. I could see the Fomorian, but he couldn't see me. He stumbled around in the druid fog, bellowing in anger. Twice he almost trampled Shay's still-inert body. It didn't matter if he did. I couldn't stop him. He would eventually find Corcan, rip open his body, and use the blood to let more of his kind out of the sea barrier.

Trying to breathe as shallowly as possible, I stared up at the full moon. I wasn't any good with Moon spells. As Briallen said, they work best for women. I eased myself up against the wall as the thing clawed against the ground nearby. With painful steps, I inched my way around the perimeter. If I could get out, I could get help. There had to be a fairy outside the walls who could at least help me contain the thing.

I was halfway to the exit when I stopped. Confused, I looked up again. The moon stared back at me. It wasn't supposed to be there. It was the first night of the new moon. The sky should be empty. Why would I see a moon that shouldn't be there? An ancient, dry voice welled up in my memory.

Not your moon.

Not your moon. I tried to think, but I was too tired. If it wasn't my moon, what was it? Virgil somehow knew I'd see a moon that wasn't mine. He didn't know what it meant. Damned gargoyle. I didn't know what it meant either. I wished Briallen were with me. She would matter-of-factly point out the obvious to me. I felt dizzy and slumped against the wall.

I jerked my head up. Had I blacked out? The Fomorian seemed farther away than before. Or closer. I couldn't really remember. I felt like lying down. Maybe just for a bit. Something slipped out of my memory. Briallen. Something about Briallen. Briallen would know what to do with the moon. But she was locked in her trance. Right. Only I could wake her. That was what she had said. She should see this moon. A sick feeling welled up in my stomach. What would happen to her if I died? Would she sleep forever? Or would she waste away until she died?

I could almost see the darkness in my mind now. It was biding its time, like it knew it would win eventually. I laughed. It was only going to win a dead body.

The Fomorian was snuffling along the perimeter of the wall now. He was looking for me, and he would find me. I felt bad about Briallen. I hoped she wouldn't be too disappointed. I fumbled in my pocket for the cell phone. I decided to leave a message for her if she woke up. She would need to know what she was up against. No signal. I tossed the phone away, wincing at the pain. The Fomorian swung his head around at the noise and moved toward it.

I wished she could know I had my ability back at the end. She would have been happy for me. My head felt heavy, and I let my chin fall to my chest. I tried to will away the pain and focus on happy memories. Times when I didn't know how tough it was going to be, when I thought practicing simple levitations in Briallen's house was the tough stuff.

I picked my head up. The darkness in my head hadn't won yet. It was returning, but I could still feel my abilities. I still had them, and I was about to die an idiot. I had one more shot. It would probably kill me, but I had to try. I placed my hands against the ground and pulled as much essence out of the earth as I could. My vision flashed red as my mind screamed at the effort. I was the only one who could reach her. I didn't need a fucking cell phone. When

I couldn't hold any more, I released all the essence in one massive sending. I called Briallen.

Exhausted, I collapsed to the ground. Blood stung my eyes. I pawed at them feebly. The creature still haunted the edges of the fort. My vision blurred as I let my head loll against the ground. I stared up into the sky, the strange moon a pale blur. Its surface seemed to ripple. I tried to clear my vision, but the moon just rippled again. It folded in on itself, a twist of white light that cascaded down from the sky like an unwinding ribbon. Soundlessly, it hit me like a tidal wave.

My body convulsed as essence coursed through my veins. Spikes of pain shot through my broken body, and I screamed. I think I did lose consciousness for a moment. I opened my eyes. The darkness had fled from my mind again. The pain went with it. I couldn't feel anything. Nothing but Power.

Amazed, I pulled myself to my feet. My body vibrated with more Power than I had ever felt. I could feel Briallen. My eyes swept the parade ground, but didn't see her. But I could feel her. Realization swept over me. She was inside me. Somehow, I could feel Briallen's essence inside me. And feel her Power. I could tap it.

I lifted the dagger. The runes on the blade flared with a ghostly pale fire. It became a thing alive in my hand, pulsating. And growing. Essence flowed down my arm. The blade stretched and grew into a burning sword of red flame.

Sensing the surge of power from me, the Fomorian turned. I watched his eye home in on me. He charged through the fog, black lighting coursing around him. I grasped the sword with both hands and pointed the blade. With a shout, I tapped all the essence inside me. A crackle of blazing red energy burst from the focused tip of the blade. Crimson fire raced across the field. A ball of fierce hot light engulfed the Fomorian, blinding me with its intensity. I heard a screeching wail of pain.

And then nothing.

Phantom black spots flickered in my eyes as my vision cleared. The Fomorian was gone. Scorched earth marked the spot where he had stood.

I swayed on my feet. My body felt like an empty husk. I couldn't feel anything inside. Not Briallen. Not even my own essence. I had purged everything out of me. The darkness in my head settled back in, cutting off any ability to tap essence. Again. I fell to the ground.

I watched the seawall fall back and heard the crashing surge of a flood outside the fort. The strange moon faded away, and the stars came out. Cold, crisp stars in the blanket of night sky. Only for a moment though. The clouds that had hung over the city all day swirled back and blotted out the light.

Time felt suspended. I don't know how long I lay there. I could feel blood and sweat saturating my clothes. I could sense broken bones and worse inside me. But I didn't feel any pain. A bad sign. A very bad sign. Not far off, Corcan and Shay lay, still not moving. In the dark entryway to the fort, I could make out Murdock's inert body. And Keeva. Keeva, I didn't feel at all. Not her essence. Not her body. Nothing. She was gone. Meryl had dreamed it. She had seen this final moment. It was going to end with everyone around me dead and me not far behind. I whispered an apology to all of them.

A fat drop of rain hit me on the face. Then another and another. Curtains of water gushed down as the clouds opened. It felt cold and good in a distant way. In the darkness of the passage beyond Murdock, something moved. A tall, pale shape shimmered there, moving toward me. The image resolved itself into that of a woman walking. She paused on the edge of the parade ground, seeming to take in the carnage. Slowly, she came to me across the grass, stark white and beautiful. Even her hair shone white. She smiled through tears streaming down her face. Gently, she reached out a hand and placed it on my forehead.

"Sleep," Briallen said. And I did.

17

An insistent beeping roused me from deep sleep. I had the vague notion I should fling my arm out and destroy an alarm clock. The thought woke me even more, but only mentally. My body felt leaden. The beeping sound clarified, resolving into a steady rhythm. I recognized it now. It wasn't an alarm. It was a heart monitor. With an effort, I dragged my eyelids up.

Old acoustical tiles covered the ceiling. Directly over my head, someone with a probably annoyingly cheerful personality had put a yellow smiley face sticker. I could feel an essence comfortably radiating against my side. Curled into a ball near my waist, Stinkwort slept. Next to the bed, Briallen sat in a vinyl-covered armchair. She was sleeping, too. I hadn't imagined her at the fort. Her skin was paler than ever, and her hair was stark white.

The heart monitor beeped away. An IV stand with several bags dangling from it stood at the head of the bed. A tangle of plastic tubing ran from the bags and disappeared under wads of white tape on my arm. A brace on my right leg made the bedcover look like a mountain range. A plaster cast was on my left arm. The doorway and windows in the room were wreathed in lavender and dill. Using my famous skills of deduction, I realized I was back in Avalon Memorial.

A vase on the nightstand held a bouquet of black roses. Careful not to rouse Stinkwort, I reached for the card. The front had another smiley face, this one with two black Xs instead of eyes and a tongue sticking out of its mouth. I opened it.

Dear Connor. Don't Die. XXOO, Meryl. P.S. Nice going on that whole end of the world thing.

I smiled. I guess I was wrong about the relentlessly cheerful smiley face owner. I placed the card back on the nightstand. It slid off and fluttered to the floor. I didn't even try to catch it.

"We have to stop meeting like this," said Briallen.

Exhausted, I moved only my eyes to look at her. She was sitting up straighter, but however long her nap had been didn't erase the fatigue from her face.

"How's Murdock?"

"He's fine. He's two floors down."

I frowned. It was unusual for Avalon to treat humans. "Why's he here?"

"Power backlash of some kind. It's playing with his essence, but he appears fine. He doesn't remember anything after showing up at the fort. Want to tell me what happened?"

"First, tell me about the others."

She leaned forward. "Shay's exhausted, but fine, at least physically. When they brought him here after Castle Island, he woke up screaming. Apparently he was having blackouts and his memories came back. He was at some of the murders. Gillen found the remnants of a possession spell on him."

"Makes sense," I said. "I couldn't figure out why Shay kept having so many connections to what was happening.

Gethin must have used him to find victims and gain access to Corcan Sidhe."

Briallen nodded in agreement. "He's blaming himself for what happened, but, really, he was defenseless against someone like that."

Poor Shay. I hoped he was strong enough to get past it. "What about Corcan?"

"I'm told he's healthier than ever. The ritual had a positive effect on him." She paused.

"Keeva's dead," I said.

Briallen took my hand and squeezed. "No, hon'. She's alive. Why did you think she was dead?"

Relief swept over me. "I thought I watched her die. What did she say?"

"She said she put a barrier over the fort to contain the spell."

"That's it?"

"That's it."

I nodded. Keeva being modest was interesting.

"Okay. Me. What's wrong?"

"Let's see . . . a ruptured spleen, a collapsed lung, torn knee ligaments, your arm is fractured in three places, a concussion . . ." She smiled. "You've been out of it for nine days. Let's just say for now that you're not dead and leave it at that."

I didn't say anything for a moment. I could feel emotional heat rise in my face. Briallen knew me pretty well. She knew I didn't like crying. "I had my ability back, Briallen. It's gone again, but I had it back and I still failed."

She rubbed my hand. "You didn't fail. You beat the thing, averted a catastrophe, and everyone escaped relatively unharmed."

"Relatively."

She rolled her eyes. "Fine. I won't argue with you today."

"Was that really you at the end?"

She leaned back in her chair. "Yes and no. Your sending

blew the door off my sanctum. I knew I wouldn't get to you in time. So, I sent as much of my essence to you as I could.

"I almost killed you, too, didn't I?"

She smiled. "I won't lie. I took a huge risk and drained myself almost to nothing. But you didn't almost kill me."

"How did you send the image of the moon when you were in a trance?"

She gave me a curious look.

"I saw a full moon when there shouldn't have been any. A gargoyle told me it wasn't my moon. It's what made me think of you. I thought you sent it."

She shook her head. "I don't know what you saw. You were in a dimensional vortex. Who knows where you really were at that moment? The Wheel turns as it will, Connor. I have no idea why a gargoyle would know that about the Power of the Moon, but I'm glad it did."

We didn't speak for a long moment. Talking of the moon brought me back to the fort. I remember watching the fireworks and the flits and the thought crossing my mind that it felt familiar. It wasn't just Meryl's dream either. She had seen the end—the bodies and the injuries. I had seen flashes of everything else before that. The lights. The sword. And the bug-eyed monster. In retrospect, I realized what that meant.

"I dreamed the whole thing," I said. "Well, not the whole thing. Most of it. Just not enough. Like you said, I'm not a Dreamer, at least I wasn't that I knew of. I didn't understand that I was dreaming the future until just now. I thought I was just having nightmares."

Briallen tilted her head to the side and pursed her lips. "Maybe this mystery thing in your head is forcing your abilities in new directions."

"I don't want new directions. I want my abilities back."

She sighed. "One of these days you're going to be pleased by the curves that life throws you, Connor, and I, for one, can't wait to experience the novelty."

I smiled at her. "So tell me about this dagger that turns into a sword."

She shrugged. "Actually, it's a sword that turns into a dagger."

"And . . . ?"

"And, that's it. Don't look a gift horse in the mouth."

I let it lie. Briallen would tell me what she wanted me to know in her own good time. I glanced down at the still-sleeping Stinkwort. "What happened to Gethin?"

"I'll let Joe tell you. It's his story."

There was a knock, and Keeva stuck her head in the door. "Oh, sorry, I can come back."

Briallen stood. "No, I was just leaving. If Gillen Yor finds me still here, he'll raise bloody hell. He's a little territorial." She bent over and kissed me on the cheek. We looked at each other in silence for a moment, small smiles on our faces.

She turned and nodded at Keeva. Keeva lowered her gaze and bowed as though she were at court. It was nice to know she respected somebody. She waited until Briallen was gone before she dropped herself into the armchair. She placed an envelope on her lap.

"I thought you died," I said. She looked like hell. Not as pale as Briallen, but definitely not her usual vibrant self.

She gave me a disgusted look. "That spell you gave me ricocheted and bound me into the damn wall." I suppressed a smile. Of all methods I had envisioned torturing Keeva with over the years, trapping her in a wall hadn't come up. She ran a hand through her hair. "Fortunately, the binding broke when you killed the Fomorian."

I tried to sound reasonable. "So, I did a good thing."

"And when the seawall fell, I got sucked out into the harbor in the backlash. I had no energy left to fly, and it took me three hours to swim back in."

"Trapped in a wall and swept out to sea. Bad day." I lost the battle with the smile. We both laughed. It felt good.

"I thought you died, too," she said.

"I don't know why I didn't."

She grew very serious. "Never question life, Connor. Question its point all you want, but not life itself."

"So now you're a philosopher, too?"

"I'm just saying we don't always get to know why things work out the way they do."

She opened the envelope, pulled a picture out, and handed it to me. It was a black-and-white of a crowded street. One figure's face was circled. Gethin macLorcan.

"That was taken in Munich early last fall," Keeva said. "He lived there with his mother. That's her next to him." Gerda Alfheim looked tall and elegant just standing in a long dark coat. Her eyes had a furtive look but she didn't seem aware of the photographer. I didn't particularly go in for elves, but I could see why macDuin had been attracted to her.

"As a known terrorist, Gerda Alfheim was under surveillance. From what macDuin told me, Gerda lured him to Germany because Gethin was dying. MacDuin refused to help with the blood ritual. It was all a ruse though. They knew he would refuse. Gethin secretly came here while Lorcan was there, somehow got his hands on some passwords, and gained access to the Guildhouse. He stole the stones and a couple of old grimoires."

"So why didn't macDuin tell anyone?"

"Because of the Fey Summit. Maeve appointed macDuin to appease the Teutonic Consortium. He was afraid he would be implicated in the murders, and the elves would use fairies sympathetic to their cause to start an insurgency against Maeve and ruin the Summit. He really had given up his superior race politics. He was protecting Maeve. He wanted peace. It took a long time for people to believe that and trust him. But that's not why that photo was taken. Take a look between them at the face in the background."

I held the photo up. Someone stood just beyond Gethin, mostly hidden by him, but about three-quarters of his profile was in view. My jaw dropped, and I looked at Keeva.

She nodded. "That's definitely Bergin Vize."

I let the photo fall and stared up at the ceiling. The stupid smiley face grinned back at me and winked. I made a mental note to kill Meryl after I stopped laughing.

"If you remember, macDuin was in the same terrorist cell as Vize during the war. That's how he met Gerda. But I don't think macDuin knew about the Fomorian spell. The Guild thinks it was Vize's idea."

"So this whole thing was about Bergin Vize trying to kill me again?"

Keeva laughed in surprise. "You weren't even supposed to be involved. You're on disability, remember? Vize had no way of knowing you would be at the fort."

"He must not be very happy with me right now."

"No, I don't think so. In fact, we have extra security on you. Both he and Gerda are nowhere to be found."

I sighed. "I just don't understand why they hate the world so much that they would destroy it."

"They don't see it that way, Connor. Their world has already been destroyed. They're trying to restore it, and themselves, to its former glory. If it takes releasing some of the most heinous beings that ever walked, so be it."

I looked right into her eyes. "What I don't understand is why you helped cover it up."

She straightened up indignantly. "I didn't cover up anything. I thought I was working on a missing person case for my boss. MacDuin used me."

"And macDuin knew just the right ass-kisser to ask."

She stood and glared down at me. "You sound awfully cocky for someone who gave me a spell that almost killed me."

"Maybe I wouldn't have almost died if you had memorized it better."

"Maybe I wouldn't have had to memorize it if you had told me what was going on sooner."

A nasty retort bubbled up to my lips. I clamped my mouth shut and closed my eyes. "You're right," I said. The look on her face was priceless. "If I had asked for your help sooner, maybe we could have saved some lives."

She looked down at her feet. "It's not easy for people like us to ask for help."

I smiled. I had had my suspicions for days. Only someone from the Guild would know Meryl's filing system, and I knew it wasn't likely macDuin was giving me hints. "You left the ogham runes on my door and on Murdock's car."

She fidgeted. "I don't know what you're talking about."

"Yes, you do. You wanted me to help but you wouldn't come right out and ask. In fact, I think you were following me all this time to see if I came up with anything. I led you to Corcan, and he led you to Gethin, didn't he? That's how you caught him!"

She sighed heavily and stood. "Anyway, I just stopped by to let you know the whole story. MacDuin suspended the Bergen Vize investigation, probably after he saw that picture. The new Community Liaison Officer is opening it up again."

"And that would be . . . ?"

She walked to the door and threw a smile over her shoulder as she left. "The ass-kisser, who else?"

Leave it to Keeva to find a way to climb the corporate ladder in the midst of disaster. At least she knew that I knew she owed me a favor now. That's always helpful with recalcitrant Guild members.

Stinkwort sat up and stretched. "Hell, is she gone yet?"

"You know she is. And I know you woke up ten minutes ago."

He walked to the edge of the bed scratching his butt. "The 'new Community Liaison Officer' wouldn't know a sleeping flit from one jumping up her nose." He fluttered over to the nightstand and stuck his head in my water glass.

"You gave a pretty awesome display at the fort."

He pulled his head out and shook water out of his hair. He sat down and grinned. "Yeah, I did, if I say so myself."

"So what happened after you left?"

He made himself comfortable on the nightstand. "Man, I haven't been to a blast like that since the old days. Maeve throws a mean party."

"I meant Gethin, Joe."

He shrugged. "Oh. Maeve was happy to see him in a pissed-as-hell kind of way. After she pulled his wings off with her bare hands, she had him beheaded. Then we had the party."

I figured as much. Maeve had worked hard to keep things peaceful with the elves, to say nothing of all the murders Gethin had committed. Fairy justice was swift and often final.

"Why so quiet? I thought you'd be happy."

I looked at him. "I am, sort of. I don't feel bad for him at all. I just wish it never happened. Maybe if I had stopped Bergin Vize two years ago, it wouldn't have."

Stinkwort rolled his eyes. "Here we go again."

"No, really, Joe. Like it or not, in some way, Bergin Vize is my responsibility."

"So what do you want to do about it?"

I smirked at him. "I think after I get back on my feet, I might need a vacation. How would you like to see the Black Forest?"

about the author

Mark Del Franco lives with his partner, Jack, in Boston, Massachusetts. Mark secretly is trying to kill Jack's houseplants. He is currently developing a sequel to *Unshapely Things,* as well as other fiction projects. Please visit www.markdelfranco.com for more information about the Convergent world.

THE ULTIMATE IN FANTASY!

From magical tales of distant worlds to stories of those with abilities beyond the ordinary, Ace and Roc have everything you need to stretch your imagination to its limits.

Marion Zimmer Bradley/Diana Paxon

Guy Gavriel Kaye

Dennis McKiernan

Patricia McKillip

Robin McKinley

Sharon Shinn

Katherine Kurtz

Barb and J. C. Hendees

Elizabeth Bear

T. A. Barron

Brian Jacques

Robert Asprin

Penguin Group (USA) Online

What will you be reading tomorrow?

Tom Clancy, Patricia Cornwell, W.E.B. Griffin,
Nora Roberts, William Gibson, Robin Cook,
Brian Jacques, Catherine Coulter, Stephen King,
Dean Koontz, Ken Follett, Clive Cussler,
Eric Jerome Dickey, John Sandford,
Terry McMillan, Sue Monk Kidd, Amy Tan,
John Berendt…

You'll find them all at
penguin.com

*Read excerpts and newsletters,
find tour schedules and reading group guides,
and enter contests.*

Subscribe to Penguin Group (USA) newsletters
and get an exclusive inside look
at exciting new titles and the authors you love
long before everyone else does.

PENGUIN GROUP (USA)

3 1901 03896 6240